Plato's *Apology of Socrates*

Oklahoma Series in Classical Culture

Plato's *Apology of Socrates*

A Commentary

PAUL ALLEN MILLER
CHARLES PLATTER

UNIVERSITY OF OKLAHOMA PRESS : NORMAN

Library of Congress Cataloging-in-Publication Data

Miller, Paul Allen, 1959–
Plato's Apology of Socrates : a commentary / Paul Allen Miller, Charles Platter.
p. cm. — (Oklahoma series in classical culture ; v. 36)
Includes Greek text of Plato's Apology with introduction, notes, and commentary in English.
Includes bibliographical references and index.
ISBN 978-0-8061-4025-4 (pbk. : alk. paper) 1. Plato. Apology. 2. Plato—Criticism and interpretation. 3. Socrates—Trials, litigation, etc. I. Platter, Charles, 1957– II. Plato. Apology. III. Title.
PA4279.A8M55 2010
184—dc22

2009010278

Plato's Apology of Socrates: A Commentary is Volume 36 in the Oklahoma Series in Classical Culture.

The paper in this book meets the guidelines for permanence and durability of the Committee on Production Guidelines for Book Longevity of the Council on Library Resources, Inc. ∞

1 2 3 4 5 6 7 8 9 10

You see, I think that people today are so deeply asleep that unless, you know, you're putting on those sort of superficial plays that just help your audience to sleep more comfortably, it's hard to know what to do in the theater.

Andre Gregory and Wallace Shawn, *My Dinner with Andre*

Contents

Acknowledgments

We would like to thank the following people, without whose help this book would not have existed in it current form. Gratitude is first of all owed to Ellen Greene, editor of the Oklahoma Series in Classical Culture at the University of Oklahoma Press, to whom we first proposed this idea and who helped shepherd it through the approval process from beginning to end. Next we would like to thank our friends and colleagues, Mark Beck and Stephen Fineberg, each of whom read the complete manuscript and made numerous important suggestions and corrections. Invaluable assistance was also provided by Virginia Lewis, Deana Zeigler, and David Driscoll, graduate students at the University of Georgia who helped proofread and correct the manuscript, as well as Casey Moore, Leihua Weng, Travus Helmly, Janet Safford, Erik Heymann, and Cagney McGonegal, who as students at the University of South Carolina were the first group to use the complete text and provided important feedback and suggestions. All remaining errors are, of course, our own. Special thanks are due to Louise Kinman Platter for her work on the index.

Finally, we wish to thank the wonderful staff at the University of Oklahoma Press: our copyeditor, Sarah Nestor; Special Projects Editor Alice Stanton; Assistant to the Director and Publisher Astrud Reed; and Senior Associate Director and Publisher John Drayton.

Abbreviations

acc.	accusative
act.	active
adj.	adjective
aor.	aorist
art.	article
compar.	comparative
contr.	contraction
dat.	dative
def.	definite
fem.	feminine
fr.	fragment
fut.	future
gen.	genitive
idiom.	idiomatic
imper.	imperative
impers.	impersonal
impf.	imperfect
indecl.	indeclinable
indic.	indicative
infin.	infinitive
intrans.	intransitive
lit.	literally
masc.	masculine

mid.	middle
neut.	neuter
nom.	nominative
obj.	object
opt.	optative
part.	participle
pass.	passive
pers.	person
pf.	perfect
pl.	plural
pluperf.	pluperfect
prep.	preposition
pres.	present
sg.	singular
subj.	subjunctive
superl.	superlative
trans.	translation

Editorial Note

We have based the text for *Plato's Apology* on the 1900 Oxford Classical Text of John Burnet, noting departures from Burnet in the appendix. We have also divided the *Apology* into thirty-three chapters in order to include supplementary material in the introductions to each chapter and in the essays following the text.

The citations we have used in this commentary are traditional, based on the page and paragraph numbers from the edition of the French humanist Henri Etienne, often referred to by his Latin name, Stephanus. These numbers and letters (a–e) can be found in the margins of the text. The paragraphs are further subdivided into lines. The *Apology* thus begins at Stephanus page 17, paragraph a, line 1 (written 17a1). Our basic policy for expressions that spill over into the next line is to cite only the line in which the first word occurs. More complex phrases and long sentences are sometimes cited with inclusive page numbers.

For words quoted in isolation from their context we follow standard practice and convert all grave accents to acute. Thus, we print φροντιστής quoted in isolation (18b8) but in context κατὰ τούτους (17b6).

Because many readers will come to this book as intermediate students of Greek, we have tried to err on the side of generosity when providing assistance. It goes without saying that we have done far too much for some and nowhere near enough for others.

EDITORIAL NOTE

The running vocabulary presents less common words and expressions the first time they appear in the text. Readers should learn them at that time. We do not include in the running vocabulary words that are generally learned in first-year Greek, but all words can be found in the glossary (pp. 197–222). We give parsing help for verbs that use different stems to form their principal parts and for the less frequently encountered tenses and moods.

Plato's *Apology of Socrates*

Introduction

We have chosen not to produce a highly detailed survey of the historical and cultural contexts of Plato's *Apology of Socrates*. The amount of relevant material for such a study is vast, and much of it is collected usefully in works such as those by Brickhouse and Smith (1989) and Nails (2002).

Instead, we have tried to frame our task more simply with the needs of the intermediate Greek student in mind: what is the minimum amount of factual information necessary for someone encountering the work in the original language for the first time? To answer that question, we have divided what follows into two categories. Section I gives a basic outline of the historical context of Socrates' trial, focusing on the oligarchic revolution of 404 and the counterrevolution that followed. This section concludes with brief remarks about judicial procedure in Athens and the physical setting of the trial. Section II situates Plato and Socrates within fifth- and fourth-century Athenian society and emphasizes their place within the history of Western culture. It concludes with a discussion of what is sometimes known as the "Socratic question," the fact that Socrates wrote nothing and that much of what we know about him, including the *Apology*, comes through Plato.

In addition to this introduction, following the *Apology* text, we have supplied each of the chapters with short essays. There we introduce additional background information designed to clarify the points raised by Socrates and to encourage readers to think critically about them from a historically informed position. These essays can be assigned and used as the basis for class discussions, or they can be the starting point for paper topics or for general reflection.

I. THE HISTORICAL BACKGROUND

The "Thirty Tyrants"

Socrates' trial took place in 399 B.C.E., after the end of the Peloponnesian War between Athens and Sparta (431–404). After the surrender of Athens, the Spartan victors chose a group of thirty citizens (the Thirty) to dismantle the democratic government and replace it with the "ancestral laws" (νόμοι πάτριοι), by which Athens was now to be governed (Xenophon, *Hellenica,* 2.3.2). These men, led by Critias, Plato's uncle, used their authority to restructure the courts and purge the city of their opponents. Many of those who were not executed fled to the Piraeus, where they were joined by Thrasybulus and began to organize resistance under his leadership. In 403 they were attacked by the oligarchs, whom they defeated, killing Critias and also Plato's uncle Charmides, who had been an important collaborator of the Thirty.

Amnesty

Most of the oligarchs who survived fled to Eleusis, where they had prepared a refuge for themselves. The exiled democrats, who included in their number Socrates' close friend Chaerephon, as Socrates reminds the jury (*Apology* 21a), returned to Athens. An amnesty was negotiated (with the help of the Spartan commander Pausanias) that extended to all but the Thirty and a few others.

Aftermath

Socrates himself did not go into exile and was regarded with suspicion by some democratic leaders, although he was sixty-five at the time of the revolution. He makes it quite clear that he was no supporter of the Thirty and tells a story about a time when he explicitly disobeyed their orders (*Apology* 32c–d). Whatever doubts the democrats may have had about Socrates, the amnesty agreement prevented anyone from prosecuting him for having given even tacit support to the oligarchs. In 399, however, he was brought to trial on a charge of impiety (ἀσέβεια) by three Athenians: Meletus and Lycon, about whom little is known, and Anytus, a prominent democratic leader.

The Charges against Socrates

Socrates quotes the charges against him at 28b–c: "Socrates does wrong, both because he corrupts the youth, and because he does not recognize the gods the city recognizes." At the beginning of the *Memorabilia* (1.1.1), Xenophon quotes a similar charge. Diogenes Laertius (2.40) repeats the charge and adds that the penalty sought by the prosecution was death. Religious offenses in ancient Athens were taken seriously, as the welfare of the city was understood to depend upon the continued support of the gods. At the same time, religious practice, so often an emotional issue, could be exploited cynically by one's political opponents.

Pretrial Hearing

Following the accusation, a formal hearing was held before the King-Archon, the official responsible for cases involving violations of religious law.[1] If the King-Archon decided that there was sufficient evidence to bring the accused to trial, as he clearly did, the case was sent to the Heliaea, the court that heard cases regarding impiety.

1. This aspect of the process is tightly woven into the fabric of the Platonic dialogues. Socrates leaves the conversation at the end of the *Theaetetus* to go to the hearing, and he encounters Euthyphro, in the dialogue of the same name, as he leaves the meeting with the King-Archon.

The Courtroom

The trial took place outdoors. The courtroom was a semipublic setting that allowed spectators to hear the speeches and react to them. At the same time, the court was physically separated from the public, probably by a low wall that allowed officers of the court to maintain order and to make certain that only actual members of the jury were allowed to vote.

The Jury

The pool of jurors was chosen annually. On any given day when the courts were in session, interested jurors assembled early and, through a complex procedure designed to guard against jury packing, received a token that gave them entrance to the appropriate court. Although precision is not possible due to the lack of evidence, Socrates' jury probably consisted of 500 jurors, or perhaps 501 to avoid the possibility of a tie.

The Trial

On the day of the trial, after the traditional prayers and sacrifices had been made, each side was given an equal amount of time to present its case. A vote was then taken to determine the guilt or innocence of the defendant. If the vote was in his favor, he walked away a free man. Further, if the prosecutor did not secure one-fifth of the vote, the latter was subject to a fine for frivolous prosecution (cf. *Apology* 36b). But if the jury voted to convict, as was the case for Socrates, a second penalty phase ensued. The original indictment would have included the penalty proposed by the prosecution, and at this time the accusors justified their reasoning. The defendant then had the opportunity to suggest a different penalty, as Socrates does beginning at 35e1. After this speech, the jury voted again for one of the two alternatives. In the *Apology*, they accepted the proposal of the prosecution and sentenced Socrates to death.

II. SOCRATES AND PLATO

In the *Apology*, we read the response of a philosopher on trial for his life. It is a work admirable for the luminosity of its writing, its depiction of the philosopher's reply to an uncomprehending and hostile public, its dramatization of a crucial moment in Western intellectual history, and its unwavering defense of the value of the philosophical life.

Plato's *Apology* is only one version of Socrates' defense. There were a number of different versions of this speech in circulation. Each portrayed Socrates' trial and conviction in a different light, depending on whether the writer was a supporter of Socrates or an opponent.[2] The fact that the trial had such a galvanizing effect on so many people indicates that Socrates was no ordinary man and that he remained a source of controversy and contention in death at least as much as in life.

To understand why Plato felt it necessary to produce his own version of Socrates' defense speech, we must first try to understand what has made Socrates such an object of fascination and controversy. There are many answers to this question, and we cannot possibly hope to cover them adequately in such a small space. Nonetheless, there are several points that the beginning reader needs to consider.

First Philosopher

Socrates was in a real sense the first philosopher of the Western tradition. While there were certainly men before him whom we now call pre-Socratic philosophers, the very fact that they are so labeled denotes that the arrival of Socrates marks a fundamental break in the history of formal thought in the West. The nature of that break, as it is presented to us by Aristotle (*Metaphysics* 1) and by the fragments of those earlier thinkers, is as follows: while the

2. Danzig 2003 offers the most up-to-date account of this controversy and of Plato's and Xenophon's contributions to it.

pre-Socratics were, by and large, concerned with cosmogonic and physical speculations, Socrates turned philosophical inquiry inward and asked "who am I?" and "how should I live?" He does not ask what the basic physical or metaphysical elements of the universe are, but what the nature of the self is, how one cares for it, and how one does so in the company of others.

The Socratic Method

Socrates' "method," at least as it is presented by Plato, Xenophon, Aristotle, and others, was to inquire into the nature of the good, the self, justice, wisdom, and so forth by asking his fellow citizens what they thought these things were. In so doing, he also asked them to defend their beliefs and assumptions, while demanding that they maintain a high standard of logical consistency. Such questioning often revealed the existence of unfounded or contradictory sets of beliefs, which could not be defended and hence demanded revision. Thus, Socrates was not a dogmatic philosopher or a builder of elaborate systems, nor did he present a series of abstract speculations as received truth or the product of his genius. Rather, he defined philosophy as an ongoing mode of inquiry into the foundations of our communal and individual lives—one that is undertaken in dialogue with others.

Philosophy's Challenge

By demanding that individuals examine in a rigorous manner their beliefs and assumptions concerning the values they held most dear, Socrates was also necessarily a provocative figure, who often occasioned anger and resentment from those he questioned. His actions, which often cast him in the role of a dissident within his community, clearly made him enemies. He did not simply accept the received verities of Athenian ideology and religion, but demanded that his fellow citizens subject those "truths" to rigorous examination. Socrates, in effect, founded philosophy as a form of political and social criticism if not direct civil disobedience.

The "Socratic Question"

Socrates was a philosopher who did not write. In fact, the memory of Socrates largely survives into the modern world owing to the works of Plato. The son of an aristocratic family that was deeply embedded in the politics of Athens, Plato was well placed to become one of the ambitious and cynical young men who populate his dialogues. Instead, he appears to have committed himself to Socrates and to philosophy at an early age. Plato was twenty-eight, according to Diogenes Laertius (3.6), when Socrates was executed. He devoted the rest of his long life (he died in 348 B.C.E.) to trying to understand what this formative influence on his life meant and how to live in accord with his understanding of it. Plato produced a large body of work, much of which is centered around the conversations of Socrates. While other portraits of Socrates were in circulation in antiquity, and especially in the immediate wake of his execution, Plato's became authoritative, and it is through Plato that the founder of Western philosophy has come down to us.

Platonic Writing

Plato's Socrates achieved preeminence for at least two reasons. First, Plato is a writer of extraordinary talent. His characters are drawn vividly; his language is clear and precise; his syntax is conversational and his wit brilliant. Every word in a Platonic dialogue is chosen for maximum impact. Indeed, Plato's attention to revision (*philoponia*) was legendary in antiquity.[3] The result is that even when the language appears to be casual and improvised, we can assume that a great deal of labor has gone into making it appear that way.

Second, Plato was an original philosopher of genius. This description may seem a bit of a paradox for a man who devoted his life to

3. See, for example, Dionysius of Halicarnassus, *De compositione verborum* 25; Quintilian 8.6.64; Diogenes Laertius 3.37.

conserving the memory of his teacher, but it is nevertheless true. Further, there is a great deal of debate in the scholarly literature about which dialogues are early and which are late, which dialogues are closer to the teachings of Socrates and which are more clearly the products of Plato's invention. The controversies here are many, and it is not necessary for the first-time reader of the *Apology* to feel a need to decide on such matters. What seems clear, however, and what nobody seriously denies, is that Plato does not simply set himself the task of recording Socrates' speeches and conversations. He is not a journalist. Rather, he strives from first to last to come to grips with both Socrates as a man and the challenge he offered to received modes of thought. To do that effectively, Plato was required to develop his own understanding of these matters, eventually writing long and complex works such as the *Republic*, *Symposium*, *Parmenides*, *Philebus*, and *Timaeus*. These could only have been produced through a process of considerable reflection and elaboration and not through the simple transcription of a set of conversations, no matter their brilliance, subtlety, or depth.

The result of this complex authorial situation is that we must always speak of Plato *and* Socrates when responding to the *Apology*. There is no doubt that Socrates was a very real individual, who provoked both fierce hostility and fond attachment among his fellow citizens. He stands at the head of a long list of truth tellers and inquirers who have challenged the received opinions of their governments and their peers in the name of the love of wisdom (*philo-sophia*). But the Socrates we have in the text of the *Apology*, although he exists in other recorded versions that have come down to us from antiquity, especially those of Xenophon, is largely a product of the literary and philosophical genius of Plato. With the *Apology*, then, we stand at the beginning of the Western literary, philosophical, and political tradition, and this is why no one can seriously call him- or herself educated who has not closely pondered the meaning and art of this seminal text.

III. BIBLIOGRAPHY

Adam, A. M. 1914. *The Apology of Socrates.* Cambridge, UK: Cambridge University Press.

Ahbel-Rappe, Sara, and Rachana Kametkar, eds. 2006. *A Companion to Socrates*. London: Blackwell.

Allen, R. E. 1970. *Plato's* Euthyphro *and the Early Theory of Forms.* London: Routledge and Kegan Paul.

———. 1980. *Socrates and Legal Obligation.* Minneapolis: University of Minnesota Press.

Bosher, K. 2007. "Circle or Square?: Imagining the Early Greek Orchestra." Paper presented at the annual meeting of the American Institute of Archaeology, San Diego, Calif.

Brickhouse, Thomas C., and Nicholas D. Smith. 1989. *Socrates on Trial.* Princeton: Princeton University Press.

———. 1992. *The Trial and Execution of Socrates: Sources and Controversies.* New York and Oxford: Oxford University Press.

———. 2004. *Routledge Guidebook to Plato and the Trial of Socrates.* London and New York: Routledge.

Brisson, Luc. 1998. *Plato the Mythmaker*. Translated and edited by Gerard Nadaff. Chicago: University of Chicago Press.

Burnet, John. 1924. *Plato's Euthyphro, Apology, and Crito.* Oxford: Oxford University Press.

Burnyeat, Myles F. 2003. "*Apology* 30b2–4: Socrates, Money, and the Grammar of ΓΙΓΝΕΣΘΑΙ." *Journal of Hellenic Studies* 123: 1–25.

———. 2004. "On the Source of Burnet's Construal of *Apology* 30b2–4: A Correction." *Journal of Hellenic Studies* 124: 139–42.

Carter, L. B. 1986. *The Quiet Athenian.* Oxford: Clarendon Press.

Colaiaco, James A. 2001. *Socrates against Athens: Philosophy on Trial*. New York and London: Routledge.

Croiset, A. 1920–. *Platon, Oeuvres complètes*. Paris: Association Guillaume Budé.

Danzig, Gabriel. 2003. "Apologizing for Socrates: Plato and Xenophon on Socrates' Behavior in Court." *Transactions of the American Philological Association* 133: 281–321.

Davidson, Arnold I., ed. 1997. *Foucault and His Interlocutors.* Chicago: University of Chicago Press.

Denniston, J. D. 1954. *The Greek Particles.* Oxford: Clarendon Press.

deRomilly, Jacqueline. 1992. Translated by Janet Lloyd. *The Great Sophists of Periclean Athens.* Oxford: Clarendon Press.

Destree, Pierre, and Nicholas P. Smith, eds. 2005. *Socrates' Divine Sign: Religious Practice and Value in Socratic Philosophy.* Kelowna, B.C.: Academic Printing and Publishing.

Dodds, E. R. 1951. *The Greeks and the Irrational.* Berkeley: University of California Press.

———. 1966. *Plato: Gorgias.* Oxford: Clarendon Press.

Dover, K. J. 1972. *Aristophanic Comedy.* Berkeley: University of California Press.

———. 1974. *Greek Popular Morality in the Time of Plato and Aristotle.* Oxford: Blackwell.

Dow, S. 1939. "Aristotle, the Kleroteria, and the Courts." *Harvard Studies in Classical Philology* 50: 1–34.

Dyer, Louis. 1908. *Apology of Socrates and Crito, with Extracts from the Phaedo and Symposium and from Xenophon's Memorabilia.* Revised by Thomas Day Seymour. Boston and New York: Ginn & Co.

Foucault, Michel. 2005. *The Hermeneutics of the Subject: Lectures at the Collège de France 1981–1982.* Edited by Frédéric Gros. Translated by Graham Burchell. Series editors, François Ewald and Alessandro Fontana. English series editor, Arnold J. Davidson. New York: Picador.

Fowler, Robert, ed. 2004. *The Cambridge Companion to Homer.* Cambridge: Cambridge University Press.

Gantz, Timothy. 1993. *Early Greek Myth: A Guide to Literary and Artistic Sources.* Baltimore: Johns Hopkins University Press.

Gentili, Bruno. 1988. *Poetry and Its Public in Ancient Greece from Homer to the Fifth Century.* Translated by A. Thomas Cole. Baltimore and London: Johns Hopkins University Press.

Grube, G. M. A., trans. 1988. *The Trial and Death of Socrates: Euthyphro, Apology, Crito, and Death Scene from Phaedo.* Indianapolis: Hackett Publishing.

Guthrie, W. K. C. 1975. *A History of Greek Philosophy.* Vol. 4. Cambridge: Cambridge University Press.

Habinek, Thomas. 2005. *Ancient Rhetoric and Oratory*. Oxford: Blackwell.

Hadot, Pierre. 1997. "Forms of Life and Forms of Discourse in Ancient Philosophy," translated by Arnold I. Davidson and Paula Wissing. In *Foucault and His Interlocutors*, edited by Arnold I. Davidson, 203–24. Chicago: University of Chicago Press.

———. 2002. *What is Ancient Philosophy?* Translated by Michael Chase. Cambridge, Mass., Belknap Press of Harvard University Press.

Halliwell, Stephen. 1991. "The Uses of Laughter in Greek Culture." *Classical Quarterly*, n.s., 41: 279–96.

Hans, James S. 2006. *Socrates and the Irrational*. Charlottesville: University of Virginia Press.

Harris, W. V. 1989. *Ancient Literacy*. Cambridge, Mass.: Harvard University Press.

Havelock, Eric A. 1963. *Preface to Plato*. Cambridge, Mass.: Harvard University Press.

Helm, James J. 1997. *Plato: Apology*. Rev. ed. Chicago: Bolchazy-Carducci.

Hunter, Richard. 2004. *Plato's* Symposium. Oxford: Oxford University Press.

———. 2004. "Homer and Greek Literature." In *The Cambridge Companion to Homer*, edited by Robert Fowler, 235–53. Cambridge: Cambridge University Press.

Irwin, T. H. 1992. "Plato: The Intellectual Background." In *The Cambridge Companion to Plato*, edited by Richard Kraut, 51–89. Cambridge: Cambridge University Press.

Kennedy, George. 1963. *The Art of Persuasion in Greece*. Princeton: Princeton University Press.

Kerford, G. B. 1981. *The Sophistic Movement*. Cambridge: Harvard University Press.

King, Martin Luther. 1986. *A Testament of Hope: The Essential Writings and Speeches of Martin Luther King, Jr.* Edited by James Melvin Washington. San Francisco: Harper Collins.

Kirk, G. S., J. E. Raven, and M. Schofield [1983]. *The Presocratic Philosophers*. 2nd ed. Cambridge: Cambridge University Press.

Kraut, Richard. 1992. *The Cambridge Companion to Plato*. Cambridge and New York: Cambridge University Press.

———. 2006. "The Examined Life." In *A Companion to Socrates,* edited by Sara Ahbel-Rappe and Rachana Kametkar, 228–42. London: Blackwell.

Lang, M. 1978. *Socrates in the A*gora. Athens: American School of Classical Studies.

Larson, Thomas L., ed. 1963. *Plato: Totalitarian or Democrat?* Englewood Cliffs, N.J.: Prentice-Hall.

Ledbetter, Grace M. 2003. *Poetics before Plato: Interpretation and Authority in Early Greek Theories of Poetry.* Princeton: Princeton University Press.

Long, A. A. 2006. "How Does Socrates' Divine Sign Communicate with Him?" In *A Companion to Socrates,* edited by Sara Ahbel-Rappe and Rachana Kametkar, 63–74. London: Blackwell.

MacDowell, Douglas. 1995. *Aristophanes and Athens: An Introduction to the Plays.* Oxford: Oxford University Press.

Mara, Gerald M. 1997. *Socrates' Discursive Democracy: Logos and Ergon in Platonic Political Philosophy*. Albany: State University of New York Press.

McCoy, Marina. 2008. *Plato on the Rhetoric of Philosophers and Sophists.* Cambridge: Cambridge University Press.

Mikalson, Jon D. 1983. *Athenian Popular Religion*. Chapel Hill and London: University of North Carolina Press.

Miller, Paul Allen. 1994. "Epos and Iambos or Archilochus Meets the Wolfman." In *Lyric Texts and Lyric Consciousness: The Birth of a Genre from Archaic Greece to Augustan Rome*, 9–36. London: Routledge.

———. 2007. "Lacan, the *Symposium*, and Transference." In *Postmodern Spiritual Practices: The Reception of Plato and the Construction of the Subject in Lacan, Derrida, and Foucault,* 100–32. Columbus: Ohio State University Press.

Momigliano, Arnaldo. 1971. *The Development of Greek Biography: Four Lectures.* Cambridge: Harvard University Press.

Morgan, Michael L. 1992. "Plato and Greek Religion." In *The Cambridge Companion to Plato,* edited by Richard Kraut, 227–47. Cambridge and New York: Cambridge University Press.

Nagy, Gregory. 1979. *The Best of the Achaeans: Concepts of the Hero in Archaic Greek Poetry*. Baltimore: Johns Hopkins University Press.

Nails, Deborah. 2002. *The People of Plato: A Prosopography of Plato and Other Socratics.* Indianapolis: Hackett Publishing.

Nehamas, Alexander. 1998. *The Art of Living: Socratic Reflections from Plato to Foucault*. Berkeley: University of California Press.

Nietzsche, Friedrich. 2003. *The Birth of Tragedy: Out of the Spirit of Music,* translated by Shaun Whiteside. London: Penguin.

Nightingale, Andrea Wilson. 1995. *Genres in Dialogue: Plato and the Construct of Philosophy*. Cambridge and New York: Cambridge University Press.

O'Sullivan , L. L. 1997. "Athenian Impiety Trials in the Late Fourth Century B. C." *Classical Quarterly,* n.s. 47, 136–52.

Penner, Terry. 1992. "Socrates and the Early Dialogues." In *The Cambridge Companion to Plato,* edited by Richard Kraut, 121–69. Cambridge and New York: Cambridge University Press.

Places, E. D. 1964. *Lexique: La langue philosophique et religieuse de Platon*. 2 vols. Paris: Les Belles Lettres.

Platter, Charles. 2005. "Was Plato the Founder of Totalitarianism?" *Classical Studies and the Ancient World. History in Dispute*, vol. 21, edited by Paul Allen Miller and Charles Platter, 154–63. Detroit: Gale.

———. 2007. *Aristophanes and the Carnival of Genres*. Baltimore: Johns Hopkins University Press.

Reeve, C. D. C. 1989. *Socrates in the* Apology: *An Essay on Plato's* Apology of Socrates. Indianapolis: Hackett.

Riddell, J. 1973. *The Apology of Plato, with a Revised Text and English Notes, and a Digest of Platonic Idioms*. New York: Arno Press.

Roochnik, David. 2004. *Retrieving the Ancients: An Introduction to Greek Philosophy.* London: Blackwell.

Rose, Gilbert. 1989. *Plato's Apology: Text and Commentary.* Indianapolis: Bryn Mawr Commentaries, Hackett Publishing.

Sayre, Kenneth M. "Plato's Dialogues in Light of the *Seventh Letter*." In *Platonic Writings, Platonic Readings,* edited by Charles L. Griswold, Jr., 93–109. New York: Routledge.

Schiappa, Edward. 2002. *Protagoras and Logos*. Columbia: University of South Carolina Press.

Sealey, Robert. 1983. "The Athenian Courts of Homicide." *Classical Philology* 78: 275–96.

Slings, S. R. 1994. *Plato's* Apology of Socrates*: A Literary and Philosophical Study with a Running Commentary*. Leiden, New York, and Cologne: E. J. Brill.

Smith, Nicholas D., and Paul B. Woodruff, eds. 2000. *Reason and Religion in Socratic Philosophy*. New York: Oxford University Press.

Smyth, H. W. 1956. *Greek Grammar*. Revised by Gordon M. Messing. Cambridge: Harvard University Press.

Stokes, Michael C. 2005. *Dialectic in Action: An Examination of Plato's* Crito. Swansea: Classical Press of Wales.

Strauss, Barry S. 1993. *Fathers and Sons in Athens: Ideology and Society in the Era of the Peloponnesian War.* London: Routledge.

Tarrant, H. T. H. 1993. *The Last Days of Socrates.* London and New York: Penguin Books.

Thomas, Rosalind. 1989. *Oral Tradition and Written Record in Classical Athens*. Cambridge and New York: Cambridge University Press.

———. 1992. *Literacy and Orality in Ancient Greece*. Cambridge and New York: Cambridge University Press.

Thoreau, Henry David. 2003. *Walden and Civil Disobedience*. Edited by Jonathon Levin. New York: Barnes & Noble.

Tredennick, Hugh, trans. 1969. *Plato: The Last Days of Socrates: Euthyphro, The Apology, Crito, Phaedo*. London: Penguin.

Veyne, Paul. 1988. *Did the Greeks Believe in Their Myths?: An Essay on the Constitutive Imagination*. Translated by Paula Wissing. Chicago: University of Chicago Press.

Vlastos, Gregory. 1991. *Socrates: Ironist and Moral Philosopher*. Ithaca, N.Y.: Cornell University Press.

Weber, F. J. 1986. *Platons Apologie der Sokrates*. Paderborn, Ger.: Ferdenand Schöningen.

Weiss, Roslyn. 2006. *The Socratic Paradox and Its Enemies.* Chicago: University of Chicago Press.

Wilson, Emily. 2007. *The Death of Socrates*. Cambridge: Harvard University Press.

Woodbury, Leonard. 1981. "Anaxagoras and Athens." *Phoenix* 35: 295–315.

Worthington, Ian, ed. 2007. *A Companion to Greek Rhetoric*. Oxford: Blackwell.

Apology of Socrates

CHAPTER 1

(17a1–18a6)

Socrates introduces two important themes for the rest of the dialogue in the first sentence: (1) the effect of speech on the hearer, and (2) the relation between what one *thinks* one knows and the truth. These topics, however, are introduced casually and seem at first to have no further significance than "what effect my accusers have had upon you, I don't know." For additional discussion of the chapter and questions for study, see essay 1.

Ὅτι μὲν ὑμεῖς, ὦ ἄνδρες Ἀθηναῖοι, πεπόνθατε ὑπὸ τῶν a
ἐμῶν κατηγόρων, οὐκ οἶδα· ἐγὼ δ᾽ οὖν καὶ αὐτὸς ὑπ᾽ αὐτῶν
ὀλίγου ἐμαυτοῦ ἐπελαθόμην, οὕτω πιθανῶς ἔλεγον. καίτοι
ἀληθές γε ὡς ἔπος εἰπεῖν οὐδὲν εἰρήκασιν. μάλιστα δὲ

πεπόνθατε pf. act. indic. < πάσχω *experience*
κατηγόρων < κατήγορος, -ου, ὁ *accuser*
ὀλίγου *almost, just short of*
πιθανῶς *persuasively*
εἰρήκασιν pf. act. indic. < λέγω *say*

17a1 **ὅτι** = ὅ τι "Whatever."
ὦ ἄνδρες Ἀθηναῖοι Although this is supposed to be a defense speech, in various places Socrates goes out of his way to antagonize the jury. One way he does this is by choosing to address jury members only as "Athenians." He saves the commoner and more respectful form of address, ὦ ἄνδρες δικασταί, "O judges," for the jurors who vote to acquit him and pointedly adds that only they could rightly be addressed in this way (see 40a2–3). In another version of this same speech by Xenophon, Socrates is even more antagonistic.
πεπόνθατε The verb is essentially passive in meaning, so ὑπό + genitive commonly follows to indicate the person responsible.

17a2 **δ᾽οὖν** "Anyway." The particle intensifies the contrast signaled by μέν . . . δέ.
καί Adverbial here, as often: "even."

17a3 **ἐμαυτοῦ** Object of ἐπελαθόμην < ἐπιλανθάνομαι. Verbs of remembering and forgetting regularly take the genitive.

17a4 **ὡς ἔπος εἰπεῖν** Unlike the English, "so to speak," this idiom limits the scope of the statement. Translate "almost, practically."

αὐτῶν ἓν ἐθαύμασα τῶν πολλῶν ὧν ἐψεύσαντο, τοῦτο ἐν ᾧ ἔλεγον ὡς χρῆν ὑμᾶς εὐλαβεῖσθαι μὴ ὑπ' ἐμοῦ ἐξαπατηθῆτε
b ὡς δεινοῦ ὄντος λέγειν. τὸ γὰρ μὴ αἰσχυνθῆναι ὅτι αὐτίκα ὑπ' ἐμοῦ ἐξελεγχθήσονται ἔργῳ, ἐπειδὰν μηδ' ὁπωστιοῦν φαίνωμαι δεινὸς λέγειν, τοῦτό μοι ἔδοξεν αὐτῶν ἀναισχυντότατον εἶναι, εἰ μὴ ἄρα δεινὸν καλοῦσιν οὗτοι λέγειν τὸν τἀληθῆ λέγοντα· εἰ μὲν γὰρ τοῦτο λέγουσιν, ὁμολογοίην ἂν ἔγωγε οὐ κατὰ τούτους εἶναι ῥήτωρ. οὗτοι μὲν οὖν, ὥσπερ

ἐθαύμασα < θαυμάζω *marvel at*
χρῆν = ἔχρην, impf. of χρή *it is necessary*
εὐλαβεῖσθαι < εὐλαβέομαι *beware, take care*
ἐξαπατηθῆτε < ἐξαπατάω *deceive*
αἰσχυνθῆναι aor. pass. infin. < αἰσχύνω *shame*
ἐξελεγχθήσονται fut. pass. < ἐξελέγχω *examine closely, refute*
ὁπωστιοῦν *in any way at all*
ἀναισχυντότατον *most shameless*
ὁμολογοίην < ὁμολογέω *agree*
ῥήτωρ, -ορος, ὁ *orator*
ὥσπερ *just as*

17a5 **αὐτῶν** Agrees with πολλῶν.
ὧν Genitive by attraction.
τοῦτο "Of their many lies, I marveled at *this one* in particular."

17a6 **μή** The negative introduces a clause of fearing dependent on εὐλαβεῖσθαι.

17b1 **ὡς δείνου ὄντος** "On the grounds that [I] am (ὄντος) skilled at speaking (δεινοῦ λέγειν)." The genitives are governed by the ὑπό (ὑπ') in 17a6. The prosecutors have apparently warned the jurors that Socrates' speech will be full of deception. This was a charge often leveled at professional teachers of rhetoric (sophists) and their students. Athenian oratory is full of disclaimers designed to counter such attacks. Litigants often strike the pose of simple men who speak the truth (see Lysias 19.1.2; Isaeus 10.1). Like them, Socrates denies any particular eloquence. Nevertheless, his pause at 17b4 to consider ironically that he may have misunderstood what his accusers meant by δεινὸς λέγειν clearly illustrates his *skill at speaking*.

17b1 **τό . . . μὴ αἰσχυνθῆναι** "The idea that [they] would not be shamed . . ." The articular infinitive functions as the subject of ἔδοξεν (b3) and is the antecedent of τοῦτο.

17b3 **αὐτῶν** "Of them" (the accusers).

17b4 **εἰ μὴ ἄρα** "Unless, of course." ἄρα ironically draws attention to the special sense of δεινὸς λέγειν that Socrates pretends to discover.

17b5 **τἀληθῆ** = τὰ ἀληθῆ
λέγουσιν "They mean."
ὁμολογοίην Potential optative.

17b6 **οὐ κατὰ τούτους** "Not after *their* fashion."
μὲν οὖν οὖν ("so, . . .") resumes the discussion interrupted by Socrates' musing on what his accusers meant by δεινός. μέν sets up a contrast with ὑμεῖς δέ (17b8).

ἐγὼ λέγω, ἤ τι ἢ οὐδὲν ἀληθὲς εἰρήκασιν, ὑμεῖς δέ μου ἀκού-
σεσθε πᾶσαν τὴν ἀλήθειαν—οὐ μέντοι μὰ Δία, ὦ ἄνδρες
Ἀθηναῖοι, κεκαλλιεπημένους γε λόγους, ὥσπερ οἱ τούτων,
ῥήμασί τε καὶ ὀνόμασιν οὐδὲ κεκοσμημένους, ἀλλ᾽ ἀκού- c
σεσθε εἰκῇ λεγόμενα τοῖς ἐπιτυχοῦσιν ὀνόμασιν—πιστεύω
γὰρ δίκαια εἶναι ἃ λέγω—καὶ μηδεὶς ὑμῶν προσδοκησάτω
ἄλλως· οὐδὲ γὰρ ἂν δήπου πρέποι, ὦ ἄνδρες, τῇδε τῇ
ἡλικίᾳ ὥσπερ μειρακίῳ πλάττοντι λόγους εἰς ὑμᾶς εἰσιέναι.

ἤ τι ἢ οὐδέν *little or nothing*
εἰκῇ *at random*
ἐπιτυχοῦσιν aor. act. part. < ἐπιτυγχάνω *chance upon*
ὀνόμασιν < ὄνομα, -τος, τό *name*
προσδοκησάτω 3rd pers. aor. act. imper. < προσδοκάω *expect*
πρέποι opt. < πρέπει (impers.) *be fitting*
μειρακίῳ < μειράκιον, -ου, τό *youth*
πλάττοντι < πλάττω *shape, fashion*
εἰσιέναι < εἴσειμι *go into*

17b7–c5 From me, you shall hear the unvarnished truth; it is not fitting for a man of my age to play rhetorical games.

17b8 **μου . . . ἀλήθειαν** ἀκούω takes an accusative of the thing heard and a genitive of the person.

μὰ Δία "No, by Zeus." μά is a negative interjection, used with οὐ or independently.

17b9 **κεκαλλιεπημένους . . . λόγους** "Artful language . . . arranged with phrases and words," that is, "with artfully arranged phrases and words." The participles go with λόγους in form but with ῥήμασί τε καὶ ὀνόμασιν in sense. Socrates' diction parodies the type of speech he is imagining. Note the rhyming endings (*homoioteleuton*), evocative of the style of Gorgias of Leontini, one of the most influential sophists of the fifth century. His visit to Athens in 427 B.C.E. provides the occasion for Plato's dialogue *Gorgias*.

οἱ τούτων Supply λόγοι.

17c2 **ἐπιτυχοῦσιν** The claim cannot be taken at face value. As we have already seen, Plato chooses Socrates' words carefully. Note how the loose structure of this sentence gives the impression of improvisation.

17c3 **δίκαια** For the idea that simple words are inherently more likely to be trusted than clever ones, see on 17b1.

ἃ λέγω The relative clause (antecedent omitted) functions as the subject of εἶναι.

17c4 **οὐδὲ . . . ἂν . . . πρέποι** Supply μοι with the potential optative, which also accounts for the case of μειρακίῳ below.

δήπου "Surely." The word is used ironically, as often in Plato.

17c5 **τῇ ἡλικίᾳ**, "At my age."

καὶ μέντοι καὶ πάνυ, ὦ ἄνδρες Ἀθηναῖοι, τοῦτο ὑμῶν δέομαι
καὶ παρίεμαι· ἐὰν διὰ τῶν αὐτῶν λόγων ἀκούητέ μου ἀπο-
λογουμένου δι' ὧνπερ εἴωθα λέγειν καὶ ἐν ἀγορᾷ ἐπὶ τῶν
τραπεζῶν, ἵνα ὑμῶν πολλοὶ ἀκηκόασι, καὶ ἄλλοθι, μήτε
d θαυμάζειν μήτε θορυβεῖν τούτου ἕνεκα. ἔχει γὰρ οὑτωσί.

δέομαι *ask*
παρίεμαι *beg*
εἴωθα pf. (with pres. meaning) < ἤθω *be accustomed*
ἄλλοθι *elsewhere*
θορυβεῖν < **θορυβέω** *make an uproar*
οὑτωσί *thus*

17c6 **καὶ μέντοι καί** "Yes, indeed, and."

17c6–d1. The sentence raises the question of whether the jurors might wonder and create a disturbance because they are unused to hearing everyday speech in a court setting or because, as we see later in the speech, Socrates' normal manner of speaking with his fellow citizens causes consternation and wonder.

17c7-8 **διὰ τῶν αὐτῶν λόγων . . . δι' ὧνπερ** "By the very same words which." Socrates' request is both conventional and idiosyncratic. Demosthenes 25.14 has a speaker making a similar plea. At the same time, Socrates' lack of pretense and fondness for homely examples are axiomatic in both Plato and Xenophon (although generally understood to be ironic). Note that he makes a similar request prior to the conversation with Meletus (27b).

17c8 **ἐν ἀγορᾷ** The agora was the social center of Athenian public life. As Burnet (1924) notes, words such as ἀγορά, ἄστυ, and ἀγρός appear so commonly that they are treated as virtual proper nouns and thus appear without the article.

ἐπὶ τῶν τραπεζῶν The variety of coined money circulating in Athens stimulated the development of private banks conducted at "tables" in the agora, where money could be exchanged and transactions could be witnessed by a third party.

17d1 **θαυμάζειν . . . θορυβεῖν** Both infinitives depend on δέομαι and παρίεμαι, above. Although the *Apology* is not a court transcript, Plato goes out of his way to include details that suggest otherwise. Unlike modern courtrooms, where extraneous noise is strongly discouraged, Athenian juries could be quite noisy. Burnet (1924) correctly notes that the verb θορυβεῖν can refer either to heckling or to applause. Although Socrates here refers to the former, his speech to those who vote for a lesser punishment after his conviction indicates the presence of hard-core supporters as well. Athenian rules of jury selection made jury-packing difficult, however, with potential jurors assigned randomly to courtrooms. Nevertheless, there were plenty of opportunities for spectators to make their opinions known, whether they were members of the jury or not.

οὑτωσί The adverb is made more emphatic by the addition of the deictic iota. Note that its accent is fixed and is not affected by the normal accentuation of the adverb.

νῦν ἐγὼ πρῶτον ἐπὶ δικαστήριον ἀναβέβηκα, ἔτη γεγονὼς
ἑβδομήκοντα· ἀτεχνῶς οὖν ξένως ἔχω τῆς ἐνθάδε λέξεως.
ὥσπερ οὖν ἄν, εἰ τῷ ὄντι ξένος ἐτύγχανον ὤν, συνεγιγνώσκετε δήπου ἄν μοι εἰ ἐν ἐκείνῃ τῇ φωνῇ τε καὶ τῷ τρόπῳ
ἔλεγον ἐν οἷσπερ ἐτεθράμμην, καὶ δὴ καὶ νῦν τοῦτο ὑμῶν 18
δέομαι δίκαιον, ὥς γέ μοι δοκῶ, τὸν μὲν τρόπον τῆς λέξεως
ἐᾶν—ἴσως μὲν γὰρ χείρων, ἴσως δὲ βελτίων ἂν εἴη—αὐτὸ
δὲ τοῦτο σκοπεῖν καὶ τούτῳ τὸν νοῦν προσέχειν, εἰ δίκαια
λέγω ἢ μή· δικαστοῦ μὲν γὰρ αὕτη ἀρετή, ῥήτορος δὲ
τἀληθῆ λέγειν.

ἀναβέβηκα pf. act. indic. < ἀναβαίνω appear in court
ἔτη < ἔτος, -ους, τό *year*
γεγονώς pf. act. part. < γίγνομαι *attain, become*
ἑβδομήκοντα (indeclinable) *seventy*
ἀτεχνῶς *literally*
τῷ ὄντι really
συνεγιγνώσκετε impf. act. < συγγιγνώσκω *pardon*
φωνῇ < φωνή, -ῆς, ἡ *voice, speech style*
τρόπῳ < τρόπος, -ου, ὁ *manner*
ἐτεθράμμην pluperf. pass. < τρέφω *raise, bring up*
ἐᾶν pres. act. infin. < ἐάω *allow*
δικαστοῦ < δικαστής, -οῦ, ὁ *judge, juror*

17d2 **ἐπὶ δικαστήριον ἀναβέβηκα** "I am appearing before the court." ἐπὶ δικαστήριον ἀναβαίνειν is a technical legal term.
ἔτη . . . ἑβδομήκοντα Later, Socrates, will say that such longevity would never have been possible had he not abstained from politics. The fact that he regards his complete absence from the courts as worthy of mention gives some indication of the litigious nature of Athenian society.

17d3 **τῆς ἐνθάδε λέξεως** "The style of speech here."

17d4 **ὥσπερ οὖν ἄν** The condition is present contrary-to-fact. ἄν (both of them) goes with συνεγιγνώσκετε. The metaphor hinted at with ξένως (c3) now becomes a full-blown analogy.

18a1 **καὶ δὴ καὶ νῦν** "And so, now."

18a3 **ἴσως μὲν γὰρ χείρων, ἴσως δὲ βελτίων ἂν εἴη** "Perhaps it may be worse, perhaps better." On one level, this sentence asks the jurors to withold judgment on the untutored forensic oratory of Socrates. On another, it raises the possibility that his seemingly spontaneous style may well be superior to that of his rhetorically trained opponents.
αὐτὸ δὲ τοῦτο "This very thing," referring to εἰ δίκαια λέγω ἢ μή below.

18a5 **αὕτη** < οὗτος not αὐτός. ἀρετή is predicate, as omission of the article shows: "This is the virtue [i.e., the defining quality] of . . ."

CHAPTER 2

(18a7–19a7)

Overview of the defense: Socrates defends himself against the charges of his fellow Athenians, both those present in the court (οἱ ὕστεροι κατήγοροι) and those who have slandered him for a long time (οἱ πρῶτοι κατήγοροι). For additional discussion of the chapter and questions for study, see essay 2.

Πρῶτον μὲν οὖν δίκαιός εἰμι ἀπολογήσασθαι, ὦ ἄνδρες
Ἀθηναῖοι, πρὸς τὰ πρῶτά μου ψευδῆ κατηγορημένα καὶ τοὺς
πρώτους κατηγόρους, ἔπειτα δὲ πρὸς τὰ ὕστερον καὶ τοὺς
b ὑστέρους. ἐμοῦ γὰρ πολλοὶ κατήγοροι γεγόνασι πρὸς ὑμᾶς
καὶ πάλαι πολλὰ ἤδη ἔτη καὶ οὐδὲν ἀληθὲς λέγοντες, οὓς
ἐγὼ μᾶλλον φοβοῦμαι ἢ τοὺς ἀμφὶ Ἄνυτον, καίπερ ὄντας

κατηγορημένα pf. pass. part. < κατηγορέω *accuse, charge*

18a7 **δίκαιος** "Justified," a common usage. Note the recurrent use of vocabulary derived from δίκη (see, for example, 18a1, a4, and a5). As a result of their frequent appearances, these words come to have thematic connotations beyond their literal definitions. They remind the jury that their constant concern should be what is just. Moreover, the words are designed to spur a more general philosophical reflection on the nature of justice.

18a8 **μου** Genitive with a verb of accusation (κατηγορεῖν). Nouns derived from such verbs also take a genitive object. See 18b1 below.

18a9 **τὰ ὕστερον** "The later ones." That is, the most recent false charges. Socrates decides to deviate from the accusation at hand to address charges made by an earlier set of accusers. This is perhaps not a good legal strategy and raises again a question alluded to earlier (see on 17a1) regarding Socrates' attitude toward his judges and whether he is really trying to save his life. Xenophon writes in his *Apology* that Socrates had determined that it was time for him to die and so deliberately provoked the jury (4).

18b3 **τοὺς ἀμφὶ Ἄνυτον** "Those around Anytus." Anytus was a prominent leader of the democratic faction and is represented in Plato's *Meno* as resentful of Socrates' criticism of his associates. He was later exiled by the Thirty (see introduction), with whom some democrats may have associated Socrates, and lost most of his considerable inheritance. His coprosecutors may have

καὶ τούτους δεινούς· ἀλλ' ἐκεῖνοι δεινότεροι, ὦ ἄνδρες, οἳ ὑμῶν τοὺς πολλοὺς ἐκ παίδων παραλαμβάνοντες ἔπειθόν τε καὶ κατηγόρουν ἐμοῦ μᾶλλον οὐδὲν ἀληθές, ὡς ἔστιν τις Σωκράτης σοφὸς ἀνήρ, τά τε μετέωρα φροντιστὴς καὶ τὰ

παραλαμβάνοντες < παραλαμβάνω *take in hand, take aside*

---

had similar motivations. Lycon's son was executed by the Thirty. For a discussion of the prosecutors, see on 23e3–24a1.

18b5 **ἐκ παίδων** "From the time you were children."

18b5-6 **ἔπειθον . . . κατηγόρουν** The imperfects suggest ongoing action.

18b6 **ὡς** Here introducing indirect statement after κατηγόρουν.

ἔστιν When ἔστιν signifies the existence of something, it is accented on the first syllable and appears at the beginning of the clause. Translate: "there is."

18b6-7 **μᾶλλον οὐδὲν ἀληθές** "Nothing very true." μᾶλλον does not appear in all manuscripts.

18b7 **σοφός** Socrates imagines the term used contemptuously by his detractors. In traditional societies such as fifth-century Athens, terms that suggest innovation of any kind often appear suspect and lacking the proper respect for received wisdom. See, for example, the portrayal of Socrates' school in Aristophanes' *Clouds*; see also Places (1964, 3) on σοφός. Xenophon gives a pointed example at *Symposium* 6.6, where the Syracusan impresario says scornfully to Socrates: "Aren't you called 'the thinker' (φροντιστής)?"

τὰ μετέωρα, "Middle air." Close attention to the movements of heavenly bodies and to weather signs was well established in Greek culture and is abundantly demonstrated in the second half of Hesiod's *Works and Days*. Speculation about the mechanical causes of these phenomena was less well regarded and considered impractical. In *Clouds*, Aristophanes refers to people such as Socrates as μετεωροσοφισταί, "sophists of the middle air" (360). In fact, our first look at Socrates there finds him hanging in a basket "walking on air and investigating the sun" (225; cf. *Apology* 19c2–5).

φροντιστής Derived from φροντίς, "thought," and pejorative, like σοφός above. Mockery of intellectual activity was common in the late fifth century, especially in comedy. By putting such language in the mouths of the first accusers, Socrates also begins to introduce ideas that will culminate in the references to Aristophanes' famous play, *Clouds*, below. There Aristophanes imagines Socrates as not only making use of *phrontis*, but literally inhabiting it. His school is called a *phrontisterion*, a "thinking place." Socrates was not the only philosopher to find himself the butt of a joke. Thales of Miletus was said to have fallen into a well while gazing at τὰ ἐν οὐρανοῦ (Plato, *Theaetetus* 174a; cf. *Apology* 19b5), and Anaxagoras was nicknamed *Nous*, "Mind," after the principle that he had identified as organizing the universe (Diogenes Laertius 2.6). See also essay 14 (pp. 167–69).

τὰ ὑπὸ γῆς ἅπαντα ἀνεζητηκώς The parody of philosophy students in Aristophanes' *Clouds* influences Socrates' language directly. In an early scene from the play, a student explains to Strepsiades, an old Athenian, the strange behavior of his fellow students: ζητοῦσιν οὗτοι τὰ κατὰ γῆς "They are investigating things underground." Strepsiades replies, "Oh! You mean onions!" (188–89).

ὑπὸ γῆς πάντα ἀνεζητηκὼς καὶ τὸν ἥττω λόγον κρείττω
c ποιῶν. οὗτοι, ὦ ἄνδρες Ἀθηναῖοι, ⟨οἱ⟩ ταύτην τὴν φήμην κατασκεδάσαντες, οἱ δεινοί εἰσίν μου κατήγοροι· οἱ γὰρ ἀκούοντες ἡγοῦνται τοὺς ταῦτα ζητοῦντας οὐδὲ θεοὺς νομίζειν. ἔπειτά εἰσιν οὗτοι οἱ κατήγοροι πολλοὶ καὶ πολὺν χρόνον ἤδη κατηγορηκότες, ἔτι δὲ καὶ ἐν ταύτῃ τῇ ἡλικίᾳ λέγοντες πρὸς ὑμᾶς ἐν ᾗ ἂν μάλιστα ἐπιστεύσατε, παῖδες ὄντες ἔνιοι

ἀνεζητηκώς pf. act. part. < ἀναζητέω *seek out*
φήμην < φήμη, -ης, ἡ *report*
κατασκεδάσαντες aor. act. part. < κατασκεδάννυμι *spread*
νομίζειν *acknowledge, believe in*
ἔτι δὲ καί *moreover*
ἡλικίᾳ < ἡλικία, -ας, ἡ *age, time of life*

18b8-c1 **τὸν ἥττω λόγον κρείττω ποιῶν** "Making the weaker argument the stronger." Note the contracted masc. sg. acc. forms of the comparatives ἥττω and κρείττω (= ἥττονα and κρείττονα). As Socrates implies, the phrase is a cliché used unreflectively by opponents of the new education, with its emphasis on public speaking (cf. *Clouds* 112, where the same phrase occurs). Such criticism often attacked the sophists, a diverse group of men with widely different interests, united only, it seems, in their willingness to teach rhetoric for a fee. A possible implication of the representation of Socrates in *Clouds* is that he, too, is a sophist, a charge he strenuously denies. Such teachers were nevertheless in high demand by young men eager to gain influence in the Assembly and were resented by some of the entrenched elites. The beginning of Plato's *Protagoras* captures the equivocal position of the sophists neatly. There we meet an ambitious young man, burning to become a student of Protagoras, but who blushes at the thought of being called a sophist (312a).

18c1 **<οἱ>** Bracketed text does not appear in the surviving manuscripts but has been restored by the editor, who thinks that it was there originally. The insertion allows us to take οὗτοι . . . οἱ ταύτην τὴν φήμην κατασκεδάσαντες as the subject and οἱ δεινοί . . . μου κατήγοροι as the predicate: "these men who have broadcast this rumor are my dangerous accusers." δεινοί preserves something of its original sense (< δέος, "fear").

18c3 **θεοὺς νομίζειν** "Acknowledge the gods," as is clear from Socrates' remark at *Euthyphro* 3b describing to Euthyphro the charges of Meletus: "For he says that I am a maker of gods, and he brings charges because, in making new gods, I do not honor the old ones (τοὺς ἀρχαίους [θεοὺς] οὐ νομίζοντα). The phrase is therefore to be distinguished from νομίζειν θεοὺς εἶναι (26d2), "believe that the gods exist," a charge Socrates takes pains to rebut.

18c4 **κατήγοροι** Subject of the sentence, agreeing with κατηγορηκότες (c5), λέγοντες (c6), and κατηγοροῦντες (c8).
πολλοί Predicate adjective.

18c6 **ᾗ** The antecedent is ἡλικίᾳ (dative of time within which).
ἂν . . . ἐπιστεύσατε Here, with the aorist indicative, ἄν indicates potential in the past: "when you were likely to believe."

ὑμῶν καὶ μειράκια, ἀτεχνῶς ἐρήμην κατηγοροῦντες ἀπολο-
γουμένου οὐδενός. ὃ δὲ πάντων ἀλογώτατον, ὅτι οὐδὲ τὰ
ὀνόματα οἷόν τε αὐτῶν εἰδέναι καὶ εἰπεῖν, πλὴν εἴ τις d
κωμῳδοποιὸς τυγχάνει ὤν. ὅσοι δὲ φθόνῳ καὶ διαβολῇ
χρώμενοι ὑμᾶς ἀνέπειθον—οἱ δὲ καὶ αὐτοὶ πεπεισμένοι
ἄλλους πείθοντες—οὗτοι πάντες ἀπορώτατοί εἰσιν· οὐδὲ γὰρ

ἐρήμην < ἐρήμη, -ης, ἡ *undefended*
κωμῳδοποιός, -οῦ, ὁ comic poet
φθόνῳ < φθόνος, -ου, ὁ *envy, resentment*
διαβολῇ < διαβολή, -ῆς, ἡ *slander*
χρώμενοι < χράομαι *use*
ἀνέπειθον impf. act. < ἀναπείθω *try to persuade, seduce*
ἀπορώτατοι *impossible to deal with*

παῖδες ὄντες ἔνιοι "When some of you were children."

18c7 **ἐρήμην κατηγοροῦντες** Supply δίκην. A technical legal expression: "prosecuting an undefended case." The phrase is glossed by the genitive absolute that follows for the benefit of jurors less familiar with legal jargon than Plato's Socrates, an irony that should not escape us, given his lack of courtroom experience. The overarching issue, however, is that Socrates did not choose to leave his "case" undefended but was compelled to do so by the anonymity of his accusers.

18c8 **ὃ δὲ πάντων ἀλογώτατον** Supply τοῦτ' ἐστι. ἀλογώτατον operates on both literal and metaphorical levels. In the most conventional sense, Socrates' situation is ἄλογος, that is, "unreasonable," since it was not possible to make a reply, or *ἀπολογεῖσθαι*, to those who were not present. More literally, ἄλογος (ἀ- + λόγος) means "without speech, unutterable." Inasmuch as Socrates cannot name the accusers, their names are literally *ἀλογώτατα*, "most unutterable." Finally, this kind of anonymous slander represents the opposite of the philosophical mode of life for which Socrates stands. It is without *λόγος* in its most profound sense, neither able to offer an account of itself (cf. 39c7), nor willing to submit to the process of questioning and examination of others in dialogue (δια*λόγος*).

18d1 **οἷόν τε** Supply ἐστί. Idiomatic: "it is possible."

18d2 **κωμῳδοποιός** Aristophanes (ca. 451–388) is the primary referent (see also 19c2), and his *Clouds* (423) has just been alluded to at 18b7. Other comic poets, however, like Ameipsias (*Connus*, 423) and Eupolis (*Colaces*, 421), had also written about Socrates. In addition, Aristophanes rewrote *Clouds* around 417 and mentions Socrates in *Birds* (414) and *Frogs* (405) just a few years before the trial.

ὅσοι δέ . . . The first accusers turn out to be extremely numerous: the original slanderers (ὅσοι δέ), those "of you" whom they persuaded (οἱ αὐτοί, in the next line), and a third generation of slanderers persuaded by the second.

ἀνέπειθον Impf. of repeated actions.

ἀναβιβάσασθαι οἷόν τ᾽ ἐστὶν αὐτῶν ἐνταυθοῖ οὐδ᾽ ἐλέγξαι
οὐδένα, ἀλλ᾽ ἀνάγκη ἀτεχνῶς ὥσπερ σκιαμαχεῖν ἀπολογού-
μενόν τε καὶ ἐλέγχειν μηδενὸς ἀποκρινομένου. ἀξιώσατε
οὖν καὶ ὑμεῖς, ὥσπερ ἐγὼ λέγω, διττούς μου τοὺς κατηγόρους
γεγονέναι, ἑτέρους μὲν τοὺς ἄρτι κατηγορήσαντας, ἑτέρους δὲ
e τοὺς πάλαι οὓς ἐγὼ λέγω, καὶ οἰήθητε δεῖν πρὸς ἐκείνους
πρῶτόν με ἀπολογήσασθαι· καὶ γὰρ ὑμεῖς ἐκείνων πρότερον
ἠκούσατε κατηγορούντων καὶ πολὺ μᾶλλον ἢ τῶνδε τῶν
ὕστερον.
Εἶεν· ἀπολογητέον δή, ὦ ἄνδρες Ἀθηναῖοι, καὶ ἐπιχειρη-
19 τέον ὑμῶν ἐξελέσθαι τὴν διαβολὴν ἣν ὑμεῖς ἐν πολλῷ χρόνῳ

ἀναβιβάσασθαι < ἀναβιβάζω *bring into court*
ἐνταυθοῖ *to this place*
ἐλέγξαι aor. act. infin. < ἐλέγχω *examine, refute*
ἀξιώσατε < ἀξιόω *believe, think*
ἄρτι *just now*
οἰήθητε aor. pass. imper. < οἴομαι *think*
εἶεν *very well then*
ἐξελέσθαι aor. mid. infin. < ἐξαιρέω *remove*

18d5 **ἀναβιβάσασθαι** Supply εἰς τὸ δικαστήριον.
ἐλέγξαι The verb and its compounded form ἐξελέγχειν (cf. 17b2) suggest both examination and refutation. They occur frequently in Plato's dialogues to describe Socrates' characteristic style of conversation.

18d6 **ἀτεχνῶς ὥσπερ** "Practically like."
σκιαμαχεῖν "Fight in the dark," and therefore "randomly" (as at *Republic* 520c). The verb can also mean "shadowbox," that is, practice fighting moves without a partner. The first sense predominates. Note the parallelism created by the two genitive absolutes: ἐλέγχειν *μηδενὸς ἀποκρινομένου* and κατηγοροῦντες *ἀπολογομένου οὐδενός* (18c7).

18d8 **οὖν καὶ ὑμεῖς** οὖν often signals the return of the discussion to the main point after a digression. Translate: "So, you also . . ."

18d9 **γεγονέναι** The perfect aspect is relevant. The first accusers began their work in the past, and its effects continue into the present.

18e1 **τοὺς πάλαι** Supply κατηγορήσαντας.

18e2 **καὶ γάρ** "In fact."

18e3 **τῶνδε τῶν ὕστερον** That is, Meletus and his crew. Supply ἠκούσατε κατηγορούντων from the first part of the sentence: "In fact, you heard them accusing [me] earlier and much longer than [you heard] these men [accusing me] later."

18e5 **ἀπολογητέον . . . ἐπιχειρητέον** These neuter verbal adjectives, like the Latin gerundive, express necessity: "there must be a defense . . . and an attempt."

19a1 **ἐξελέσθαι** "Remove the slander *from* you." ἐξ- governs ὑμῶν.

ἔσχετε ταύτην ἐν οὕτως ὀλίγῳ χρόνῳ. βουλοίμην μὲν οὖν ἂν τοῦτο οὕτως γενέσθαι, εἴ τι ἄμεινον καὶ ὑμῖν καὶ ἐμοί, καὶ πλέον τί με ποιῆσαι ἀπολογούμενον· οἶμαι δὲ αὐτὸ χαλεπὸν εἶναι, καὶ οὐ πάνυ με λανθάνει οἷόν ἐστιν. ὅμως τοῦτο μὲν ἴτω ὅπῃ τῷ θεῷ φίλον, τῷ δὲ νόμῳ πειστέον καὶ ἀπολογητέον.

ἔσχετε aor. act. indic. < ἔχω *acquired*
ὅμως *all the same, nonetheless*
λανθάνει < λανθάνω *escape the notice of*
ἴτω 3rd person imper. < εἶμι *go*
ὅπῃ *where, in what way*
πειστέον neut. verbal adj. < πείθομαι (+ dat.) *one must obey*

19a2 **ταύτην** The antecedent is διαβολήν: "this one which."
μὲν οὖν This combination asserts the strong emotional interest of the speaker, here affirmative (and ironic). Translate: "I would *really* like . . ."

19a4 **πλέον τί . . . ποιῆσαι** "Succeed," literally, "do something more," an example of rhetorical understatement (litotes). The infinitive is dependent on βουλοίμην.

19a5 **οὐ πάνυ λανθάνει οἷόν ἐστιν** Technically, the subject of λανθάνει is οἷόν ἐστιν, but the idiom does not translate literally into English. Try instead: "It doesn't really escape me how it is."

19a6 **τῷ θεῷ** No specific divinity is intended. The remark, coupled with a similar statement at 35d7–8, works to undermine further the charges of atheism without committing Socrates to a very specific statement of belief.

CHAPTER 3

(19a7–d7)

Socrates defends himself against the old accusers' charge of being interested in science. The search for the causes of natural phenomena was considered suspect by many cultual conservatives in fifth-century Athens, inasmuch as such investigations sought to offer mechanical explanations for things that heretofore had been left to religion and mythology. As will become clear later in the speech, Socrates only had a very minimal interest in such speculations, preferring to concentrate on problems of self-knowledge.

Nonetheless, to many, Socrates' consistent questioning of all received notions seemed as corrosive to traditional morality as the natural philosophers' attempt to substitute rational causes for the explanations offered by poetry, religion, and myth. This critical approach to tradition was the basis, at least in part, of the charge that Socrates had corrupted the youth. For additional discussion of the chapter and questions for study, see essay 3.

Ἀναλάβωμεν οὖν ἐξ ἀρχῆς τίς ἡ κατηγορία ἐστὶν ἐξ ἧς
b ἡ ἐμὴ διαβολὴ γέγονεν, ᾗ δὴ καὶ πιστεύων Μέλητός με ἐγρά-

ἀπολογητέον neut. verbal adj. < ἀπολογέομαι *one must make a defense*
ἀναλάβωμεν aor. act. subj. < ἀναλαμβάνω *resume*
ἐγράψατο < γράφω (mid.) *indict*

19b1 **ἡ ἐμὴ διαβολή** The possessive adjective has the force of the objective genitive: "the slander against me."
ᾗ The antecedent is διαβολή. Socrates assumes that Meletus and his cronies would not dare bring him to trial without the implicit support of the older accusers, an impression strengthened by δή, which emphasizes

ψατο τὴν γραφὴν ταύτην. εἶεν· τί δὴ λέγοντες διέβαλλον οἱ διαβάλλοντες; ὥσπερ οὖν κατηγόρων τὴν ἀντωμοσίαν δεῖ ἀναγνῶναι αὐτῶν· "Σωκράτης ἀδικεῖ καὶ περιεργάζεται ζητῶν τά τε ὑπὸ γῆς καὶ οὐράνια καὶ τὸν ἥττω λόγον κρείττω ποιῶν καὶ ἄλλους ταὐτὰ ταῦτα διδάσκων." τοιαύτη τίς ἐστιν· c
ταῦτα γὰρ ἑωρᾶτε καὶ αὐτοὶ ἐν τῇ Ἀριστοφάνους κωμῳδίᾳ, Σωκράτη τινὰ ἐκεῖ περιφερόμενον, φάσκοντά τε ἀεροβατεῖν καὶ ἄλλην πολλὴν φλυαρίαν φλυαροῦντα, ὧν ἐγὼ οὐδὲν οὔτε

ἀντωμοσίαν < ἀντωμοσία, -ας, ἡ *formal charge, affidavit*
ἀναγνῶναι aor. act. infin. < ἀναγιγνώσκω *read*
ἀδικεῖ < ἀδικέω *do wrong*
περιεργάζεται < περιεργάζομαι *busy oneself*
ἥττω (= ἥττονα) < ἥττων *weaker*
κρείττω (= κρείττονα) < κρείττων *stronger*
ἑωρᾶτε < ὁράω *see*
φάσκοντα < φάσκω *assert*

---

the relative. Meletus is said to have written the indictment on behalf of the poets Socrates has angered (23e). In the *Euthyphro* he is referred to as young and unknown, and this sense of his relative obscurity is echoed in the *Apology* (36a–b). In addition, see on 23e5–24a1.

ἐγράψατο γράφεσθαι takes an accusative of the charge and of the person charged.

19b2 **τί δὴ λέγοντες** "By saying what, precisely?" For the use of δή, see on 19b1.

19b3 **ἀντωμοσίαν** Literally, "the swearing against." The formal charge was read aloud before the trial began. The thought here is compressed. The simplest approach is to take δεῖ ἀναγνῶναι both in the main clause *and* in the ὥσπερ-clause: "So it is necessary to read their (αὐτῶν) indictment just as [it is necessary to read] that of the prosecutors."

19b5 **ζητῶν τά τε ὑπὸ γῆς καὶ οὐράνια καὶ τὸν ἥττω λόγον κρείττω ποῖων** See on 18c1. In *Clouds* Aristophanes had portrayed Socrates and his students as involved in both activities.

19c1 **ἄλλους ταὐτὰ ταῦτα διδάσκων** ταὐτά = τὰ αυτά, "the same things." διδάσκω takes a double accusative to indicate the recipient and the content of the lesson.

τοιαύτη τίς ἐστιν "It's something like this." τοιαύτη agrees with ἀντωμοσία.

19c3 **Σωκράτη τινά** "Some Socrates." Socrates distances himself from Aristophanes' caricature of him in *Clouds*.

περιφερόμενον In *Clouds*, we first meet Socrates suspended in a basket so his thoughts can become as rarefied as the "middle air" that he proposes to study.

ἀεροβατεῖν Quoted from *Clouds* 225.

19c4 **φλυαρίαν φλυαροῦντα** Cognate accusative: "talk nonsense."

ὧν The relative is governed by πέρι in the next line. The position of the accent on the first syllable indicates that the preposition follows its object (anastrophe). The word order is extremely disturbed here (hyperbaton).

μέγα οὔτε μικρὸν πέρι ἐπαΐω. καὶ οὐχ ὡς ἀτιμάζων λέγω τὴν τοιαύτην ἐπιστήμην, εἴ τις περὶ τῶν τοιούτων σοφός ἐστιν—μή πως ἐγὼ ὑπὸ Μελήτου τοσαύτας δίκας φεύγοιμι—ἀλλὰ γὰρ ἐμοὶ τούτων, ὦ ἄνδρες Ἀθηναῖοι, οὐδὲν μέτεστιν.
d μάρτυρας δὲ αὖ ὑμῶν τοὺς πολλοὺς παρέχομαι, καὶ ἀξιῶ ὑμᾶς ἀλλήλους διδάσκειν τε καὶ φράζειν, ὅσοι ἐμοῦ πώποτε ἀκηκόατε διαλεγομένου—πολλοὶ δὲ ὑμῶν οἱ τοιοῦτοί εἰσιν—

ἐπαΐω *understand*
ἀτιμάζων < ἀτιμάζω *treat with dishonor*
ἐπιστήμην < ἐπιστήμη, -ης, ἡ *knowledge*
ἀλλὰ γάρ *but as a matter of fact*
μέτεστιν *have a share in*
μάρτυρας < μάρτυς, -υρος, ὁ *witness*
φράζειν < φράζω *point out*
διαλεγομένου < διαλέγομαι *converse*

19c5 **οὐχ . . . ἀτιμάζων** In *Phaedo*, the dialogue where the death of Socrates is narrated, Socrates recalls that as a young man he was deeply interested in natural science and the structure of the cosmos, but that he later became disillusioned with it (96–97). In this passage, Socrates' appreciation of the sciences gives way to an ironic implication that these matters are unknowable (εἴ τις περὶ τῶν τοιούτων, etc.).

19c6 **ἐπιστήμην** The word is normally distinguished by Plato from δόξα, "opinion, belief." Here it is used ironically.

19c7 **μή πως ἐγὼ . . . τοσαύτας δίκας φεύγοιμι** Opt. of wish: "I hope I don't have to defend myself against such great charges."

19d2 **διδάσκειν τε καὶ φράζειν** The logical order of the two events is inverted (hysteron proteron). The request that the jurors teach each other might look like a Socratic mannerism, but it is not. Compare this passage to Andocides' speech, *On the Mysteries* 46, where he, too, calls upon members of the jury to verify his version of events and to "teach" each other.

19d3 **διαλεγομένου** On the most basic level, Socrates merely says that members of the jury have heard him in conversation. The end result of such conversations, as reported by Plato anyway, is often an exasperated ἀπορία, or perplexity, on the part of the interlocutor. The dialogues with politicians, poets, and craftsmen that Socrates summarizes a little later (21c5–22e6) seem definitely to have been of this sort. The recollection of these conversations would quickly disprove the charge that Socrates engaged in scientific speculations or taught rhetoric. Nonetheless, it is not clear that bringing to mind these conversations would have been effective in winning the jury over to Socrates' side.

φράζετε οὖν ἀλλήλοις εἰ πώποτε ἢ μικρὸν ἢ μέγα ἤκουσέ τις ὑμῶν ἐμοῦ περὶ τῶν τοιούτων διαλεγομένου, καὶ ἐκ τούτου γνώσεσθε ὅτι τοιαῦτ᾽ ἐστὶ καὶ τἆλλα περὶ ἐμοῦ ἃ οἱ πολλοὶ λέγουσιν.

19d4 **φράζετε** This extremely conversational sentence shifts its syntax midway through (anacolouthon). The original construction, based on ἀξιῶ + subject acc. and infin., breaks off in favor of the imperative.

19d6 **τοιαῦτ᾽** "Of such a sort," that is, "equally baseless" (Burnet 1924).

19d

CHAPTER 4

(19d8–20c3)

Socrates answers the charge that he teaches for money, like the sophists. For additional discussion of the chapter and questions for study, see essay 4.

Ἀλλὰ γὰρ οὔτε τούτων οὐδέν ἐστιν, οὐδέ γ' εἴ τινος ἀκηκόατε ὡς ἐγὼ παιδεύειν ἐπιχειρῶ ἀνθρώπους καὶ χρήματα
e πράττομαι, οὐδὲ τοῦτο ἀληθές. ἐπεὶ καὶ τοῦτό γέ μοι δοκεῖ καλὸν εἶναι, εἴ τις οἷός τ' εἴη παιδεύειν ἀνθρώπους ὥσπερ Γοργίας τε ὁ Λεοντῖνος καὶ Πρόδικος ὁ Κεῖος καὶ Ἱππίας ὁ

οἷός τ' εἴη (idiom.) *is able*

19d8 **τούτων οὐδὲν ἐστιν** "None of these things are [true]."
οὐδέ γε "Not *even* . . ."

19d9 **χρήματα πράττομαι** The Platonic dialogues highlight Socrates' refusal to participate in the pursuit of wealth. Indeed, he is portrayed in the same light even in Aristophanes' decidedly unfriendly portrait of him in *Clouds*. Elsewhere in the *Apology*, Socrates explicitly denies that he makes money by conversing with others (31c, 33b). Among some upper-class Athenians, there is a prejudice against working for another on the grounds that whoever does so is not really free (see Xenophon, *Mem.* 2.8). For such people, the accusation that Socrates took money for teaching would not sit well. In Plato's *Apology*, the issue is different: the professed ignorance of Socrates means that there is nothing he is qualified to teach, and if he cannot teach, he certainly cannot teach for a fee. Moreover, as he later shows, even those who claim to have wisdom often do not, while the kind of self-knowledge Socrates has on offer cannot be reduced to a commodity. See on 20c1–3.

19e3–4 **Γοργίας . . . Πρόδικος . . . Ἱππίας** Gorgias of Leontini in Sicily, Prodicus of the island of Ceos, and Hippias of Elis in the Peloponnese were famous sophists of the late fifth century (for more complete biographical information, see Nails 2002). They figure prominently in the Platonic dialogues. Gorgias is known to have visited Athens in 427 as an ambassador, and his visit is the dramatic occasion for Plato's *Gorgias*, in which Socrates compares rhetoricians to flatterers and philosophers to doctors who prescribe a

Ἠλεῖος. τούτων γὰρ ἕκαστος, ὦ ἄνδρες, οἷός τ' ἐστὶν ἰὼν
εἰς ἑκάστην τῶν πόλεων τοὺς νέους—οἷς ἔξεστι τῶν ἑαυτῶν
πολιτῶν προῖκα συνεῖναι ᾧ ἂν βούλωνται—τούτους πείθουσι
τὰς ἐκείνων συνουσίας ἀπολιπόντας σφίσιν συνεῖναι χρή- 20
ματα διδόντας καὶ χάριν προσειδέναι. ἐπεὶ καὶ ἄλλος ἀνήρ
ἐστι Πάριος ἐνθάδε σοφὸς ὃν ἐγὼ ᾐσθόμην ἐπιδημοῦντα·
ἔτυχον γὰρ προσελθὼν ἀνδρὶ ὃς τετέλεκε χρήματα σοφισταῖς

προῖκα *for free*
συνεῖναι < σύνειμι *associate with*
χάριν προσειδέναι < χάριν πρόσοιδα (idiom.) *be grateful*
ἐνθάδε *here, now*
ᾐσθόμην < αἰσθάνομαι *perceive*
ἐπιδημοῦντα < ἐπιδημέω *be residing*
ἔτυχον aor. act. indic. < τυγχάνω (+ part.) *happen to do something*
προσελθών aor. act. part. < προσέρχομαι *approach*
τετέλεκε pf. act. indic. < τελέω *spend*
σοφισταῖς < σοφιστής, -οῦ, -ὁ *sophist*

---

bitter medecine. Hippias appears prominently in two dialogues, *Hippias Major* and *Hippias Minor*. Both Prodicus and Hippias appear in the hilarious opening scene of *Protagoras*, which represents the house of Callias (see below) as virtually a camp for sophists.

19e4–20a2 **οἷός τ' ἐστιν** This sentence is artfully constructed to mimic the organic, often ungrammatical quality of everyday speech and to suggest a contrast with the elaborate periods of the rhetorically trained speaker. We expect a complementary infinitive with οἷός τ' ἐστιν, but the relative clause intervenes, and when Socrates returns to the main clause, he abandons the idiom and begins again with πείθουσι (agreeing in number with τούτων [e4] rather than ἕκαστος).

19e5 **οἷς ἔξεστι . . .** "who can associate for free with any fellow citizens they wish."

19e6 **ᾧ** Dative following συνεῖναι. The second relative clause has been incorporated into the first (see trans. above).

19e6–a2 **συνεῖναι . . . προσειδέναι** Dependent on πείθουσι. Coordinate both with ἀπολιπόντας, the aorist participle here expressing prior time.

20a1 **ἐκείνων** That is, of their fellow citizens (obj. gen. with τὰς . . . συνουσίας).
σφίσιν Indirect reflexive, occurring in a subordinate clause and referring back to the subject of the sentence (i.e., to Gorgias, Hippias, and Prodicus).

20a2 **ἐπεί** Another elliptical use of ἐπεί. Translate "As a consequence."
Πάριος Adj. Paros is an island in the northern Aegean Sea.

πλείω ἢ σύμπαντες οἱ ἄλλοι, Καλλίᾳ τῷ Ἱππονίκου· τοῦτον οὖν ἀνηρόμην—ἐστὸν γὰρ αὐτῷ δύο ὑεῖ— "Ὦ Καλλία," ἦν δ' ἐγώ, "εἰ μέν σου τὼ ὑεῖ πώλω ἢ μόσχω ἐγενέσθην, εἴχομεν ἂν αὐτοῖν ἐπιστάτην λαβεῖν καὶ μισθώσασθαι ὃς

πλείω = πλείονα < πλέων *more*
σύμπαντες < σύμπας, -παν *all*
ἀνηρόμην aor. mid. indic. < ἀνέρομαι *ask*
ὑεῖ (nom. dual) < ὑός, -οῦ, ὁ *son*
ἦν δ'ἐγώ (idiom.) *I said*
πώλω (nom. dual) < πῶλος, -ου, ὁ *colt*
μόσχω < μόσχος, -ου, ὁ *calf*
εἴχομεν < **ἔχω** (+ infin.) *be able to*
ἐπιστάτην < ἐπιστάτης , -ου, ὁ *overseer*
μισθώσασθαι aor. mid. infin. < μισθόω *hire*

20a5 **Καλλίᾳ τῷ Ἱππονίκου** Callias was an Athenian nobleman from a distinguished family with an interest in intellectual matters, fabulous wealth, and a tendency toward self-indulgence. Plato's *Protagoras* is set at Callias's house, as is Xenophon's *Symposium*. The education of his sons may have been a standard theme in Socratic literature, since the absence of a need to economize would have allowed the subject to be treated in the abstract. In addition to Plato's use of the topic here, the lesser-known Socratic writer Aeschines of Sphettios wrote a dialogue (*Aspasia*) in which Socrates advised Callias to send his sons to Aspasia, the former mistress of Pericles, for their education. Callias was a fellow demesman of Socrates and related to Plato by marriage.

Socrates here poses a set of questions to Callias about his sons' education. This is the first specimen in the *Apology* of the style of conversation for which Socrates was known. It has several features paralleled frequently elsewhere in the dialogues: the examination of someone who claims a certain expertise; argument from analogy; and the use of humble metaphors to discuss lofty matters.

20a6 **ἐστόν** 3rd sg. pres. dual < εἰμί.

20a7 **τὼ ὑεῖ** Dual nom. of the masc. def. art. and ὗος. Note that the same endings appear below with πώλω and μόσχω. Not much is known of the sons. One was named Protarchus and appears prominently in Plato's *Philebus*.

ἐγενέσθην, εἴχομεν ἄν A mixed counterfactual condition. The aorist (middle dual) in the protasis suggests that we translate the verb as "had been born" rather than "were."

20a8 **αὐτοῖν** Dual dat. < αὐτός "For the two of them."

ὃς ἔμελλεν "Who was going to . . . ," that is, "whose job it would be to . . ."

ἔμελλεν αὐτὼ καλώ τε κἀγαθὼ ποιήσειν τὴν προσήκουσαν b
ἀρετήν, ἦν δ' ἂν οὗτος ἢ τῶν ἱππικῶν τις ἢ τῶν γεωργικῶν· νῦν δ' ἐπειδὴ ἀνθρώπω ἐστόν, τίνα αὐτοῖν ἐν νῷ ἔχεις ἐπιστάτην λαβεῖν; τίς τῆς τοιαύτης ἀρετῆς, τῆς ἀνθρωπίνης τε καὶ πολιτικῆς, ἐπιστήμων ἐστίν; οἶμαι γάρ σε ἐσκέφθαι διὰ τὴν τῶν ὑέων κτῆσιν. ἔστιν τις," ἔφην ἐγώ, "ἢ οὔ;" "Πάνυ γε," ἦ δ' ὅς. "Τίς," ἦν δ' ἐγώ, "καὶ ποδαπός, καὶ πόσου διδάσκει;" "Εὔηνος," ἔφη, "ὦ Σώκρατες, Πάριος,

---

ἱππικῶν < ἱππικός, -ή, -όν *equestrian*
γεωργικῶν < γεωργικός, -ή, -όν *agricultural*
νῷ < νοῦς, νοῦ, ὁ *mind*
ἀνθρωπίνης < ἀνθρωπίνος, -η, -ον *human, attainable by a person*
πολιτικῆς < πολιτικός, -ή, -όν *of a citizen*
ἐσκέφθαι pf. mid. infin. < σκέπτομαι *examine, consider*
κτῆσιν < κτῆσις, -εως, ἡ *possession*
ποδαπός *from where*

20b1 **καλώ τε κἀγαθώ** Predicate adjectives, agreeing with πώλω ("colt") and μόσχω ("calf"). The crasis in καλὸς κἀγαθός (also present in the abstract noun καλοκἀγαθία, the verb καλοκἀγαθέω, etc.) suggests that the phrase had become a slogan to describe members of the aristocracy. It cannot have been common to apply the phrase to farm animals, and it was just this sort of undignified comparison that infuriated some aristocratic interlocutors of Socrates. At *Gorgias* 494d1, for example, Callicles tellingly accuses Socrates of being a "*mob*-orator" (δημηγόρος). On Socrates' use of homely metaphors, see Alcibiades in the *Symposium* 221d7–222a6.

τὴν προσήκουσαν ἀρετήν "With respect to their appropriate excellence," that is, with respect to whatever qualities make a calf or a foal good.

20b2 **ἦν δ' ἄν** "He would be." The clause is the apodosis of a present counterfactual condition (impf. + ἄν) without a protasis.

20b3 **νῦν δ'** "As it is . . ."

20b6 **ἔστιν τις** Note the accent: "Is there anyone . . . ?"

20b7 **ἦ δ' ὅς** Idiomatic: "he said." So also ἦν δ' ἐγώ in the next line.

20b8 **πόσου** Genitive of price, as in Callias's answer below. Note the contrast between Socrates' careful and complete use of connectives (τίς . . . *καὶ* ποδαπός, *καὶ* πόσου) and Callias's response, which leaves them all out (asyndeton).

Εὔηνος Evenus of Paros is best known as an elegiac poet. Some fragments have survived. He is represented in Plato's *Phaedo* (60d) as being curious about Socrates' decision to write poetry after his condemnation and in the *Phaedrus* (267a3) as the authority for certain rhetorical terms.

πέντε μνῶν." καὶ ἐγὼ τὸν Εὔηνον ἐμακάρισα εἰ ὡς ἀληθῶς
c ἔχοι ταύτην τὴν τέχνην καὶ οὕτως ἐμμελῶς διδάσκει. ἐγὼ
γοῦν καὶ αὐτὸς ἐκαλλυνόμην τε καὶ ἡβρυνόμην ἂν εἰ ἠπιστάμην
ταῦτα· ἀλλ' οὐ γὰρ ἐπίσταμαι, ὦ ἄνδρες Ἀθηναῖοι.

ἐμακάρισα < μακαρίζω *bless, deem happy*
ἐμμελῶς *properly, at a reasonable price*
ἐκαλλυνόμην < καλλύνω (mid.) *be proud*
ἡβρυνόμην < ἁβρύνω (mid.) *give oneself airs*

20b9 **πέντε μνῶν** The sum looks modest in comparison to those commanded by celebrity teachers such as Protagoras, who in the previous generation were said to have charged one hundred minas. Nevertheless, such a price would have made Evenus's instruction beyond the range of all but the wealthy. In Xenophon's *Oeconomicus* (2.3), five minas is estimated to be the total value of all Socrates' estate, a modest but not insignificant sum.

ὡς ἀληθῶς That is, if he "truly" had the ability and did not just claim to have it. The qualification, of course, negates the amazement that Socrates claims to have felt.

29c1 **ἔχοι** The εἰ-clause is the protasis of a future-less-vivid condition, emphasizing the unlikely (to Socrates) possibility that Evenus could make good on his claims to teach. The general thought of the sentences (expressed ironically) is: "I was amazed, first at the idea that Evenus should have this skill [optative], and second, that he teaches it [indicative] so cheaply."

τέχνην This is an important word in the Platonic lexicon, with many nuances and complexities. One common translation is "craft." It refers to an "art" or a "skill" that can be reduced to a method, as opposed to an open field of intellectual and ethical inquiry (cf. *Phaedrus* 274d–e). It is at times contrasted with ἐπιστήμη and σοφία (see Places 1964).

20c1–3 Socrates here speaks less of his own ignorance than of his conviction that ἀρετή cannot be reduced to a τέχνη capable of being transferred to another in exchange for money (Nightingale 1995, 50). Further, by explicitly denying that he has any such knowledge, he implicitly shows that he is not a sophist who sells his services to the highest bidder

20c2 **γοῦν** = γε οὖν, a common crasis. The combination calls attention to the justification for a statement that is only partly valid and is sometimes referred to as the "γοῦν of partial proof."

ἐκαλλυνόμην . . . ἡβρυνόμην ἂν . . . εἰ ἠπιστάμην The present counterfactual condition has two apodoses, both coming before the protasis.

CHAPTER 5

(20c4–21a8)

"If you are not a teacher, where then do these rumors come from?" Socrates begins the exposition of his practice by addressing this question. Here we find the famous story of Chaerephon's trip to the Delphic oracle. For additional discussion of the chapter and questions for study, see essay 5.

Ὑπολάβοι ἂν οὖν τις ὑμῶν ἴσως· "Ἀλλ', ὦ Σώκρατες, τὸ σὸν τί ἐστι πρᾶγμα; πόθεν αἱ διαβολαί σοι αὗται γεγόνασιν; οὐ γὰρ δήπου σοῦ γε οὐδὲν τῶν ἄλλων περιττότερον πραγματευομένου ἔπειτα τοσαύτη φήμη τε καὶ λόγος γέγονεν, εἰ μή τι ἔπραττες ἀλλοῖον ἢ οἱ πολλοί. λέγε οὖν ἡμῖν τί

ὑπολάβοι aor. act. opt. < ὑπολαμβάνω *understand, suppose*
πρᾶγμα, -τος, τό *thing, matter*
πόθεν *from where*
περιττότερον < περιττός, -ή, -όν *extraordinary, remarkable*
πραγματευομένου < πραγματεύομαι *be busy, conduct oneself*
ἀλλοῖον < ἀλλοῖος, -α, -ον *of another sort, different*

20c5 **τὸ σὸν . . . πρᾶγμα** "What, then, is your business?" The position of τὸ σόν is emphatic.

20c6 **οὐ** Governs the main verb, γέγονεν (c7).

δήπου = δή ("Certainly") + που ("I suppose"). The move from certainty to doubt in the word makes it natural in ironic or incredulous questions, as here.

τῶν ἄλλων Genitive of comparison after οὐδέν . . . περιττότερον, which is the object of the genitive absolute σοῦ . . . πραγματευομένου. The speaker implies that "Where there's smoke, there's fire": it is probably not by chance that Socrates has this reputation.

20c8 **εἰ μή τι ἔπραττες** The protasis of a present counterfactual condition and equivalent in meaning to the genitive absolute above. The apodosis has to be inferred from the question in 20c5–6.

d ἐστιν, ἵνα μὴ ἡμεῖς περὶ σοῦ αὐτοσχεδιάζωμεν." ταυτί μοι δοκεῖ δίκαια λέγειν ὁ λέγων, κἀγὼ ὑμῖν πειράσομαι ἀποδεῖξαι τί ποτ' ἐστὶν τοῦτο ὃ ἐμοὶ πεποίηκεν τό τε ὄνομα καὶ τὴν διαβολήν. ἀκούετε δή. καὶ ἴσως μὲν δόξω τισὶν ὑμῶν παίζειν· εὖ μέντοι ἴστε, πᾶσαν ὑμῖν τὴν ἀλήθειαν ἐρῶ. ἐγὼ γάρ, ὦ ἄνδρες Ἀθηναῖοι, δι' οὐδὲν ἀλλ' ἢ διὰ σοφίαν τινὰ τοῦτο τὸ ὄνομα ἔσχηκα. ποίαν δὴ σοφίαν ταύτην; ἥπερ ἐστὶν ἴσως ἀνθρωπίνη σοφία· τῷ ὄντι γὰρ κινδυνεύω ταύτην εἶναι σοφός. οὗτοι δὲ τάχ' ἄν, οὓς ἄρτι

αὐτοσχεδιάζωμεν pres. act. subj. < αὐτοσχεδιάζω *judge carelessly*
πειράσομαι < πειράομαι *try, attempt*
ἀποδεῖξαι aor. act. infin. < ἀποδείκνυμι *show, demonstrate*
παίζειν < παίζω *play*
ἐρῶ fut. indic. < λέγω *say*
σοφίαν < σοφία *wisdom*
ἔσχηκα pf. act. indic. < ἔχω *have*
κινδυνεύω (+ inf.) *run the risk of, be likely to*
ταχ' < ταχα *perhaps, possibly*

20d1 **ταυτί** The deictic iota added to ταῦτα strengthens it. Note the alliteration δοκεῖ δίκαια λέγειν ὁ λέγων.

20d2 **κἀγώ** = καὶ ἐγώ

20d4 **δή** This usage is colloquial with imperatives for emphasis: "So listen!"
καί . . . μέν introduces a new point. Note the absence of a corresponding δέ. He begins as if he were going to say, "I may seem to be joking [μέν], but [δέ] I am not." Instead, he substitutes the imperative ἴστε for the δέ-clause and drives ahead.

20d6 **ἀλλ'** = ἄλλο

20d7 **σοφίαν** Socrates is σοφός because he is wise, not because he is a σοφιστής.
ποίαν δή The δή makes the ποίαν (the antecedent is σοφία) more specific: "Precisely what kind of . . . ?" ποίαν anticipates ἥπερ in the next line: "The very kind which . . ."

20d8 **ἀνθρωπίνη** A split between human and divine wisdom is assumed in most Greek literature. Here the distinction reveals an important ironic dimension. As Socrates will go on to say, the only real wisdom belongs to the god, and human wisdom will consist of recognizing this limitation (i.e., "this ignorance").

20d9 **ταύτην** Accusative of respect, referring to σοφία.

20d9–e1 **οὗτοι δὲ τάχ' ἂν . . . σοφοὶ εἶεν** οὗτοι refers to the teachers of rhetoric just discussed (ἄρτι, see 20b9–c1). The unnatural word order (hyperbaton) is extreme, with subject οὗτοι and predicate σοφοί separated by twelve words. By pointing ironically to the fact that the wisdom the sophists lay claim to is superhuman (i.e., inaccessible to men), Socrates suggests that what they claim to teach is not wisdom at all. Thus Socrates' modest claim to possess merely human wisdom turns out to be a boast of sorts, since his wisdom is real even if limited. δέ is strongly adversative here, even without μέν: "But those men I just mentioned . . ."

ἔλεγον, μείζω τινὰ ἢ κατ' ἄνθρωπον σοφίαν σοφοὶ εἶεν, ἢ e
οὐκ ἔχω τί λέγω· οὐ γὰρ δὴ ἔγωγε αὐτὴν ἐπίσταμαι, ἀλλ' ὅστις φησὶ ψεύδεταί τε καὶ ἐπὶ διαβολῇ τῇ ἐμῇ λέγει. καί μοι, ὦ ἄνδρες Ἀθηναῖοι, μὴ θορυβήσητε, μηδ' ἐὰν δόξω τι ὑμῖν μέγα λέγειν· οὐ γὰρ ἐμὸν ἐρῶ τὸν λόγον ὃν ἂν λέγω, ἀλλ' εἰς ἀξιόχρεων ὑμῖν τὸν λέγοντα ἀνοίσω. τῆς γὰρ ἐμῆς, εἰ δή τίς ἐστιν σοφία καὶ οἵα, μάρτυρα ὑμῖν παρέξομαι

ἀξιόχρεων < ἀξιόχρεως *responsible, trustworthy*
ἀνοίσω fut. act. indic. < ἀναφέρω *refer*

20e1 **μείζω** (= μείζονα) Acc. of respect, agreeing with τινά . . . σοφίαν.

20e2 **ἢ οὐκ ἔχω τί λέγω** Translate: "Or I don't know how to express it." λέγω is deliberative subjunctive.

δή "Certainly."

ἔγωγε "I, in any case . . ."

20e3 **φησί** Supply τοῦτο.

ἐπὶ διαβολῇ τῇ ἐμῇ "To slander me."

20e4 **θορυβήσητε** μή + aorist subjunctive in prohibitions. The imagined reactions of Socrates' audience are a centerpiece of Plato's dramatic recreation. Athenian trials are likely to have been boisterous affairs, anyway. The courtrooms were probably open air and surrounded only by low walls, except on the side of the entrance, where admission was restricted. Consequently, in addition to the jurors, bystanders were often present. Other orators make reference to this fact (see, for example, Demosthenes *On the Crown*, 196).

τι . . . μέγα λέγειν "Boast."

20e5–6 **οὐ γὰρ ἐμόν . . . ἀνοίσω** More colloquially: "The story I will tell is not my own, but the source is reliable."

20e6 **ἀξιόχρεων** Masc. sg. acc., agreeing with τὸν λέγοντα in predicative position.

τῆς ἐμῆς Supply σοφίας. The genitives are dependent on μάρτυρα.

20e7 **εἰ δή τίς ἐστιν σοφία καὶ οἵα** "If, really, there is anything to it at all."

παρέξομαι The verb takes two accusatives here ("supply the god as a witness").

τὸν θεὸν τὸν ἐν Δελφοῖς. Χαιρεφῶντα γὰρ ἴστε που. οὗτος
21 ἐμός τε ἑταῖρος ἦν ἐκ νέου καὶ ὑμῶν τῷ πλήθει ἑταῖρός τε
καὶ συνέφυγε τὴν φυγὴν ταύτην καὶ μεθ' ὑμῶν κατῆλθε.
καὶ ἴστε δὴ οἷος ἦν Χαιρεφῶν, ὡς σφοδρὸς ἐφ' ὅτι ὁρμήσειεν.
καὶ δή ποτε καὶ εἰς Δελφοὺς ἐλθὼν ἐτόλμησε τοῦτο μαντεύσασθαι—καί, ὅπερ λέγω, μὴ θορυβεῖτε, ὦ ἄνδρες—ἤρετο γὰρ

ἐκ νέου *from youth*
συνέφυγε aor. act. indic. < συμφεύγω *flee along with*
κατῆλθε aor. act. indic. < κατέρχομαι *return, come back*
σφοδρός, -ά, -όν *passionate, enthusiastic*
ὁρμήσειεν aor. act. opt. < ὁρμάω *rush into, undertake*
ἐτόλμησε < τολμάω *dare*
μαντεύσασθαι < μαντεύομαι *ask the oracle*
ἤρετο impf. indic. < ἔρομαι *ask*

20e8 **Δελφοῖς** Apollo's shrine in Delphi housed the Pythian priestess through whom he prophesied. People came from all over the Greek world and beyond to consult the oracle.

Χαιρεφῶντα (ca. 469–ca. 399) Apparently dead by the time of the trial, Chaerephon was well known as a great admirer and close friend of Socrates, as can be seen from references to the pair in comedy: for example, *Clouds* 104 (423 B.C.E.), and *Birds* 1553–64 (414 B.C.E.). In 404, with the Thirty in power (see introduction), he chose exile with the democratic faction and returned the next year when the democracy was restored (that Socrates did not join them may have seemed an act of disloyalty, despite his advanced age). Socrates thus assumes that the jurors will regard Chaerephon as one of their own and, therefore, worthy of trust. Xenophon also mentions Chaerephon's trip to the oracle in his *Apology*, but he reports a slightly different response from Apollo (14).

ἴστε που "I think you know . . ." που is common where speakers pretend to be unsure of the facts at hand.

21a1 **ἑταῖρος** In the first instance, the word means "companion." The word also has a political sense of "partisan supporter," however, the sense in which it is to be understood in the second instance. πλῆθος is a euphemism for the democratic faction opposed to the actions of the aristocratic clubs (ἑταιρεῖαι) from which the oligarchs drew support. See on 36b8.

21a3 **ἐφ' ὅτι** τοῦτο, the antecedent of the ὅ in ὅτι, has been incorporated into the relative clause: "how impetuous he was toward whatever . . ."

ὁρμήσειεν The optative here expresses a general occurance in the past.

21a4 **καὶ δή . . . καί** "Moreover."

21a5 **ὅπερ λέγω** "With respect to the very thing I am saying." The present tense here suggests continuity in the sense of "keep saying." The precise reference, however, is to 20e4.

δὴ εἴ τις ἐμοῦ εἴη σοφώτερος. ἀνεῖλεν οὖν ἡ Πυθία μηδένα σοφώτερον εἶναι. καὶ τούτων πέρι ὁ ἀδελφὸς ὑμῖν αὐτοῦ οὑτοσὶ μαρτυρήσει, ἐπειδὴ ἐκεῖνος τετελεύτηκεν.

ἀνεῖλεν aor. act. indic. < ἀναιρέω (of an oracle) *respond*
μαρτυρήσει < μαρτυρέω *testify*
τετελεύτηκεν pf. act. indic. < τελευτάω *die*

21a6 The fact that Chaerephon thought to ask a question about the wisdom of Socrates shows that the tradition of Socrates as an ἀνὴρ σοφός (see, for example, 18b7) has a history outside of the *Apology.* This idea is corroborated by the language of Aristophanes' *Clouds,* where the school of Socrates is referred to as a ψυχῶν σοφῶν . . . φροντιστήριον, a "thinkery of wise souls" (94). That Aristophanes' popular representation matches Chaerephon's "insider's view" is interesting, particularly considering the energy that Plato's Socrates expends in denying that he has any wisdom at all, at least as wisdom is popularly understood.

δή Emphasizes the γάρ.

εἴη The optative is common in indirect questions in secondary sequence. Translate: "was."

ἀνεῖλεν ἀναιρεῖν This is the technical term for a reply from the Pythian priestess.

ἡ Πυθία The oracles of Apollo at Delphi were delivered by his priestess, the Pythia, so called from the cult title Apollo took on slaying the serpent that had previously held the site on which the shrine was built. They were then shaped into hexameter verse by the *prophetai* or resident interpretors.

21a8 **ἀδελφός . . . οὑτοσί** His name was Chaerecrates. The deictic iota implies that he is in the audience. Note how the postponement of οὑτοσί creates a sense of drama. If this incident was part of the actual trial, a statement by Chaerecrates might be read at this point to confirm Socrates' account.

CHAPTER 6

(21b1–e2)

Socrates claims to have been as puzzled as the jurors by this oracular statement, since he is convinced that he knows nothing. He thus sets out either to unravel its meaning or to disprove it by going about the city in quest of one wiser than himself. Wisdom, it will turn out, is not positive knowledge, in the sense of a τέχνη or the mastery of a set of facts, but self-knowledge. For additional discussion of the chapter and questions for study, see essay 6.

b Σκέψασθε δὴ ὧν ἕνεκα ταῦτα λέγω· μέλλω γὰρ ὑμᾶς διδάξειν ὅθεν μοι ἡ διαβολὴ γέγονεν. ταῦτα γὰρ ἐγὼ ἀκούσας ἐνεθυμούμην οὑτωσί· "Τί ποτε λέγει ὁ θεός, καὶ τί ποτε αἰνίττεται; ἐγὼ γὰρ δὴ οὔτε μέγα οὔτε σμικρὸν σύνοιδα ἐμαυτῷ σοφὸς ὤν· τί οὖν ποτε λέγει φάσκων ἐμὲ σοφώ-

---

ὅθεν *from where*
ἐνεθυμούμην impf. < ἐνθυμέομαι *consider*
αἰνίττεται < αἰνίττομαι *speak in riddles*
σύνοιδα *be aware*

21b1 **ὧν ἕνεκα** "Why."

21b3-4 **ποτε . . . ποτε** The parallelism is emphatic, followed up by an emotional γὰρ δή (a souped-up version of explanatory γάρ), and climaxing with Socrates' emphatic denial that he is wise.

21b4 **αἰνίττεται** The tradition of riddling Delphic oracles was well established in Socrates' time. The most famous is certainly the story of the Lydian king Croesus recounted in book one of the *Histories* of Herodotus. Already in the the sixth century B.C.E., however, the pre-Socratic (and famously oracular) philosopher Heraclitus of Miletus had said of Apollo: οὔτε λέγει οὔτε κρύπτει, ἀλλὰ σημαίνει, "he neither speaks nor conceals, but gives a sign" (Kirk, Raven, and Schofield 1993, fr. 244).

21b5 **ὤν** When forms of οἶδα introduce indirect statement, the main verb of the reported clause becomes a participle.

τατον εἶναι; οὐ γὰρ δήπου ψεύδεταί γε· οὐ γὰρ θέμις αὐτῷ." καὶ πολὺν μὲν χρόνον ἠπόρουν τί ποτε λέγει· ἔπειτα μόγις πάνυ ἐπὶ ζήτησιν αὐτοῦ τοιαύτην τινὰ ἐτραπόμην. ἦλθον ἐπί τινα τῶν δοκούντων σοφῶν εἶναι, ὡς ἐνταῦθα εἴπερ που ἐλέγξων τὸ μαντεῖον καὶ ἀποφανῶν τῷ c
χρησμῷ ὅτι "Οὑτοσὶ ἐμοῦ σοφώτερός ἐστι, σὺ δ' ἐμὲ ἔφησθα." διασκοπῶν οὖν τοῦτον—ὀνόματι γὰρ οὐδὲν δέομαι λέγειν,

---

ἠπόρουν < ἀπορέω *be at a loss*
ζήτησιν < ζήτησις, -εως, -ἡ *investigation*
ἐτραπόμην aor. mid. indic. < τρέπω *turn*
ἀποφανῶν fut. act. part. < ἀποφαίνω *show, represent*
χρησμῷ < χρησμός, -οῦ, ὁ *oracular reply*
διασκοπῶν < διασκοπέω *examine, consider*

21b6 **θέμις** The noun is derived from τίθημι and glossed as "law" or "right," but usually in the sense of something divinely ordained or "laid down." The moral uprightness Socrates attributes to the gods is not consistent with their portrayal in Homer, Hesiod, and tragedy. The pre-Socratic philosopher Xenophanes of Colophon (sixth century B.C.E.) says: "Homer and Hesiod have attributed to the gods everything that is shame and reproach among men, stealing and committing adultery and deceiving each other" (Kirk, Raven and Schofield 1993, fr. 166). The fact that the gods themselves do not appear to agree on the nature of piety is also discussed in the *Euthyphro*, the dialogue that is set not long before the trial of Socrates (see introduction).

21b7 **πολὺν χρόνον** Acc. of duration of time.

τί ποτε λέγει Note how the presence of the direct interrogative τί in place of ὅτι, together with the present tense λέγει, gives the impression that we are inside Socrates' head as he ponders the meaning of the oracle.

21b8 **μόγις πάνυ** "With great difficulty." "He would naturally shrink from the idea of proving the god a liar," says Burnet, which is certainly the surface meaning of Socrates' words. This sense is emphasized further by ζήτησιν . . . τοιαύτην τινα, where the vagueness of the expression suggests that the experience was so unusual for Socrates that he still does not really have words to describe it. Socrates' *aporia* may have been genuine. Still, some audience members might have suspected that these expressions of confusion were feigned. The oracle as reported in Xenophon is a good deal less cryptic.

αὐτοῦ That is, Apollo.

21b9 **ἦλθον** Socrates' dramatic rendering of his investigation begins abruptly, without conjunctions or particles.

δοκούντων "Reputed to be." The distinction between appearance (δοκεῖν) and reality (εἶναι) is fundamental to the *Apology* and to the Platonic dialogues in general (see, for example, 21c6–7).

ὡς The future participle with ὡς is commonly used to indicate purpose.

21c3 **τοῦτον** The pronoun refers back to τινά (21b9). Why does Socrates not give the man's name? Burnet thought that the line referred directly to Anytus, who is represented as having a testy exchange with Socrates in Plato's *Meno*. There is no direct evidence for this claim, however.

ἧν δέ τις τῶν πολιτικῶν πρὸς ὃν ἐγὼ σκοπῶν τοιοῦτόν τι ἔπαθον, ὦ ἄνδρες Ἀθηναῖοι, καὶ διαλεγόμενος αὐτῷ—ἔδοξέ μοι οὗτος ὁ ἀνὴρ δοκεῖν μὲν εἶναι σοφὸς ἄλλοις τε πολλοῖς ἀνθρώποις καὶ μάλιστα ἑαυτῷ, εἶναι δ' οὔ· κἄπειτα ἐπειρώμην αὐτῷ δεικνύναι ὅτι οἴοιτο μὲν εἶναι σοφός, εἴη δ' οὔ.
d ἐντεῦθεν οὖν τούτῳ τε ἀπηχθόμην καὶ πολλοῖς τῶν παρόντων· πρὸς ἐμαυτὸν δ' οὖν ἀπιὼν ἐλογιζόμην ὅτι τούτου μὲν τοῦ ἀνθρώπου ἐγὼ σοφώτερός εἰμι· κινδυνεύει μὲν γὰρ ἡμῶν οὐδέτερος οὐδὲν καλὸν κἀγαθὸν εἰδέναι, ἀλλ' οὗτος μὲν οἴεταί τι εἰδέναι οὐκ εἰδώς, ἐγὼ δέ, ὥσπερ οὖν οὐκ οἶδα,

---

πολιτικῶν < πολιτικός, -ή, -όν *statesman*
ἐπειρώμην impf. < πειράω *try*
ἐντεῦθεν *from there*
ἀπηχθόμην aor. mid. indic. < ἀπεχθάνομαι *become hated*
ἀπιών part. < ἄπειμι *go away*
ἐλογιζόμην impf. < λογίζομαι *reckon*
εἰδώς part. < οἶδα *know*

21c4 **σκοπῶν** "In the course of my investigation."
τοιοῦτόν τι "A certain kind of thing."

21c5 **διαλεγόμενος . . . ἔδοξε** The syntax of Plato's sentences frequently recreate oral mannerisms (see on 19e4–20a2). Here Socrates abandons the nominative, on the basis of which we should expect a verb in the first-person singular, and shifts the syntax midsentence (anacolouthon) to impersonal ἔδοξε.

21c6–7 **δοκεῖν μέν . . . εἶναι δ' οὐ** As mentioned above, it is difficult to overstate the importance of the contrast between seeming and being for Plato in general and for the *Apology* in particular. It is an idea that clearly sets him apart from those in the conformist mainstream, for whom appearance ("seeming") is enough. Note the striking effect of the laconic δέ-clause.

21c7 **ἐπειρώμην** As Socrates will imply later, inadvertent ignorance is no crime, and the person corrected should naturally be grateful for the assistance. That the unnamed politician grew angry instead is shameful, if not particularly surprising.

21c8 **οἴοιτο . . . εἴη** In indirect statement after ὅτι, verbs usually appear in the optative (as here) if they are introduced by a verb of saying, showing, and so forth *in a past tense* (ἐπειρώμην . . . δεικνύναι).

21d2 **δ' οὖν** "And so."
ἀπιών "As I left."

21d4 **καλὸν κἀγαθόν** Neuter. It goes without saying that anyone in fifth-century Athens who regarded himself as καλὸς κἀγαθός felt that his actions were similarly noble. Socrates' most revolutionary act may have been to insist on evaluating the individual on the basis of his *deeds* rather than on the basis of wealth or inherited status.

21d5 **εἰδώς** The participle is concessive.

οὐδὲ οἴομαι· ἔοικα γοῦν τούτου γε σμικρῷ τινι αὐτῷ τούτῳ σοφώτερος εἶναι, ὅτι ἃ μὴ οἶδα οὐδὲ οἴομαι εἰδέναι. ἐντεῦθεν ἐπ' ἄλλον ᾖα τῶν ἐκείνου δοκούντων σοφωτέρων εἶναι καί μοι ταὐτὰ ταῦτα ἔδοξε, καὶ ἐνταῦθα κἀκείνῳ καὶ ἄλλοις **e**
πολλοῖς ἀπηχθόμην.

ἔοικα *I am likely*
ᾖα 1st sg. impf. < εἶμι *go*

21d6 **γοῦν** = γε οὖν "So, to that extent . . ."
τούτου That is, the politician.
σμικρῷ τινι αὐτῷ τούτῳ "By just this one small thing." Dat. of degree of difference.

21d7 **ἅ** The antecedent of ἅ is an unexpressed ταῦτα that would be the object of εἰδέναι: "that what I don't know I don't think I know."

21e1 **κἀκείνῳ** (= καὶ ἐκείνῳ) The demonstratives are a little confusing here. ἐκείνου (d8) refers to the first of the politicians Socrates visited, ἐκείνῳ (e1) to the second politician.

CHAPTER 7

(21e3–22c9)

Socrates continues his examination of the oracle by speaking with the poets. For additional discussion of the chapter and questions for study, see essay 7.

Μετὰ ταῦτ' οὖν ἤδη ἐφεξῆς ᾖα, αἰσθανόμενος μὲν καὶ
λυπούμενος καὶ δεδιὼς ὅτι ἀπηχθανόμην, ὅμως δὲ ἀναγκαῖον
ἐδόκει εἶναι τὸ τοῦ θεοῦ περὶ πλείστου ποιεῖσθαι—ἰτέον
οὖν, σκοποῦντι τὸν χρησμὸν τί λέγει, ἐπὶ ἅπαντας τούς τι
22 δοκοῦντας εἰδέναι. καὶ νὴ τὸν κύνα, ὦ ἄνδρες Ἀθηναῖοι—
δεῖ γὰρ πρὸς ὑμᾶς τἀληθῆ λέγειν—ἦ μὴν ἐγὼ ἔπαθόν τι
τοιοῦτον· οἱ μὲν μάλιστα εὐδοκιμοῦντες ἔδοξάν μοι ὀλίγου

ἐφεξῆς *successively*
αἰσθανόμενος < αἰσθάνομαι *perceive*
λυπούμενος < λυπέω *cause pain, grief*
δεδιώς < δείδω *fear*
ἀναγκαῖον < ἀναγκαῖος, -η, -ον *necessary*
ἰτέον neut. verbal adj. (impers.) < εἶμι *it is necessary to go*
εὐδοκιμοῦντες < εὐδοκιμέω *seem good*

21e5 **τὸ τοῦ θεοῦ** Apollo's oracle (obj. of ποιεῖσθαι).
περὶ πλείστου ποιεῖσθαι "Take very seriously."
ἰτέον Supply μοι, agreeing with σκοποῦντι: "So I had to go investigate . . ." Note how Socrates emphasizes divine necessity over his own volition.

22e6 **τι** Obj. of εἰδέναι.

22a1 **νὴ τὸν κύνα** "Yes, by the dog!" This is a characteristic oath of Socrates, who also swears by the gods. However, it is not unique to him. The scholia on the *Apology* preserve a fragment from a comedy of Cratinus (fr. 249) in which a speaker refers to those who swear by the dog and the goose but not by the gods (see also Aristophanes *Wasps*, 83).

22a2 **ἦ μήν** "Very truly."

22a3 **μάλιστα** The adverb is in the attributive position, modifying οἱ . . . εὐδοκιμοῦντες.
ὀλίγου δεῖν "Almost," an idomatic use of the absolute infinitive (Smyth 1956, 2012).

δεῖν τοῦ πλείστου ἐνδεεῖς εἶναι ζητοῦντι κατὰ τὸν θεόν, ἄλλοι δὲ δοκοῦντες φαυλότεροι ἐπιεικέστεροι εἶναι ἄνδρες πρὸς τὸ φρονίμως ἔχειν. δεῖ δὴ ὑμῖν τὴν ἐμὴν πλάνην ἐπιδεῖξαι ὥσπερ πόνους τινὰς πονοῦντος ἵνα μοι καὶ ἀνέλεγκτος ἡ μαντεία γένοιτο. μετὰ γὰρ τοὺς πολιτικοὺς ᾖα

πλάνην < πλάνη, -ης, ἡ *wandering*
πονοῦντος < πονέω *work hard*
ἀνέλεγκτος, -ον *thoroughly tested*

22a4 **τοῦ πλείστου ἐνδεεῖς** "Most deficient" (lit., "lacking the most"). For Socrates, the world is upside down.

μοι . . . ζητοῦντι Note how the entire phrase is bracketed by the two datives.

κατὰ τὸν θεόν The evident simplicity of the expression obscures Socrates' more controversial claim. Apollo did not *command* anything at all. He made a statement about Socrates' wisdom that the latter decided to interpret in a certain way. ζητεῖν κατὰ τὸν θεόν is only an accurate description of Socrates' activities if one accepts his less-than-straightforward interpretation of the oracle. Note also the imagery of philosophy as a pursuit rather than as a body of doctrine (see also on 21b8).

22a5 **ἐπιεικέστεροι** "More suitable," the predicate of ἄλλοι: "and other men appearing more worthless (φαυλότεροι) appeared *more suitable* in regards to intelligent thought (τὸ φρονίμως ἔχειν)." Note the effect created by placing side by side the antonyms φαυλότεροι and ἐπιεικέστεροι. Socrates here redefines terms commonly used in a social or class context in terms of moral and intellectual virtue.

22a6 **δή** The particle emphasizes δεῖ. Its effect is intensified by the fact that the two words are homonyms.

22a6–7 **πλάνην . . . πόνους . . . πονοῦντος** Socrates casts himself as a latter-day Heracles, whose labors are commonly described in Greek literature as πόνοι. Note the alliteration. The comparison to Heracles is important for the way that Socrates presents his quest. He could, after all, quit here, having asserted that in his experience, those with the best reputation for wisdom were frequently found wanting. By styling himself a Heracles, however, a single encounter will not be enough, and instead he presents his experience as a *series* of labors: politicians, poets (the traditional source of didactic moral reflection), and craftsmen (a group likely to have been well represented on the jury due to the proximity of their jobs in the agora to the court). The result of this series is that the critique of the politicians, traditional targets of invective in comedy and elsewhere, expands to include the entire city. Socrates will come back to this topic later in a famous metaphor in which he compares himself to a stinging fly that keeps a noble but lazy horse (Athens) from dozing its life away (30e).

22a7 **ἐπιδεῖξαι** Literally, "display," but the verb and the related noun ἐπιδείξις are common for describing oratorical performances.

22a8 **ἀνέλεγκτος** Socrates' mission, as he represents it, was undertaken to vindicate the words of Apollo, however implausible they seemed to him.

ἐπὶ τοὺς ποιητὰς τούς τε τῶν τραγῳδιῶν καὶ τοὺς τῶν
b διθυράμβων καὶ τοὺς ἄλλους, ὡς ἐνταῦθα ἐπ' αὐτοφώρῳ
καταληψόμενος ἐμαυτὸν ἀμαθέστερον ἐκείνων ὄντα. ἀνα-
λαμβάνων οὖν αὐτῶν τὰ ποιήματα ἅ μοι ἐδόκει μάλιστα
πεπραγματεῦσθαι αὐτοῖς, διηρώτων ἂν αὐτοὺς τί λέγοιεν,

καταληψόμενος < καταλαμβάνω *find, understand*
ἀμαθέστερον comp. < ἀμαθής, -ές *ignorant*
πεπραγματεῦσθαι pf. mid. infin. < πραγματεύομαι *work over*
διηρώτων impf. act. < διερωτάω *interrogate*

22a9 **τοὺς ποιητάς** It is no longer conventional to assume a connection between poetry and wisdom. To an ancient audience, however, the association was very close, since poetry claimed its inspiration from the Muses, themselves the daughters of Zeus (see *Theogony* 22–34 for Hesiod's description of his encounter with them). Both the *Iliad* and the *Odyssey* begin by asking the Muse to provide information about the subjects of their songs. Poetry's divine origin allowed poets to claim that their songs were "true," despite the fact that their subjects were set in distant times and places. From there it was a short step to the claim that poetry is the source of wisdom itself. For an amusing critique of the claim that poetry is knowledge, see Plato's *Ion*, a conversation between Socrates and Ion. The latter is a genial but somewhat self-important rhapsode (professional reciter of Homeric poetry).

τραγῳδιῶν The Greater Dionysia and the Lenaea, where tragedy was performed, were state-sponsored, communal, and highly ritualized events. Tragedy was thus not only an entertainment, but an important part of how the city represented itself, both to its own citizens and to the inhabitants of other Greek cities attending the festival.

22b1 **διθυράμβων** The dithyramb was a type of poetry, traditionally associated with Dionysus, that treated mythological themes. It was performed at civic festivals by choruses of boys or men.

τοὺς ἄλλους That is, writers of comedies, elegies, lyrics, and so forth.

ἐπ' αὐτοφώρῳ "Red-handed." Note ὡς + fut. part. to indicate the *purpose* of Socrates' visit. For φώρ, "thief," compare the Latin cognate *fur*.

22b2 **ἐκείνων** Genitive of comparison.

22b3 **ποιήματα** Socrates chooses a very neutral word here. ποιήματα (noun < ποιέω) simply identifies the poem as something created by artifice. By choosing it in place of words such as ᾠδή or ἀοιδή "song" (< ἀείδω, "sing"), which are associated with inspired song (cf. *Iliad* 1.1), Socrates tacitly undermines the claim that poetry has access to revealed wisdom. At 23c2, he will concede its divine origin but suggest that the poet, like the prophet, channels the word of the gods without understanding it.

22b4 **αὐτοῖς** A dative of agent is common with verbs in the perfect passive (πεπραγματεῦσθαι).

διηρώτων ἄν The imperfect + ἄν is used to express habitual action in the past.

λέγοιεν The optative appears frequently in indirect questions introduced by a verb in a past tense. Note that λέγω here means "mean."

ἵν᾽ ἅμα τι καὶ μανθάνοιμι παρ᾽ αὐτῶν. αἰσχύνομαι οὖν
ὑμῖν εἰπεῖν, ὦ ἄνδρες, τἀληθῆ· ὅμως δὲ ῥητέον. ὡς ἔπος
γὰρ εἰπεῖν ὀλίγου αὐτῶν ἅπαντες οἱ παρόντες ἂν βέλτιον
ἔλεγον περὶ ὧν αὐτοὶ ἐπεποιήκεσαν. ἔγνων οὖν αὖ καὶ
περὶ τῶν ποιητῶν ἐν ὀλίγῳ τοῦτο, ὅτι οὐ σοφίᾳ ποιοῖεν
ἃ ποιοῖεν, ἀλλὰ φύσει τινὶ καὶ ἐνθουσιάζοντες ὥσπερ οἱ c
θεομάντεις καὶ οἱ χρησμῳδοί· καὶ γὰρ οὗτοι λέγουσι μὲν

αἰσχύνομαι < αἰσχύνω *shame*
ῥητέον neut. verbal adj. *it must be said*
ἐπεποιήκεσαν 3rd pl. pluperf. act. < ποιέω *make*

22b6 **τἀληθῆ** = τὰ ἀληθῆ. The object is dramatically postponed until the final position in the sentence.

ὡς ἔπος εἰπεῖν See on 17a4.

22b7 **αὐτῶν** Gen. of comparison with βέλτιον.

οἱ παρόντες That is, at that time, not the present audience.

ἂν . . . ἔλεγον Past tenses of the indicative + ἄν can be used to indicate probability in the past: "[they] would probably speak . . ."

22b8 **αὐτοί** Like αὐτῶν above, referring to the poets.

ἐπεποιήκεσαν For poets as "makers," see on 22b3.

αὖ καί "In turn also." Socrates connects this experience with what he found to be the case with the politicians, then he goes on to distinguish the two by means of the ὅτι-clause.

22b9 **ἐν ὀλίγῳ** Supply χρόνῳ.

σοφίᾳ Traditionally, σοφία was an attribute of poets, so Socrates makes a radical suggestion in denying it to them.

ποιοῖεν Optative in indirect speech after a past-tense verb.

22c1 **φύσει** "Inborn capacity, nature." Here the word is understood in opposition to τέχνη and σοφία and locates the source of an ability for which the possessor cannot (and does not need to) give a rational explanation. If the composition of poetry is irrational, it is not surprising that the poets cannot give a coherent account of their work.

ἐνθουσιάζοντες The participle is related to ἔνθεος, literally "having a god inside," and is used to describe both poetic inspiration and divine possession. Socrates' treatment of the poets recalls that of the politicians; nonetheless, the participle, however ironic, betrays a certain respect for their work. The poets may not know what they are doing and so fall short of philosophy, but they are in some sense touched by the divine.

22c2 **θεομάντεις . . . χρησμῳδοί** A θεομάντις is someone possessed by a god, which can be good or bad. A χρησμῳδός receives, and possibly promulgates, the oracles of a god. They are also mentioned together in Plato's *Meno* (99c), where Socrates cites them as examples of people who act without φρόνησις ("good judgment") in language that is strongly reminiscent of the *Apology*.

πολλὰ καὶ καλά, ἴσασιν δὲ οὐδὲν ὧν λέγουσι. τοιοῦτόν τί μοι ἐφάνησαν πάθος καὶ οἱ ποιηταὶ πεπονθότες, καὶ ἅμα ᾐσθόμην αὐτῶν διὰ τὴν ποίησιν οἰομένων καὶ τἆλλα σοφωτάτων εἶναι ἀνθρώπων ἃ οὐκ ἦσαν. ἀπῇα οὖν καὶ ἐντεῦθεν τῷ αὐτῷ οἰόμενος περιγεγονέναι ᾧπερ καὶ τῶν πολιτικῶν.

ποίησιν < ποίησις, -εως, ἡ *activity of creating poetry*
ἀπῇα 1st sg. impf. < ἄπειμι *go away*
περιγεγονέναι pf. act. infin. < περιγίγνομαι *be superior to*

22c3 **πολλὰ καὶ καλά** = πολλὰ καλά, an example of *hendiadys*, a common rhetorical figure by which one idea is expressed through two.

ὧν The relative is attracted into the case of the implied antecedent τούτων.

τοιοῦτόν τι . . . πάθος "A similar experience."

22c5–6 The key syntactic units of the sentence are: ᾐσθόμην . . . οἰομένων . . . εἶναι. The basic grammatical principles are as follows: (1) verbs of perception typically have their objects in the genitive; (2) verbs of knowing, learning, and perceiving often use a participle to express indirect statement; and (3) οἴομαι uses a subject-accusative + infinitive construction to express indirect statement. Principles (1) and (2) explain the form of οἰομένων; (3) accounts for εἶναι.

22c5 **καὶ τἆλλα** "Also in respect to other things." τἆλλα (= τὰ ἄλλα) is the antecedent of ἅ (also an accusative of respect) below.

22c6 **σοφωτάτων** Predicate of οἰομένων.

22c7 **τῷ αὐτῷ** "The same thing"; that is, by recognizing that I was not wise.

περιγεγονέναι Verbs that express superiority and inferiority typically take a genitive of comparison as their object. Here περιγεγονέναι goes with both the main clause and the relative clause, but only its genitive complement in the relative clause, is expressed (τῶν πολιτικῶν). For the main clause, supply τῶν ποιητῶν.

CHAPTER 8

(22c9–e5)

After being disappointed with the poets, Socrates goes to the craftsmen (χειροτέχναι), who, while certainly in possession of a τέχνη, irrationally use that expertise to claim a more general wisdom. For additional discussion of the chapter and questions for study, see essay 8.

Τελευτῶν οὖν ἐπὶ τοὺς χειροτέχνας ᾖα· ἐμαυτῷ γὰρ
συνῄδη οὐδὲν ἐπισταμένῳ ὡς ἔπος εἰπεῖν, τούτους δέ γ' ᾔδη d
ὅτι εὑρήσοιμι πολλὰ καὶ καλὰ ἐπισταμένους. καὶ τούτου
μὲν οὐκ ἐψεύσθην, ἀλλ' ἠπίσταντο ἃ ἐγὼ οὐκ ἠπιστάμην
καί μου ταύτῃ σοφώτεροι ἦσαν. ἀλλ', ὦ ἄνδρες Ἀθηναῖοι,
ταὐτόν μοι ἔδοξαν ἔχειν ἁμάρτημα ὅπερ καὶ οἱ ποιηταὶ καὶ

τελευτῶν < τελευτάω *come to an end*
σύνῄδη 3rd sg. impf. < σύνοιδα *be conscious, aware*
ἁμάρτημα, -τος, τό *error*

22c9 **τελευτῶν** "Finally." The participle of τελευτάω sometimes functions adverbially, as here.

22d1 **συνῄδη** When the subject of the participle is the same as the subject of the main verb, the participle can agree either with the subject (cf. 21b) *or* with the complement (as here).

ὡς ἔπος εἰπεῖν The phrase emphasizes οὐδέν: "nothing, to put it in a word."

τούτους Object of εὑρήσοιμι. The position is emphatic.

δέ γ' The combination is strongly adversative.

22d3 **ἃ ἐγὼ οὐκ ἠπιστάμην** Socrates' claims about his ignorance of the crafts should probably be taken with some caution. Ancient tradition has Socrates following the craft of his father, Sophroniscus, who was said to be a stonecutter. Socrates himself, in *Theaetetus*, refers to his mother, Phaenarete, as a midwife (149a), and he claims to have taken after her (metaphorically) by helping to give birth to the wisdom of others. For the ancient sources on the biography of Socrates, see Nails 2002, 263–69.

οἱ ἀγαθοὶ δημιουργοί—διὰ τὸ τὴν τέχνην καλῶς ἐξεργάζεσθαι ἕκαστος ἠξίου καὶ τἆλλα τὰ μέγιστα σοφώτατος
εἶναι—καὶ αὐτῶν αὕτη ἡ πλημμέλεια ἐκείνην τὴν σοφίαν
e ἀποκρύπτειν· ὥστε με ἐμαυτὸν ἀνερωτᾶν ὑπὲρ τοῦ χρησμοῦ
πότερα δεξαίμην ἂν οὕτως ὥσπερ ἔχω ἔχειν, μήτε τι σοφὸς
ὢν τὴν ἐκείνων σοφίαν μήτε ἀμαθὴς τὴν ἀμαθίαν, ἢ ἀμφότερα ἃ ἐκεῖνοι ἔχουσιν ἔχειν. ἀπεκρινάμην οὖν ἐμαυτῷ
καὶ τῷ χρησμῷ ὅτι μοι λυσιτελοῖ ὥσπερ ἔχω ἔχειν.

δημιουργοί < δημιουργός, -οῦ, ὁ *craftsman*
ἠξίου 3rd sg. impf. act. < ἀξιόω *believe, judge*
πλημμέλεια, -ας, ἡ *error*
ἀποκρύπτειν < ἀποκρύπτω *conceal something* (*acc.*) *from someone* (*acc.*)
ὑπερ (+ gen.) *on behalf of*
πότερα . . . ἤ *whether . . . or*
δεξαίμην aor. opt. mid. < δέχομαι *take*
λυσιτελοῖ pres. opt. < λυσιτελέω *be beneficial*

22d6 **ἀγαθοί** The distinction is puzzling, since distinctions in ability have played no role in Socrates' story to this point.
διὰ τὸ τὴν τέχνην καλῶς ἐξεργάζεσθαι The articular infinitive is the object of the preposition: "by performing their art well."

22d7 **τὰ μέγιστα** That is, all the big questions about politics, ethics, and metaphysics, as opposed to the limited (and perhaps trivial) wisdom they possessed about their craft.

22d8 **ἐκείνην τὴν σοφίαν** "That wisdom they *did* have."

22e1 **ἀποκρύπτειν** Traditionally, there are two ways of construing this passage: (1) understand the infinitive as dependent on ἔδοξαν (d5), or (2) read ἀπέκρυπτεν, as the text appears in several manuscripts.

22e3 **σοφίαν . . . ἀμαθίαν** Accusatives of respect. ἐκείνων goes with both.
ἀμφότερα That is, "both" their (limited) wisdom and their (appalling) ignorance.

22e4 **ἔχειν** Parallel with the ἔχειν at 22e2, dependent on δεξαίμην ἄν.

CHAPTER 9

(22e6–23c1)

These examinations explain how Socrates' reputation for wisdom, as well as the enmity against him, arose. For additional discussion of the chapter and questions for study, see essay 9.

Ἐκ ταυτησὶ δὴ τῆς ἐξετάσεως, ὦ ἄνδρες Ἀθηναῖοι,
πολλαὶ μὲν ἀπέχθειαί μοι γεγόνασι καὶ οἷαι χαλεπώταται 23
καὶ βαρύταται, ὥστε πολλὰς διαβολὰς ἀπ' αὐτῶν γεγονέναι,
ὄνομα δὲ τοῦτο λέγεσθαι, σοφὸς εἶναι· οἴονται γάρ με
ἑκάστοτε οἱ παρόντες ταῦτα αὐτὸν εἶναι σοφὸν ἃ ἂν ἄλλον
ἐξελέγξω. τὸ δὲ κινδυνεύει, ὦ ἄνδρες, τῷ ὄντι ὁ θεὸς σοφὸς
εἶναι, καὶ ἐν τῷ χρησμῷ τούτῳ τοῦτο λέγειν, ὅτι ἡ

ἐξετάσεως < ἐξέτασις, -εως, ἡ *close examination, scrutiny*
ἀπέχθειαι < ἀπέχθεια, -ας, ἡ *enmity, hatred*
βαρύταται super. < βαρύς, -εῖα, -ύ *heavy, onerous*
ἑκάστοτε *each time*

22e6 **δή** δή of identity: "precisely this." The particle is made more emphatic by the deictic iota on ταυτησί.

23a1 **μέν** The particle stands in isolation (it is unrelated to the δέ at 23a3). It sets up the expectation of a δέ-clause, but the ὥστε-clause intervenes and the anticipated μέν . . . δέ construction does not emerge.

23a3 **σοφὸς εἶναι** Note the case of σοφός. Names frequently are reported in the nominative (with a redundant εἶναι, on which see Smyth 1956, 1615). Burnet cites Aeschines' speech *On the Embassy* (99), where he says of Demosthenes: προσείληφε τὴν τῶν πονηρῶν κοινὴν ἐπωνυμίαν, συκοφάντης ("He earned the generic name for worthless men—sychophant"). Here σοφός gets the same treatment.

23a3-4 **με . . . αὐτόν** "I myself" (in contrast to ἄλλον).

23a5 **τὸ δέ** "But in fact . . ." The τό is used as a weak demonstrative pronoun (lit.: "but with respect to this . . ."). Socrates now ventures a new interpretation of the oracle.

ἀνθρωπίνη σοφία ὀλίγου τινὸς ἀξία ἐστὶν καὶ οὐδενός. καὶ
φαίνεται τοῦτον λέγειν τὸν Σωκράτη, προσκεχρῆσθαι δὲ
b τῷ ἐμῷ ὀνόματι, ἐμὲ παράδειγμα ποιούμενος, ὥσπερ ἂν
⟨εἰ⟩ εἴποι ὅτι "Οὗτος ὑμῶν, ὦ ἄνθρωποι, σοφώτατός ἐστιν,
ὅστις ὥσπερ Σωκράτης ἔγνωκεν ὅτι οὐδενὸς ἄξιός ἐστι τῇ
ἀληθείᾳ πρὸς σοφίαν." ταῦτ' οὖν ἐγὼ μὲν ἔτι καὶ νῦν
περιιὼν ζητῶ καὶ ἐρευνῶ κατὰ τὸν θεὸν καὶ τῶν ἀστῶν καὶ
ξένων ἄν τινα οἴωμαι σοφὸν εἶναι· καὶ ἐπειδάν μοι μὴ
δοκῇ, τῷ θεῷ βοηθῶν ἐνδείκνυμαι ὅτι οὐκ ἔστι σοφός. καὶ

προσκεχρῆσθαι pf. mid. infin. < προσχράομαι *use in addition*
παράδειγμα, -τος, τό *example, lesson*
περιιών < περίειμι *go about*
ἐρευνῶ < ἐρευνάω *examine*
ἀστῶν < ἀστός, -οῦ, ὁ *townsman, citizen*
ἐπειδάν *whenever*
ἐνδείκνυμαι *demonstrate*

23a7 **ὀλίγου τινος . . . καὶ οὐδενός** Both terms are dependent on ἀξία. καί is used occasionally to express alternatives where we would expect ἤ (Denniston 1954, 292). Translate "even."

23b1 **παράδειγμα ποιούμενος** The participial phrase explains in what sense Socrates meant προσκεχρῆσθαι τῷ ἐμῷ ὀνόματι.

23b2 **<εἰ>** The brackets indicate that the editor feels the word needs to be added, despite the fact that it does not appear in any of the manuscripts. It was written in the margin of an early manuscript by an anonymous reader and included by Henri Etienne (Stephanus) in his early printed edition.
ὅτι Do not translate.

23b4 **τῇ ἀληθείᾳ** The noun is used adverbially.
ταῦτ' οὖν = διὰ ταῦτα
ἔτι καὶ νῦν "Even still now." In this sentence we get the full statement of what, for Plato's Socrates, is the essential philosophical paradox: human wisdom deserving of the name consists in the recognition of human ignorance before the most important questions of human life.

23b5 **κατὰ τὸν θεόν** "According to the command of the god" (see on 22a4).
ἀστῶν καὶ ξενῶν Partitive genitives, depending on τινά.

23b6 **ἄν** = ἐάν
μὴ δοκῇ Supply σοφός εἶναι.

23b7–8 Socrates' interpretation of the oracle completely shifts its original emphasis, with the result that his mission now takes on an evangelistic quality: everyone with any claim to wisdom, Socrates implies, needs to accept this conclusion about its limitations.

ὑπὸ ταύτης τῆς ἀσχολίας οὔτε τι τῶν τῆς πόλεως πρᾶξαί μοι σχολὴ γέγονεν ἄξιον λόγου οὔτε τῶν οἰκείων, ἀλλ' ἐν πενίᾳ μυρίᾳ εἰμὶ διὰ τὴν τοῦ θεοῦ λατρείαν. **c**

πενίᾳ < πενία, -ας, ἡ *poverty*
λατρείαν < λατρεία, -ας, ἡ *service*

23b8 **ἀσχολίας** The idea of leisure and its absence brings up the question of Socrates' vocation again. Note that by interpreting the oracle as a religious duty, he implicitly addresses the charge of atheism that Meletus will raise. Further, if assiduous service to the god produces ἀσχολία, it will leave no free time, or σχολή, for traditional adult male citizen activities such as politics and moneymaking. Finally, this particular idea of service inevitably puts Socrates in contact with wealthy youths, who, because of the position they occupy between childhood and adult life, have plenty of σχολή (23c3) to devote to Socratic conversation.

τι τῶν τῆς πόλεως "Any of the city's business." For Greeks, and in particular for Athenians, an individual was defined by his relationship to the polis. Socrates, in saying that he had accomplished nothing for the city, confesses to what many would have counted as a positive vice. The separation between public and private life, which we take for granted, was not generally admitted. For Athenian attitudes toward those who chose not to participate in public affairs, see on 31c5.

23b9 **ἄξιον λόγου** He will, however, mention a few examples of his civic behavior in the pages that follow.

23c1 **πενίᾳ μυρίᾳ** Xenophon (*Oeconomicus* 2.1–4) reports Socrates as saying that his property could be worth five minas. This would put him into the lowest of the property classes into which all Athenian citizens were enrolled, that of the *thetes*. This assessment does not accord with all of the evidence, however. In any event, he possessed sufficient wealth earlier in his life to outfit himself for service as a hoplite, and the fact that Socrates seems clearly to travel in the highest social circles may indicate that, despite his indisputable disdain for money, his family was well connected. Much of the evidence is collected by Nails (2002) in her entries for Socrates, Phaenarete (mother), Chaerodemus (stepfather), and Patrocles (half-brother).

CHAPTER 10

(23c2–24b3)

Over time resentment against Socrates increased, especially as his young companions began to imitate him and aggressively questioned their elders and those in positions of authority. For additional discussion of the chapter and questions for study, see essay 10.

Πρὸς δὲ τούτοις οἱ νέοι μοι ἐπακολουθοῦντες—οἷς μάλιστα σχολή ἐστιν, οἱ τῶν πλουσιωτάτων—αὐτόματοι, χαίρουσιν ἀκούοντες ἐξεταζομένων τῶν ἀνθρώπων, καὶ αὐτοὶ πολλάκις ἐμὲ μιμοῦνται, εἶτα ἐπιχειροῦσιν ἄλλους ἐξετάζειν· κἄπειτα οἶμαι εὑρίσκουσι πολλὴν ἀφθονίαν οἰομένων μὲν εἰδέναι τι ἀνθρώπων, εἰδότων δὲ ὀλίγα ἢ οὐδέν. ἐντεῦθεν οὖν οἱ ὑπ᾽ αὐτῶν ἐξεταζόμενοι ἐμοὶ ὀργίζονται, οὐχ αὑτοῖς,

---

ἐπακολουθοῦντες < ἐπακολουθέω *follow after*
πλουσιωτάτων super. < πλούσιος, -α, -ον *wealthy*
αὐτόματοι < αὐτόματος, -η, -ον *on one's own*
ἐξεταζομένων < ἐξετάζω *examine, scrutinize*
εἶτα *then, next*
ἐπιχειροῦσιν < ἐπιχειρέω *try*
ἀφθονίαν < ἀφθονία, -ας, ἡ *abundance*
εἰδότων part. < οἶδα *know*
ὀργίζονται < ὀργίζομαι *grow angry*

23c5 **μιμοῦνται** It is clear that the motives of Socrates are different from those of the wealthy youths who "imitate" him, even if we think (reasonably) that his interpretation of the Delphic oracle is ironic and that he has chosen this vocation because *he* feels it is the best way to live. For the youths, Socratic testing is entertainment and an amusing form of rebellion against their elders. Socrates does not discount this motivation entirely (cf. ἀηδές 33c4).

23c6 **οἶμαι** Socrates' words suggest that he is speculating, that is, that he has not witnessed these demonstrations personally.

23c7 **οἰομένων . . . εἰδότων** The genitives are partitive and depend on ἀφθονίαν. **εἰδέναι τι** Here equivalent to "be wise," as can be seen by the contrast with (εἰδότων) ὀλίγα ἢ οὐδέν.

23c8 **αὑτοῖς** Note the rough breathing mark on the reflexive pronoun.

καὶ λέγουσιν ὡς Σωκράτης τίς ἐστι μιαρώτατος καὶ δια- d φθείρει τοὺς νέους· καὶ ἐπειδάν τις αὐτοὺς ἐρωτᾷ ὅτι ποιῶν καὶ ὅτι διδάσκων, ἔχουσι μὲν οὐδὲν εἰπεῖν ἀλλ' ἀγνοοῦσιν, ἵνα δὲ μὴ δοκῶσιν ἀπορεῖν, τὰ κατὰ πάντων τῶν φιλοσοφούντων πρόχειρα ταῦτα λέγουσιν, ὅτι "τὰ μετέωρα καὶ τὰ ὑπὸ γῆς" καὶ "θεοὺς μὴ νομίζειν" καὶ "τὸν ἥττω λόγον κρείττω ποιεῖν." τὰ γὰρ ἀληθῆ οἴομαι οὐκ ἂν ἐθέλοιεν λέγειν, ὅτι κατάδηλοι γίγνονται προσποιούμενοι μὲν εἰδέναι, εἰδότες δὲ οὐδέν. ἅτε οὖν οἶμαι φιλότιμοι

μιαρώτατος super. < μιαρός, -ά, -όν *impure, defiled*
διαφθείρει < διαφθείρω *corrupt, ruin*
ἀγνοοῦσιν < ἀγνοέω *be ignorant*
μετέωρα < μετέωρος, -α, -ον *midair, above the earth*
ἐθέλοιεν < ἐθέλω *wish*
κατάδηλοι < κατάδηλος, -ον *plain, obvious*
προσποιούμενοι < προσποιέω *claim, pretend*
ἅτε *since*
φιλότιμοι < φιλότιμος, -ον *ambitious*

23d1 **Σωκράτης τις** The words recall the accusation Socrates puts into the mouths of the "first accusers" (18b7).

23d2 **διαφθείρει τοὺς νέους** "Corrupts the youth." This is the slander mentioned at 21b2. At the same time, Socrates implicitly argues that the charge is little more than a face-saving gesture on the part of those who resent having their ignorance exposed.

23d2-3 **ὅτι . . . ὅτι** In both cases the indirect interrogative is the object of the participle.

23d4 **δοκῶσιν** Here as elsewhere the difference between seeming and being is of crucial importance.

23d4–5 **τὰ κατὰ πάντων τῶν φιλοσοφούντων πρόχειρα ταῦτα** "These stock charges against those practicing philosophy." For a restatement of the charges, see 18b7–c4. It is important to note that the first time any form of the word φιλοσοφία is found in the *Apology*, it appears as a verb. For the idea of philosophy as something you do, see on 22a4.

23d8 **κατάδηλοι** The word is best translated here by an adverb such as "obviously." It goes without saying that the statement is not calculated to win over anyone who has experienced this kind of treatment from Socrates or his imitators.

23d9 **εἰδέναι, εἰδότες δὲ οὐδέν** This idea is stated in a less compressed form at 23c6–7. Note that the state of mind in such people is precisely the opposite of that of Socrates, who—although, like them, he knows nothing—nevertheless recognizes his ignorance.

e ὄντες καὶ σφοδροὶ καὶ πολλοί, καὶ συντεταμένως καὶ πιθανῶς λέγοντες περὶ ἐμοῦ, ἐμπεπλήκασιν ὑμῶν τὰ ὦτα καὶ πάλαι καὶ σφοδρῶς διαβάλλοντες. ἐκ τούτων καὶ Μέλητός μοι ἐπέθετο καὶ Ἄνυτος καὶ Λύκων, Μέλητος μὲν ὑπὲρ τῶν ποιητῶν ἀχθόμενος, Ἄνυτος δὲ ὑπὲρ τῶν δημιουργῶν καὶ

σφοδροί < σφοδρός, -ά, -όν *passionate*
συντεταμένως *vigorously*
ἐμπεπλήκασιν pf. act. indic. < ἐμπίμπλημι *fill up*
ὦτα neut. acc., pl. < οὖς, ὠτός, τό ear
ἐπέθετο aor. mid. indic. < ἐπιτίθημι *set upon, attack*

23e3–24a1 **Meletus, Anytus, and Lycon** The three accusers are not well represented in the Platonic dialogues. Lycon appears nowhere else. There is a brief discussion of Meletus at the beginning of *Euthyphro*, where the point of the conversation is that no one knows who he is. Only Anytus has a prominent role. In *Meno* he warns Socrates, after they have a series of sharp exchanges, that his way of talking will get him into trouble (95a). Various ancient sources preserve the (unlikely) tradition that the Athenians later repented and avenged themselves upon the accusers (Nails 2002, 38).

Meletus is often confused with his father, who had the same name and may have been the poet mentioned by Aristophanes as early as the 420s (fr. 117) and as late as 405 in *Frogs* (1302). The name is not rare in Attic Greek, however, so speculation is hazardous.

Lycon was a contemporary of Socrates. His family had apparently attained some prominence, as he was regularly mocked in comedy, and his son Autolycus was the victor in the pancration at the Panathenaea in 422. Autolycus was later executed by the Thirty in 404/403. Xenophon portrays father and son as particularly close (*Symposium*). By the terms of the amnesty agreement (see introduction), Lycon would have been forbidden to mention his son's death at the trial, but he might nevertheless have joined in the prosecution if he thought that associates of Socrates were responsible for the death. He is by far the least prominent of the accusers.

Anytus is the most prominent accuser. An energetic man who had inherited a tannery from his father, he was general in 409 and supported the moderate oligarchic faction around Theramenes under the Thirty. He was later expelled by them and joined the exiled democrats at Phyle, where he was made a general again. With the fall of the Thirty, he returned to Athens with Thrasybulus and was a respected leader.

23e5 **ὑπέρ** The preposition should be understood loosely. Of course, we are not to imagine a conspiracy between these groups. Still, having accusers who could appeal to different constituencies would be part of a strategy to create a broad base of support. At *Apology* 36a8–b2 Socrates says that he would not have been convicted had this "alliance" not been in place.

τῶν πολιτικῶν, Λύκων δὲ ὑπὲρ τῶν ῥητόρων· ὥστε, ὅπερ 24
ἀρχόμενος ἐγὼ ἔλεγον, θαυμάζοιμ' ἂν εἰ οἷός τ' εἴην ἐγὼ ὑμῶν ταύτην τὴν διαβολὴν ἐξελέσθαι ἐν οὕτως ὀλίγῳ χρόνῳ οὕτω πολλὴν γεγονυῖαν. ταῦτ' ἔστιν ὑμῖν, ὦ ἄνδρες Ἀθηναῖοι, τἀληθῆ, καὶ ὑμᾶς οὔτε μέγα οὔτε μικρὸν ἀποκρυψάμενος ἐγὼ λέγω οὐδ' ὑποστειλάμενος. καίτοι οἶδα σχεδὸν ὅτι αὐτοῖς τούτοις ἀπεχθάνομαι, ὃ καὶ τεκμήριον ὅτι ἀληθῆ λέγω καὶ ὅτι αὕτη ἐστὶν ἡ διαβολὴ ἡ ἐμὴ καὶ τὰ αἴτια
ταῦτά ἐστιν. καὶ ἐάντε νῦν ἐάντε αὖθις ζητήσητε ταῦτα, b
οὕτως εὑρήσετε.

ἀρχόμενος < ἄρχω *begin*
θαυμάζοιμι < θαυμάζω *wonder*
ἐξελέσθαι aor. mid. infin. < ἐξαιρέω *remove*
γεγονυῖαν pf. act. part. < γίγνομαι *exist*
ὑποστειλάμενος < ὑποστέλλω *withhold*
σχεδόν *nearly, almost*
τεκμήριον, -ου, τό *evidence, proof*
αἴτια < αἴτιον, -ου, τό *cause*

24a1 **ὅπερ . . . ἔλεγον** The allusion is to 19a.

24a6 **οἶδα σχεδόν** "I'm pretty sure."

24a7 **τούτοις αὐτοῖς** The antecedent of these pronouns is not at all clear, and commentators are divided; some understand them as referring to Socrates' habit of exposing intellectual pretence ("these same things"), others as referring to "these same men," that is, the accusers. Both are possible, but the first seems most relevant to the point Socrates is making.

24b1 **ἐάντε . . . ἐάντε** ἐάν for εἰ, introducing a future-more-vivid condition (ἐάν with subj. + fut. indic.): "whether . . . or."

24b2 **εὑρήσετε** Supply ταῦτα as the object of the verb.

CHAPTER 11

(24b3–c9)

Here begins the defense against the charges Meletus has brought: that Socrates has corrupted the youth and does not worship the gods of the city. For additional discussion of the chapter and questions for study, see essay 11.

Περὶ μὲν οὖν ὧν οἱ πρῶτοί μου κατήγοροι κατηγόρουν αὕτη ἔστω ἱκανὴ ἀπολογία πρὸς ὑμᾶς· πρὸς δὲ Μέλητον τὸν ἀγαθὸν καὶ φιλόπολιν, ὥς φησι, καὶ τοὺς ὑστέρους μετὰ ταῦτα πειράσομαι ἀπολογήσασθαι. αὖθις γὰρ δή, ὥσπερ ἑτέρων τούτων ὄντων κατηγόρων, λάβωμεν αὖ τὴν

ἔστω 3rd imper. < εἰμί *be*
ἱκανή < ἱκανός, -ή, -όν *sufficient*

24b3 **μὲν οὖν** As it often does, this combination of particles resumes the narrative interrupted by Socrates' digression on Apollo's oracle (20c3).

24b4 **ἔστω** 3rd imper. < εἰμί: "let it be."

24b5 **τὸν ἀγαθὸν τε καὶ φιλόπολιν, ὥς φησι** Socrates is apparently quoting from Meletus's description of himself in his speech for the prosecution. His tone recalls the irony of Antony in Shakespeare's *Julius Caesar* III (ii): "And Brutus is an *honourable* man."

24b6 **γὰρ δή** δή emphasizes γάρ, drawing attention to the beginning of a narrative, here the accusation of the prosecutors (Denniston 1954, 243).

24b7 **ἑτέρων τούτων ὄντων** In parallel with τούτων (b8).

τούτων ἀντωμοσίαν. ἔχει δέ πως ὧδε· Σωκράτη φησὶν ἀδικεῖν τούς τε νέους διαφθείροντα καὶ θεοὺς οὓς ἡ πόλις νομίζει οὐ νομίζοντα, ἕτερα δὲ δαιμόνια καινά. τὸ μὲν δὴ c

---

καινά < καινός, -ή, -όν *new, strange*

24b8 **ἀντωμοσίαν** The formal indictment (also called an ἔγκλημα, "summons") refers to a proceedings that took place prior to the trial at the office of the Archon Basileus, the official responsible for cases having to do with ἀσέβεια ("impiety"), before whom both parties swore (ἀντ-ωμοσία < ὄμνυμι, "swear") to their version of the facts. It is precisely upon Socrates' departure from that meeting that he encounters Euthyphro at the beginning of the dialogue of the same name. The ἀντωμοσία as given falls into three parts: (1) corrupting the youth, (2) failing to honor the gods of Athens, and (3) introducing new divinities. Plato's description is in general agreement with the versions of Xenophon (*Memorabilia* 1.1.1) and Diogenes Laertius (2.40).

ἔχει . . . πως ὧδε "It goes something like this . . ." If the actual words of the indictment had been crucial to Socrates' case, he could have asked the herald to read from the official copy. He chooses not to make that request.

24b9 **διαφθείροντα** It is not clear that this was a common charge. The fourth-century orator Aeschines refers to legislation dating from the time of Solon (sixth century) and even earlier that was directed at ensuring the σωφροσύνη of boys (παῖδες), youths (μειράκια), and on up, but he is not at all specific. At any rate, there are no other recorded prosecutions on this charge. Burnet thought the fact that Isocrates (fourth century) pretends to defend himself against this charge in his περὶ τῆς ἀντιδόσεως ("On the Exchange") shows that it was a plausible accusation. That Isocrates' model was Socrates himself, and not common Athenian legal practice, cannot be discounted, however. Note, for example, the reference to his age (*Antid.* 9) and the open legal fiction that structures the work (*Antid.* 14), as well as numerous other echoes. It should also be noted that διαφθείρω often has sexual connotations. See Lysias (1.92.8). The charge, therefore, suggests the possibility of corruption that is physical as well as moral.

24c1 **νομίζει οὐ νομίζοντα** The participle agrees with Σωκράτη: "not honoring the gods the city honors."

δαιμόνια Literally, "divine things." The word openly alludes to Socrates' well-documented belief in a divine sign (δαιμόνιον) that guided his actions (see also 31c–d). Reference to it appears frequently in the dialogues, for example, in *Euthyphro* (3b5–6), where Euthyphro clearly associates the indictment with Socrates' divine sign. Certainly one of the most striking things about the *daimonion* is the fact that, according to Plato, it only intervened to stop him whenever he was about to do something wrong (in Xenophon, *Apology*, it can be positive). Socrates credits it with his decision not to enter politics, for example (31d3–4). The negative force of the divine sign plays an important role later in the *Apology*. After the jury votes to convict him, Socrates consoles his supporters by telling them that the *daimonion* did not intervene to stop him when he left home that morning, and therefore everything that has happened is for the best (40a–b). For further discussion, see essay 15.

ἔγκλημα τοιοῦτόν ἐστιν· τούτου δὲ τοῦ ἐγκλήματος ἓν ἕκαστον ἐξετάσωμεν.

Φησὶ γὰρ δὴ τοὺς νέους ἀδικεῖν με διαφθείροντα. ἐγὼ δέ γε, ὦ ἄνδρες Ἀθηναῖοι, ἀδικεῖν φημι Μέλητον, ὅτι σπουδῇ χαριεντίζεται, ῥᾳδίως εἰς ἀγῶνα καθιστὰς ἀνθρώπους, περὶ πραγμάτων προσποιούμενος σπουδάζειν καὶ κήδεσθαι ὧν οὐδὲν τούτῳ πώποτε ἐμέλησεν· ὡς δὲ τοῦτο οὕτως ἔχει, πειράσομαι καὶ ὑμῖν ἐπιδεῖξαι.

ἔγκλημα, -τος, τό *accusation*
ῥᾳδίως *lightly, easily*
ἀγῶνα < ἀγών, -ῶνος, ὁ *trial*
καθιστάς pres. act. part. < καθίστημι *bring*
σπουδάζειν < σπουδάζω *take seriously*
κήδεσθαι < κήδω (mid.) *have a care for*

24c2 **ἓν ἕκαστον** "Each part."

24c5 **σπουδῇ χαριεντίζεται** "He fools around in earnest." Socrates mocks Meletus in advance by suggesting that the prosecution's case is an elaborate (and inappropriate) joke. The notion of "care" embedded in σπουδῇ (and picked up a little later with σπουδάζειν [24c7] and κήδεσθαι, "care for" [24c8]) anticipates the relentless series of puns made by Socrates on the name of Meletus and its relationship to μελετᾶω, "care for" and related words: ἐμέλησεν (24c8, 26b2), μέλον (24d4), μεμέληκεν (24d9, 25c3), ἀμέλειαν (25c3). Yet Socrates' comment is also ironic, for the combination of serious and comic is often a characteristic of his own practice. See, for example, *Phaedrus* (234d7), *Gorgias* (481b7), and *Protagoras* (336d3), where Socrates' interlocutors cannot tell whether he's kidding or not. The same idea is implicit earlier in the speech, when Socrates begins to tell the story about the Delphic oracle (παίζειν 20d5).

24c7 **ὧν** Supply a word like τούτων, "these things" for an antecedent.

CHAPTER 12

(24c9–25c4)

Meletus is cross-examined about his claim that Socrates corrupts the youth. For additional discussion of the chapter and questions for study, see essay 12.

καί μοι δεῦρο, ὦ Μέλητε, εἰπέ· ἄλλο τι ἢ περὶ πλείστου ποιῇ ὅπως ὡς βέλτιστοι οἱ νεώτεροι ἔσονται; d

Ἔγωγε.

Ἴθι δή νυν εἰπὲ τούτοις, τίς αὐτοὺς βελτίους ποιεῖ; δῆλον γὰρ ὅτι οἶσθα, μέλον γέ σοι. τὸν μὲν γὰρ διαφθείροντα ἐξευρών, ὡς φῄς, ἐμέ, εἰσάγεις τουτοισὶ καὶ κατη-

---

δεῦρο *come now!*
ὡς βέλτιστοι *as good as possible*
ἐξευρών aor. act. part. < ἐξευρίσκω *find out, discover*
εἰσάγεις < εἰσάγω *bring in* (to court)

24c9 **καί μοι δεῦρο** Athenian law allowed either party to question the other through a process called ἐρώτησις (< ἐρωτάω, "ask") and required a response. By choosing to include this feature in his version of the speech of Socrates, Plato also recreates a specimen of the question-and-answer style that dominates the dialogues.

ἄλλο τι ἤ . . . Translate: "Isn't it the case that . . . ?" (lit., "Is anything else the case, or . . .?"

24d1 **περὶ πλείστου ποιῇ** "You consider of the greatest importance," that is, "you take care."

24d1 **ὅπως** "That" (cf. Smyth 1956, 2211).

24d3 **ἴθι** Sg. imper. < εἶμι, "go."

τούτοις Understand τοῖς δικασταῖς.

βελτίους (masc. acc. pl.) Contracted form of βελτίονας.

24d4 **μέλον** Impersonal accusative absolute. "Since it is a concern . . ."

γε lays additional stress upon the word and thus emphasizes the pun on Meletus's name. Socrates' irony here is revealing: those who claim to have a care for virtue are generally not possessed of any real, testable knowledge but rely on conventional opinion, personal prejudice, and rote repetition.

24d5 **ἐξευρών** The participle has causal force: "since you have discovered."

γορεῖς· τὸν δὲ δὴ βελτίους ποιοῦντα ἴθι εἰπὲ καὶ μήνυσον αὐτοῖς τίς ἐστιν. —Ὁρᾷς, ὦ Μέλητε, ὅτι σιγᾷς καὶ οὐκ ἔχεις εἰπεῖν; καίτοι οὐκ αἰσχρόν σοι δοκεῖ εἶναι καὶ ἱκανὸν τεκμήριον οὗ δὴ ἐγὼ λέγω, ὅτι σοι οὐδὲν μεμέληκεν; ἀλλ' εἰπέ, ὠγαθέ, τίς αὐτοὺς ἀμείνους ποιεῖ;

Οἱ νόμοι.

e 'Αλλ' οὐ τοῦτο ἐρωτῶ, ὦ βέλτιστε, ἀλλὰ τίς ἄνθρωπος, ὅστις πρῶτον καὶ αὐτὸ τοῦτο οἶδε, τοὺς νόμους;

Οὗτοι, ὦ Σώκρατες, οἱ δικασταί.

Πῶς λέγεις, ὦ Μέλητε; οἵδε τοὺς νέους παιδεύειν οἷοί τέ εἰσι καὶ βελτίους ποιοῦσιν;

Μάλιστα.

Πότερον ἅπαντες, ἢ οἱ μὲν αὐτῶν, οἱ δ' οὔ;

Ἅπαντες.

Εὖ γε νὴ τὴν Ἥραν λέγεις καὶ πολλὴν ἀφθονίαν τῶν ὠφελούντων. τί δὲ δή; οἵδε οἱ ἀκροαταὶ βελτίους ποιοῦσιν

μήνυσον aor. imper. < μηνύω *disclose, indicate*
σιγᾷς < σιγάω *be silent*
καίτοι *and yet*
αἰσχρόν < αἰσχρός, -ά, -όν *shameful*
μεμέληκεν pf. act. indic. < μέλει *it is a care*
παιδεύειν < παιδεύω *teach*

24d7 **σιγᾷς** Silence on the part of the one being subjected to a line of Socratic questioning is a common sign of resistance to the *aporia* that inevitably follows. Socrates, or the audience, is usually able to cajole the reluctant responder into continuing, however. Compare Thrasymachus at *Republic* 350d and Callicles in the *Gorgias* 501c.

24d9 **οὗ δὴ ἐγὼ λέγω** "Of exactly what I am saying."

24e7 **πότερον** Untranslated. As is common in replies, the language is abbreviated: "[Do you mean] everybody, or [is it the case that] some [educate] and some don't?"

24e9 **νὴ τὸν Ἥραν** "Yes, by Hera."

εὖ . . . λέγεις A colloquialism. Translate "Good answer!" (Weber 1986). Compare *Laches* 180b3. γε is emphatic. Note that λέγεις also modifies πολλὴν ἀφθονίαν.

24e10 **ὠφελούντων** "Benefactors." The participle is used substantively and is dependent on ἀφθονίαν.

τί δὲ δή "What, then?" This is a very common transitional question in Plato.

ἀκροαταί "Listeners." These should be imagined to include not just the jury, but the spectators as well. See on 17c10.

ἢ οὔ; 25

Καὶ οὗτοι.

Τί δέ, οἱ βουλευταί;

Καὶ οἱ βουλευταί.

Ἀλλ᾽ ἄρα, ὦ Μέλητε, μὴ οἱ ἐν τῇ ἐκκλησίᾳ, οἱ ἐκκλησιασταί, διαφθείρουσι τοὺς νεωτέρους; ἢ κἀκεῖνοι βελτίους ποιοῦσιν ἅπαντες;

Κἀκεῖνοι.

Πάντες ἄρα, ὡς ἔοικεν, Ἀθηναῖοι καλοὺς κἀγαθοὺς ποιοῦσι πλὴν ἐμοῦ, ἐγὼ δὲ μόνος διαφθείρω. οὕτω λέγεις;

Πάνυ σφόδρα ταῦτα λέγω.

Πολλήν γέ μου κατέγνωκας δυστυχίαν. καί μοι ἀπό-
κριναι· ἦ καὶ περὶ ἵππους οὕτω σοι δοκεῖ ἔχειν; οἱ μὲν
βελτίους ποιοῦντες αὐτοὺς πάντες ἄνθρωποι εἶναι, εἷς δέ b

ἔοικεν *seems* (impers.)
κατέγνωκας pf. act. indic. < καταγιγνώσκω *recognize*
δυστυχίαν < δυστυχία, -ας, ἡ *bad luck*
ἀποκρίναι aor. mid. imper. < ἀποκρίνομαι *answer*

25a3 **βουλευταί** The *boule* consisted of five hundred citizens, who prepared the agenda for the general assembly (*ecclesia*). Socrates will later tell a story about his own service on the *boule* (32b).

25a5 **ἄρα . . . μή** "Can it be that . . . ?" (Denniston 1954, 47).

ἐκκλησιασταί The *ecclesia* met on the Pnyx, a small, rocky hill southwest of the Acropolis, and in theory was composed of all citizens (i.e., all adult males with citizen parents). ἐκκλησιασταί, however, is an uncommon word, and Burnet (1924) may be correct that after the periphrastic οἱ ἐν τῇ ἐκκλησίᾳ, it appears as an afterthought ("You could call them *ecclesiastai*").

25a6 **κἀκεῖνοι** = καὶ ἐκεῖνοι.

25a9 **ἄρα** "Evidently . . ."

25a12 **γε** "Certainly."

ἀπόκριναι Meletus must pay now for his exaggerations and his shameless pandering to the vanity of the jury (e.g., ἅπαντες 24e8). If it is true that Socrates *alone* corrupts the youth and that everybody else improves them, then, as Socrates says, "That's a lot of benefactors!" But if caring for the young is like caring for horses (see 20a2–c3), it is hardly likely that one person alone hurts them and everybody else—whether or not they have ever been on a horse in their lives—improves them. It is typical of Socrates to argue that a job will be best performed by a trained expert. Such thinking also provides the basis for the division of labor in the ideal city described in the *Republic*.

25a13–b1 **μέν . . . δέ** Supply in both clauses δοκεῖ from 24a13.

τις ὁ διαφθείρων; ἢ τοὐναντίον τούτου πᾶν εἷς μέν τις ὁ βελτίους οἷός τ' ὢν ποιεῖν ἢ πάνυ ὀλίγοι, οἱ ἱππικοί, οἱ δὲ πολλοὶ ἐάνπερ συνῶσι καὶ χρῶνται ἵπποις, διαφθείρουσιν; οὐχ οὕτως ἔχει, ὦ Μέλητε, καὶ περὶ ἵππων καὶ τῶν ἄλλων ἁπάντων ζῴων; πάντως δήπου, ἐάντε σὺ καὶ Ἄνυτος οὐ φῆτε ἐάντε φῆτε· πολλὴ γὰρ ἄν τις εὐδαιμονία εἴη περὶ τοὺς νέους εἰ εἷς μὲν μόνος αὐτοὺς διαφθείρει, οἱ δ' ἄλλοι
c ὠφελοῦσιν. ἀλλὰ γάρ, ὦ Μέλητε, ἱκανῶς ἐπιδείκνυσαι ὅτι οὐδεπώποτε ἐφρόντισας τῶν νέων, καὶ σαφῶς ἀποφαίνεις τὴν σαυτοῦ ἀμέλειαν, ὅτι οὐδέν σοι μεμέληκεν περὶ ὧν ἐμὲ εἰσάγεις.

συνῶσι pres. subj. < συνειμί *be with, associate with*
ὠφελοῦσιν < ὠφελέω *aid, profit*
ἐφρόντισας < φροντίζω *think, reflect upon*
σαφῶς *clearly*
ἀποφαίνεις < ἀποφαίνω *display, make known*

25b2–3 **εἷς μέν . . . οἱ δέ** There is a slight anacolouthon in this sentence, as it shifts from participial in the μέν-clause (οἷός τ' ὤν) to indicative (διαφθείρουσιν) in the δέ-clause.

25b8 **μόνος** The word, together with εἷς, emphasizes the absurdity of Meletus's claim that *every* Athenian except Socrates benefits the young. Socrates' sarcasm is dependent on the validity of his analogy between training horses and training the young to be "as good as possible." A recurrent question in the Platonic dialogues is whether excellence (ἀρετή) is a kind of knowledge, in which case it should be teachable like any other subject. Here Socrates simply assumes the analogy to ridicule Meletus.

25c3 **τὴν σαυτοῦ ἀμέλειαν** "Your own lack of concern." Unfortunately, the English translation obscures an important pun on the name of *Mel*etus, whose name suggests a connection with μελετάω "be concerned" (so also in the case of μεμέληκεν at 25c3), despite the fact that he does not seem to have cared enough to think much about the principles on which he claims to act. Also, by bringing up the "care of the self," Socrates sets Meletus up as the antithesis of his own thoughtful behavior and the moderation he attempts to encourage among all Athenians (compare, for example, his assertions at 30b and 31b). Note how Socratic questioning leads the interlocutor to convict himself of ignorance and/or bad faith.

οὐδέν Adverbial, "not at all."

περὶ ὧν The full form of the construction, shortened to avoid repetition, would be περὶ τούτων περὶ ὧν.

25c

CHAPTER 13

(25c5–26a7)

Socrates examines the argument that he is a bad influence on the young and finds it incoherent: "Why on earth would I willingly corrupt those in my company, since I would be among the first harmed by their corruption?" For additional discussion of the chapter and questions for study, see essay 13.

Ἔτι δὲ ἡμῖν εἰπέ, ὦ πρὸς Διὸς Μέλητε, πότερόν ἐστιν οἰκεῖν ἄμεινον ἐν πολίταις χρηστοῖς ἢ πονηροῖς; ὦ τάν, ἀπόκριναι· οὐδὲν γάρ τοι χαλεπὸν ἐρωτῶ. οὐχ οἱ μὲν πονηροὶ κακόν τι ἐργάζονται τοὺς ἀεὶ ἐγγυτάτω αὐτῶν ὄντας, οἱ δ' ἀγαθοὶ ἀγαθόν τι;

Πάνυ γε.

πολίταις < πολίτης, -ου, ὁ *citizen*
χρηστοῖς < χρηστός, -ή, -όν *useful, good*
πονηροῖς < πονηρός, -ά, -όν *worthless, bad*
τοι *certainly*
ἐργάζονται < ἐργάζομαι *do something* (acc.) *to someone* (acc.)

25c5 **εἰπέ, ὦ πρὸς Διὸς Μέλητε** This is an example of interlaced word order. ὦ is an interjection, which normally accompanies the vocative and is untranslated. πρὸς Διὸς is an oath that calls upon Zeus to witness Meletus's testimony and should be construed with εἰπέ. Translate "in the eyes of Zeus" or "with god as your witness."

25c6 **ὦ τάν** Attic form of address, equivalent roughly to "O sir," but the etymology is uncertain.

25c9 **οἱ δ' ἀγαθοί ἀγαθόν τι** Supply ἐργάζονται τοὺς ἀεὶ ἐγγυτάτω αὐτῶν.

d Ἔστιν οὖν ὅστις βούλεται ὑπὸ τῶν συνόντων βλάπτεσθαι μᾶλλον ἢ ὠφελεῖσθαι; ἀποκρίνου, ὦ ἀγαθέ· καὶ γὰρ ὁ νόμος κελεύει ἀποκρίνεσθαι. ἔσθ' ὅστις βούλεται βλάπτεσθαι;

Οὐ δῆτα.

Φέρε δή, πότερον ἐμὲ εἰσάγεις δεῦρο ὡς διαφθείροντα τοὺς νέους καὶ πονηροτέρους ποιοῦντα ἑκόντα ἢ ἄκοντα;

Ἑκόντα ἔγωγε.

Τί δῆτα, ὦ Μέλητε; τοσοῦτον σὺ ἐμοῦ σοφώτερος εἶ τηλικούτου ὄντος τηλικόσδε ὤν, ὥστε σὺ μὲν ἔγνωκας ὅτι οἱ μὲν κακοὶ κακόν τι ἐργάζονται ἀεὶ τοὺς μάλιστα πλησίον

βλάπτεσθαι < βλάπτω *harm*
ἀποκρίνου pres. mid. imper. < ἀποκρίνομαι *answer*
κελεύει < κελεύω *order*
ἑκόντα < ἑκών, -οῦσα, -όν *willing*
ἄκοντα < ἄκων, -ουσα, -ον *unwilling*
τηλικούτου < τηλικοῦτος, -αύτη, -οῦτο *of such an age*

25d1 Socrates employs here a version of an argument that appears frequently in Plato: no one ever does wrong willingly, because wrongdoing produces a chaotic society. In a chaotic society, one cannot be secure. Therefore, it is not in the interest of anyone to do wrong intentionally. One could act in error, thinking incorrectly that something was good when in fact it is bad, but one would not do it again once the mistake had been noted.
ἔστιν . . . ὅστις "Is there anyone who . . . ?"

25d2 **ἀποκρίνου** Clearly we are to imagine a pause after Socrates' question during which Meletus attempts to avoid answering, another example of Plato's determination to create verisimilitude.

25d3 **κελεύει** A law purporting to establish this fact, and which may have been in effect at the end of the fifth century, is quoted by Demosthenes (*Against Stephanus* 2.10).

25d4 **δῆτα** The particle is emphatic, making Meletus's reply a strong denial. It is a common reply by speakers in Plato. In the context of Meletus's refusal to answer, however, the emphasis draws attention not to the certainty of his conviction, but to his evident irritation at having to answer to Socrates.

25d5 **φέρε δή** "Come then," a common phrase that marks the transition from one part of the argument to the next.
πότερον Often, as here, the word indicates that alternatives will follow. In such cases πότερον itself is better not translated. See on 24e7.
ὡς διαφθείροντα τοὺς νέους "On the grounds that I am corrupting the young men."

25d6 **ἑκόντα ἢ ἄκοντα** Both adjectives (here better translated as adverbs) agree with ἐμέ.

25d7 **ἑκόντα ἔγωγε** "Willingly, I tell you."

25d8–9 **τοσοῦτον σὺ ἐμοῦ σοφοτέρος . . . ὤν** "Are you so much wiser at your age than I am at mine . . ."

25d10 **τοὺς μάλιστα πλησίον ἑαυτῶν** "The people closest to them."

ἑαυτῶν, οἱ δὲ ἀγαθοὶ ἀγαθόν, ἐγὼ δὲ δὴ εἰς τοσοῦτον ἀμα- e
θίας ἥκω ὥστε καὶ τοῦτ᾽ ἀγνοῶ, ὅτι ἐάν τινα μοχθηρὸν
ποιήσω τῶν συνόντων, κινδυνεύσω κακόν τι λαβεῖν ὑπ᾽ αὐτοῦ,
ὥστε τοῦτο ⟨τὸ⟩ τοσοῦτον κακὸν ἑκὼν ποιῶ, ὡς φῂς σύ;
ταῦτα ἐγώ σοι οὐ πείθομαι, ὦ Μέλητε, οἶμαι δὲ οὐδὲ ἄλλον
ἀνθρώπων οὐδένα· ἀλλ᾽ ἢ οὐ διαφθείρω, ἢ εἰ διαφθείρω,
ἄκων, ὥστε σύ γε κατ᾽ ἀμφότερα ψεύδῃ. εἰ δὲ ἄκων δια- 26
φθείρω, τῶν τοιούτων ἁμαρτημάτων οὐ δεῦρο νόμος
εἰσάγειν ἐστίν, ἀλλὰ ἰδίᾳ λαβόντα διδάσκειν καὶ νου-
θετεῖν· δῆλον γὰρ ὅτι ἐὰν μάθω, παύσομαι ὅ γε ἄκων ποιῶ.
σὺ δὲ συγγενέσθαι μέν μοι καὶ διδάξαι ἔφυγες καὶ οὐκ
ἠθέλησας, δεῦρο δὲ εἰσάγεις, οἷ νόμος ἐστὶν εἰσάγειν τοὺς
κολάσεως δεομένους ἀλλ᾽ οὐ μαθήσεως.

μοχθηρόν < μοχθηρός, -ά, -όν *worthless*
ἰδίᾳ *privately*
νουθετεῖν < νουθετέω *admonish*
συγγενέσθαι aor. mid. infin. < συγγίνομαι *associate with*
οἷ *to which place, where*
κολάσεως < κόλασις, -εως, ἡ *punishment*
μαθήσεως < μάθησις, -εως, ἡ *instruction, learning*

25e1 **οἱ δὲ ἀγαθοί** Supply ἐργάζονται.
εἰς τοσοῦτον "To such a degree."
25e2 **τοῦτ᾽** The pronoun is explained by the ὅτι-clause that follows.
25e3 **συνόντων** The participle (masc. gen. pl. < σύνειμι) is partitive with τινά. μοχθηρόν is the predicate.
25e5 **οὐδὲ ἄλλον** Supply σοι πείθεσθαι (in indirect statement after οἶμαι).
26a1 **ἄκων** Supply διαφθείρω a second time here.
κατ᾽ ἀμφότερα "Either way."
26a3 **εἰσάγειν** Dependent (with the infinitives that follow) on οὐ . . . νόμος . . . ἐστίν: "it's not customary . . ."
λάβοντα The participle (masc. sg. acc.) agrees with the implied subject of the infinitives dependent on νόμος ἐστίν (repeated from the previous clause without the οὐ). Note the parallel between this sentence and 26a6–7.
26a4 **δηλόν** Supply ἐστι. The expression is impersonal.
παύσομαι Supply ποιῶν.
ὅ The antecedent (τοῦτο) has been omitted.
26a5 **σὺ δέ** The δέ is adversative: "but you . . ."
26a7 **κολάσεως . . . μαθήσεως** Both genitives are dependent on the participle δεομένους.

26a

CHAPTER 14

(26a8–27a7)

"Meletus, do you say I corrupt the youth by teaching them not to believe in the gods? You must have me confused with a pre-Socratic philosopher." For additional discussion of the chapter and questions for study, see essay 14.

Ἀλλὰ γάρ, ὦ ἄνδρες Ἀθηναῖοι, τοῦτο μὲν δῆλον ἤδη
b οὑγὼ ἔλεγον, ὅτι Μελήτῳ τούτων οὔτε μέγα οὔτε μικρὸν
πώποτε ἐμέλησεν. ὅμως δὲ δὴ λέγε ἡμῖν, πῶς με φῂς
διαφθείρειν, ὦ Μέλητε, τοὺς νεωτέρους; ἢ δῆλον δὴ ὅτι
κατὰ τὴν γραφὴν ἣν ἐγράψω θεοὺς διδάσκοντα μὴ νομίζειν
οὓς ἡ πόλις νομίζει, ἕτερα δὲ δαιμόνια καινά; οὐ ταῦτα
λέγεις ὅτι διδάσκων διαφθείρω;

Πάνυ μὲν οὖν σφόδρα ταῦτα λέγω.

Πρὸς αὐτῶν τοίνυν, ὦ Μέλητε, τούτων τῶν θεῶν ὧν νῦν ὁ λόγος ἐστίν, εἰπὲ ἔτι σαφέστερον καὶ ἐμοὶ καὶ τοῖς ἀν-

---

26a8 **μέν** Untranslated here. The strong adversative adverb ὅμως in the δέ-clause (strengthened by the δή) will supply all the contrast the sentence needs.

26b1 **οὑγώ** = ὁ ἐγώ.

οὔτε μέγα οὔτε σμικρόν The expresson is adverbial: "at all" (literally, "neither in a big way nor a small one"). Note again the relentless punning on *Mel*etus, whose name does not appear to fit him well.

26b2 **ἐμέλησεν** The subject is impersonal.

πῶς Note the use of the direct, and therefore more forceful, interrogative in a place where the indirect form ὅπως would be equally possible.

26b3 **ἢ δῆλον δή** Supply ἐστί: "or is it perfectly clear that . . . ?"

26b4 **νομίζειν** The indirect statement continues to be dependent on φῄς (above): "that I teach them not to recognize . . ."

26b7 **μὲν οὖν** In replies, μὲν οὖν indicates a strong emotional response, positive or negative. Here, obviously, Meletus is made to express his emphatic agreement.

26b8–9 **ὧν νῦν ὁ λόγος ἐστίν** "Who are now under discussion."

26b9 **ἔτι** Used ironically. Socrates pretends that what Meletus says is *clear* to begin with. In fact, the claims of Meletus will not be clarified by the ensuing

δράσιν τουτοισί. ἐγὼ γὰρ οὐ δύναμαι μαθεῖν πότερον λέγεις c
διδάσκειν με νομίζειν εἶναί τινας θεούς—καὶ αὐτὸς ἄρα νομίζω
εἶναι θεοὺς καὶ οὐκ εἰμὶ τὸ παράπαν ἄθεος οὐδὲ ταύτῃ ἀδικῶ
—οὐ μέντοι οὕσπερ γε ἡ πόλις ἀλλὰ ἑτέρους, καὶ τοῦτ᾽ ἔστιν
ὅ μοι ἐγκαλεῖς, ὅτι ἑτέρους, ἢ παντάπασί με φῂς οὔτε
αὐτὸν νομίζειν θεοὺς τούς τε ἄλλους ταῦτα διδάσκειν.

Ταῦτα λέγω, ὡς τὸ παράπαν οὐ νομίζεις θεούς.

Ὦ θαυμάσιε Μέλητε, ἵνα τί ταῦτα λέγεις; οὐδὲ ἥλιον d
οὐδὲ σελήνην ἄρα νομίζω θεοὺς εἶναι, ὥσπερ οἱ ἄλλοι ἄνθρωποι;

τὸ παράπαν *completely*
ἐγκαλεῖς < ἐγκαλέω *charge*
παντάπασι *completely*
θαυμάσιε voc. < θαυμάσιος, -α, -ον *wondrous, marvelous*

---

discussion at all, except to the extent that they are shown even more clearly to be incoherent.

26c2 The argument at this point turns on a difference between the original charge that declared Socrates did not honor the gods (νομίζειν τοὺς θεούς, 24c) and a new possibility introduced by Socrates (and snapped up by Meletus) that he does not believe the gods exist at all (νομίζειν τοὺς θεοὺς εἶναι). While the latter possibility is certainly more dramatic (and perhaps even true), it will turn out to be fatal to the argument of Meletus, which accuses Socrates of introducing new gods. After all, says Socrates, a man who introduces new gods can hardly be an utter atheist, can he?

26c4 **οὐ . . . οὕσπερ** The antecedent is θεούς: "not the same ones."
μέντοι . . . γε "To be sure." Socrates ironically pretends to accept the charge of neglecting the gods of Athens.

26c5 **ἑτέρους** Supply νομίζω.
με . . . αὐτόν The pronoun is emphatic: "I myself." Note that διδάσκειν takes two accusatives, of the thing taught (ταῦτα) and of the persons taught (τοὺς ἄλλους).

26d1 **ἵνα τί** "Why?"
οὐδὲ ἥλιον οὐδὲ σελήνην The divinity of the sun and moon, while probably assumed by most Athenians, did not play an important role in public cult. This question seems designed to introduce ideas attributed to Anaxagoras of Clazomene, Socrates' older contemporary and an associate of the Athenian politician Pericles (495–429 B.C.E.). He is said to have been prosecuted for impiety (ἀσέβεια).

Μὰ Δί', ὦ ἄνδρες δικασταί, ἐπεὶ τὸν μὲν ἥλιον λίθον φησὶν εἶναι, τὴν δὲ σελήνην γῆν.

Ἀναξαγόρου οἴει κατηγορεῖν, ὦ φίλε Μέλητε; καὶ οὕτω καταφρονεῖς τῶνδε καὶ οἴει αὐτοὺς ἀπείρους γραμμάτων εἶναι ὥστε οὐκ εἰδέναι ὅτι τὰ Ἀναξαγόρου βιβλία τοῦ Κλαζομενίου γέμει τούτων τῶν λόγων; καὶ δὴ καὶ οἱ νέοι ταῦτα παρ' ἐμοῦ μανθάνουσιν, ἃ ἔξεστιν ἐνίοτε εἰ πάνυ πολλοῦ δραχμῆς

καταφρονεῖς < καταφρονέω *hold in contempt*
ἀπείρους < ἄπειρος, -α, -ον *inexperienced*
γέμει < γέμω *be full of*
ἐνίοτε *from time to time*

26d4 **ὦ ἄνδρες δικασταί** Meletus uses the standard form of address for Athenian jurors, in contrast to Socrates. See on 17a1. In a spluttering outburst, he accuses Socrates of accepting the speculations of the pre-Socratic philosophers. Much of their work attempts to give a rational account of the physical processes (both celestial and terrestrial) that make up human life. See Kirk, Raven, and Schofield (1993).

26d7 **τῶνδε** The pronoun is dependent on καταφρονεῖς and refers to the jurors.

ἀπείρους γραμμάτων That is, "uncultured." Burnet notes that this remark implies the existence of a reading public in Athens. This is certainly true to a degree. In Aristophanes' *Frogs* (52), produced in 405, the god Dionysus talks about reading a tragedy of Euripides. See also Euripides, *Erechtheus* fr. 369 (422 B.C.E.?). Socrates' remarks should not be taken at face value, however. The evidence for private libraries and a substantial book trade is scant before the end of the fifth century. See Harris (1989) and Thomas (1989, 1992). Whatever reading public there was in Athens at the time of Socrates' trial, it certainly cannot be presumed to have included the entire jury.

26d8 **ὥστε οὐκ** ὥστε + infinitive normally takes μή, but οὐκ appears here because the clause is part of a larger indirect statement dependent on οἴει.

βιβλία Like other pre-Socratic philosophers, Anaxagoras supposedly wrote a book περὶ φύσεως. This would have been written on rolls of papyrus (imported from Egypt). The earliest surviving papyri date from the second half of the fourth century.

26d10 **ἅ** That is, the doctrines of Anaxagoras.

δραχμῆς The price Socrates mentions would not be high for the young men to whom Socrates alludes, whose families measured their wealth by the talent of silver (= 6,000 drachmas). Day laborers, for example, earned much less (1 drachma per day in the late fifth century, according to inscriptions). Presumably, the price of books would be more of an obstacle for them. It may have been for the jurors as well. They were paid 3 obols (1/2 drachma) per day. The reliance of jurors upon such subsidies had been mocked publicly in works such as the *Wasps* of Aristophanes, although the jury stipend was not necessarily their only source of income.

ἐκ τῆς ὀρχήστρας πριαμένοις Σωκράτους καταγελᾶν, ἐὰν e
προσποιῆται ἑαυτοῦ εἶναι, ἄλλως τε καὶ οὕτως ἄτοπα ὄντα; ἀλλ᾽, ὦ πρὸς Διός, οὑτωσί σοι δοκῶ; οὐδένα νομίζω θεὸν εἶναι;

Οὐ μέντοι μὰ Δία οὐδ᾽ ὁπωστιοῦν.

πριαμένοις < πρίαμαι *purchase*
καταγελᾶν < καταγελάω *laugh at*

26e1 **ἐκ τῆς ὀρχήστρας** "From the orchestra." This is a much contested passage on which most commentators and translators simply pronounce without acknowledging the alternatives. These can be divided into three classes. First, ὀρχήστρα refers to a dance floor in the agora where books were sold (Dyer and Seymour 1908, Adam 1914, Grube 1988, Rose 1989, Helm 1997). Second, ὀρχήστρα refers to the dance floor at the front of the stage at the theater of Dionysus, where the chorus sang. Hence the reference is to plays by Euripides and others in which the doctrines of Anaxagoras were sung (Riddell 1973, Rose 1989). Third, ὀρχήστρα refers to the dance floor at the front of the stage of the theater of Dionysus where the chorus sang, which apparently during the majority of the year, when there were no performances, served as a book market (Croiset 1920–, Tredennick 1967, Nails 2002).

There are numerous objections to these interpretations, however. Briefly, with regard to the first, there is no evidence for a dancing floor in the agora beyond the dubious interpretation of this passage, nor any ancient source that refers to a part of the agora known as the ὀρχήστρα. As for the second, since there was an orchestra in the theater, commentators point to passages in tragedy that seem to echo Anaxagoras. None are simple transcriptions of the philosopher's doctrines. Further, there is no record of theater tickets costing more than two obols, a third of the sum mentioned by Socrates. The main disadvantage of the third interpretation is that we must assume the existence of a book market—for which there is no corroborating evidence beyond the testimony of the present passage.

We are inclined to favor the third interpretation, since it requires the fewest assumptions. At the same time, it is worth noting that the word ὀρχήστρα is itself quite rare in our fifth-century sources (see Bosher 2007), and so all interpretations are bound to be somewhat speculative.

καταγελᾶν Dependent on ἔξεστιν above. The clauses, rearranged, go together as follows: "Do they learn these things from me, which if Socrates were to claim them as his own it is possible for the young men (who buy them from time to time in the orchestra—and for a drachma at most) to laugh at him?"

26e2 **ἄλλως τε καὶ οὕτως ἄτοπα ὄντα** "Especially since they [the ideas] are so strange." In the *Phaedo* (98c2), Socrates again uses ἄτοπα to describe the ideas of Anaxagoras. Yet the same term is used of Socrates at *Symposium* 215a, *Theaetetus* 149a, and *Gorgias* 494d.

Ἄπιστός γ' εἶ, ὦ Μέλητε, καὶ ταῦτα μέντοι, ὡς ἐμοὶ
δοκεῖς, σαυτῷ. ἐμοὶ γὰρ δοκεῖ οὑτοσί, ὦ ἄνδρες Ἀθηναῖοι,
πάνυ εἶναι ὑβριστὴς καὶ ἀκόλαστος, καὶ ἀτεχνῶς τὴν γραφὴν ταύτην ὕβρει τινὶ καὶ ἀκολασίᾳ καὶ νεότητι γράψασθαι.
27 ἔοικεν γὰρ ὥσπερ αἴνιγμα συντιθέντι διαπειρωμένῳ "Ἆρα
γνώσεται Σωκράτης ὁ σοφὸς δὴ ἐμοῦ χαριεντιζομένου καὶ
ἐναντί' ἐμαυτῷ λέγοντος, ἢ ἐξαπατήσω αὐτὸν καὶ τοὺς ἄλλους τοὺς ἀκούοντας;" οὗτος γὰρ ἐμοὶ φαίνεται τὰ ἐναντία
λέγειν αὐτὸς ἑαυτῷ ἐν τῇ γραφῇ ὥσπερ ἂν εἰ εἴποι· "Ἀδικεῖ
Σωκράτης θεοὺς οὐ νομίζων, ἀλλὰ θεοὺς νομίζων." καίτοι
τοῦτό ἐστι παίζοντος.

ἀκόλαστος, -η, -ον *undisciplined*
νεότητι < νεότης, -ητος, ἡ *youthful recklessness*
χαριεντιζομένου < χαριεντίζομαι *make a joke*
ἐξαπατήσω < ἐξαπατάω *deceive*

26e6 **ἄπιστός γ' εἶ** "I don't believe you." It is hard to improve upon Riddell's (1973) paraphrase of this sentence, "Very well; nobody else will believe that and I am pretty sure you do not yourself."

26e9 **ὕβρει . . . νεότητι** This is not the metaphysical ὕβρις of tragedy that brings about divine retribution, but a crime clearly recognized in Attic law, in cases as different as assault and adultery. Basically, ὕβρις is committed when someone blatently disregards the rights of another citizen. Such acts are often perceived to be mitigated by their association with youthful pranks (see Demosthenes 54.13–14), an association that Socrates appears to make as well (νεότητι). Note also his repeated insinuations that Meletus is not serious (24c5, 27a3, 27a7). There is high irony here, as Socrates, who is being prosecuted for being a bad citizen, accuses Meletus of a crime that strikes at the heart of citizenship.

ἀκολασίᾳ One of the concepts that the Socrates of Plato regularly opposes to σωφροσύνη ("moderation").

27a1 **ἔοικεν . . . διαπειρωμένῳ** "He seems like someone who composed a riddle as a test," literally, "while testing" (διαπειρωμένῳ). A fine example of Socratic irony: a mistake on the part of the interlocutor is treated facetiously as a test of Socrates himself.

27a2 **σοφὸς δή** As Denniston (1954) notes, δή is often used in the manner of quotation marks: "the 'wise' Socrates." Socrates imagines a Meletus resentful of Socrates' reputation for wisdom and constructing his "riddle" to expose him. Of course, as has already been made clear, Socrates has a very low regard for Meletus's abilities, so his scenario of a Meletus envious of Socrates' "undeserved" reputation for wisdom is itself ironic.

27a3 **ἐναντί' ἐμαυτῷ λέγοντος** ἐναντί(α) is neut. acc. pl. The participle is genitive following γιγνώσκω. The Socratic dialogues of Plato are full of characters who, in the course of their conversations with Socrates, are forced to realize that different aspects of their beliefs are inconsistent and often in conflict.

27a7 **παίζοντος** Gen. of characteristic: "This, I tell you, is [the work of] a man who is joking."

27a

CHAPTER 15

(27a8–28a1)

Socrates demonstrates that Meletus contradicts himself in the indictment. For additional discussion of the chapter and questions for study, see essay 15.

Συνεπισκέψασθε δή, ὦ ἄνδρες, ᾗ μοι φαίνεται ταῦτα
λέγειν· σὺ δὲ ἡμῖν ἀπόκριναι, ὦ Μέλητε. ὑμεῖς δέ, ὅπερ
κατ' ἀρχὰς ὑμᾶς παρῃτησάμην, μέμνησθέ μοι μὴ θορυβεῖν b
ἐὰν ἐν τῷ εἰωθότι τρόπῳ τοὺς λόγους ποιῶμαι.

Ἔστιν ὅστις ἀνθρώπων, ὦ Μέλητε, ἀνθρώπεια μὲν νομίζει πράγματ' εἶναι, ἀνθρώπους δὲ οὐ νομίζει; ἀποκρινέσθω, ὦ ἄνδρες, καὶ μὴ ἄλλα καὶ ἄλλα θορυβείτω· ἔσθ' ὅστις ἵππους μὲν οὐ νομίζει, ἱππικὰ δὲ πράγματα; ἢ αὐλητὰς μὲν οὐ

συνεπισκέψασθε < συνεπισκοπέω *examine together*
παρῃτησάμην < παραιτέομαι *ask earnestly, beg*
μέμνησθε pf. act. indic. < μιμνήσκω *remember*
εἰωθότι pf. part. < ἔθω *be accustomed*
ἀποκρινέσθω 3rd sg. imper. < ἀποκρίνομαι *answer*
ἄλλα καὶ ἄλλα *one thing after another*
θορυβείτω 3rd sg. imper. < θορυβέω *make a racket, interrupt*
αὐλητάς < αὐλητής, -οῦ, ὁ *flute player*

27a8 **ᾗ** The relative pronoun is used adverbially: "how."

27b1 **κατ' ἀρχάς . . . θορυβεῖν** He alludes to the request he made at 17c–d. Again, Plato includes details to heighten the verisimilitude of the speech.

27b3 Socrates now proceeds to explain the contradiction in Meletus's "riddle." It contains two parts: first, that a belief in divine things (δαιμόνια) implies a belief in divinities (δαίμονες); second, that divinities are gods (θεοί). This problem was not important for the original charge. Since then, however, Socrates has baited Meletus into accusing him of being a complete atheist (26c) and can now ignore the charge of religious nonconformism to concentrate on refuting Meletus's latest claim.

νομίζει εἶναι, αὐλητικὰ δὲ πράγματα; οὐκ ἔστιν, ὦ ἄριστε
ἀνδρῶν· εἰ μὴ σὺ βούλει ἀποκρίνεσθαι, ἐγὼ σοὶ λέγω καὶ
τοῖς ἄλλοις τουτοισί. ἀλλὰ τὸ ἐπὶ τούτῳ γε ἀπόκριναι·
c ἔσθ' ὅστις δαιμόνια μὲν νομίζει πράγματ' εἶναι, δαίμονας δὲ
οὐ νομίζει;

Οὐκ ἔστιν.

Ὡς ὤνησας ὅτι μόγις ἀπεκρίνω ὑπὸ τουτωνὶ ἀναγκαζόμενος. οὐκοῦν δαιμόνια μὲν φῄς με καὶ νομίζειν καὶ διδάσκειν, εἴτ' οὖν καινὰ εἴτε παλαιά, ἀλλ' οὖν δαιμόνιά γε νομίζω κατὰ τὸν σὸν λόγον, καὶ ταῦτα καὶ διωμόσω ἐν τῇ ἀντιγραφῇ. εἰ δὲ δαιμόνια νομίζω, καὶ δαίμονας δήπου πολλὴ ἀνάγκη νομίζειν μέ ἐστιν· οὐχ οὕτως ἔχει; ἔχει δή·

αὐλητικά < αὐλητικός, -ή, όν *pertaining to flutes*
ὤνησας aor. indic. act. < ὀνίνημι *profit*
ἀπεκρίνω 2nd sing. aor. indic. < ἀποκρίνομαι *answer*
διωμόσω aor. indic. mid. < διόμνυμι *swear*
ἀντιγραφῇ < ἀντιγραφή, -ῆς, ἡ *response to a charge, plea*

27b7 **οὐκ ἔστιν** Socrates answers his own question. We must assume a pause after πράγματα, during which Socrates waits in vain for Meletus's reply.

27b8 **λέγω** Hortatory subjunctive: "Let me say."

27b9 **τὸ ἐπὶ τούτῳ** "The next thing." τούτῳ (emphasized by γε) refers to the question Socrates has just answered.

27c1 **δαιμόνια** The introduction of "divine things" into the discussion is important for Socrates' argument. He has not yet mentioned the "divine sign" that regularly advised him to refrain from political life, but Socrates discusses it later (31d–e) and accuses Meletus of caricaturing it. Here, however, by linking δαιμόνια and θεοί, Socrates will lay the groundwork for his claim that there is nothing inconsistent (or illegal) about believing in both. *Euthyphro*, a dialogue that takes place before the trial, begins with a discussion of the charges brought by Meletus. There Socrates' interlocutor, Euthyphro, assumes that the reference to "introducing new divinities" in the indictment (*Apol.* 24c) is code for the δαιμόνιον of Socrates (2b).

δαίμονας Gods are referred to as δαίμονες, particularly if the god's identity is unknown. In the *Iliad*, for example, the Greek warrior Teucer unexpectedly breaks the string of his bow and blames a δαίμων. The term is used more broadly, however. Hesiod's Golden Age men are called δαίμονες as well (*Works and Days* 122).

27c4 **ὡς ὤνησας** [Understand ἐμέ]: "how you benefited me!"

27c6 **ἀλλ' οὖν . . . γε** "Nevertheless, they're still . . . δαίμονας." As often, the γε (translated here as "still") follows the word it emphasizes.

27c9 **ἔχει δή** "It certainly does!" Socrates answers his own question. δή strengthens an affirmative response.

τίθημι γάρ σε ὁμολογοῦντα, ἐπειδὴ οὐκ ἀποκρίνῃ. τοὺς δὲ
δαίμονας οὐχὶ ἤτοι θεούς γε ἡγούμεθα ἢ θεῶν παῖδας; φῂς d
ἢ οὔ;

Πάνυ γε.

Οὐκοῦν εἴπερ δαίμονας ἡγοῦμαι, ὡς σὺ φῄς, εἰ μὲν θεοί τινές εἰσιν οἱ δαίμονες, τοῦτ' ἂν εἴη ὃ ἐγώ φημί σε αἰνίττεσθαι καὶ χαριεντίζεσθαι, θεοὺς οὐχ ἡγούμενον φάναι με θεοὺς αὖ ἡγεῖσθαι πάλιν, ἐπειδήπερ γε δαίμονας ἡγοῦμαι· εἰ δ' αὖ οἱ δαίμονες θεῶν παῖδές εἰσιν νόθοι τινὲς ἢ ἐκ νυμφῶν ἢ ἔκ τινων ἄλλων ὧν δὴ καὶ λέγονται, τίς ἂν ἀνθρώπων θεῶν μὲν παῖδας ἡγοῖτο εἶναι, θεοὺς δὲ μή; ὁμοίως γὰρ
ἂν ἄτοπον εἴη ὥσπερ ἂν εἴ τις ἵππων μὲν παῖδας ἡγοῖτο e

ἤτοι *surely*
αἰνίττεσθαι < αἰνίττομαι *speak in riddles*
ἄτοπον < ἄτοπος, -ον *strange*

27c10 **τίθημι γάρ σε ὁμολογοῦντα** "I'll take it that you agree," lit.: "I put you down as agreeing."

27d1 **φῂς ἢ οὔ** Supply φπς again with οὔ.

27d4 **θεοί τινές** "Gods of some kind."

27d5 **ὅ** Accusative of respect.

27d6 **φάναι** The infinitive is equivalent to an articular infinitive and in apposition to τοῦτ': this is what I mean by riddling, "to say that . . ."

27d6–7 **θεούς . . . θεούς . . .** The syntax is deliberately complicated, mirroring what Socrates perceives as the latent incoherence of Meletus's charge. The first θεούς is the object of the participle ἡγούμενον, which modifies με, the subject of ἡγεῖσθαι. The second θεούς is the object of ἡγεῖσθαι. In each case, we must assume εἶναι.

οὐχ ἡγούμενον . . . ἡγεῖσθαι Note how the aspect of the (concessive) participle and the infinitive reinforce each other in describing two beliefs that are supposed to coexist at the same time: "that although I don't believe, on the other hand I do."

27d7 **ἐπειδήπερ γε** "Inasmuch as." Both –περ and γε qualify Socrates' statement and show that he is accepting Meletus's claims about him (for the sake of the argument) rather than expressing his own opinion.

27d8 **θεῶν παῖδες . . . νόθοι τινές** "certain illegitimate children of the gods."

27d9 **ὧν** = ἐξ ὧν For λέγονται, supply εἶναι.

27d10 **θεοὺς δὲ μή** "But no gods." The extreme brevity of the construction heightens the contrast.

27e1 **ὥσπερ ἄν** Supply εἴη. The phrase is coordinated with the ὁμοίως–clause above: "It would be equally odd, just as it would be if . . ."

ἢ καὶ ὄνων, τοὺς ἡμιόνους, ἵππους δὲ καὶ ὄνους μὴ ἡγοῖτο εἶναι. ἀλλ', ὦ Μέλητε, οὐκ ἔστιν ὅπως σὺ ταῦτα οὐχὶ ἀποπειρώμενος ἡμῶν ἐγράψω τὴν γραφὴν ταύτην ἢ ἀπορῶν ὅτι ἐγκαλοῖς ἐμοὶ ἀληθὲς ἀδίκημα· ὅπως δὲ σύ τινα πείθοις ἂν καὶ σμικρὸν νοῦν ἔχοντα ἀνθρώπων, ὡς οὐ τοῦ αὐτοῦ ἔστιν καὶ δαιμόνια καὶ θεῖα ἡγεῖσθαι, καὶ αὖ τοῦ αὐτοῦ μήτε
28 δαίμονας μήτε θεοὺς μήτε ἥρωας, οὐδεμία μηχανή ἐστιν.

ὄνων < ὄνος, -ου, ὁ *donkey*
ἡμιόνους < ἡμίονος, -ου, ὁ *mule*
ἀποπειρώμενος < ἀποπειράομαι *test*
ἀδίκημα < ἀδίκημα -τος, τό *wrong, injury*

27e2 **ἡμιόνους** The noun is in apposition to παῖδες. Just as the δαίμονες are the offspring of gods and mortal women, so mules are the offspring of horses bred with donkeys. ἡμιόνους also puns on ἡμιθέους, "demigod."

27e3 **οὐκ ἔστιν ὅπως . . . ουχί** "There is no way that . . . not," a true double negative, since the negations belong to different clauses.

27e4 **οὐχὶ ἀποπειρώμενος ἐγράψω** "That you didn't bring this indictment as a test (lit. "testing"). ἡμῶν is the object of ἀποπειρώμενος.

ἢ ἀπορῶν ὅτι "Unless, at a loss as to what . . ."

27e5 **ἐγκαλοῖς** Optative in place of subjunctive in an indirect (deliberative) question after a verb in the past tense. ἀπορῶν, as a present participle, expresses time contemporaneous with the aorist ἐγράψω and thus is treated as though it were a past tense.

ὅπως is introduced by οὐδεμία μηχανή ἐστιν (28a2), which is postponed for maximum effect.

27e7 **ὡς οὐ τοῦ αὐτοῦ** Gen. of characteristic: "that it is not [characteristic] of the same person to . . ."

28a

CHAPTER 16

(28a2–d10)

Socrates moves from a refutation of Meletus's indictment to a general defense of the philosophic life. For additional discussion of the chapter and questions for study, see essay 16.

Ἀλλὰ γάρ, ὦ ἄνδρες Ἀθηναῖοι, ὡς μὲν ἐγὼ οὐκ ἀδικῶ
κατὰ τὴν Μελήτου γραφήν, οὐ πολλῆς μοι δοκεῖ εἶναι ἀπολογίας, ἀλλὰ ἱκανὰ καὶ ταῦτα· ὃ δὲ καὶ ἐν τοῖς ἔμπροσθεν
ἔλεγον, ὅτι πολλή μοι ἀπέχθεια γέγονεν καὶ πρὸς πολλούς,
εὖ ἴστε ὅτι ἀληθές ἐστιν. καὶ τοῦτ' ἔστιν ὃ ἐμὲ αἱρήσει, ἐάνπερ αἱρῇ, οὐ Μέλητος οὐδὲ Ἄνυτος ἀλλ' ἡ τῶν πολλῶν διαβολή τε καὶ φθόνος. ἃ δὴ πολλοὺς καὶ ἄλλους καὶ ἀγαθοὺς
ἄνδρας ᾕρηκεν, οἶμαι δὲ καὶ αἱρήσει· οὐδὲν δὲ δεινὸν μὴ ἐν b
ἐμοὶ στῇ.

ᾕρηκεν pf. act. indic. < αἱρέω *seize*
στῇ aor. act. subj. (intrans.) < ἵστημι *stop, stand*

28a3 **πολλῆς . . . εἶναι . . . ἀπολογίας** Lit. "be of much defense." On the one hand, the weak accusations of Meletus do not *need* much defense in order for Socrates to dispatch them. On the other, Socrates' refutation of Meletus does not constitute much of a defense. Both senses are operative. Thus, Socrates justifies the relative shortness of his response to the actual indictment. At the same time, he prepares the way for a return to the topic of popular prejudice against him.

28a4 **ἱκανὰ καὶ ταῦτα** Take with μοι δοκεῖ εἶναι.
ἐν τοῖς ἔμπροσθεν Supply λόγοις.

28a8 **ἅ** That is, διαβολή and φθόνος. The difference in the genders of the two nouns causes the relative pronoun to shift to the neuter.

28b1 **δεινόν** The adjective is related to the noun δέος, "fear," and so can introduce a clause of fearing.
μὴ ἐν ἐμοὶ στῇ "that it will stop with me."

Ἴσως ἂν οὖν εἴποι τις· "εἶτ' οὐκ αἰσχύνῃ, ὦ Σώκρατες,
τοιοῦτον ἐπιτήδευμα ἐπιτηδεύσας ἐξ οὗ κινδυνεύεις νυνὶ ἀποθανεῖν;" ἐγὼ δὲ τούτῳ ἂν δίκαιον λόγον ἀντείποιμι, ὅτι "Οὐ
καλῶς λέγεις, ὦ ἄνθρωπε, εἰ οἴει δεῖν κίνδυνον ὑπολογίζεσθαι
τοῦ ζῆν ἢ τεθνάναι ἄνδρα ὅτου τι καὶ σμικρὸν ὄφελός ἐστιν,
ἀλλ' οὐκ ἐκεῖνο μόνον σκοπεῖν ὅταν πράττῃ, πότερον δίκαια ἢ
ἄδικα πράττει, καὶ ἀνδρὸς ἀγαθοῦ ἔργα ἢ κακοῦ. φαῦλοι
c γὰρ ἂν τῷ γε σῷ λόγῳ εἶεν τῶν ἡμιθέων ὅσοι ἐν Τροίᾳ
τετελευτήκασιν οἵ τε ἄλλοι καὶ ὁ τῆς Θέτιδος ὑός, ὃς
τοσοῦτον τοῦ κινδύνου κατεφρόνησεν παρὰ τὸ αἰσχρόν τι
ὑπομεῖναι ὥστε, ἐπειδὴ εἶπεν ἡ μήτηρ αὐτῷ προθυμουμένῳ

ἐπιτηδεύσας < ἐπιτηδεύω *pursue, practice*
ἀντείποιμι aor. act. opt. < ἀντιλέγω *reply*
κίνδυνον < κίνδυνος, -ου, ὁ *danger*
ὑπολογίζεσθαι < ὑπολογίζομαι *take into account*
ζῆν < ζάω *live*
ὅτου = οὗτινος < ὅστις *whoever*
ὄφελος, -ους, τό *use, good*
φαῦλοι < φαῦλος, -η, -ον *worthless, insignificant*
ἡμιθέων < ἡμίθεος, -ου, ὁ *demigod, hero*
τετελευτήκασιν pf. act. indic. < τελευτάω *die*
κατεφρόνησεν < καταφρονέω *despise*
προθυμουμένῳ < προθυμέομαι *be eager, zealous*

28b3 **εἶτ'** = εἶτα The word appears frequently in Plato and comedy, often indicating real or feigned indignation.

28b4 **τοιοῦτον . . . ἐξ οὗ** "Such a practice, from which."

ἀποθανεῖν Here, as often, ἀποθνῄσκω is used as the passive of ἀποκτείνω.

28b5 **τούτῳ** "To this man."

28b6 **οὐ καλῶς λέγεις** "You're wrong."

28b7 **τοῦ ζῆν ἢ τεθνάναι** Both articular infinitives are dependent on κίνδυνον.

ὅτου τι καὶ σμικρὸν ὀφελός ἐστιν "Of whom there is even a small value," that is, "who is worth anything at all."

28b8 **σκοπεῖν** Dependent on οἴει (28b6).

28b9 **φαῦλοι** Predicate adjective; the subject is ὅσοι.

28c2 **οἵ τε ἄλλοι** While English prefers to say "Achilles and the others," Greek usually puts the emphatic term last.

Θέτιδος Thetis is a minor sea goddess who married the mortal Peleus and became the mother of Achilles. She appears several times in the *Iliad* to advise and comfort her son.

28c3–4 **παρὰ τὸ . . . ὑπομεῖναι** "As opposed to enduring anything shameful."

28c4–5 **προθυμουμένῳ Ἕκτορα ἀποκτεῖναι** In the *Iliad*, Achilles returns to battle in order to avenge the death of his friend Patroclus, who has been killed by Hector.

῞Εκτορα ἀποκτεῖναι, θεὸς οὖσα, οὑτωσί πως, ὡς ἐγὼ οἶμαι· '῏Ω παῖ, εἰ τιμωρήσεις Πατρόκλῳ τῷ ἑταίρῳ τὸν φόνον καὶ ῞Εκτορα ἀποκτενεῖς, αὐτὸς ἀποθανῇ—αὐτίκα γάρ τοι,' φησί, 'μεθ' ῞Εκτορα πότμος ἑτοῖμος'—ὁ δὲ τοῦτο ἀκούσας τοῦ μὲν θανάτου καὶ τοῦ κινδύνου ὠλιγώρησε, πολὺ δὲ μᾶλλον δείσας τὸ ζῆν κακὸς ὢν καὶ τοῖς φίλοις μὴ τιμωρεῖν, d
'Αὐτίκα,' φησί, 'τεθναίην, δίκην ἐπιθεὶς τῷ ἀδικοῦντι, ἵνα μὴ ἐνθάδε μένω καταγέλαστος παρὰ νηυσὶ κορωνίσιν ἄχθος ἀρούρης.' μὴ αὐτὸν οἴει φροντίσαι θανάτου καὶ κινδύνου;"

Οὕτω γὰρ ἔχει, ὦ ἄνδρες 'Αθηναῖοι, τῇ ἀληθείᾳ· οὗ ἄν τις ἑαυτὸν τάξῃ ἡγησάμενος βέλτιστον εἶναι ἢ ὑπ' ἄρχοντος ταχθῇ, ἐνταῦθα δεῖ, ὡς ἐμοὶ δοκεῖ, μένοντα κινδυνεύειν, μηδὲν ὑπολογιζόμενον μήτε θάνατον μήτε ἄλλο μηδὲν πρὸ τοῦ αἰσχροῦ.

ἀποκτεῖναι aor. act. infin. < ἀποκτείνω *kill*
τιμωρήσεις < τιμωρέω *avenge*
φόνον < φόνος, -ου, ὁ *murder*
αὐτίκα *right away, at once*
πότμος, -ου, ὁ *fate*
ὠλιγώρησε < ὀλιγωρέω *think little of*
τεθναίην pf. act. opt. < θνήσκω *die*
καταγέλαστος, -ον *laughed at, ridiculous*
κορωνίσιν < κορωνίς, -ίδος, ἡ *curved*
φροντίσαι < φροντίζω *think upon, reflect*
τάξῃ aor. act. subj. < τάττω *station*
ἄρχοντος < ἄρχων -ντος, ὁ *commander*
τάχθῃ aor. pass. subj. < τάττω

28c5 **οὑτωσί πως** "Something like this." This phrase, along with the parenthetical ὡς ἐγὼ οἶμαι, excuses any mistakes in advance. Socrates quotes from Thetis's speech to Achilles in book 18 of the *Iliad*: αὐτίκα γάρ τοι ἔπειτα μεθ' ῞Εκτορα πότμος ἑτοῖμος, "Immediately after Hector your fate is prepared" (96).

28c8 **ὅ δέ** Pronominal use of the article: "And he . . ."

28d2 **δίκην ἐπιθεὶς τῷ ἀδικοῦντι** That is, to Hector. This formula for vengeance nicely encapsulates the traditional Greek understanding of retributive justice.

28d3 **παρὰ νηυσὶ κορωνίσιν** The phrase is formulaic in Homer. Note the non-Attic ending for the dative plural.

28d4 **ἄχθος ἀρούρης** "A weight upon the earth," a memorable Homeric phrase. **μή** Introduces a question expecting a "No" answer.

28d6 **οὗ ἄν** Take with ἐνταῦθα (d7): "Wherever . . . in that place . . ."

28d8 **ταχθῇ** The metaphor is from hoplite warfare, in which, for the survival of all, it is crucial that each man occupy the position to which he is assigned.

28d10 **τοῦ αἰσχροῦ** "Shame." The neuter singular of the adjective is often used in place of an abstract noun.

CHAPTER 17

(28d10–30c1)

Socrates explains how he follows the maxim outlined in the previous chapter, not abandoning the philosophical post to which Apollo had assigned him. For additional discussion of the chapter and questions for study, see essay 17.

ἐγὼ οὖν δεινὰ ἂν εἴην εἰργασμένος, ὦ ἄνδρες
e Ἀθηναῖοι, εἰ ὅτε μέν με οἱ ἄρχοντες ἔταττον, οὓς ὑμεῖς εἵλεσθε
ἄρχειν μου, καὶ ἐν Ποτειδαίᾳ καὶ ἐν Ἀμφιπόλει καὶ ἐπὶ
Δηλίῳ, τότε μὲν οὗ ἐκεῖνοι ἔταττον ἔμενον ὥσπερ καὶ ἄλλος

εἵλεσθε aor. mid. indic. < αἱρέω *choose*

28d10–29a1 This elaborate sentence, in the form of an inverted condition (future-less-vivid: ἄν + opt., εἰ + opt), is Socrates' response to the imaginary questioner at 28b3 who said, "Aren't you ashamed to have followed a way of life that has gotten you into so much trouble?" The structure is as follows: δεινὰ ἂν εἴην εἰργασμένος . . . εἰ, ὅτε μέν με . . . ἔταττον . . . τότε . . . ἔμενον . . . τοῦ δὲ θεοῦ τάττοντος [gen. abs.] . . . λίποιμι τὴν τάξιν.

εἴην εἰργασμένος Pf. optative middle. Trans.: "I would be acting terribly, if . . ."

28e1 **οἱ ἄρχοντες** Many offices in fifth-century Athens were chosen by lot. Indeed, this is how Socrates himself ended up as a member and perhaps the chief officer of the βουλή, the council of five hundred that prepared the business for the ἐκκλησία (see Xenophon, *Memorabilia* 4.4.2; see also *Hellenica* 1.7). Military commanders, however, were elected, as can be seen from εἵλεσθε (below).

28e2–3 **ἐν Ποτειδαίᾳ . . . Ἀμφιπόλει . . . Δηλίῳ.** Three battles from the Peloponnesian War, in which Socrates appears to have distinguished himself. At the Battle of Potidaea (432), Socrates rescued the wounded Alcibiades, as the latter describes in Plato's *Symposium* (219e–221b). Delium (424) was an Athenian defeat where Socrates' courageous retreat is praised by Alcibiades in the passage referred to above and by the commanding general, Laches, in the dialogue that bears his name (181b). Amphipolis (422), too, was an Athenian defeat (see Thucydides 5.6–5.11), but nothing is known about Socrates' exploits there.

τις καὶ ἐκινδύνευον ἀποθανεῖν, τοῦ δὲ θεοῦ τάττοντος, ὡς ἐγὼ
ᾠήθην τε καὶ ὑπέλαβον, φιλοσοφοῦντά με δεῖν ζῆν καὶ ἐξετάζοντα ἐμαυτὸν καὶ τοὺς ἄλλους, ἐνταῦθα δὲ φοβηθεὶς ἢ θάνατον
ἢ ἄλλ' ὁτιοῦν πρᾶγμα λίποιμι τὴν τάξιν. δεινόν τἂν εἴη, καὶ 29
ὡς ἀληθῶς τότ' ἄν με δικαίως εἰσάγοι τις εἰς δικαστήριον,
ὅτι οὐ νομίζω θεοὺς εἶναι ἀπειθῶν τῇ μαντείᾳ καὶ δεδιὼς
θάνατον καὶ οἰόμενος σοφὸς εἶναι οὐκ ὤν. τὸ γάρ τοι
θάνατον δεδιέναι, ὦ ἄνδρες, οὐδὲν ἄλλο ἐστὶν ἢ δοκεῖν
σοφὸν εἶναι μὴ ὄντα· δοκεῖν γὰρ εἰδέναι ἐστὶν ἃ οὐκ οἶδεν. οἶδε
μὲν γὰρ οὐδεὶς τὸν θάνατον οὐδ' εἰ τυγχάνει τῷ ἀνθρώπῳ

ᾠήθην aor. pass. indic. (act. sense) < οἴομαι *think*
ὑπέλαβον aor. act. indic. < ὑπολαμβάνω *suppose*
φοβηθείς aor. pass. part. (act. sense) < φοβέομαι *fear*
τάξιν < τάξις, -ιος, ἡ *station*
δικαστήριον, -ου, τό *law court*
ἀπειθῶν < ἀπειθέω *disobey*
δεδιώς pf. act. part. < δείδω *fear*

28e3 **ὥσπερ καὶ ἄλλος τις** "Like anybody else." Socrates represents his obedience as somewhat ordinary.

28e5 **δεῖν** Indirect statement, dependent on τάττοντος (e3). Note that Socrates sees philosophy not just as a process of examining others, but also himself.

29a1 **δεινόν τἂν** (= τοι ἄν) . . . "It really would be terrible." δεινόν recalls the point made at 28d9 (δεινά), which may have been forgotten in the intervening lines.

29a3 **ὅτι** "On the grounds that."

ἀπειθῶν The participle is causal, as Socrates explains *why* minding his own business would be equivalent to atheism.

29a4 **εἶναι** Infinitive in indirect statement after οἰόμενος.

οὐκ ὤν Supply σοφός. The participle is concessive. The striking brevity of the construction (brachyology) recalls Socrates' description of the attempt to disprove Apollo's oracle (e.g., at 21c7).

τοι "I assure you." θάνατον is the object of the articular infinitive τό . . . δεδιέναι (< δείδω). The fear of death is irrational, because it presumes that we have enough knowledge to know that it is something to fear. Persisting in this irrational fear, therefore, is another example of pretending to know things you don't (i.e., it is identical to the experience of the politicians, poets, and craftsmen whom Socrates met).

29a5 **δοκεῖν** Treat as parallel with τό . . . δεδιέναι: " I assure you, Athenian men, that fearing death is nothing more than a man thinking himself to be wise, without being so." The accusative participle and the accusative predicate adjective (σοφόν) agree with the implied subject of the infinitives.

29a7 **μέν** Best left untranslated. The contrasting thought is expressed at δεδίασι δ' (29a9).

πάντων μέγιστον ὂν τῶν ἀγαθῶν, δεδίασι δ' ὡς εὖ εἰδότες
b ὅτι μέγιστον τῶν κακῶν ἐστι. καί τοῦτο πῶς οὐκ ἀμαθία ἐστὶν αὕτη ἡ ἐπονείδιστος, ἡ τοῦ οἴεσθαι εἰδέναι ἃ οὐκ οἶδεν; ἐγὼ δ', ὦ ἄνδρες, τούτῳ καὶ ἐνταῦθα ἴσως διαφέρω τῶν πολλῶν ἀνθρώπων, καὶ εἰ δή τῳ σοφώτερός του φαίην εἶναι, τούτῳ ἄν, ὅτι οὐκ εἰδὼς ἱκανῶς περὶ τῶν ἐν Ἅιδου οὕτω καὶ οἴομαι οὐκ εἰδέναι· τὸ δὲ ἀδικεῖν καὶ ἀπειθεῖν τῷ βελτίονι καὶ θεῷ καὶ ἀνθρώπῳ, ὅτι κακὸν καὶ αἰσχρόν ἐστιν οἶδα. πρὸ οὖν τῶν κακῶν ὧν οἶδα ὅτι κακά ἐστιν, ἃ μὴ οἶδα εἰ καὶ ἀγαθὰ ὄντα τυγχάνει οὐδέποτε φοβήσομαι οὐδὲ φεύξομαι· ὥστε οὐδ' εἴ
c με νῦν ὑμεῖς ἀφίετε Ἀνύτῳ ἀπιστήσαντες, ὃς ἔφη ἢ τὴν ἀρχὴν οὐ δεῖν ἐμὲ δεῦρο εἰσελθεῖν ἤ, ἐπειδὴ εἰσῆλθον, οὐχ

ἐπονείδιστος, -ον *shameful, reproachful*
διαφέρω *differ from; be superior to*
οὐδέποτε *not at any time, never*
ἀφίετε pres. imper. < ἀφίημι *release, let go*
ἀπιστήσαντες < ἀπιστέω *disbelieve.*
ἐπειδή *since, when*

29a8 **ὡς** "As if." Supply τὸν θάνατον.

29b2 **ἡ τοῦ οἴεσθαι** Supply ἀμαθία before the articular infinitive.

29b3 **τούτῳ** Dative of degree of difference.

τῶν πολλῶν ἀνθρώπων Genitive of comparison with διαφέρω.

29b4 **εἰ δή** δή frequently appears after εἰ to soften the supposition, that is, "If I *really* am wiser [and it's not just a mistake the god made]" versus "If I am wiser."

τῳ = τινι.

του = τινος. Genitive of comparison.

29b8 **ὧν** Relative pronoun attracted into the case of the antecedent.

ἅ Object of φοβήσομαι and φεύξομαι.

ὄντα Supplementary participle with τυγχάνει.

29c1–30c1 A very complex sentence in the form of a conditional with a three-part protasis, leading to an apodosis (εἴποιμ' 29d2) that introduces an extended hypothetical quotation (29d2–30c1).

29c2 **τὴν ἀρχήν** Accusative absolute: "at the beginning."

οὐ δεῖν ἐμὲ δεῦρο εἰσελθεῖν Refusing to face the charges would have meant exile, a possibility that Socrates addresses in *Crito*. Burnet (1924) thought that this phrase represented an actual quotation from Anytus's speech, which is possible. There is no evidence, however, that any such speech by Anytus was ever published, although among the pseudo-Socratic literature an "Accusation of Socrates" was written by Polycrates and is mentioned by Isocrates (*Busirus* 4). Plato could, of course, be quoting from memory and giving a general sense of Anytus's remarks, and it is clear that he takes pains to make it *look like* Socrates is quoting. Socrates' arrival at court, after

οἷόν τ᾽ εἶναι τὸ μὴ ἀποκτεῖναί με, λέγων πρὸς ὑμᾶς ὡς εἰ
διαφευξοίμην ἤδη ἂν ὑμῶν οἱ ὑεῖς ἐπιτηδεύοντες ἃ Σωκράτης διδάσκει πάντες παντάπασι διαφθαρήσονται, —εἴ μοι
πρὸς ταῦτα εἴποιτε· "Ὦ Σώκρατες, νῦν μὲν Ἀνύτῳ οὐ πει-
σόμεθα ἀλλ᾽ ἀφίεμέν σε, ἐπὶ τούτῳ μέντοι, ἐφ᾽ ᾧτε μηκέτι
ἐν ταύτῃ τῇ ζητήσει διατρίβειν μηδὲ φιλοσοφεῖν· ἐὰν δὲ
ἁλῷς ἔτι τοῦτο πράττων, ἀποθανῇ" —εἰ οὖν με, ὅπερ εἶπον, d
ἐπὶ τούτοις ἀφίοιτε, εἴποιμ᾽ ἂν ὑμῖν ὅτι "Ἐγὼ ὑμᾶς, ὦ ἄνδρες
Ἀθηναῖοι, ἀσπάζομαι μὲν καὶ φιλῶ, πείσομαι δὲ μᾶλλον τῷ
θεῷ ἢ ὑμῖν, καὶ ἕωσπερ ἂν ἐμπνέω καὶ οἷός τε ὦ, οὐ μὴ

διαφευξοίμην fut. opt. < διαφεύγω *be acquitted*
ᾧτε < ὅστε, ἥτε, ὅτε *who, which*
διατρίβειν < διατρίβω *spend time*
ἁλῷς aor. act. subj. < ἁλίσκομαι *be caught*
ἀσπάζομαι *embrace*
ἕωσπερ (+ subj.) *so long as*
ἐμπνέω *draw breath*
οἷός τε ὦ < οἷός τε εἰμί be able

---

all, could have been perceived by supporters and defenders alike as an act of defiance in and of itself. Such an interpretation is certainly consistent with much of Socrates' behavior throughout the speech, from his persistent refusal to address the audience as "judges" to the "punishment" he will later propose for himself (37a).

29c3 **οἷόν τ' εἶναι** For the construction, see on 19e5. Note the change to neuter for the impersonal subject.

μή Negates the articular infinitive (τό . . . ἀποκτεῖναι).

23c5–6 **εἴ μοι . . . εἴποιτε . . .** The structure of the condition (future less vivid) is as follows: εἴ μοι εἴποιτε . . . εἴ με . . . ἀφοῖτε (29d1) . . . εἴποιμ᾽ ἄν . . . There is a slight anacolouthon. The εἰ-clauses continue the construction begun at 29c1: εἰ ἀφίετε . . . (simple present).

29c6 **ταῦτα** That is, the claim that the failure to execute Socrates would lead to the corruption of the youth.

29c7 **ἐπὶ τούτῳ** "upon this condition . . . that" τούτῳ is the antecedent of the relative pronoun ᾧτε.

29d2 **ἐπὶ τούτοις** That is, on the conditions given in the ἐπὶ τούτῳ-clause above.

29d3–4 **πείσομαι δὲ μᾶλλον τῷ θεῷ ἢ ὑμῖν** This passage is one of the foundational Western texts for thinking about civil disobedience and, more generally, the conflict between public behavior and private beliefs (see also Sophocles, *Antigone*).

29d4 **ἕωσπερ ἄν** Emphatic version of ἕως ἄν (+ subj.), introducing an indefinite temporal clause.

οἷός τ' ὦ See on 19e5.

οὐ μή The double negative is emphatic.

παύσωμαι φιλοσοφῶν καὶ ὑμῖν παρακελευόμενός τε καὶ ἐνδεικνύμενος ὅτῳ ἂν ἀεὶ ἐντυγχάνω ὑμῶν, λέγων οἷάπερ εἴωθα, ὅτι 'Ὦ ἄριστε ἀνδρῶν, Ἀθηναῖος ὤν, πόλεως τῆς μεγίστης καὶ εὐδοκιμωτάτης εἰς σοφίαν καὶ ἰσχύν, χρημάτων μὲν οὐκ αἰσχύνῃ ἐπιμελούμενος ὅπως σοι ἔσται ὡς πλεῖστα,
e καὶ δόξης καὶ τιμῆς, φρονήσεως δὲ καὶ ἀληθείας καὶ τῆς ψυχῆς ὅπως ὡς βελτίστη ἔσται οὐκ ἐπιμελῇ οὐδὲ φροντίζεις;' καὶ ἐάν τις ὑμῶν ἀμφισβητήσῃ καὶ φῇ ἐπιμελεῖσθαι,

---

παρακελευόμενος < παρακελεύομαι *exhort*
ἐνδεικνύμενος < ἐνδείκνυμι *point out*
ἰσχύν < ἰσχύς, -ύος, ἡ *strength*
ἐπιμελούμενος < ἐπιμελέομαι *care for*
δόξης < δόξα, -ης, ἡ *reputation, opinion*
τιμῆς < τιμή, -ῆς, ἡ *honor*
φρονήσεως < φρόνησις, -εως, ἡ *thought*
ἀμφισβητησῇ aor. act. subj. < ἀμφισβητέω *dispute*
ἐπιμελεῖσθαι < ἐπιμελέομαι *care for*

29d6 **ὑμῶν** Partitive with ὅτῳ.
οἷάπερ "Just the kind of things."

29d7–e3 If this is actually the way Socrates was accustomed to approach his fellow citizens, however deserving of his remonstrations they may have been, it is little wonder that he was the recipient of ἡ τῶν πολλῶν διαβολή τε καὶ φθόνος (28a8).

29d7 **εἴωθα** Supply λέγειν.
ὅτι Do not translate.
ἄριστε Socrates turns this common and facile address into an ironic deflation of Athenian self-conceit. It is precisely their unwillingness to dedicate themselves to ἀρετή that has brought the criticism of Socrates upon them.

29d9 **ὅπως** Here introducing an indirect question and dependent on ἐπιμελούμενος, like χρημάτων above. Although common in Greek, this type of construction is archaic in English. See, for example, the King James translation of Matthew 6.28, which translates literally the *koine* of the original: "Consider the lilies of the field, how they grow" (= "Consider how the lilies of the field grow").

29e1 **δόξης καὶ τιμῆς** These two terms are regarded with suspicion throughout the Platonic dialogues, and a critique of his fellow citizens' excessive reliance on what *seems* best is implicit in Socrates' account of his quest, during the course of which he spoke to many who *seemed* wise but were not (21c–22e). τιμή is a core value for the Homeric hero, representing acknowledgment of his value to the social group. In fact, the entire plot of the *Iliad* revolves around the loss of τιμή that Achilles suffers at the hands of Agamemnon. This sense is still visible in the fifth century, where the term often denotes public offices and civic distinctions. Such honors are harmless in themselves, but Socrates suggests that the unscrupulous use them as a means for creating the *appearance* of accomplishment, while neglecting excellence (ἀρετή) itself.

οὐκ εὐθὺς ἀφήσω αὐτὸν οὐδ' ἄπειμι, ἀλλ' ἐρήσομαι αὐτὸν καὶ
ἐξετάσω καὶ ἐλέγξω, καὶ ἐάν μοι μὴ δοκῇ κεκτῆσθαι ἀρετήν,
φάναι δέ, ὀνειδιῶ ὅτι τὰ πλείστου ἄξια περὶ ἐλαχίστου ποι- 30
εῖται, τὰ δὲ φαυλότερα περὶ πλείονος. ταῦτα καὶ νεωτέρῳ
καὶ πρεσβυτέρῳ ὅτῳ ἂν ἐντυγχάνω ποιήσω, καὶ ξένῳ καὶ
ἀστῷ, μᾶλλον δὲ τοῖς ἀστοῖς, ὅσῳ μου ἐγγυτέρω ἐστὲ γένει.
ταῦτα γὰρ κελεύει ὁ θεός, εὖ ἴστε, καὶ ἐγὼ οἴομαι οὐδέν πω
ὑμῖν μεῖζον ἀγαθὸν γενέσθαι ἐν τῇ πόλει ἢ τὴν ἐμὴν τῷ θεῷ
ὑπηρεσίαν. οὐδὲν γὰρ ἄλλο πράττων ἐγὼ περιέρχομαι ἢ

ἀφήσω fut. act. indic. < αφίημι *set free*
ὀνειδιῶ fut. act. indic. < ὀνειδίζω *reproach*
πρεσβυτέρῳ < πρεσβύτερος, -α, -ον *older*
ἐντυγχάνω pres. act. subj. *encounter*
ἐγγυτέρω < ἐγγυς *nearer*
γένει < γένος, -ους, τό *kinship*

30a1 **φάναι δέ** "But to say he does."
περὶ ἐλαχίστου ποιεῖται Idiomatic: "consider least important." The object of the verb is τὰ πλείστου ἄξια, "the most valuable things."

30a2 **περὶ πλείονος** Supply ποιεῖται from above: "consider more important."

30a2–4 "I shall test stranger and citizen alike." Socrates' refusal to show deference to his fellow citizens would have been viewed by many as a provocation. In fact, his only concession is to be even more exacting in his criticism of them. This novel behavior marks the beginning of a philosophical conception of universal humanity.

30a4 **ὅσῳ** Dative of degree of difference.
γένει Dative of respect. Socrates here uncovers another paradox of philosophy, as he understands it, that philosophy's search for an absolute truth independent of history is nonetheless rooted in the local political conditions of the citizen-philosopher.

30a7 **ὑπηρεσίαν** "Service." The metaphor derives from the subordinate position of the rowers on a ship, who sit at (lit., "under") their oars (ἐρετμοί). It is interesting to note, however, that the rowers were the backbone of Athenian naval power. They were also among the most democratic factions in the city, since they were composed of citizens who lacked the wealth to serve as hoplites. While Socrates was no great lover of Athenian democracy, the decoupling of political power from the external markings of social status was among the first necessary steps on the road to a truly philosophical reflection on the nature of the state, its rulers, and its stakeholders. Thus, in his service to the god, Socrates, like the rowers, exercises a profession that is despised by those who represent the traditional ideology, which he calls into question, yet one which, as he sees it, is essential to the well-being of the polis and its citizens.

πείθων ὑμῶν καὶ νεωτέρους καὶ πρεσβυτέρους μήτε σωμάτων
b ἐπιμελεῖσθαι μήτε χρημάτων πρότερον μηδὲ οὕτω σφόδρα
ὡς τῆς ψυχῆς ὅπως ὡς ἀρίστη ἔσται, λέγων ὅτι ʻΟὐκ ἐκ
χρημάτων ἀρετὴ γίγνεται, ἀλλ᾽ ἐξ ἀρετῆς χρήματα καὶ τὰ
ἄλλα ἀγαθὰ τοῖς ἀνθρώποις ἅπαντα καὶ ἰδίᾳ καὶ δημοσίᾳ.᾽
εἰ μὲν οὖν ταῦτα λέγων διαφθείρω τοὺς νέους, ταῦτ᾽ ἂν εἴη
βλαβερά· εἰ δέ τίς μέ φησιν ἄλλα λέγειν ἢ ταῦτα, οὐδὲν
λέγει. πρὸς ταῦτα," φαίην ἄν, "ὦ ἄνδρες Ἀθηναῖοι, ἢ
πείθεσθε Ἀνύτῳ ἢ μή, καὶ ἢ ἀφίετέ με ἢ μή, ὡς ἐμοῦ οὐκ
c ἂν ποιήσοντος ἄλλα, οὐδ᾽ εἰ μέλλω πολλάκις τεθνάναι."

σωμάτων < σῶμα, -τος, τό *body*
δημοσίᾳ < δημόσιος, -α, -ον *of the people*
βλαβερά < βλαβερός, -ά, -όν *harmful*

30a8 **ὑμῶν** Partitive with νεωτέρους καὶ πρεσβυτέρους.

σωμάτων Note that "bodies" here are classified with external possessions and are contrasted with the soul.

30b1 **ἐπιμελεῖσθαι** Dependent on πείθων. Socrates here appropriates the vocabulary of public concern as it was employed in the institutions of fifth-century Athenian politics to describe the assumption of well-defined duties, for which one must be accountable after the term of office. Weber (1986) argues that this move is not accidental and insightfully connects it with Socrates' reformulation of citizenship in terms of individual ethics, with the result that "the ἐπιμέλεια τῆς ψυχῆς is, following Socrates, something just as natural as the assumption of public office."

πρότερον μηδὲ οὕτω σφόδρα ὡς τῆς ψυχῆς "Before, nor with as much eagerness as for the soul." The rejection of material goals and the exhortation to care for the soul is a crucial part of Socrates' revolutionary approach to thought (see Hadot 2002, 22–38).

30b2 **ἔσται** The implied subject is ψυχή. Note the elaborate chiasmus of ἐκ χρημάτων ἀρετή . . . ἐξ ἀρετῆς χρήματα, made more striking by the presence of the same words in different cases (polyptoton).

ὅτι Do not translate.

30b8–c1 **ἐμοῦ οὐκ ἂν ποιήσοντος ἄλλα** ἄν with the future participle is unusual. Some editors consequently emend to ἂν ποιήσαντος, which would be equivalent to the apodosis of a future-less-vivid condition (optative + ἄν). There is no manuscript support for such a change, however. Translate: "since I will act no differently."

30c1 **οὐδ᾽ εἰ** "Even if." μέλλω + infin. is equivalent to a future indicative.

CHAPTER 18

(30c2–31c3)

"My service to the god, far from being a liability, is a divine blessing on the city." For additional discussion of the chapter and questions for study, see essay 18.

Μὴ θορυβεῖτε, ὦ ἄνδρες Ἀθηναῖοι, ἀλλ' ἐμμείνατέ μοι οἷς ἐδεήθην ὑμῶν, μὴ θορυβεῖν ἐφ' οἷς ἂν λέγω ἀλλ' ἀκούειν· καὶ γάρ, ὡς ἐγὼ οἶμαι, ὀνήσεσθε ἀκούοντες. μέλλω γὰρ οὖν ἄττα ὑμῖν ἐρεῖν καὶ ἄλλα ἐφ' οἷς ἴσως βοήσεσθε· ἀλλὰ μηδαμῶς ποιεῖτε τοῦτο. εὖ γὰρ ἴστε, ἐάν με ἀποκτείνητε τοιοῦτον ὄντα οἷον ἐγὼ λέγω, οὐκ ἐμὲ μείζω βλάψετε ἢ ὑμᾶς αὐτούς· ἐμὲ μὲν γὰρ οὐδὲν ἂν βλάψειεν οὔτε Μέλητος

ἐμμείνατε < ἐμμένω *stay with*
ὀνήσεσθε ftr. indic. < ὀνίνημι *profit, derive benefit*
μηδαμῶς *in no way*
ἀποκτείνητε < ἀποκτείνω *kill*

30c2 **ἐμμείνατε . . . ὑμῶν** The metaphor is spatial. Socrates asks the jurors to "stay" with his previous request that they not interrupt.

30c3 **οἷς** Dative with ἐμμείνατε. The relative clause has been incorporated into the main clause by ellipsis of its antecedent. So also with ἐφ' οἷς later in the line. The requests to which he refers were at 17d1 and 20e4.

30c4 **γὰρ οὖν** οὖν emphasizes the γάρ in the manner of γὰρ δή and heightens the provocativeness of Socrates' claim both to benefit the audience *and* to give them something to shout (βοήσεσθε) about.

30c5 **ἄττα** (= τινά) **. . . καὶ ἄλλα** Hendiadys: "certain others."

30c7 **οἷον ἐγὼ λέγω** "Such as I claim to be."

μείζω Masc. acc. sg. (contracted form of μείζονα).

30c8 **ὑμᾶς αὐτούς** The reflexive pronoun for the first- and second-person plural is formed from the personal pronoun + the appropriate form of αὐτός, -ή, -ό.

μέν The clause begins as if Socrates were going to elaborate the contrast made in the previous sentence between the possibility that the jury members could injure him (μέν) and that they might injure themselves in so doing (δέ). Instead, Socrates digresses briefly, and when he concludes he picks up the contrast with νῦν οὖν (d6) and abandons the second part of the μέν . . . δέ construction.

οὔτε Ἄνυτος—οὐδὲ γὰρ ἂν δύναιτο—οὐ γὰρ οἴομαι θεμιτὸν
d εἶναι ἀμείνονι ἀνδρὶ ὑπὸ χείρονος βλάπτεσθαι. ἀποκτείνειε
μεντἂν ἴσως ἢ ἐξελάσειεν ἢ ἀτιμώσειεν· ἀλλὰ ταῦτα οὗτος
μὲν ἴσως οἴεται καὶ ἄλλος τίς που μεγάλα κακά, ἐγὼ δ' οὐκ
οἴομαι, ἀλλὰ πολὺ μᾶλλον ποιεῖν ἃ οὑτοσὶ νῦν ποιεῖ, ἄνδρα
ἀδίκως ἐπιχειρεῖν ἀποκτεινύναι. νῦν οὖν, ὦ ἄνδρες Ἀθηναῖοι, πολλοῦ δέω ἐγὼ ὑπὲρ ἐμαυτοῦ ἀπολογεῖσθαι, ὥς τις
ἂν οἴοιτο, ἀλλὰ ὑπὲρ ὑμῶν, μή τι ἐξαμάρτητε περὶ τὴν τοῦ
e θεοῦ δόσιν ὑμῖν ἐμοῦ καταψηφισάμενοι. ἐὰν γάρ με ἀποκτείνητε, οὐ ῥᾳδίως ἄλλον τοιοῦτον εὑρήσετε, ἀτεχνῶς—εἰ
καὶ γελοιότερον εἰπεῖν—προσκείμενον τῇ πόλει ὑπὸ τοῦ θεοῦ

ἐξελάσειεν aor. act. opt. < ἐξελαύνω *send into exile*
ἀτιμώσειεν < ἀτιμόω *punish with the loss of citizen rights*
ἀποκτεινύναι pres. act. infin. < ἀποκτείνυμι *kill*
ἐξαμάρτητε aor. act. subj. < ἐξαμαρτάνω *make a mistake*
δόσιν < δόσις, -εως, ἡ *gift*
προσκείμενον < πρόσκειμαι *be attached to*

30c9 **θεμιτόν** The adjective is derived from θέμις, "that which has been laid down (< τίθημι)," and, by extension, "law, right." It possesses a certain solemnity often associated with divine decrees. In Hesiod (*Theogony* 901), the Titan Themis is Zeus's second wife and a personification of his divine authority.

30d2 **μεντἂν** Crasis of μέντοι ἄν. μέντοι is condescending. See Denniston (1954, 402, iii). Translate: "He *could* perhaps . . ."

ἀτιμώσειεν This is the reading of Stobaeus in the *Florilegium* (fifth century C.E.). The manuscripts read ἀτιμάσειεν (< ἀτιμάω, "dishonor"). Both verbs make sense in the context, but ἐξελαύνειν refers to a specific legal procedure, so it is arguable that the other verb should as well. On this argument, ἀτιμάσειεν would have been an error made by an ancient copyist unfamiliar with the details of Attic law who substituted a more familiar (and less specific) word.

οὗτος Presumably he is referring to Meletus.

30d3 **που** "I suppose." Take with ἄλλος τις.

30d4 **ἀλλὰ πολὺ μᾶλλον** Supply οἴομαι and use μεγάλα κακά as the predicate of the indirect statement (subject = ἅ . . . ποιεῖ, in apposition with ἄνδρα . . . ἀποκτεινύναι).

30d6 **πολλοῦ δέω** A common idiom. "I am far from."

30d7 **ἐξαμάρτητε** Subjunctive in a clause of fearing, dependent on ἀπολογεῖσθαι.

30e1 **ἐμοῦ καταψηφισάμενοι** "By convicting me." The ψηφ-root in the participle refers to the bronze "pebbles" (ψῆφοι) used by the jurors to cast their votes. For illustrations see Lang (1978).

30e2 **ἀτεχνῶς** "Truly," adding emphasis to a striking expression. Weber (1986).

ὥσπερ ἵππῳ μεγάλῳ μὲν καὶ γενναίῳ, ὑπὸ μεγέθους δὲ νωθεστέρῳ καὶ δεομένῳ ἐγείρεσθαι ὑπὸ μύωπός τινος, οἷον δή μοι δοκεῖ ὁ θεὸς ἐμὲ τῇ πόλει προστεθηκέναι τοιοῦτόν τινα, ὃς ὑμᾶς ἐγείρων καὶ πείθων καὶ ὀνειδίζων ἕνα ἕκαστον οὐδὲν παύομαι τὴν ἡμέραν ὅλην πανταχοῦ προσκαθίζων. 31
τοιοῦτος οὖν ἄλλος οὐ ῥᾳδίως ὑμῖν γενήσεται, ὦ ἄνδρες, ἀλλ' ἐὰν ἐμοὶ πείθησθε, φείσεσθέ μου· ὑμεῖς δ' ἴσως τάχ' ἂν ἀχθόμενοι, ὥσπερ οἱ νυστάζοντες ἐγειρόμενοι, κρούσαντες ἄν με, πειθόμενοι Ἀνύτῳ, ῥᾳδίως ἂν ἀποκτείναιτε, εἶτα τὸν λοιπὸν βίον καθεύδοντες διατελοῖτε ἄν, εἰ μή τινα ἄλλον ὁ

γενναίῳ < γενναῖος, -α, -ον *noble*
μεγέθους < μέγεθος, -ους, τό *greatness, size*
νωθεστέρῳ comp. < νωθής, -ές *sluggish*
ἐγείρεσθαι < εγείρω *be roused*
προστεθηκέναι pf. act. infin. < προστίθημι *put beside*
προσκαθίζων < προσκαθίζω *land on*
φείσεσθε fut. act. indic. < φείδομαι *spare*
νυστάζοντες < νυστάζω *doze*
καθεύδοντες < καθεύδω *sleep*
διατελοῖτε < διατελέω *continue*

30e4 **γενναίῳ . . . νωθεστέρῳ** The comparison of Athens to a horse that is noble but lazy is not flattering. It contrasts markedly with the famous eulogy of Athens as "the school of Greece" in Pericles' Funeral Oration (Thucydides 2.41).

30e5 **ἐγείρεσθαι** Dependent on δεομένῳ.

μύωπος This is one of the best-known passages from the *Apology*, depicting Socrates as the annoying "fly" who continually pesters his fellow citizens. Many readers have seen a link between Socrates' comparison and the genre of the Aesopic fable, which, to judge from references in Herodotus and Old Comedy, was well known in the fifth century. The connection is worth exploring. At the beginning of *Phaedo* (60d), the dramatization of his death, we learn that Socrates has spent some time in prison putting fables of Aesop into verse.

οἷον Untranslated predicate accusative of ἐμέ, object of προστεθηκέναι. It anticipates τοιοῦτόν τινα in the next line.

31a2 **ὑμῖν** Dative of possession.

31a4 **ἂν** This ἄν, plus the two in 31a5, goes with ἀποκτείναιτε (optative in the apodosis of a future-less-vivid condition). The image of the stinging fly and the lazy horse is developed further, as the sentence subtly slides between the literal and the metaphorical.

κρούσαντες . . . με The image preserves the idea of Socrates as a fly but imagines him getting crushed not by an irritated horse, but by Athenians influenced by Anytus. The verb means "to strike" but also "to examine by tapping" when checking to see if a pot is cracked.

θεὸς ὑμῖν ἐπιπέμψειεν κηδόμενος ὑμῶν. ὅτι δ' ἐγὼ τυγχάνω
ὢν τοιοῦτος οἷος ὑπὸ τοῦ θεοῦ τῇ πόλει δεδόσθαι, ἐνθένδε
b ἂν κατανοήσαιτε· οὐ γὰρ ἀνθρωπίνῳ ἔοικε τὸ ἐμὲ τῶν
μὲν ἐμαυτοῦ πάντων ἠμεληκέναι καὶ ἀνέχεσθαι τῶν οἰκείων
ἀμελουμένων τοσαῦτα ἤδη ἔτη, τὸ δὲ ὑμέτερον πράττειν ἀεί,
ἰδίᾳ ἑκάστῳ προσιόντα ὥσπερ πατέρα ἢ ἀδελφὸν πρεσβύ-
τερον πείθοντα ἐπιμελεῖσθαι ἀρετῆς. καὶ εἰ μέν τι ἀπὸ
τούτων ἀπέλαυον καὶ μισθὸν λαμβάνων ταῦτα παρεκελευόμην, εἶχον ἄν τινα λόγον· νῦν δὲ ὁρᾶτε δὴ καὶ αὐτοὶ

κηδόμενος < κήδω (mid.) *care for*
δεδόσθαι pf. pass. infin. < δίδωμι *give*
ἔνθενδε *from what follows*
κατανοήσαιτε aor. opt. < κατανοέω *understand*
ἠμεληκέναι pf. act. infin. < ἀμελέω *neglect*
ἀνέχεσθαι < ἀνέχω *hold up, bear up*
ἀπέλαυον < ἀπολαύω *benefit from*
μισθόν < μισθός, -οῦ, ὁ *wage*
παρεκελευόμην < παρακελεύομαι *urge*

31a7 **ὅτι δ' ἐγὼ τυγχάνω ὤν** Indirect speech introduced by ἂν κατανοήσαιτε.

31b1 **οὐ . . . ἀνθρωπίνῳ ἔοικε** "Aren't natural for a man" (lit. "are not similar to a human thing"). ἔοικε has three articular infinitive subjects: τό . . . ἠμεληκέναι, [τὸ] ἀνέχεσθαι, and τό . . . πράττειν with ἐμέ as their subject.

31b2 **ἠμεληκέναι** This is one of a series of verbs derived from the same stem as ἐπιμέλεια, "care." Socrates here does not *care* for his χρήματα (30b1), but he neglects his worldly affairs so as to urge his fellow citizens to care (ἐπιμελεῖσθαι 29e3–4, 30a9, 31b5) for their true selves, defined as their souls (ψυχή 29e1, 30b2).

τῶν οἰκείων Neuter plural.

31b3 **τὸ . . . ὑμέτερον** "*Your* business," as opposed to τῶν οἰκείων.

31b4 **ἰδίᾳ** Socrates' public behavior is very different from that of Meletus mentioned at 26a3. Plato's use of ἰδίᾳ in both passages emphasizes the contrast. Socrates in effect establishes philosophy as an extrademocratic practice that takes place outside the realm of the δῆμος (cf. 30b4), which defined the center of civic life in democratic Athens. Socrates' activities might reasonably be viewed by some as a threat to the existing political order.

προσιόντα Masc. acc. sg. participle < πρόσειμι, agreeing with ἐμέ (b1).

31b5 **ἐπιμελεῖσθαι ἀρετῆς** The infinitive is dependent on πείθοντα. Note the repeated focus on internal development characteristic of Socrates' approach to civic virtue.

31b5–7 **εἰ . . . ἀπέλαυον . . . εἶχον ἄν** Present counterfactual condition.

31b7 **λόγον** That is, some justification for neglecting my personal affairs. Socrates ironically adopts the thought patterns of his fellow citizens, who, he implies, only act for material gain.

ὅτι οἱ κατήγοροι τἆλλα πάντα ἀναισχύντως οὕτω κατηγοροῦντες τοῦτό γε οὐχ οἷοί τε ἐγένοντο ἀπαναισχυντῆσαι
παρασχόμενοι μάρτυρα, ὡς ἐγώ ποτέ τινα ἢ ἐπραξάμην c
μισθὸν ἢ ᾔτησα. ἱκανὸν γάρ, οἶμαι, ἐγὼ παρέχομαι τὸν
μάρτυρα ὡς ἀληθῆ λέγω, τὴν πενίαν.

ἀναισχύντως *shamelessly*
ἀπαναισχυντῆσαι < ἀπαναισχυντέω *be shameless enough to say*
παρασχόμενοι aor. mid. part. < παρέχω *offer*

31b8 **τἆλλα πάντα** "In all other respects."
31c1 **ὡς ἐγώ** Introducing indirect statement after a noun of speaking (μάρτυρα).
31c3 **τὴν πενίαν** The poverty of Socrates is relative, though he clearly had no interest in accumulating money. For the value of his household, see on 20b8.

CHAPTER 19

(31c4–32a3)

"Why then have I preferred this private form of service to the more usual public show of devotion to one's fellow citizens?" For additional discussion of the chapter and questions for study, see essay 19.

Ἴσως ἂν οὖν δόξειεν ἄτοπον εἶναι, ὅτι δὴ ἐγὼ ἰδίᾳ μὲν ταῦτα συμβουλεύω περιιὼν καὶ πολυπραγμονῶ, δημοσίᾳ δὲ οὐ τολμῶ ἀναβαίνων εἰς τὸ πλῆθος τὸ ὑμέτερον συμβου-

δόξειεν aor. act. opt. < δοκέω *seem*
συμβουλεύω *give advice*
πολυπραγμονῶ < πολυπραγμονέω *be meddlesome*
τολμῶ < τολμάω *dare*
πλῆθος *multitude; democratic faction*

31c5 **πολυπραγμονῶ** Here Socrates appropriates a term with a well-established public meaning and gives it a new private one. πολυπραγμοσύνη, "over-busyness," is a highly charged term within the political struggles between democrats and oligarchs that dominated Athenian life in the last part of the fifth century (see Carter 1986). Oligarchs who opposed what they saw as democratic interference in the affairs of other city-states styled themselves as ἀπράγμονες, by which they meant to suggest that they knew how to mind their own business, in contrast to the "busyness" of their enemies. In Aristophanes' *Birds,* two citizens abandon Athens in search of a τόπος ἀπράγμων, where they can live in peace. In Pericles' Funeral Oration, by contrast, Thucydides has the democrat Pericles say the following: "We alone consider that a man who has no share of public life is not someone who minds his own business (ἀπράγμονα), but worthless ἀχρηστόν" (2.40). Plato's Socrates contests the view that πολυπραγμοσύνη can only exist as part of a public career and makes a case for his own version of "business." In other passages, it is the ἀπραγμοσύνη of the philosopher that is worn (ironically) as a badge of pride. Compare *Gorgias* 526c4, with the accompanying commentary in Dodds (1966); compare also *Republic* 433a.

31c6 **ἀναβαίνων** That is, before the assembly. Note the skillful way Plato uses two participles derived from verbs of motion to contrast the actions of "going up" to address the assembly and "going about" addressing individuals."

λεύειν τῇ πόλει. τούτου δὲ αἴτιόν ἐστιν ὃ ὑμεῖς ἐμοῦ
πολλάκις ἀκηκόατε πολλαχοῦ λέγοντος, ὅτι μοι θεῖόν τι καὶ
δαιμόνιον γίγνεται, ὃ δὴ καὶ ἐν τῇ γραφῇ ἐπικω- d
μῳδῶν Μέλητος ἐγράψατο. ἐμοὶ δὲ τοῦτ' ἔστιν ἐκ παιδὸς
ἀρξάμενον, φωνή τις γιγνομένη, ἣ ὅταν γένηται, ἀεὶ ἀποτρέπει με τούτου ὃ ἂν μέλλω πράττειν, προτρέπει δὲ οὔποτε.
τοῦτ' ἔστιν ὅ μοι ἐναντιοῦται τὰ πολιτικὰ πράττειν, καὶ
παγκάλως γέ μοι δοκεῖ ἐναντιοῦσθαι· εὖ γὰρ ἴστε, ὦ ἄνδρες

πολλαχοῦ *in many places, often*
ἀποτρέπει < ἀποτρέπω *dissuade from*
προτρέπει < προτρέπω *persuade to do*
ἐναντιοῦται < ἐναντιόομαι *oppose*
παγκάλως *absolutely, correctly*

31c8 **θεῖόν τι καὶ δαιμόνιον** "Something holy and divine." For the δαιμόνιον of Socrates, see on 24c1.

31d1 **ἐπικωμῳδῶν** Although ἐπικωμῳδέω appears only here in classical literature, the uncompounded form appears in oratory in the general sense of "mock." See Lysias (24.18), where the context is also that of an accusation that one's opponent is joking (see on 27a7). Within a speech that has already named Aristophanes' *Clouds* as a prominent voice among the "first accusors," however, Socrates cannot use comedy as a metaphor without also invoking the real thing and so binding together the two groups of accusors.

31d2 **ἐκ παιδός** See on 21a1: ἐκ νέου.

31d3–4 **ἀποτρέπει . . . προτρέπει** The effect of Socrates' divine sign in Plato is completely negative. It cannot, therefore, be cited as in any way dictating the content or nature of Socratic philosophy.

31d4 **τούτου** Genitive of separation with ἀποτρέπει.

31d6 **παγκάλως γέ μοι δοκεῖ ἐναντιοῦσθαι** Since the δαιμόνιον only says "No," as opposed to more loquacious forms of divine signaling, Socrates can only speculate about the rationale behind its intervention. Here, however, he uses that speculation to justify his (relative) lack of civic involvement. This is similar to his behavior in the case of the oracle, where his practice of testing was only indirectly related to the god's words. Taken together, these anecdotes help to identify Socrates' approach to philosophy as a highly idiosyncratic reinterpretation of traditional piety.

Ἀθηναῖοι, εἰ ἐγὼ πάλαι ἐπεχείρησα πράττειν τὰ πολιτικὰ
πράγματα, πάλαι ἂν ἀπολώλη καὶ οὔτ' ἂν ὑμᾶς ὠφελήκη
e οὐδὲν οὔτ' ἂν ἐμαυτόν. καί μοι μὴ ἄχθεσθε λέγοντι τἀληθῆ·
οὐ γάρ ἐστιν ὅστις ἀνθρώπων σωθήσεται οὔτε ὑμῖν οὔτε
ἄλλῳ πλήθει οὐδενὶ γνησίως ἐναντιούμενος καὶ διακωλύων
πολλὰ ἄδικα καὶ παράνομα ἐν τῇ πόλει γίγνεσθαι, ἀλλ'
32 ἀναγκαῖόν ἐστι τὸν τῷ ὄντι μαχούμενον ὑπὲρ τοῦ δικαίου,
καὶ εἰ μέλλει ὀλίγον χρόνον σωθήσεσθαι, ἰδιωτεύειν ἀλλὰ
μὴ δημοσιεύειν.

ἀπολώλη 1st sg. pluperf. act. < ἀπόλλυμι *be destroyed*
ὠφελήκη 1st sg. pluperf. act. < ὠφελέω *help, aid*
ἄχθεσθε < ἄχθομαι *be angry*
σωθήσεται fut. pass. < σῴζω *save*
γνησίως *genuinely*
διακωλύων < διακωλύω *hinder, prevent*
παράνομα < παράνομος, -ον *unlawful*
μαχούμενον fut. part. < μάχομαι *fight*

31d7–8 **εἰ . . . ἐπεχείρησα . . . ἂν ἀπολώλη . . . ὠφελήκη** (< ὀφείλω) Past counterfactual condition, with the pluperfect substituted for the aorist in the double apodosis.

31d8–e1 **ἄν** Note the threefold repetition of ἄν, not at all necessary for the sentence to be intelligible but creating an emphatic tricolon, with which the sentence concludes. The rhetorical fireworks continue in the next sentence with a cluster of negatives: οὐ . . . οὔτε . . . οὔτε . . . οὐδενί.

31e4 **γίγνεσθαι** Infinitive following a verb of hindering (διακωλύων).

32a1 **τόν . . . μαχόυμενον** Subject of σωθήσεσθαι.

32a2–3 **ἰδιωτεύειν . . . μὴ δημοσιεύειν** "To be a private citizen . . . not to be involved in politics." Complementary infinitives with ἀναγκαῖον.

32a

CHAPTER 20

(32a4–32e1)

"My past experiences substantiate this claim." For additional discussion of the chapter and questions for study, see essay 20.

Μεγάλα δ' ἔγωγε ὑμῖν τεκμήρια παρέξομαι τούτων, οὐ λόγους ἀλλ' ὃ ὑμεῖς τιμᾶτε, ἔργα. ἀκούσατε δή μοι τὰ συμβεβηκότα, ἵνα εἰδῆτε ὅτι οὐδ' ἂν ἑνὶ ὑπεικάθοιμι παρὰ τὸ δίκαιον δείσας θάνατον, μὴ ὑπείκων δὲ ἅμα κἂν ἀπολοίμην. ἐρῶ δὲ ὑμῖν φορτικὰ μὲν καὶ δικανικά, ἀληθῆ δέ.

τεκμήρια < τεκμήριον, -ου, τό *proof*
συμβεβηκότα pf. act. part. < συμβαίνω *occur*
ὑπεικάθοιμι aor. act. opt. < ὑπείκω *yield*
φορτικά < φορτικός, -ή, -όν *vulgar*
δικανικά < δικανικός, -ή, -όν *pertaining to the law courts*

32a5–8 **ἀκούσατε δή . . .** The structure of this very complex sentence is as follows: imperative (ἀκούσατε), followed by a purpose clause (ἵνα εἰδῆτε . . .) and indirect statement (ὅτι . . . ἀπολοίμην) with a potential optative (οὐδ' . . . θάνατον), a negated participle in the nominative (μὴ ὑπείκων) reasserting Socrates' principled stand, and a final protasis (κἂν . . . ἀπολοίμην) that reiterates his willingness to die.

32a6 **ἑνί** "To even one man."

ὑπεικάθοιμι The -θ- infix is characteristic of poetry and may give the passage a heroic flavor (Smyth 1956, 490), but the word is rare. Notice the chiastic arrangement of the optatives and participles: ὑπεικάθοιμι . . . δείσας (concessive) . . . ὑπείκων . . . ἀπολοίμην.

32a8 **φορτικά . . . δικανικά** The anecdotes that Socrates tells support his claims, but since it is Socrates doing the telling, they could be viewed as boastful and hence "vulgar." In addition, the lawcourts are full of defendants reminding the jurors of their many services to the city, and for this reason an uncharitable listener could regard his behavior as just the kind of thing you would expect from a defendant. Unlike much of what one hears under such circumstances, Socrates implies what he has to say is true. The stories are carefully chosen. The first shows Socrates standing by his convictions

ἐγὼ γάρ, ὦ ἄνδρες Ἀθηναῖοι, ἄλλην μὲν ἀρχὴν οὐδεμίαν
b πώποτε ἦρξα ἐν τῇ πόλει, ἐβούλευσα δέ· καὶ ἔτυχεν ἡμῶν
ἡ φυλὴ Ἀντιοχὶς πρυτανεύουσα ὅτε ὑμεῖς τοὺς δέκα
στρατηγοὺς τοὺς οὐκ ἀνελομένους τοὺς ἐκ τῆς ναυμαχίας
ἐβουλεύσασθε ἀθρόους κρίνειν, παρανόμως, ὡς ἐν τῷ ὑστέρῳ
χρόνῳ πᾶσιν ὑμῖν ἔδοξεν. τότ' ἐγὼ μόνος τῶν πρυτάνεων

ἀρχήν < ἀρχή, -ῆς, ἡ *office*
ἐβούλευσα < βουλεύω *serve as a member of the boule*
φυλή, -ῆς, ἡ *tribe*
πρυτανεύουσα < πρυτανεύω *serve as a* prytanis
ἀνελομένους aor. mid. part. < ἀναιρέω *pick up*
ναυμαχίας < ναυμαχία, -ας, ἡ *sea fight*
ἀθρόους < ἀθρόος, -α, -ον *all together*
κρίνειν < κρίνω *judge, try*

---

against the angry democratic majority. The second takes place during the short-lived rule of the Thirty (see introduction). By choosing these two stories, Socrates effectively positions himself as politically nonpartisan in his pursuit of truth and his refusal to do wrong. In so doing, however, he can only count on the support of those jurors who are similarly above factional loyalty.

32a9 **ἄλλην . . . ἀρχήν** The adjective anticipates Socrates' statement that he was once a member of the βουλή: except for this service, he held no *other* office.

32b1 **ἐβούλευσα** See on 25a3.

32b2 **Ἀντιοχίς** One of the ten tribes, named after Athenian heroes, into which the citizen body was divided.

πρυτανεύουσα Supplementary participle with ἔτυχεν. Each of the tribes contributed fifty members annually to the βουλή, which prepared business for the assembly, and these groups rotated in turn as πρυτανεῖς, which formed the executive arm of the *boule*.

τοὺς δέκα στρατηγούς The reference is to the Battle of Arginusae, when the Athenian fleet was victorious over the Spartans. After the battle a storm prevented the Athenians from collecting the bodies of the fallen soldiers. The event produced great popular anger in Athens, as Xenophon describes (*Hellenika*, 1.7).

32b4 **ἐβουλεύσασθε** Some manuscripts have ἐβούλεσθε here, a reading that is perfectly intelligible but also a likely banalization from the more specific verb describing the official actions of the βουλή.

παρανόμως "Illegally." Athenian legal practice did not permit defendants to be tried as a group on capital charges.

ἐν τῷ ὑστέρῳ χρόνῳ See Xenophon, *Hellenika*, 1.7.35. Their remorse did little for the unfortunate generals, who had already been executed.

32b5 **ἐγὼ μόνος** Xenophon says that a few others tried to intervene but that they eventually backed down, threatened with prosecution themselves, and that only Socrates held out to the end.

ἠναντιώθην ὑμῖν μηδὲν ποιεῖν παρὰ τοὺς νόμους καὶ ἐναντία
ἐψηφισάμην· καὶ ἑτοίμων ὄντων ἐνδεικνύναι με καὶ ἀπάγειν
τῶν ῥητόρων, καὶ ὑμῶν κελευόντων καὶ βοώντων, μετὰ τοῦ
νόμου καὶ τοῦ δικαίου ᾤμην μᾶλλόν με δεῖν διακινδυνεύειν c
ἢ μεθ' ὑμῶν γενέσθαι μὴ δίκαια βουλευομένων, φοβηθέντα
δεσμὸν ἢ θάνατον. καὶ ταῦτα μὲν ἦν ἔτι δημοκρατουμένης
τῆς πόλεως· ἐπειδὴ δὲ ὀλιγαρχία ἐγένετο, οἱ τριάκοντα αὖ
μεταπεμψάμενοί με πέμπτον αὐτὸν εἰς τὴν θόλον προσέταξαν

ἠναντιώθην aor. pass. indic. < ἐναντιόω *be opposed*
ἐναντία *on the other side*
ἐψηφισάμην < ψηφίζομαι *vote*
ἐνδεικνύναι pres. act. infin. < ἐνδείκνυμι *indict*
ἀπάγειν < ἀπάγω *lead away, arrest*
βοώντων < βοάω *shout*
ᾤμην impf. mid. < οἶμαι *think*
διακινδυνεύειν < διακινδυνεύω *face all dangers*
δεσμόν < δεσμός, -οῦ, ὁ *bond, imprisonment*
δημοκρατουμένης < δημοκρατέομαι *have a democratic constitution*
ὀλιγαρχία, -ίας, < *oligarchy*
μεταπεμψαμένοι < μεταπέμπω *send for*
προσέταξαν < προστάττω *command*

32b6 **ἐναντία** "On the other side," that is, "against them."

32b7–8 **ἑτοίμων ὄντων . . . τῶν ῥητόρων** Genitive absolute. So also, ὑμῶν κελευόντων καὶ βοώντων.

32b8 **ἐνδεικνύναι** Complementary infinitive with ἑτοίμων.

ὑμῶν Socrates uses the second person to describe the actions of the βουλή since the body acts collectively on behalf of all Athenians, as does the court.

32c2 **φοβηθέντα** The participle agrees with the με in c1. See on 28e for Socrates' willingness to endure danger. There he says that he would deserve to be prosecuted if he followed the orders of men but shirked his duty when the god commanded. In this passage, he shows one of the forms his understanding of service to the god might take.

32c3 **δημοκρατουμένης τῆς πόλεως** Genitive absolute. The Battle of Arginusae was fought in 406 B.C.E.

32c4 **οἱ τριάκοντα** For more information, see introduction.

32c5 **με πέμπτον** "Me and four others."

θόλον Mention of the Tholos, a circular building in the agora, provides continuity between Socrates' two stories, despite the change in government. The πρυτανεῖς with whom Socrates served in the aftermath of Arginusae met in the Tholos (also called the πρυτανεῖον), where they entertained foreign dignitaries. πρυτανεῖς took their meals and slept there as well, to ensure the presence of legally competent officials in cases of emergency. When the Thirty came to power, they too made use of the symbolic value of the Tholos in an attempt to legitimize their rule in the eyes of their fellow citizens.

ἀγαγεῖν ἐκ Σαλαμῖνος Λέοντα τὸν Σαλαμίνιον ἵνα ἀποθάνοι· οἷα δὴ καὶ ἄλλοις ἐκεῖνοι πολλοῖς πολλὰ προσέταττον, βουλόμενοι ὡς πλείστους ἀναπλῆσαι αἰτιῶν. τότε μέντοι ἐγὼ
d οὐ λόγῳ ἀλλ' ἔργῳ αὖ ἐνεδειξάμην ὅτι ἐμοὶ θανάτου μὲν μέλει, εἰ μὴ ἀγροικότερον ἦν εἰπεῖν, οὐδ' ὁτιοῦν, τοῦ δὲ μηδὲν

ἀναπλῆσαι aor. act. infin. < ἀναπίμπλημι *fill up*
ἀγροικότερον *rather vulgarly*

32c6 **Σαλαμῖνος** The island of Salamis, off the coast of Attica, famous from the naval victory of the Athenians against the Persians in 480, had been an Athenian possession since the sixth century.

Λέοντα The arrest and execution of Leon of Salamis is mentioned by various writers (Andocides, *On the Mysteries*, 1.94; Lysias 13.44; Xenophon, *Hellenika* 2.3.39). A general and a supporter of the democracy, he was said to be of impeccable personal character.

ἀποθάνοι Optative in a purpose clause in secondary sequence.

32c6–7 **οἷα . . . ἄλλοις . . . πολλοῖς πολλά** "Many such things to many people." Note the elaborate chiastic (a b b a) structure Plato uses for this clause. He clearly wishes to draw special attention to it, thereby distancing Socrates and himself from the excesses of the Thirty. This was necessary, since many might conclude from Socrates' frequent criticisms of Athenian democracy that he was therefore a supporter (see on 20e8). Such a perception would have been reinforced by the fact that Critias, one of the leaders of the Thirty (and an uncle of Plato), had been one of the young men who gathered around Socrates. He is, in fact, portrayed as such by Plato in the *Protagoras* and the *Charmides*. He is not to be confused with his grandfather, who is the main speaker of the *Timaeus* and the eponymous *Critias* (for the family tree, see Nails 2002, 106–11).

Xenophon's *Memorabilia* (1.2.30) likewise labors to show that Socrates was not a supporter of the oligarchs and claims that there was bad blood between Socrates and Critias even before Critias had come to power. To illustrate the basis of their hostility, he tells a story about Critias's pursuit of Euthydemus, which caused Socrates to remark, "Critias seems to have the feelings of a pig: he can no more keep away from Euthydemus than pigs can keep from rubbing stones." For the sources, see Nails 2002, 100.

32c8 **ἀναπλῆσαι αἰτιῶν** "Taint with guilt." They wanted to dilute their own guilt by implicating as many citizens as possible in their crimes.

32d1 **αὖ** The repetition of the adverb emphasizes the degree to which Socrates' actions were motivated by his sense of justice, not his attachment to one regime or another. When the democracy acted unjustly, he resisted. Then, *in turn* (αὖ c4), the oligarchy took power and he, *in turn* (αὖ again), showed that he did not fear death.

32d2 **ἀγροικότερον** The line of thinking seems to be that a cultivated person makes fine distinctions and articulates them, whereas another speaking ἀγροικοτέρον puts things baldly, as Socrates does here.

ἄδικον μηδ᾽ ἀνόσιον ἐργάζεσθαι, τούτου δὲ τὸ πᾶν μέλει. ἐμὲ γὰρ ἐκείνη ἡ ἀρχὴ οὐκ ἐξέπληξεν, οὕτως ἰσχυρὰ οὖσα, ὥστε ἄδικόν τι ἐργάσασθαι, ἀλλ᾽ ἐπειδὴ ἐκ τῆς θόλου ἐξήλθομεν, οἱ μὲν τέτταρες ᾤχοντο εἰς Σαλαμῖνα καὶ ἤγαγον Λέοντα, ἐγὼ δὲ ᾠχόμην ἀπιὼν οἴκαδε. καὶ ἴσως ἂν διὰ ταῦτα ἀπέθανον, εἰ μὴ ἡ ἀρχὴ διὰ ταχέων κατελύθη. καὶ
τούτων ὑμῖν ἔσονται πολλοὶ μάρτυρες. e

ἀνόσιον < ἀνόσιος, -ον *impious*
ἀρχή, -ῆς, ἡ *regime*
ἐξέπληξεν < ἐκπλήττω *strike with panic*
ἰσχυρά < ἰσχυρός, -ά, -όν *powerful, strong*
ᾤχόντο impf. < οἴχομαι *go, depart*
κατελύθη < καταλύω *destroy, dissolve*

32d2–3 **τοῦ . . . ἐργάζεσθαι** Articular infinitive dependent on μέλει.
32d3 **τὸ πᾶν** "Entirely."
32d4 **οὖσα** The participle is concessive.

CHAPTER 21

(32e2–33b8)

"My only crime is to have been willing to discuss the right and the just with all who cared to listen, young and old, rich and poor." For additional discussion of the chapter and questions for study, see essay 21.

Ἀρ᾽ οὖν ἄν με οἴεσθε τοσάδε ἔτη διαγενέσθαι εἰ ἔπραττον τὰ δημόσια, καὶ πράττων ἀξίως ἀνδρὸς ἀγαθοῦ ἐβοήθουν τοῖς δικαίοις καί, ὥσπερ χρή, τοῦτο περὶ πλείστου ἐποιούμην; πολλοῦ γε δεῖ, ὦ ἄνδρες Ἀθηναῖοι· οὐδὲ γὰρ ἂν ἄλλος
33 ἀνθρώπων οὐδείς. ἀλλ᾽ ἐγὼ διὰ παντὸς τοῦ βίου δημοσίᾳ τε εἴ πού τι ἔπραξα τοιοῦτος φανοῦμαι, καὶ ἰδίᾳ ὁ αὐτὸς οὗτος, οὐδενὶ πώποτε συγχωρήσας οὐδὲν παρὰ τὸ δίκαιον οὔτε ἄλλῳ οὔτε τούτων οὐδενὶ οὓς δὴ διαβάλλοντες ἐμέ φασιν ἐμοὺς μαθητὰς εἶναι. ἐγὼ δὲ διδάσκαλος μὲν οὐδενὸς

διαγενέσθαι aor. mid. infin. < διαγίγνομαι *pass through*
συγχωρήσας < συγχωρέω *go along with, collude with*
μαθητάς < μαθητής, -οῦ, ὁ *pupil*
διδάσκαλος, -ου, ὁ *teacher*

32e3 **τὰ δημόσια** "Public business."

32e4 **τοῖς δικαίοις** Neuter abstraction: "justice."

32e5 **πολλοῦ γε δεῖ** "Far from it."

ἄν In the apodosis of a past counterfactual condition. Supply the protasis and τοσάδε ἔτη διαγενέσθαι from the previous sentence.

33a1–3 The mixture of aorist (ἔπραξα) and future (φανοῦμαι) is odd. Two ideas seem to be conflated: the idea that Socrates' public behavior has been consistent with his private actions, and the idea that this will continue to be the case in the future.

33a2 **τοιοῦτος** Precisely *what* sort of men he means is explained by οὐδενὶ πώποτε συγχωρήσας . . . (below).

ἰδίᾳ ὁ αὐτὸς οὗτος "The same person in private affairs."

33a5–b3 "I am not a teacher, but a conversationalist."

πώποτ' ἐγενόμην· εἰ δέ τίς μου λέγοντος καὶ τὰ ἐμαυτοῦ
πράττοντος ἐπιθυμοῖ ἀκούειν, εἴτε νεώτερος εἴτε πρεσβύτερος,
οὐδενὶ πώποτε ἐφθόνησα, οὐδὲ χρήματα μὲν λαμβάνων διαλέγομαι μὴ λαμβάνων δὲ οὔ, ἀλλ' ὁμοίως καὶ πλουσίῳ καὶ **b**
πένητι παρέχω ἐμαυτὸν ἐρωτᾶν, καὶ ἐάν τις βούληται
ἀποκρινόμενος ἀκούειν ὧν ἂν λέγω. καὶ τούτων ἐγὼ εἴτε
τις χρηστὸς γίγνεται εἴτε μή, οὐκ ἂν δικαίως τὴν αἰτίαν
ὑπέχοιμι, ὧν μήτε ὑπεσχόμην μηδενὶ μηδὲν πώποτε μάθημα
μήτε ἐδίδαξα· εἰ δέ τίς φησι παρ' ἐμοῦ πώποτέ τι μαθεῖν ἢ
ἀκοῦσαι ἰδίᾳ ὅτι μὴ καὶ οἱ ἄλλοι πάντες, εὖ ἴστε ὅτι οὐκ
ἀληθῆ λέγει.

ἐπιθυμεῖ < ἐπιθυμέω *desire*
ἐφθόνησα < φθονέω *begrudge*
πλουσίῳ < πλουσίος, -α, -ον *rich, wealthy*
πένητι < πένης, -ητος, ὁ *poor man*
ὑπέχοιμι < ὑπέχω *offer, incur (mid.)*
μάθημα, -ατος, τό *lesson*

33a6–7 **τὰ ἐμαυτοῦ πράττοντος . . . ἀκούειν** "Listen to me practicing my way of life." ἀκούω takes the genitive, but πράττω normally refers to the realm of action, not speech. Socrates' ἔργον, however, is precisely his λόγος.

33b1 **μὴ λαμβάνων δὲ οὔ** Supply χρήματα as the object of the participle and διαλέγομαι to go with οὔ: "Nor do I refuse to converse if I don't get paid."

33b2 **ἐρωτᾶν** Infinitive of purpose: "for questioning." Note again that Socrates offers himself for questioning, as well as questioning others. But as the next line makes clear, they must be willing to answer as well.

33b3–8 "Anyone who says I ever taught him does not speak the truth." On one level, this is absolutely true. The goal of Socratic conversation is not the transmission of preexisting information, but self-examination and testing. Thus, he cannot cause someone to become good or bad. Only the individual under "examination" brings about that change.

33b5 **ὧν** The antecedent is τούτων.

33b5–6 **ὑπεσχόμην . . . μάθημα μήτε ἐδίδαξα** "I never offered a lesson or taught one."

CHAPTER 22

(33b9–34b5)

"Nonetheless, young men congregate around me, because they enjoy hearing those who pretend to be wise interrogated." For additional discussion of the chapter and questions for study, see essay 22.

Ἀλλὰ διὰ τί δή ποτε μετ' ἐμοῦ χαίρουσί τινες πολὺν
c χρόνον διατρίβοντες; ἀκηκόατε, ὦ ἄνδρες Ἀθηναῖοι, πᾶσαν
ὑμῖν τὴν ἀλήθειαν ἐγὼ εἶπον· ὅτι ἀκούοντες χαίρουσιν
ἐξεταζομένοις τοῖς οἰομένοις μὲν εἶναι σοφοῖς, οὖσι δ' οὔ.
ἔστι γὰρ οὐκ ἀηδές. ἐμοὶ δὲ τοῦτο, ὡς ἐγώ φημι, προστέτακται ὑπὸ τοῦ θεοῦ πράττειν καὶ ἐκ μαντείων καὶ ἐξ ἐνυπνίων

διατρίβοντες < διατρίβω *consume, spend*
ἀηδές < ἀηδής, -ές *unpleasant*
προστέτακται pf. pass. indic. < προστάττω *command, assign*

33c2 **ὅτι** "It is because . . ." ὅτι picks up the τί from b9.

33c3 **ἐξεταζομένοις . . . οἰομένοις . . . σοφοῖς, οὖσι** The datives all depend on χαίρουσι. σοφοῖς is the predicate of τοῖς . . . οὖσι δ' οὐ: "who think that they are wise . . . but are not."

33c4 **προστέτακται** Socrates insists that his experience should be understood within the traditional patterns of Greek religious experience. He has already discussed the oracle from Apollo in detail. At the beginning of *Phaedo* (60e), Socrates describes a recurring dream that he interpreted as offering him encouragement to pursue a life devoted to philosophy. Note, however, that at c4 (οὐκ ἀηδές), he appears to admit that there are fringe benefits to his way of life as well.

33c5 **ἐξ ἐνυπνίων** "In dreams." Whereas there may be some irony in the story of Chaerephon's consultation with the Delphic oracle (20e6–21e2), here the emphasis on repeated dreams seems to suggest that his philosophical inquiry is based on a desire that is deeply personal and in the end transrational. Although Socrates elsewhere mentions dreams that he interprets as divine instruction or encouragement (*Crito* 44a, *Phaedo* 60e), this is the only place where he mentions dreams as an impetus for his life's mission.

καὶ παντὶ τρόπῳ ᾧπέρ τίς ποτε καὶ ἄλλη θεία μοῖρα ἀνθρώπῳ
καὶ ὁτιοῦν προσέταξε πράττειν. ταῦτα, ὦ ἄνδρες Ἀθηναῖοι,
καὶ ἀληθῆ ἐστιν καὶ εὐέλεγκτα. εἰ γὰρ δὴ ἔγωγε τῶν νέων
τοὺς μὲν διαφθείρω τοὺς δὲ διέφθαρκα, χρῆν δήπου, εἴτε d
τινὲς αὐτῶν πρεσβύτεροι γενόμενοι ἔγνωσαν ὅτι νέοις οὖσιν
αὐτοῖς ἐγὼ κακὸν πώποτέ τι συνεβούλευσα, νυνὶ αὐτοὺς
ἀναβαίνοντας ἐμοῦ κατηγορεῖν καὶ τιμωρεῖσθαι· εἰ δὲ μὴ
αὐτοὶ ἤθελον, τῶν οἰκείων τινὰς τῶν ἐκείνων, πατέρας καὶ
ἀδελφοὺς καὶ ἄλλους τοὺς προσήκοντας, εἴπερ ὑπ᾽ ἐμοῦ τι
κακὸν ἐπεπόνθεσαν αὐτῶν οἱ οἰκεῖοι, νῦν μεμνῆσθαι καὶ
τιμωρεῖσθαι. πάντως δὲ πάρεισιν αὐτῶν πολλοὶ ἐνταυθοῖ
οὓς ἐγὼ ὁρῶ, πρῶτον μὲν Κρίτων οὑτοσί, ἐμὸς ἡλικιώτης
καὶ δημότης, Κριτοβούλου τοῦδε πατήρ, ἔπειτα Λυσανίας ὁ e

μοῖρα, -ας, ἡ *fate*
εὐέλεγκτα < εὐέλεγκτος, -ον *easy to test*
διέφθαρκα pf. act. indic. < διαφθείρω *corrupt*
συνεβούλευσα < συμβουλεύω *advise*
τιμωρεῖσθαι < τιμωρέω *take vengeance on*
οἰκείων < οἰκεῖος, -α, -ον *belonging to the household, family*
προσήκοντας < προσήκω (here) *relatives*
ἐπεπόνθεσαν pluperf. act. < πάσχω *suffer, experience*
πάντως (here) *at any rate*
ἡλικιώτης, -ου, ὁ *contemporary*
δημότης, -ου, ὁ *fellow demesman*

33d1 **τοὺς μέν . . . τοὺς δέ . . .** "Some . . . others . . ."
χρῆν Imperfect of χρή, here with ἄν, as frequently.

33d2 **πρεσβύτεροι** Take with γενόμενοι: "now that they're older."
νέοις οὖσι "When they were young."

33d4 **κατηγορεῖν . . . τιμωρεῖσθαι** Infinitives dependent on χρῆν. So also μεμνῆσθαι καὶ τιμωρεῖσθαι (d8).

33d6 **τινάς** Subject of μεμνῆσθαι and τιμωρεῖσθαι.

33d9–e1 **Κρίτων . . . Κριτοβούλου** Crito was a wealthy and well-connected friend of Socrates. He plays a prominent role in both Plato's and Xenophon's accounts of the Socratic circle. In the dialogue named after him, he is an emissary of unknown well-wishers who want to persuade Socrates to accept their financial and logistical assistance in securing his escape from prison and flight into exile. His son Critobolus is also one of the men present at the death of Socrates (*Phaedo* 59b).

Σφήττιος, Αἰσχίνου τοῦδε πατήρ, ἔτι δ' Ἀντιφῶν ὁ Κηφισιεὺς οὑτοσί, Ἐπιγένους πατήρ, ἄλλοι τοίνυν οὗτοι ὧν οἱ ἀδελφοὶ ἐν ταύτῃ τῇ διατριβῇ γεγόνασιν, Νικόστρατος Θεοζοτίδου, ἀδελφὸς Θεοδότου—καὶ ὁ μὲν Θεόδοτος τετελεύτηκεν, ὥστε οὐκ ἂν ἐκεῖνός γε αὐτοῦ καταδεηθείη—καὶ Παράλιος ὅδε, ὁ Δημοδόκου, οὗ ἦν Θεάγης ἀδελφός· ὅδε δὲ
34 Ἀδείμαντος, ὁ Ἀρίστωνος, οὗ ἀδελφὸς οὑτοσὶ Πλάτων, καὶ

διατριβῇ < διατριβή, -ῆς, ἡ *pastime, way of living*
καταδεηθείη < καταδέω *beg, entreat*

33e1–2 **Λυσανίας . . . Αἰσχίνου** Not much is known about Lysanias of Sphettus, a deme of Attica, although his presence at the trial suggests that he was known as a supporter of Socrates. His son, Aeschines, is an important figure within the Socratic circle and also is part of the group mentioned in the *Phaedo*. He too was a writer of Socratic dialogues, including an *Alcibiades* and an *Aspasia*, of which some fragments remain.

33e2–3 **Ἀντιφῶν . . . Ἐπιγένους** Kephesia was a deme of northwest Athens. Of this Antiphon (not the well-known orator) little is known. His son, Epigenes, is similarly obscure, except for the reference here and his presence in *Phaedo*.

33e4–5 **Νικόστρατος . . . Θεοζοτίδου . . . Θεοδότου** Nothing much about Nicostratos is known. His father, Theozotides, was a democratic politician who proposed a decree extending pension benefits to the orphans of Athenian citizens killed in the war that drove out the oligarchs (Nails 2002, 283–84). Nothing is known of the son.

33e7–34a1 **Παράλιος . . . Δημοδόκου . . . Θεάγης** Most of the manuscripts here read Πάραλος, but our text has been emended on the basis of an inscription that refers to a Paralius who served as treasurer in 390 B.C.E. (*Inscriptiones Graeci* II^2 1400). The name is uncommon, however, and the emendation may well be incorrect. Demodocus may be the same general mentioned by Thucydides (4.75). In the *Theages* (a dialogue attributed to Plato but regarded as spurious by many), he seeks out the advice of Socrates to find a teacher for his son Theages, who is also mentioned in the *Republic*.

34a1–2 **Ἀδείμαντος, ὁ Ἀρίστωνος . . . Πλάτων** Plato's father, Ariston, is reported to have traced his ancestry back to Codrus, one of the legendary kings of Athens, and from there to Poseidon (Diogenes Laertius 3.1). His wife's lineage was equally impressive, for she counted Solon the lawgiver as one of her ancestors. Their three sons figure unequally in the Platonic dialogues. Adeimantus and Glaucon are the primary interlocutors of Socrates in the *Republic* and appear briefly at the beginning of *Parmenides*. Their brother, who actually wrote the dialogues, is shyer. In addition to this passage, he will be mentioned again at 38b as one of the friends of Socrates who have offered to contribute money to pay a fine. He is conspicuously absent from the execution of Socrates, and we learn from Phaedo, the narrator, that he was ill (59b).

Αἰαντόδωρος, οὗ Ἀπολλόδωρος ὅδε ἀδελφός. καὶ ἄλλους
πολλοὺς ἐγὼ ἔχω ὑμῖν εἰπεῖν, ὧν τινα ἐχρῆν μάλιστα μὲν ἐν
τῷ ἑαυτοῦ λόγῳ παρασχέσθαι Μέλητον μάρτυρα· εἰ δὲ τότε
ἐπελάθετο, νῦν παρασχέσθω—ἐγὼ παραχωρῶ—καὶ λεγέτω
εἴ τι ἔχει τοιοῦτον. ἀλλὰ τούτου πᾶν τοὐναντίον εὑρήσετε,
ὦ ἄνδρες, πάντας ἐμοὶ βοηθεῖν ἑτοίμους τῷ διαφθείροντι, τῷ
κακὰ ἐργαζομένῳ τοὺς οἰκείους αὐτῶν, ὥς φασι Μέλητος καὶ
Ἄνυτος. αὐτοὶ μὲν γὰρ οἱ διεφθαρμένοι τάχ' ἂν λόγον b
ἔχοιεν βοηθοῦντες· οἱ δὲ ἀδιάφθαρτοι, πρεσβύτεροι ἤδη
ἄνδρες, οἱ τούτων προσήκοντες, τίνα ἄλλον ἔχουσι λόγον
βοηθοῦντες ἐμοὶ ἀλλ' ἢ τὸν ὀρθόν τε καὶ δίκαιον, ὅτι
συνίσασι Μελήτῳ μὲν ψευδομένῳ, ἐμοὶ δὲ ἀληθεύοντι;

παραχωρῶ < παραχωρέω *yield*
διαφθαρμένοι pf. pass. part. < διαφθείρω *corrupt*
ἀδιάφθαρτοι < ἀδιάφθαρτος, -ον *uncorrupted*
συνίσασι < συνοῖδα *be conscious*
ἀληθεύοντι < ἀληθεύω *tell the truth*

34a2 **Αἰαντόδωρος . . . Ἀπολλόδωρος** Aiantodorus is not known outside of this passage. Apollodorus, however, is mentioned by Xenophon as someone who followed Socrates assiduously (*Memorabilia* 3.11.17). He was present at the death of Socrates, according to the *Phaedo*, where his excessive emotionalism is assumed (59b1). He also narrates the *Symposium*, where he is accused of having scorn for everyone who has not, like him, abandoned all his business to follow Socrates (173d).

34a4 **Μέλητον** Subject of παρασχέσθαι.

34a5 **παρασχέσθω . . . λεγέτω** Third-person imperatives.

34a6 **τι . . . τοιοῦτον** For example, a disgruntled former associate or family member.

34a7 **πάντας** Subject of βοηθεῖν.

34b4 **τόν** Supply λόγον.

CHAPTER 23

(34b6–35b8)

Conclusion: "I have made my defense. I will not debase myself and the court with the usual histrionics." For additional discussion of the chapter and questions for study, see essay 23.

Εἶεν δή, ὦ ἄνδρες· ἃ μὲν ἐγὼ ἔχοιμ' ἂν ἀπολογεῖσθαι,
σχεδόν ἐστι ταῦτα καὶ ἄλλα ἴσως τοιαῦτα. τάχα δ' ἄν τις
c ὑμῶν ἀγανακτήσειεν ἀναμνησθεὶς ἑαυτοῦ, εἰ ὁ μὲν καὶ ἐλάττω
τουτουῒ τοῦ ἀγῶνος ἀγῶνα ἀγωνιζόμενος ἐδεήθη τε καὶ

σχεδόν *nearly, almost*
ἀγανακτήσειεν < ἀγανακτέω *be angry*
ἀγωνιζόμενος < ἀγωνίζομαι *contend, fight*
ἐδεήθη < aor. pass. indic. < δέομαι *beg*

34b6 **ἅ** The relative is dependent on ταῦτα in the next line.
ἔχοιμ' Potential optative.

34c1 **ἀναμνησθεὶς ἑαυτοῦ** "Remembering himself," that is, his own behavior. Precisely *what* someone might remember and resent is explained by the μέν . . . δέ clauses that follow. Socrates' statement is not as far-fetched as it may sound to modern readers typically unacquainted with the inner workings of a court, except as represented by television drama. It was not uncommon for the kind of men who served as jurors (as opposed to the country folk who seldom came to town) to take part in legal proceedings at some time in their lives. Fifth-century Athens was a highly litigious society. Inheritance disputes were common, as were those involving business contracts. Perceived religious offenses, too, could land a citizen in court. The courts were also used as a tool of political warfare, as in the present case. Jurors who had been defendants themselves might have expected to find their own behavior vindicated, if "the wise Socrates" struggled to get himself off just as hard as they did. Socrates imagines that they may resent his refusal to beg for their mercy.

34c1–2 **ἐλάττω τουτουῒ τοῦ ἀγῶνος ἀγῶνα ἀγωνιζόμενος** "Contesting a lesser charge than this one." This elaborate play on words, which is not reflected by the translation, uses both polyptoton (< πολύ "many" + πτῶσις "fall"), the use of a single noun in various cases (< πτῶσις, *casus*, "fall, case"), and *figura etymologica*, the adjacent use of etymologically related words, to create a rhetorical tour de force, even as Socrates is also claiming to eschew the

ἱκέτευσε τοὺς δικαστὰς μετὰ πολλῶν δακρύων, παιδία τε
αὑτοῦ ἀναβιβασάμενος ἵνα ὅτι μάλιστα ἐλεηθείη, καὶ ἄλλους
τῶν οἰκείων καὶ φίλων πολλούς, ἐγὼ δὲ οὐδὲν ἄρα τούτων
ποιήσω, καὶ ταῦτα κινδυνεύων, ὡς ἂν δόξαιμι, τὸν ἔσχατον
κίνδυνον. τάχ' ἂν οὖν τις ταῦτα ἐννοήσας αὐθαδέστερον
ἂν πρός με σχοίη καὶ ὀργισθεὶς αὐτοῖς τούτοις θεῖτο ἂν μετ'
ὀργῆς τὴν ψῆφον. εἰ δή τις ὑμῶν οὕτως ἔχει—οὐκ ἀξιῶ **d**
μὲν γὰρ ἔγωγε, εἰ δ' οὖν—ἐπιεικῆ ἄν μοι δοκῶ πρὸς τοῦτον
λέγειν λέγων ὅτι "'Εμοί, ὦ ἄριστε, εἰσὶν μέν πού τινες καὶ
οἰκεῖοι· καὶ γὰρ τοῦτο αὐτὸ τὸ τοῦ 'Ομήρου, οὐδ' ἐγὼ 'ἀπὸ

ἱκέτευσε < ἱκετεύω *approach as a suppliant*
δακρύων < δάκρυον, -ου, τό *tear*
παιδία < παίδιον, -ου, τό *child*
ἀναβιβασάμενος < ἀναβιβάζω *bring into court*
ὅτι μάλιστα *as much as possible*
ἐλεηθείη aor. pass. opt. < ἐλεέω *pity*
ἔσχατον < ἔσχατος, -η, -ον *extreme, last*
ἐννοήσας < ἐννοέω *consider*
ὀργισθείς aor. pass. part. < ὀργίζω *be angry, grow angry*
ὀργῆς < ὀργή, -ῆς, ἡ *anger*
ἐπιεικῆ < ἐπιεικής, -ές *suitable, reasonable*

---

trappings of traditional courtroom performance. An ἐλάττων ἀγών would be one that is not a capital trial and hence would warrant even less the kind of courtroom histrionics Socrates here rejects.

34c6 **τὸν ἔσχατον κίνδυνον** That is, death. Socrates contrasts both his behavior and (as he imagines) that of the jurors with the relative seriousness of their respective situations.

ἄν The particle anticipates the potential optative that follows (σχοίη). Note the repetition of ἄν with the verb nevertheless.

34c7–8 **αὐθαδέστερον . . . σχοίη** "Be remorseless." ἔχω + adverb is frequently used idiomatically to mean "be in a condition."

αὐτοῖς τούτοις Causal, referring to ταῦτα (c7).

34c8 **θεῖτο . . . ψῆφον** "Vote." For the procedure, see on 30e1.

34d1 **ἀξιῶ** "Expect," but also "deem worthy." Socrates ironically says that he does not think the jurors will react in such a fashion, because such behavior would be unworthy of them.

34d2 **εἰ δ'οὖν** "But if he does . . ."

ἄν . . . λέγειν Infinitive after δοκῶ.

34d3 **ὅτι** Do not translate.

34d4 **τὸ τοῦ 'Ομήρου** "As Homer says" (literally, "with respect to the thing of Homer"). He is quoting Penelope's words to the disguised Odysseus at *Odyssey* 19.163: "You are not born from an ancient oak or rock." Socrates' refusal to seek pity from the jurors does not mean that he is a misanthropic loner without family, but simply that he is a man with high ethical standards.

δρυὸς οὐδ᾽ ἀπὸ πέτρης᾽ πέφυκα ἀλλ᾽ ἐξ ἀνθρώπων, ὥστε
καὶ οἰκεῖοί μοί εἰσι καὶ ὑεῖς γε, ὦ ἄνδρες Ἀθηναῖοι, τρεῖς, εἷς
μὲν μειράκιον ἤδη, δύο δὲ παιδία· ἀλλ᾽ ὅμως οὐδένα αὐτῶν
δεῦρο ἀναβιβασάμενος δεήσομαι ὑμῶν ἀποψηφίσασθαι." τί
δὴ οὖν οὐδὲν τούτων ποιήσω; οὐκ αὐθαδιζόμενος, ὦ ἄνδρες
e Ἀθηναῖοι, οὐδ᾽ ὑμᾶς ἀτιμάζων, ἀλλ᾽ εἰ μὲν θαρραλέως ἐγὼ
ἔχω πρὸς θάνατον ἢ μή, ἄλλος λόγος, πρὸς δ᾽ οὖν δόξαν καὶ
ἐμοὶ καὶ ὑμῖν καὶ ὅλῃ τῇ πόλει οὔ μοι δοκεῖ καλὸν εἶναι ἐμὲ
τούτων οὐδὲν ποιεῖν καὶ τηλικόνδε ὄντα καὶ τοῦτο τοὔνομα
ἔχοντα, εἴτ᾽ οὖν ἀληθὲς εἴτ᾽ οὖν ψεῦδος, ἀλλ᾽ οὖν δεδογμένον
35 γέ ἐστι τὸν Σωκράτη διαφέρειν τινι τῶν πολλῶν ἀνθρώπων.

δρυός < δρῦς, -ός, ἡ *oak*
πέτρης < πέτρη, -ης, ἡ *rock*
πέφυκα pf. act. indic. < φύω *be born*
ἀποψηφίσασθαι < ἀποψηφίζομαι *acquit*
ἀτιμάζων < ἀτιμάζω *dishonor*
θαρραλέως *courageously*
δεδογμένον . . . ἐστι 3rd sing. pf. pass. indic. (periphrastic form) < δοκέω *think*

34d6 **ὑεῖς . . . τρεῖς** Their names were Lamprocles, Sophroniscus, and Menexenus. They do not figure in the dialogues of Plato. In the *Memorabilia* of Xenophon (2.2), Socrates advises Lamprocles to get along better with his mother, Xanthippe.

34d9 **αὐθαδιζόμενος** "Acting at my own pleasure," that is, without regard for the expectations of the audience. The verb is formed from αὐτό (self) + ἥδομαι (enjoy). See on 34c8 for the virtually synonymous αὐθαδέστερον . . . σχοίη.

34e1 **θαρραλέως** A recurring theme throughout the speech is mankind's fear of death. Socrates recognizes its powerful force in determining human behavior and argues that it must be resisted. Later, in a speech of consolation to his supporters, he will envision two models of death that should not cause us to be anxious (40c–41c). For now, he pauses to consider that he has gone too far and that by forcing members of his audience to consider their own mortality and by facing death bravely himself, he may have alienated them further, making them even less receptive to philosophy. He refers to his personal bravery as irrelevant (ἄλλος λόγος) and continues by steering the speech back to something he feels they will understand—the reputation of Athens (δόξα e2).

34e3 **ἐμοί . . . ὑμῖν . . . ὅλῃ τῇ πόλει** Datives of possession.

34e4 **τούτων** The pronoun is neuter. He means things such as begging for mercy, parading one's children before the jury, and so forth.
ὄντα . . . ἔχοντα Agreeing with ἐμέ.
τοὔνομα = τὸ ὄνομα. He refers to his reputation for wisdom.

34e5–35a1 **δεδογμένον . . . ἐστι** The subject is τὸ Σωκράτη διαφέρειν (35a1): "The notion that Socrates is better than many men in some way is believed, anyway."

εἰ οὖν ὑμῶν οἱ δοκοῦντες διαφέρειν εἴτε σοφίᾳ εἴτε ἀνδρείᾳ εἴτε ἄλλῃ ᾑτινιοῦν ἀρετῇ τοιοῦτοι ἔσονται, αἰσχρὸν ἂν εἴη· οἵουσπερ ἐγὼ πολλάκις ἑώρακά τινας ὅταν κρίνωνται, δοκοῦντας μέν τι εἶναι, θαυμάσια δὲ ἐργαζομένους, ὡς δεινόν τι οἰομένους πείσεσθαι εἰ ἀποθανοῦνται, ὥσπερ ἀθανάτων ἐσομένων ἂν ὑμεῖς αὐτοὺς μὴ ἀποκτείνητε· οἳ ἐμοὶ δοκοῦσιν αἰσχύνην τῇ πόλει περιάπτειν, ὥστ' ἄν τινα καὶ τῶν ξένων ὑπολαβεῖν ὅτι οἱ διαφέροντες Ἀθηναίων εἰς ἀρετήν, οὓς b

---

ἀνδρείᾳ < ἀνδρεία, -ας, ἡ *courage*
ἑώρακα pf. act. indic. < ὁράω *see*
πείσεσθαι fut. mid. infin. < πάσχω *suffer*
περιάπτειν < περιάπτω *attach*
ὑπολαβεῖν aor. act. infin. < ὑπολαμβάνω *understand, suppose*

35a1–b3 A complex sentence in three parts that marks the climax of Socrates' argument against the usual rituals of throwing oneself on the mercy of the court.

35a1–3 The first part.

35a3 **ᾑτινιοῦν** Fem. dat. sg. ὅστις + οὖν.

τοιοῦτοι ἔσονται "Will be like that," that is, disgracing one's good name by engaging in unworthy acts. The future indicative in the protasis, as opposed to the subjunctive or the optative, connotes strong emotional involvement on the part of the speaker (cf. Smyth 1956, 2328).

35a4–7 The second part.

35a4 **οἵουσπερ . . . τινας** "Men of this very sort."

35a5 **δοκοῦντας τι εἶναι** "Seeming to be something"; that is, "having a good reputation."

θαυμασία δὲ ἐργαζόμενος "But acting in an astounding way."

35a6 **δεινόν τι οἰομένους πείσεσθαι** Socrates brings the discussion back to the irrational fear of death.

35a7 **ἀθανάτων ἐσομένων** (< εἰμί) Genitive absolute. The subject is the same as that of ἀποθανοῦνται. It is unusual for the main verb and a genitive absolute to share the same subject and so draws the reader's attention with special emphasis to this phrase.

ἄν = ἐάν.

35a7–b3 The final part and climax of the sentence. By such behavior the Athenians shame themselves before others.

35a8–b1 **ὥστ' ἄν . . . ὑπολαβεῖν** ἄν + the infinitive expresses a *possible* result.

35b1 **οἱ διαφέροντες Ἀθηναίων εἰς ἀρετήν** "The Athenians who are most outstanding (lit. 'the ones superior with respect to excellence')."

αὐτοὶ ἑαυτῶν ἔν τε ταῖς ἀρχαῖς καὶ ταῖς ἄλλαις τιμαῖς προκρίνουσιν, οὗτοι γυναικῶν οὐδὲν διαφέρουσιν. ταῦτα γάρ, ὦ ἄνδρες Ἀθηναῖοι, οὔτε ὑμᾶς χρὴ ποιεῖν τοὺς δοκοῦντας καὶ ὁπῃοῦν τι εἶναι, οὔτ', ἂν ἡμεῖς ποιῶμεν, ὑμᾶς ἐπιτρέπειν, ἀλλὰ τοῦτο αὐτὸ ἐνδείκνυσθαι, ὅτι πολὺ μᾶλλον καταψηφιεῖσθε τοῦ τὰ ἐλεινὰ ταῦτα δράματα εἰσάγοντος καὶ καταγέλαστον τὴν πόλιν ποιοῦντος ἢ τοῦ ἡσυχίαν ἄγοντος.

προκρίνουσιν < προκρίνω *choose before others, prefer*
ὁπῃοῦν *in any way whatsoever*
ἐπιτρέπειν < ἐπιτρέπω *permit*
ἐνδείκνυσθαι < ἐνδείκνυμι *demonstrate*
καταψηφιεῖσθε fut. < καταψηφίζομαι *vote against, condemn*
ἡσυχίαν < ἡσυχία, -ας, ἡ *peace, quiet*

35b2 **αὐτοί** "They themselves."
ἀρχαῖς . . . τιμαῖς Many offices in the fifth century were determined by lot, especially if they were thought to require loyalty rather than skill. Others, particularly military commands, were elective. See Aristotle, *Constitution of the Athenians* 61. ἀρχαί and τιμαί are probably synonymous here, as at Aristotle *Politics* 1281a31: τιμὰς γὰρ λέγομεν τὰς ἀρχάς.

35b3 **γυναικῶν** The casual misogyny is striking to modern readers but not exceptional for the time and place.

35b4–5 **δοκοῦντας τι εἶναι** For the idiom, see on 35a5.

35b5 **ἄν . . . ποιῶμεν** ἄν = ἐάν in the protasis of a future more vivid condition.

35b6 **μᾶλλον** The comparative looks ahead to ἤ in b8. Translate as "rather."

35b7 **τοῦ . . . εἰσάγοντος καὶ ποιοῦντος** Genitive of the person charged. εἰσάγειν is common in both forensic and dramatic contexts.
τὰ ἐλεινὰ ταῦτα δράματα "These pitiful scenes."

CHAPTER 24

(35b9–d8)

"Jurors swear to the gods to uphold justice, and those of us who truly believe in the gods should trust that they will honor their oath." For additional discussion of the chapter and questions for study, see essay 24.

Χωρὶς δὲ τῆς δόξης, ὦ ἄνδρες, οὐδὲ δίκαιόν μοι δοκεῖ
εἶναι δεῖσθαι τοῦ δικαστοῦ οὐδὲ δεόμενον ἀποφεύγειν, ἀλλὰ c
διδάσκειν καὶ πείθειν. οὐ γὰρ ἐπὶ τούτῳ κάθηται ὁ δικαστής, ἐπὶ τῷ καταχαρίζεσθαι τὰ δίκαια, ἀλλ' ἐπὶ τῷ κρίνειν
ταῦτα· καὶ ὀμώμοκεν οὐ χαριεῖσθαι οἷς ἂν δοκῇ αὐτῷ, ἀλλὰ

ἀποφεύγειν < ἀποφεύγω *escape, be acquitted*
κάθηται < κάθημαι *sit as a judge*
καταχαρίζεσθαι < καταχαρίζομαι *do a favor*
ὀμώμοκεν pf. act. indic. < ὄμνυμι *swear*
χαριεῖσθαι fut. mid. infin. < χαρίζομαι *gratify*

35b9 **χωρὶς δὲ τῆς δόξης** "Apart from the notoriety" (discussed at 35a4). Appeals to pity are also bad, because they corrupt the administration of justice and invite jurors to make decisions on the basis of sympathy rather than justice.
δίκαιόν μοι δοκεῖ The expression here takes *both* a complementary infinitive (δεῖσθαι) and a subject accusative + infinitive construction (δεόμενον ἀποφεύγειν): "It doesn't seem to me just to beg, nor for someone who begs to be acquitted."

35c2 **ἐπὶ τούτῳ** "With a view to this." The phrase anticipates the two articular infinitives below.

35c3 **ἐπὶ τῷ καταχαρίζεσθει τὰ δίκαια** "With the expectation of dispensing justice as a favor."

35c4 **ὀμώμοκεν** The subject is ὁ δικαστής.
χαριεῖσθαι The tense of the infinitive indicates action subsequent to ὀμώμοκεν. So also δικάσειν (< δικάζω).

δικάσειν κατὰ τοὺς νόμους. οὔκουν χρὴ οὔτε ἡμᾶς ἐθίζειν
ὑμᾶς ἐπιορκεῖν οὔθ' ὑμᾶς ἐθίζεσθαι· οὐδέτεροι γὰρ ἂν ἡμῶν
εὐσεβοῖεν. μὴ οὖν ἀξιοῦτέ με, ὦ ἄνδρες Ἀθηναῖοι, τοιαῦτα
δεῖν πρὸς ὑμᾶς πράττειν ἃ μήτε ἡγοῦμαι καλὰ εἶναι μήτε
d δίκαια μήτε ὅσια, ἄλλως τε μέντοι νὴ Δία πάντως καὶ ἀσεβείας φεύγοντα ὑπὸ Μελήτου τουτουΐ. σαφῶς γὰρ ἄν, εἰ
πείθοιμι ὑμᾶς καὶ τῷ δεῖσθαι βιαζοίμην ὀμωμοκότας, θεοὺς
ἂν διδάσκοιμι μὴ ἡγεῖσθαι ὑμᾶς εἶναι, καὶ ἀτεχνῶς ἀπολογούμενος κατηγοροίην ἂν ἐμαυτοῦ ὡς θεοὺς οὐ νομίζω. ἀλλὰ
πολλοῦ δεῖ οὕτως ἔχειν· νομίζω τε γάρ, ὦ ἄνδρες Ἀθηναῖοι,

δικάσειν fut. act. infin. < δικάζω *judge*
ἐπιορκεῖν < ἐπιορκέω *break an oath*
ἐθίζεσθαι < ἐθίζω *become accustomed*
εὐσεβοῖεν < εὐσεβέω *be pious*
ὅσια < ὅσιος, -α, -ον *holy*
ἀσεβείας < ἀσέβεια, -ας, ἡ *impiety*
βιαζοίμην < βιάζω *constrain, overpower by force*

35c5 **ἡμᾶς** That is, those of us who are on trial and who might indulge in this kind of activity, if we thought it would be tolerated.

35c7 **οὖν** The particle indicates that Socrates is coming back to the point made about the presumed expectation that he will throw himself at the mercy of the court, make a display of his children, and other such things (τοιαῦτα c8). Translate "So, . . ."

35d1 **ἄλλως τε** "Especially," made more emphatic by μέντοι νὴ Δία. By piling up particles and adverbs, Socrates postpones, and thus builds suspense for, the ironic paradox of defending himself impiously against a charge of impiety.

35d2 **φεύγοντα** "Since I am being prosecuted for," agreeing with με (c7).

σαφῶς γὰρ ἄν The sentence is a future-less-vivid conditional (opt. in the protasis, opt. + ἄν in the main clause. The words quoted go with the apodosis θεοὺς ἂν διδάσκοιμι . . .). Note the pleonastic repetition of ἄν at d4.

35d3 **τῷ δεῖσθαι** Articular infinitive, "by begging."

35d4 **μὴ ἡγεῖσθαι . . . εἶναι** "Not to believe the gods exist."

35d4–5 **ἀπολογούμενος κατηγοροίην ἄν** "I would prosecute myself while attempting to defend." There are no wasted words. Note how the economy of Plato's style heightens Socrates' paradox.

35d5 **ὡς** "On the grounds that . . ."

35d6 **πολλοῦ δεῖ οὕτως ἔχειν** "But this is far from the case."

νομίζω Supply τοὺς θεούς.

ὡς οὐδεὶς τῶν ἐμῶν κατηγόρων, καὶ ὑμῖν ἐπιτρέπω καὶ τῷ θεῷ κρῖναι περὶ ἐμοῦ ὅπῃ μέλλει ἐμοί τε ἄριστα εἶναι καὶ ὑμῖν.

ἐπιτρέπω *trust in*

35d7 **ὡς οὐδεὶς τῶν ἐμῶν κατηγόρων** "As none of my accusors [do]."
35d8 **ὅπῃ μέλλει . . . ἄριστα** "How it will be best."

THE VERDICT

The ἀπολογία proper ends at this point. The jurors now proceed to vote. Ballots are then counted and the verdict is announced. It is determined that Socrates has been convicted by a small margin. Next comes the penalty phase. According to the process, after accusor and accused propose penalties, the jury votes again to choose between the two. They are not allowed to substitute a penalty of their own devising. The prosecution has recommended death as a punishment, and the speech resumes with Socrates' counterproposal (ἀντιτίμησις).

CHAPTER 25

(35e1–36b2)

"The vote was much closer than I thought it would be." For additional discussion of the chapter and questions for study, see essay 25.

e Τὸ μὲν μὴ ἀγανακτεῖν, ὦ ἄνδρες Ἀθηναῖοι, ἐπὶ τούτῳ
36 τῷ γεγονότι, ὅτι μου κατεψηφίσασθε, ἄλλα τέ μοι πολλὰ
συμβάλλεται, καὶ οὐκ ἀνέλπιστόν μοι γέγονεν τὸ γεγονὸς
τοῦτο, ἀλλὰ πολὺ μᾶλλον θαυμάζω ἑκατέρων τῶν ψήφων
τὸν γεγονότα ἀριθμόν. οὐ γὰρ ᾤόμην ἔγωγε οὕτω παρ᾽
ὀλίγον ἔσεσθαι ἀλλὰ παρὰ πολύ· νῦν δέ, ὡς ἔοικεν, εἰ
τριάκοντα μόναι μετέπεσον τῶν ψήφων, ἀπεπεφεύγη ἄν.

ἀγανακτεῖν < ἀγανακτέω *be angry*
συμβάλλεται *contribute*
ἀνέλπιστον *unexpectedly*
ἑκατέρων < ἑκάτερος, -α, -ον *on either side*
μετέπεσον aor. act. indic. < μεταπίπτω *change*
ἀπεπεφεύγη pluperf. act. < ἀποφεύγω *be found innocent*

35e1–36a4 The loose construction of the entire sentence mimics the syntax of extemporaneous improvisation.

35e1–2 **τό . . . μὴ ἀγανακτεῖν** The articular infinitive is used as an accusative of respect: "concerning my lack of anger."
τούτῳ τῷ γεγονότι "At this turn of events."

36a4 **τὸν γεγονότα ἀριθμόν** "The total."
οὕτω παρ᾽ ὀλίγον "By so few."

36a5–6 **εἰ τριάκοντα . . . ἀπεπεφεύγη ἄν** The condition is a variant of the past counterfactual, with the pluperfect indicative in the apodosis in place of the aorist indicative.

36a6 **μετέπεσον** Socrates' statement is plausible. Juries in the fifth century often consisted of 500 jurors, and if the vote had been 280–220, a shift of 30 would have resulted in a tie and therefore an acquittal. For a summary of the sources, see Brickhouse and Smith (1992).

 36a

Μέλητον μὲν οὖν, ὡς ἐμοὶ δοκῶ, καὶ νῦν ἀποπέφευγα, καὶ
οὐ μόνον ἀποπέφευγα, ἀλλὰ παντὶ δῆλον τοῦτό γε, ὅτι εἰ μὴ
ἀνέβη Ἄνυτος καὶ Λύκων κατηγορήσοντες ἐμοῦ, κἂν ὦφλε b
χιλίας δραχμάς, οὐ μεταλαβὼν τὸ πέμπτον μέρος τῶν
ψήφων.

ἀνέβη aor. act. indic. < ἀναβαίνω *appear in court*
ὦφλε aor. act. indic. < ὀφλισκάνω *owe*
μεταλαβών aor. act. part. < μεταλαμβάνω *get a share of*

36a7 **καὶ νῦν** "Even now." Socrates imagines that the votes that convicted him came in equal shares from the supporters of his three accusors. Thus Meletus's share of 93.33 (the presumed 280 divided by 3) would not have been enough to convict him.

36a8–b2 **εἰ μὴ ἀνέβη . . . τῶν ψήφων** The condition is past counterfactual. Note the singular verb with the plural subject. Socrates appears to be thinking primarily of Anytus (thus the singular), then adding Lycon as an afterthought. Thereafter, he refers to them in the plural (κατηγορήσοντες). The inconsistency of number again gives the impression of off-the-cuff improvisation.

36b1 **τὸ πέμπτον μέρος** "One fifth." Frivolous prosecutions were discouraged by a rule that required the prosecutor to get one-fifth of the vote or be subject to a fine. Meletus's "share" would have fallen below that standard as Socrates reckons it.

CHAPTER 26

(36b3–37a1)

"I do not, in fact, deserve death but to be supported at city expense!" For additional discussion of the chapter and questions for study, see essay 26.

Τιμᾶται δ' οὖν μοι ὁ ἀνὴρ θανάτου. εἶεν· ἐγὼ δὲ δὴ τίνος ὑμῖν ἀντιτιμήσομαι, ὦ ἄνδρες Ἀθηναῖοι; ἢ δῆλον ὅτι τῆς ἀξίας; τί οὖν; τί ἄξιός εἰμι παθεῖν ἢ ἀποτεῖσαι, ὅτι μαθὼν ἐν τῷ βίῳ οὐχ ἡσυχίαν ἦγον, ἀλλ' ἀμελήσας ὧνπερ οἱ πολλοί, χρηματισμοῦ τε καὶ οἰκονομίας καὶ στρατηγιῶν καὶ δημηγοριῶν καὶ τῶν ἄλλων ἀρχῶν καὶ συνωμοσιῶν καὶ

τιμᾶται < τιμάω (mid.) *propose a penalty*
ἀποτεῖσαι aor. act. infin. < ἀποτίνω *pay*
χρηματισμοῦ < χρηματισμός, -οῦ, ὁ *money making*
οἰκονομίας < οἰκονομία, -ας, ἡ *household management*
στρατηγιῶν < στρατηγία, -ας, ἡ *command*
δημηγοριῶν < δημηγορία *political speech*
συνωμοσιῶν < συνωμοσία, ἡ *conspiracy*

36b5–d2 Note the highly effective rhetorical contrast between the short, simple sentences that precede it and this complex period in which Socrates ironically enumerates his "crimes."

36b3 **ὁ ἀνήρ** Presumably he refers to Meletus.

36b4 **τίνος** Genitive of value. Note also the accent.

36b5 **ἀξίας** "An appropriate one." ἀντιτιμήσομαι is understood. The gender of the adjective is determined by the implied noun τιμή.

ὅτι μαθών A rare idiom: "because."

36b6 **οὐχ ἡσυχίαν ἦγον** "I did not lead a quiet life."

ὧνπερ οἱ πολλοί Supply here something such as ἐπιμελοῦνται.

36b8 **συνωμοσιῶν** Political clubs (συνωμοσίαι < συνόμνυμι, "swear a pact") had long been a feature of Athenian society, particularly among the aristocratic families. Such groups often fell under suspicion during the democracy, on the assumption that they were incubators of antigovernmental conspiracies. Such fears, though exaggerated at times, were not completely off base. The revolutionaries of 411 were closely linked with the clubs, and Thucydides

στάσεων τῶν ἐν τῇ πόλει γιγνομένων, ἡγησάμενος ἐμαυτὸν
τῷ ὄντι ἐπιεικέστερον εἶναι ἢ ὥστε εἰς ταῦτ' ἰόντα σῴζεσθαι, c
ἐνταῦθα μὲν οὐκ ᾖα οἷ ἐλθὼν μήτε ὑμῖν μήτε ἐμαυτῷ ἔμελλον μηδὲν ὄφελος εἶναι, ἐπὶ δὲ τὸ ἰδίᾳ ἕκαστον ἰὼν εὐεργετεῖν τὴν μεγίστην εὐεργεσίαν, ὥς ἐγώ φημι, ἐνταῦθα ᾖα,
ἐπιχειρῶν ἕκαστον ὑμῶν πείθειν μὴ πρότερον μήτε τῶν
ἑαυτοῦ μηδενὸς ἐπιμελεῖσθαι πρὶν ἑαυτοῦ ἐπιμεληθείη ὅπως

στάσεων < στάσις, -εως, ἡ *faction*
ᾖα 1st sing. impf. < εἶμι *go*
οἷ *where*
εὐεργετεῖν < εὐεργετέω *do good service*

(8.54) reports that there were frequent consultations between them and Peisander in the weeks leading up to the overthrow of the democratic government. They were also heavily involved in the short-lived reign of the Thirty Tyrants. Thus Socrates' mention of συνωμοσίαι here is not simply an expression of lack of interest in practical politics, but an indirect assertion that he did not allign himself with the subversive groups that had actively worked against the democracy.

36c1 **ἐπιεικέστερον . . . ἤ** "More upright than," leading up to the result clause ὥστε . . . σῴζεσθαι.

εἰς ταῦτ' ἰόντα "By doing these things." Socrates speaks of the political associations as if they were places, hence the minor awkwardness of the sentence. The spatial metaphor, however, is maintained throughout the sentence to contrast where Socrates chose not to "go" with his habit of "going" to everyone and urging them to strive after excellence.

36c3 **ἐπὶ δὲ τό . . . εὐεργετεῖν** The sentence begins with an articular infinitive that is the object of ἐπί ("with regard to") before coming to the main verb ᾖα, "I went" (c5).

ἰδίᾳ ἕκαστον ἰών is parenthetical.

36c4 **τὴν . . . εὐεργεσίαν** Cognate accusative.

36c5 **πρότερον** Do not translate.

τῶν ἑαυτοῦ μηδενός "Anything of yours." τῶν is a partitive genitive coming off of μηδενός, the object of ἐπιμελεῖσθαι. Socrates here introduces a fundamental difference between the self and its possessions.

36c6 **ἐπιμεληθείη** Optative in a πρίν-clause after a secondary tense (ᾖα, c5).

Socrates again emphasizes the care of the self as the most crucial aspect of human life. The public activities rejected by Socrates are not intrinsically bad, provided that the pursuit of them is not just "résumé building," but the natural activity of a soul that has learned moderation. The problem is, however, that since the activities are public, their outcomes will depend in part on the immoderate behavior of others whose desires are out of control. Socratic moderation will not be enough to protect its possessor, as the present trial clearly shows. The only way out of this dilemma within a democracy is to persuade one's fellow citizens to act differently, to make the care of the self their concern as well. Socrates has devoted his career to that task.

ὡς βέλτιστος καὶ φρονιμώτατος ἔσοιτο, μήτε τῶν τῆς πόλεως, πρὶν αὐτῆς τῆς πόλεως, τῶν τε ἄλλων οὕτω κατὰ τὸν
d αὐτὸν τρόπον ἐπιμελεῖσθαι—τί οὖν εἰμι ἄξιος παθεῖν τοιοῦτος ὤν; ἀγαθόν τι, ὦ ἄνδρες Ἀθηναῖοι, εἰ δεῖ γε κατὰ τὴν
ἀξίαν τῇ ἀληθείᾳ τιμᾶσθαι· καὶ ταῦτά γε ἀγαθὸν τοιοῦτον
ὅτι ἂν πρέποι ἐμοί. τί οὖν πρέπει ἀνδρὶ πένητι εὐεργέτῃ
δεομένῳ ἄγειν σχολὴν ἐπὶ τῇ ὑμετέρᾳ παρακελεύσει; οὐκ
ἔσθ' ὅτι μᾶλλον, ὦ ἄνδρες Ἀθηναῖοι, πρέπει οὕτως ὡς τὸν
τοιοῦτον ἄνδρα ἐν πρυτανείῳ σιτεῖσθαι, πολύ γε μᾶλλον ἢ
εἴ τις ὑμῶν ἵππῳ ἢ συνωρίδι ἢ ζεύγει νενίκηκεν Ὀλυμπία-
σιν· ὁ μὲν γὰρ ὑμᾶς ποιεῖ εὐδαίμονας δοκεῖν εἶναι, ἐγὼ δὲ

φρονιμώτατος < φρόνιμος, -ον *wisest*
πρέποι < πρέπω *befitting*
σιτεῖσθαι < σιτέω *feed*
εὐδαίμονος < εὐδαίμων, -ονος *happy, fortunate*

36c7 **ἔσοιτο** Future optative in a relative clause of purpose after a secondary-tense verb. See Smyth 1956, 2554. The subject of the verb is the self (ἑαυτοῦ).
τῶν τῆς πόλεως . . . πόλεως Supply πείθειν μὴ ἐπιμελεῖσθαι from above.

A state in which decisions are made in hopes of securing more wealth, goods, prestige, and so forth (τῶν τῆς πόλεως) will by its very nature show itself to be undeserving of those things. Just as in the case of the individual, possessions and honors will be bad for a city if they are not subordinated to higher moral ideals.

36c8 **κατὰ τὸν αὐτὸν τρόπον** "In the same way," that is, caring for the attributes that make it truly excellent rather than for superficial qualities that only make it *seem* good.

36d3 **ἀξίαν** Supply δίκην.
καὶ ταῦτά γε "And indeed, with respect to these things."

36d5 **ἄγειν** Dependent on δεομένῳ.
ἐπὶ τῇ ὑμετέρᾳ παρακελεύσει "To encourage you" (lit. "for your exhortation).

36d6 **οὐκ ἔσθ' ὅτι μᾶλλον . . . πρέπει** ἔσθ' = ἔστι. Translate "There is nothing more fitting."

36d7 **πρυτανείῳ σιτεῖσθαι** For the Prytaneum, also known as the Tholos, see on 32c5. Socrates' proposal is purposely outrageous.

36d8 **συνωρίδι ἢ ζεύγει** "Two or four horse chariots." Chariot racing was arguably the most prestigious event at the Olympics and other major athletic festivals. For just that reason, it offered an opportunity to the wealthy and ambitious to display publicly their preeminence. Socrates seeks to undermine the city's infatuation with successful athletes and suggests that it would be more fitting to honor him in their place.

36d9 **εὐδαίμονας** Pride in the accomplishments of a fellow citizen produces the *appearance* of happiness in everyone.

εἶναι, καὶ ὁ μὲν τροφῆς οὐδὲν δεῖται, ἐγὼ δὲ δέομαι. εἰ e
οὖν δεῖ με κατὰ τὸ δίκαιον τῆς ἀξίας τιμᾶσθαι, τούτου
τιμῶμαι, ἐν πρυτανείῳ σιτήσεως. 37

τροφῆς < τροφή, -ῆς, ἡ *sustenance*
σιτήσεως < σίτησις, -εος, ἡ *feeding*

36e1 **τροφῆς οὐδὲν δεῖται** Because he already possesses the extreme wealth necessary to race horses.

36e2 **οὖν** The particle has resumptive force, calling our attention back to the point Socrates made at 36d3.

CHAPTER 27

(37a2–e2)

"I am serious in my proposal. I would rather die than spend my life in prison or exile, and I do not have the funds to pay a substantial fine." Xenophon argues that Socrates deliberately chose to die, since he had already lived a good life and would avoid the inevitable decline of old age (*Apology* 1–9). For additional discussion of the chapter and questions for study, see essay 27.

Ἴσως οὖν ὑμῖν καὶ ταυτὶ λέγων παραπλησίως δοκῶ λέγειν ὥσπερ περὶ τοῦ οἴκτου καὶ τῆς ἀντιβολήσεως, ἀπαυθαδιζόμενος· τὸ δὲ οὐκ ἔστιν, ὦ ἄνδρες Ἀθηναῖοι, τοιοῦτον ἀλλὰ τοιόνδε μᾶλλον. πέπεισμαι ἐγὼ ἑκὼν εἶναι μηδένα ἀδικεῖν ἀνθρώπων, ἀλλὰ ὑμᾶς τοῦτο οὐ πείθω· ὀλίγον γὰρ χρόνον ἀλλήλοις διειλέγμεθα. ἐπεί, ὡς ἐγᾦμαι, εἰ ἦν ὑμῖν νόμος,

---

παραπλησίως *similarly, in a similar way*
οἴκτου < οἶκτος, -ου, ὁ *pity*
ἀντιβολήσεως < ἀντιβόλησις, -εως, ἡ *entreaty, prayer*
τοιόνδε < τοιόσδε, -άδε, -όνδε *such a thing as follows*
πέπεισμαι pf. pass. indic. < πείθω *believe*
ἕκων *willingly*

37a3 **ὥσπερ** "Just as [I was doing]."
οἴκτου καὶ τῆς ἀντιβολήσεως He refers to his statement at 34c.
ἀπαυθαδιζόμενος See on 34d9.

37a4 **τὸ δὲ οὐκ ἔστιν . . . τοιοῦτον, ἀλλὰ τοιόνδε μᾶλλον** "It's not like that, Athenians, but more like the following."

37a5 **ἕκων εἶναι** "Willingly." For the idea that Socrates might have misbehaved inadvertently (and so deserved a stern lecture in place of an indictment), see on 25d–26a.

37a6 **ὀλίγον χρόνον** For Socrates' complaint about the short time allowed to correct the many slanders against him, see on 19a2.

37a7 **ἐγᾦμαι** = ἐγὼ οἶμαι.

37a7–b1 **εἰ ἦν ὑμῖν νόμος . . . ἐπείσθητε ἄν** Mixed counterfactual condition.

ὥσπερ καὶ ἄλλοις ἀνθρώποις, περὶ θανάτου μὴ μίαν ἡμέραν
μόνον κρίνειν ἀλλὰ πολλάς, ἐπείσθητε ἄν· νῦν δ᾽ οὐ ῥᾴδιον b
ἐν χρόνῳ ὀλίγῳ μεγάλας διαβολὰς ἀπολύεσθαι. πεπεισμένος δὴ ἐγὼ μηδένα ἀδικεῖν πολλοῦ δέω ἐμαυτόν γε ἀδικήσειν
καὶ κατ᾽ ἐμαυτοῦ ἐρεῖν αὐτὸς ὡς ἄξιός εἰμί του κακοῦ καὶ
τιμήσεσθαι τοιούτου τινὸς ἐμαυτῷ. τί δείσας; ἦ μὴ πάθω
τοῦτο οὗ Μέλητός μοι τιμᾶται, ὅ φημι οὐκ εἰδέναι οὔτ᾽ εἰ
ἀγαθὸν οὔτ᾽ εἰ κακόν ἐστιν; ἀντὶ τούτου δὴ ἕλωμαι ὧν εὖ
οἶδά τι κακῶν ὄντων τούτου τιμησάμενος; πότερον δεσμοῦ;
καὶ τί με δεῖ ζῆν ἐν δεσμωτηρίῳ, δουλεύοντα τῇ ἀεὶ καθι- c
σταμένῃ ἀρχῇ, τοῖς ἕνδεκα; ἀλλὰ χρημάτων καὶ δεδέσθαι
ἕως ἂν ἐκτείσω; ἀλλὰ ταὐτόν μοί ἐστιν ὅπερ νυνδὴ ἔλεγον·

ἕλωμαι aor. mid. subj. < αἱρέω *choose*
δεσμωτηρίῳ < δεσμωτηρίον, -ου, τό *prison*
δεδέσθαι pf. pass. infin. < δέω *bind, put in chains*
ἐκτείσω aor. mid. < ἐκτίνω *pay*

37a10 **μίαν ἡμέραν . . . πολλάς** Acc. of duration of time.

37b3 **ἀδικεῖν** Infinitive in indirect statement after πεπεισμένος.

πολλοῦ δέω "I am far from . . ." (+ infin.). Note the future tense of the two infinitives dependent on the main verb (δέω) and indicating time subsequent to it.

37b4 **του κακοῦ** "Something bad."

37b5 **ἦ** "Introducing a suggested answer, couched in interrogative form, to a question just asked" (Denniston 1954, 283).

μὴ πάθω The clause of fearing is dependent on δείσας in the previous sentence

37b6 **μοι** Dative of disadvantage.

φημί He talks about the subject at greater length at 29a–b, and our lack of knowledge about death forms the basis for his "mythologizing" at 39e5 and thereafter.

37b7 **ἕλωμαι** Deliberative subjunctive.

ὧν Partitive with τι.

37b8 **δεσμοῦ** The genitive continues to be dependent on τιμησάμενος. Imprisonment for debt was rare in Athens.

37c1-2 **τῇ . . . καθισταμένῃ ἀρχῇ** "To the officials who happen to be in power."

37c2 **τοῖς ἕνδεκα** "The Eleven." According to Aristotle (*Constitution of the Athenians* 52.1), these officials had charge of all prisoners.

οὐ γὰρ ἔστι μοι χρήματα ὁπόθεν ἐκτείσω. ἀλλὰ δὴ φυγῆς
τιμήσωμαι; ἴσως γὰρ ἄν μοι τούτου τιμήσαιτε. πολλὴ
μεντἄν με φιλοψυχία ἔχοι, ὦ ἄνδρες Ἀθηναῖοι, εἰ οὕτως
ἀλόγιστός εἰμι ὥστε μὴ δύνασθαι λογίζεσθαι ὅτι ὑμεῖς μὲν
ὄντες πολῖταί μου οὐχ οἷοί τε ἐγένεσθε ἐνεγκεῖν τὰς ἐμὰς
d διατριβὰς καὶ τοὺς λόγους, ἀλλ' ὑμῖν βαρύτεραι γεγόνασιν
καὶ ἐπιφθονώτεραι, ὥστε ζητεῖτε αὐτῶν νυνὶ ἀπαλλαγῆναι·
ἄλλοι δὲ ἄρα αὐτὰς οἴσουσι ῥᾳδίως; πολλοῦ γε δεῖ, ὦ ἄνδρες
Ἀθηναῖοι. καλὸς οὖν ἄν μοι ὁ βίος εἴη ἐξελθόντι τηλικῷδε

ὁπόθεν *from where*
ἀλόγιστος, -ον *unreasonable*
ἐνεγκεῖν aor. act. infin. < φέρω *bear*
ἐπιφθονώτεραι < ἐπίφθονος, -ον *rather hateful*
ἀπαλλαγῆναι aor. pass. infin. < ἀπαλλάττω *set free*
οἴσουσι fut. act. indic. < φέρω *bear*

37c4 **ἐκτείσω** Future indicative in a relative clause of cause.

ἀλλά "How about . . . ?" In passages where a speaker proposes and rejects various suggestions, ἀλλά is used to introduce a new possibility.

φυγῆς This is the penalty that Socrates probably was expected to offer, and Meletus's proposal may have been deliberately harsh to make sure that Socrates did not have the luxury of proposing a light penalty without risking his life. It seems plausible that in most cases (i.e., those without Socrates for a defendant), such a strategy would be effective.

37c6 **μεντἄν** = μέντοι ἄν

φιλοψυχία Some φιλο- compounds suggest not simply love, but *excessive* love. In Aristophanes' *Wasps,* men are described as φιλόκυβος, "addicted to gambling" (75), and φιλοπότης, "alcoholic" (79). Similarly, φιλοψυχία means (excessive) "love of life" and, by extension, "cowardice."

37d1–2 **βαρύτεραι . . . ἐπιφθονώτεραι** Agreeing with an implied διατρίβαι.

37d1 **γεγόνασιν** Although γίγνομαι is frequently used as a synonym for εἶναι, here it is prefered because the emphasis is on *becoming.* The accumulated resentment produced by Socrates' speeches over time *has become* irritating. In *Gorgias,* Socrates' opponent Callicles urges him to abandon philosophy, which he admits is good in moderation but irritating and childish when continued into adulthood (485a–486c). Such a person, Callicles is made to say prophetically, will be utterly unable to help himself if he is dragged into court and forced to respond to a prosecutor who has called for the death penalty.

37d3 **ἄρα** "Therefore." The argument proceeds *a fortiori,* in which a more extreme example of an idea justifies in advance all less extreme ones: "If my fellow citizens, with whom I share so much, can't stand me, how will foreigners feel?"

πολλοῦ . . . δεῖ See on 30d6.

37d4–6 Socrates shifts from irony to direct sarcasm.

ἀνθρώπῳ ἄλλην ἐξ ἄλλης πόλεως ἀμειβομένῳ καὶ ἐξελαυνομένῳ ζῆν. εὖ γὰρ οἶδ' ὅτι ὅποι ἂν ἔλθω, λέγοντος ἐμοῦ
ἀκροάσονται οἱ νέοι ὥσπερ ἐνθάδε· κἂν μὲν τούτους ἀπελαύνω, οὗτοί με αὐτοὶ ἐξελῶσι πείθοντες τοὺς πρεσβυτέρους·
ἐὰν δὲ μὴ ἀπελαύνω, οἱ τούτων πατέρες δὲ καὶ οἰκεῖοι δι' e
αὐτοὺς τούτους.

ἀμειβομένῳ < ἀμείβω *change, exchange*
ὅποι ἄν (+ subj.) *wherever*
ἀκροάσονται < ἀκροάομαι *listen*
ἀπελαύνω *drive off*
ἐξελῶσι fut. act. indic. < ἐξελαύνω *drive out, exile*

37d5 **ἄλλην** πόλιν is understood.
37d5–6 **ἐξελαυνομένῳ ζῆν** "Live as an exile."
37d6 **ἔλθω** Subjunctive in an indefinite relative clause.
λέγοντος ἐμοῦ The genitives are dependent on ἀκροάσομαι.
37d7 **κἄν** = καὶ (ἐ)άν.
37e2 **δι' αὐτοὺς τούτους** "On their behalf." Supply ἐξελῶσι from above.

CHAPTER 28

(37e3–38b9)

The close of the penalty phase: "I cannot be silent without violating the command of the god." For additional discussion of the chapter and questions for study, see essay 28.

Ἴσως οὖν ἄν τις εἴποι· "Σιγῶν δὲ καὶ ἡσυχίαν ἄγων, ὦ
Σώκρατες, οὐχ οἷός τ' ἔσῃ ἡμῖν ἐξελθὼν ζῆν;" τουτὶ δή
ἐστι πάντων χαλεπώτατον πεῖσαί τινας ὑμῶν. ἐάντε γὰρ
λέγω ὅτι τῷ θεῷ ἀπειθεῖν τοῦτ' ἐστὶν καὶ διὰ τοῦτ' ἀδύνα-
38 τον ἡσυχίαν ἄγειν, οὐ πείσεσθέ μοι ὡς εἰρωνευομένῳ· ἐάντ'
αὖ λέγω ὅτι καὶ τυγχάνει μέγιστον ἀγαθὸν ὂν ἀνθρώπῳ
τοῦτο, ἑκάστης ἡμέρας περὶ ἀρετῆς τοὺς λόγους ποιεῖσθαι
καὶ τῶν ἄλλων περὶ ὧν ὑμεῖς ἐμοῦ ἀκούετε διαλεγομένου καὶ

37e3 **σιγῶν . . . ἄγων** Conditional participles.

37e4 **ἐξελθών** The aorist participle is used to indicate time prior to the main verb: "once you've departed."

37e5–38a7 The successive future-more-vivid conditions (ἐάν + subj., fut. indic.) in these lines provide a dramatic moment in the speech as Socrates prepares to conclude. The passage offers several memorable phrases, including the famous assertion that "the unexamined life is not worth living" (38a5).

37e6 **τῷ θεῷ ἀπειθεῖν** According to Socrates' interpretation of the oracle, he is commanded to spend his life examining the opinions of those who have a reputation for wisdom. ἀπειθεῖν is used predicatively with τοῦτο.

38a1 **μοι ὡς εἰρωνευομένῳ** "On the grounds that I am speaking ironically," that is, by pretending to take seriously something he does not.

38a2 **ὄν** Supplementary participle with τυγχάνω.

38a3 **τοῦτο** The demonstrative pronoun here refers to the entire clause that follows.

ἐμαυτὸν καὶ ἄλλους ἐξετάζοντος, ὁ δὲ ἀνεξέταστος βίος οὐ
βιωτὸς ἀνθρώπῳ, ταῦτα δ᾽ ἔτι ἧττον πείσεσθέ μοι λέγοντι.
τὰ δὲ ἔχει μὲν οὕτως, ὡς ἐγώ φημι, ὦ ἄνδρες, πείθειν δὲ οὐ
ῥᾴδιον. καὶ ἐγὼ ἅμα οὐκ εἴθισμαι ἐμαυτὸν ἀξιοῦν κακοῦ
οὐδενός. εἰ μὲν γὰρ ἦν μοι χρήματα, ἐτιμησάμην ἂν χρη- **b**
μάτων ὅσα ἔμελλον ἐκτείσειν, οὐδὲν γὰρ ἂν ἐβλάβην· νῦν
δὲ οὐ γὰρ ἔστιν, εἰ μὴ ἄρα ὅσον ἂν ἐγὼ δυναίμην ἐκτεῖσαι,
τοσούτου βούλεσθέ μοι τιμῆσαι. ἴσως δ᾽ ἂν δυναίμην ἐκτεῖσαι ὑμῖν που μνᾶν ἀργυρίου· τοσούτου οὖν τιμῶμαι.

ἀνεξέταστος, -ον *unexamined*
βιωτός, -όν *livable*
εἴθισμαι pf. mid. indic. < εἰθίζω *be accustomed*
ἐβλάβην aor. pass. indic. < βλάπτω *harm*

38a5–6 **ὁ δὲ ἀνεξέταστος βίος οὐ βιωτός** ἀνεξέταστος is etymologically related to ἐξετάζοντος, as βιωτός is to βίος. Socrates' juxtaposition of them in such quick succession is a mark of high rhetorical, perhaps even Gorgianic (see on 17b9–c1), style, as can be seen from Gorgias *Palamedes* 21: βίος οὐ βιωτὸς πίστεως ἐστερημένῳ. The βίος οὐ βιωτὸς formula predates the *Apology*, however (for example, at Sophocles' *Oedipus at Colonus* 1692). See Slings 1994, 374–75. That the ultimate provenance of such phrases might be Gorgias, however, is worth considering.

38a6 **ταῦτα δ᾽** In Plato an "apodotic" δέ occasionally marks the beginning of the apodosis in a conditional sentence. Do not translate.

38a7 **τά** = ταῦτα.

38a8 **κακοῦ οὐδενός** Compare 36d2–3, where he says that an *appropriate* punishment would have to be something good.

38b1–2 The condition is mixed: present counterfactual (imperfect) in the protasis, past counterfactual (aorist + ἄν) in the apodosis: "If I had money, I would have proposed . . ."

38b2 **οὐδὲν γὰρ ἂν ἐβλάβην** The condition gets a second apodosis (past counterfactual). Socrates again reasserts the distinction between the self and its possessions. He will admit to no wrong, but he will pay a fine because the loss of money is incidental to that "self" and so of no real consequence to him.

38b5 **μνᾶν** Equivalent to one hundred drachmas. The value of Socrates' entire household, according to a passage in Xenophon, was five minas, although Socrates' eccentricity and indifference to wealth makes it hard to know whether the offer he makes is sincere or insulting. Skilled workers on the acropolis received one drachma per day. Jurors received three obols (one-half drachma).

Πλάτων δὲ ὅδε, ὦ ἄνδρες Ἀθηναῖοι, καὶ Κρίτων καὶ Κριτόβουλος καὶ Ἀπολλόδωρος κελεύουσί με τριάκοντα μνῶν τιμήσασθαι, αὐτοὶ δ' ἐγγυᾶσθαι· τιμῶμαι οὖν τοσούτου, ἐγγυηταὶ δὲ ὑμῖν ἔσονται τοῦ ἀργυρίου οὗτοι ἀξιόχρεῳ.

38b6 **Πλάτων δὲ ὅδε** For the record, this is the *only* place in the Platonic dialogues where Plato appears. He is mentioned as having been sick and so absent from the death of Socrates (*Phaedo* 59b). ὅδε is deictic: "Plato here . . ."
For Crito and Critobolus, see on 35d10–e1. For Apollodorus, see on 34a2.

38b8 **ἐγγυᾶσθαι** In indirect statement after an implied verb of speaking. The basic sense of the word is "co-sign," in the sense of accepting responsibility for another's debt in case of default. Here it appears to mean simply "agree to pay," since the amount proposed substantially exceeds the value of Socrates' property.

38b9 **ἀξιόχρεῳ** "Trustworthy" (nom. pl.).

CONCLUSION

A second pause occurs at this point, while the jury votes to determine the punishment. The votes are counted, and it is announced that the penalty proposed by Meletus has been chosen. According to Diogenes Laertius (2.42), the vote was 300–200, a percentage significantly higher than that by which they had earlier found him guilty. Socrates informally addresses those who voted for his condemnation, then attempts to console his supporters. It is not known if such speeches were actually delivered in Athenian courtrooms, although there is nothing inherently implausible about Socrates' addressing the crowd and any interested spectators (for the physical characteristics of the court, see on 20e4 and introduction) as they began to disperse (slowly, perhaps, after such an emotionally involving case).

CHAPTER 29

(38c1–39b8)

Socrates addresses those who voted for his execution. They have done him no great harm, since he would have died soon anyway, but they have done themselves no favor. For additional discussion of the chapter and questions for study, see essay 29.

Οὐ πολλοῦ γ' ἕνεκα χρόνου, ὦ ἄνδρες Ἀθηναῖοι, ὄνομα
ἕξετε καὶ αἰτίαν ὑπὸ τῶν βουλομένων τὴν πόλιν λοιδορεῖν
ὡς Σωκράτη ἀπεκτόνατε, ἄνδρα σοφόν—φήσουσι γὰρ δὴ
σοφὸν εἶναι, εἰ καὶ μή εἰμι, οἱ βουλόμενοι ὑμῖν ὀνειδίζειν—
εἰ γοῦν περιεμείνατε ὀλίγον χρόνον, ἀπὸ τοῦ αὐτομάτου ἂν
ὑμῖν τοῦτο ἐγένετο· ὁρᾶτε γὰρ δὴ τὴν ἡλικίαν ὅτι πόρρω
ἤδη ἐστὶ τοῦ βίου, θανάτου δὲ ἐγγύς. λέγω δὲ τοῦτο οὐ
πρὸς πάντας ὑμᾶς, ἀλλὰ πρὸς τοὺς ἐμοῦ καταψηφισα- d
μένους θάνατον. λέγω δὲ καὶ τόδε πρὸς τοὺς αὐτοὺς
τούτους. ἴσως με οἴεσθε, ὦ ἄνδρες, ἀπορίᾳ λόγων
ἑαλωκέναι τοιούτων οἷς ἂν ὑμᾶς ἔπεισα, εἰ ᾤμην δεῖν

λοιδορεῖν < λοιδορέω *blame*
περιεμείνατε aor. act. indic. < περιμένω *wait*
πόρρω (+ gen.) *far along*
ἑαλωκέναι pf. act. infin. < ἁλίσκομαι *be caught*

38c1 **οὐ πολλοῦ . . . ἕνεκα χρόνου** "For the sake of not much time," that is, Socrates is already old and would die soon anyway.

38c2 **ἕξετε καὶ αἰτίαν** Equivalent to a passive "be blamed" and thus followed by ὑπὸ + genitive to express personal agency.

38c4 **εἰ καί** "Even if."

38c5–6 **εἰ . . . περιεμείνατε. . . ἂν . . . ἐγένετο** Past counterfactual condition.

38c6 **τοῦτο** That is, his death.

38c7 **πόρρω . . . τοῦ βίου, θανάτου δὲ ἐγγύς** "That I am far along in life and near death." Note the chiastic arrangement by which Socrates juxtaposes βίου and θανάτου.

38d4 **οἷς** The antecedent is λόγων.
ἂν . . . ἔπεισα The aorist indicative + ἄν here expresses potentiality in the past.

ἅπαντα ποιεῖν καὶ λέγειν ὥστε ἀποφυγεῖν τὴν δίκην.
πολλοῦ γε δεῖ. ἀλλ᾽ ἀπορίᾳ μὲν ἑάλωκα, οὐ μέντοι λόγων,
ἀλλὰ τόλμης καὶ ἀναισχυντίας καὶ τοῦ μὴ ἐθέλειν λέγειν
πρὸς ὑμᾶς τοιαῦτα οἷ᾽ ἂν ὑμῖν μὲν ἥδιστα ἦν ἀκούειν—
θρηνοῦντός τέ μου καὶ ὀδυρομένου καὶ ἄλλα ποιοῦντος καὶ
e λέγοντος πολλὰ καὶ ἀνάξια ἐμοῦ, ὡς ἐγώ φημι, οἷα δὴ καὶ
εἴθισθε ὑμεῖς τῶν ἄλλων ἀκούειν. ἀλλ᾽ οὔτε τότε ᾠήθην
δεῖν ἕνεκα τοῦ κινδύνου πρᾶξαι οὐδὲν ἀνελεύθερον, οὔτε νῦν
μοι μεταμέλει οὕτως ἀπολογησαμένῳ, ἀλλὰ πολὺ μᾶλλον
αἱροῦμαι ὧδε ἀπολογησάμενος τεθνάναι ἢ ἐκείνως ζῆν. οὔτε
γὰρ ἐν δίκῃ οὔτ᾽ ἐν πολέμῳ οὔτ᾽ ἐμὲ οὔτ᾽ ἄλλον οὐδένα δεῖ

τόλμης < τόλμα, -ης, ἡ *daring*
ἀναισχυντίας < ἀναισχυντία, -ας, ἡ *shamelessness*
ἥδιστα super. < ἡδύς, -εῖα, -ύ *sweet, delightful*
θρηνοῦντος < θρηνέω *sing a dirge, lament*
ὀδυρομένου < ὀδύρομαι *moan*
ἀνελεύθερον < ἀνελεύθερος, -ον *inappropriate for a free man*
ὧδε *in this fashion*
ἐκείνως *in that fashion*
δίκῃ < δίκη, -ης, ἡ *trial*

38d5 **ὥστε ἀποφυγεῖν τὴν δίκην** "So as to get off."

38d6 **ἀπορίᾳ** Socratic irony frequently makes use of the ambivalence latent in common words or phrases. Here ἀπορία, which refers to the confusion that results when someone does not know what to say (ἀπορία λόγων), comes to mean Socrates' "inability" (i.e., his refusal) to do whatever is necessary, no matter how shameless, to avoid conviction (ἀπορία . . . τόλμης καὶ ἀναισχυντίας). In the *Gorgias*, Socrates is made to anticipate this very moment: "If I should meet my end on account of a lack of rhetorical flattery (κολακικῆς ῥητορικῆς ἐνδείᾳ), I know well that I would bear death easily" (522d).

38d8 **οἷ᾽** = οἷα. Here nominative.
ἦν Imperfect because it refers to the time while he was giving his speech.

38d9–10 **θρηνοῦντός τέ μου καὶ ὀδυρομένου καὶ ἄλλα ποιοῦντος καὶ λέγοντος** The genitives are dependent on ἀκούειν.

38e2 **ἄλλων** Object of ἀκούειν: "from others."

38e3–4 **οὔτε . . . μοι μεταμέλει** "Nor do I regret." The impersonal construction takes a supplemental participle agreeing with μοι.

38e5 **οὔτε** This negative and the ones that follow should be taken with the infinitive. The point is not that "it is not necessary to contrive," but that "it is necessary *not* to contrive." ὅπως (introducing a clause of effort) is dependent on μηχανᾶσθαι: "contrive that . . ."

τοῦτο μηχανᾶσθαι, ὅπως ἀποφεύξεται πᾶν ποιῶν θάνατον. 39
καὶ γὰρ ἐν ταῖς μάχαις πολλάκις δῆλον γίγνεται ὅτι τό γε
ἀποθανεῖν ἄν τις ἐκφύγοι καὶ ὅπλα ἀφεὶς καὶ ἐφ' ἱκετείαν
τραπόμενος τῶν διωκόντων· καὶ ἄλλαι μηχαναὶ πολλαί εἰσιν
ἐν ἑκάστοις τοῖς κινδύνοις ὥστε διαφεύγειν θάνατον, ἐάν τις
τολμᾷ πᾶν ποιεῖν καὶ λέγειν. ἀλλὰ μὴ οὐ τοῦτ' ᾖ χαλεπόν,
ὦ ἄνδρες, θάνατον ἐκφυγεῖν, ἀλλὰ πολὺ χαλεπώτερον πονη-
ρίαν· θᾶττον γὰρ θανάτου θεῖ. καὶ νῦν ἐγὼ μὲν ἅτε βραδὺς b
ὢν καὶ πρεσβύτης ὑπὸ τοῦ βραδυτέρου ἑάλων, οἱ δ' ἐμοὶ

μηχανᾶσθαι < μηχανάομαι *contrive*
ἀφείς aor. act. part. < ἀφίημι *release*
τραπόμενος aor. mid. part. < τρέπω *turn*
μηχαναί < μηχανή, -ῆς, ἡ *means*
πονηρίαν < πονηρία, -ας, ἡ *worthlessness*
θᾶττον *more swiftly*
θεῖ < θέω *run*
ἅτε *inasmuch as, since*
βραδύς, -εῖα, -ύ *slow*

39a2–3 **τό γε ἀποθανεῖν ἄν τις ἐκφύγοι** "You could certainly avoid dying." The vocabulary of flight and pursuit found throughout this passage is also that of legal prosecution and defense. Socrates, then, is playing on both notions at once.

39a3 **ὅπλα ἀφείς** Throwing away one's "weapons" or "shield" (to be able to retreat more quickly or surrender) was, unsurprisingly, regarded as a serious breech of good conduct for a soldier. Those convicted of doing so could forfeit their civic rights (Andocides 1.74), and to accuse someone of ῥιψασπία, "shield throwing," was to invite a lawsuit for κακηγορία, or "slander" (see Lysias 10.9). Thus, by casting himself as someone who will not metaphorically throw away his shield to save his life nor, both literally *and* metaphorically, abandon the post to which he was assigned, whatever the danger (28e), Socrates implies that his life has embodied the highest expressions of civic virtue.

ἱκετείαν The concept of "supplication" is familiar to readers of the *Iliad*, where the typical form involves seizing the knees of an adversary and begging for mercy. It is also the pose Odysseus claims to have adopted in one of the Cretan tales after he throws away his own shield during a raid on Egypt (*Odyssey* 14.276ff.).

39a6 **ἀλλὰ μὴ οὐ τοῦτ' ᾖ χαλεπόν** "I don't think it's difficult." Idiomatic use of the subjunctive in cautious assertions.

39b1 **θᾶττον γὰρ θανάτου θεῖ** Note the alliteration. The metaphor that has been implicit in the idea of *escaping* death now is developed explicitly in this complex personification, by which slow death finally catches an even slower Socrates and evil (κακία) runs down the accusers, speedy as they are.

κατήγοροι ἅτε δεινοὶ καὶ ὀξεῖς ὄντες ὑπὸ τοῦ θάττονος, τῆς κακίας. καὶ νῦν ἐγὼ μὲν ἄπειμι ὑφ' ὑμῶν θανάτου δίκην ὀφλών, οὗτοι δ' ὑπὸ τῆς ἀληθείας ὠφληκότες μοχθηρίαν καὶ ἀδικίαν. καὶ ἐγώ τε τῷ τιμήματι ἐμμένω καὶ οὗτοι. ταῦτα μέν που ἴσως οὕτως καὶ ἔδει σχεῖν, καὶ οἶμαι αὐτὰ μετρίως ἔχειν.

ὀξεῖς < ὀξύς, -εῖα, -ύ *sharp, clever, swift*
ὄφλων aor. act. part. < ὀφλισκάνω *owe*
ὠφληκότες pf. act. part. same verb
μοχθηρίαν < μοχθηρία, -ας, ἡ *perversity*
μετρίως *fairly*

39b5–6 **μοχθηρίαν . . . ἀδικίαν** The accusatives are the objects of ὠφληκότες.
39b6 **καὶ οὗτοι** Supply τῷ τιμήματι ἐμμένουσι from above.

CHAPTER 30

(39c1–d9)

"You may think you have freed yourselves from my reproaches by condemning me, but you have merely traded one pest for many." For additional discussion of the chapter and questions for study, see essay 30.

Τὸ δὲ δὴ μετὰ τοῦτο ἐπιθυμῶ ὑμῖν χρησμῳδῆσαι, ὦ κατα- c
ψηφισάμενοί μου· καὶ γάρ εἰμι ἤδη ἐνταῦθα ἐν ᾧ μάλιστα ἄνθρωποι χρησμῳδοῦσιν, ὅταν μέλλωσιν ἀποθανεῖσθαι. φημὶ γάρ, ὦ ἄνδρες οἳ ἐμὲ ἀπεκτόνατε, τιμωρίαν ὑμῖν ἥξειν εὐθὺς μετὰ τὸν ἐμὸν θάνατον πολὺ χαλεπωτέραν νὴ Δία ἢ οἵαν ἐμὲ ἀπεκτόνατε· νῦν γὰρ τοῦτο εἴργασθε οἰόμενοι μὲν ἀπαλλάξεσθαι τοῦ διδόναι ἔλεγχον τοῦ βίου, τὸ δὲ ὑμῖν πολὺ

χρησμῳδῆσαι < χρησμῳδέω *deliver an oracle, foretell the future*
εἴργασθε pf. mid. indic. < ἐργάζομαι *do*
ἀπαλλάξεσθαι fut. mid. infin. < ἀπαλλάττω *set free*

39c1 **τό . . . μετὰ τοῦτο** "Next."
χρησμῳδῆσαι The significance of oracles has been a recurrent theme in the *Apology*, as Socrates has consistently emphasized the connection between his chosen way of life and Chaerephon's oracle. Now, ironically, it is he who will prophesy to those who just voted to condemn him. In his version of Socrates' defense speech, Xenophon also uses this verb, but Socrates' prophecy there is cruder and more direct (*Apology* 30).

39c3 **ὅταν μέλλωσιν ἀποθανεῖσθαι** So the dying Patroclus prophecies to a skeptical Hector in the *Iliad* (16.852–61), as well as Hector to Achilles (22.358–60). See also Xenophon, *Cyropaedia* 8.7.21.

39c5 **οἵαν** Understand τιμωρίαν. The relative is used as an accusative of respect: "more harsh than the one for which [οἵαν] you execute me."

39c7 **τοῦ διδόναι ἔλεγχον** The articular infinitive is dependent on ἀπαλλάξεσθαι. Socrates' defense of his life and career, as well as his insistence on the need for everyone to be able to defend their actions and attitudes in conversation (διδόναι ἔλεγχον), puts him squarely at the beginning of the confessional tradition in Western literature. This autobiographical tradition has been followed by many, from St. Augustine in the *Confessions* through the works of Montaigne, Rousseau, Benjamin Franklin, Henry Adams, and others.

ἐναντίον ἀποβήσεται, ὡς ἐγώ φημι. πλείους ἔσονται ὑμᾶς
d οἱ ἐλέγχοντες, οὓς νῦν ἐγὼ κατεῖχον, ὑμεῖς δὲ οὐκ ᾐσθάνεσθε· καὶ χαλεπώτεροι ἔσονται ὅσῳ νεώτεροί εἰσιν, καὶ ὑμεῖς μᾶλλον ἀγανακτήσετε. εἰ γὰρ οἴεσθε ἀποκτείνοντες ἀνθρώπους ἐπισχήσειν τοῦ ὀνειδίζειν τινὰ ὑμῖν ὅτι οὐκ ὀρθῶς ζῆτε, οὐ καλῶς διανοεῖσθε· οὐ γάρ ἐσθ' αὕτη ἡ ἀπαλλαγὴ οὔτε πάνυ δυνατὴ οὔτε καλή, ἀλλ' ἐκείνη καὶ καλλίστη καὶ ῥᾴστη, μὴ τοὺς ἄλλους κολούειν ἀλλ' ἑαυτὸν παρασκευάζειν ὅπως ἔσται ὡς βέλτιστος. ταῦτα μὲν οὖν ὑμῖν τοῖς καταψηφισαμένοις μαντευσάμενος ἀπαλλάττομαι.

ἀποβήσεται fut. mid. indic. < ἀποβαίνω *turn out*
κατεῖχον impf. act. < κατέχω *restrain*
ᾐσθάνεσθε impf. mid. < αἰσθάνομαι *perceive*
ἐπισχήσειν < ἐπέχω *hold back, restrain*
ὀνειδίζειν < ὀνειδίζω *rebuke, reproach*
ζῆτε pres. act. indic. < ζάω *live*
διανοεῖσθε < διανοέομαι *think*
κολούειν < κολούω *restrain*
μαντευσάμενος < μαντεύομαι *prophecy*

39c8 **πλείους** = πλείονες (masc. nom. pl.).

39d1 **κατεῖχον** Note the unusual form of the augment. For the no-doubt irritating attempts on the part of Socrates' younger listeners to practice his techniques on their elders, see 33b–c. There are other, more serious, people in Athens having "Socratic" conversations as well, however. We should have in mind people like Apollodorus (see on 34a2; cf. also 38b8) and Aristodemus, the internal narrator of the *Symposium*, who copied Socrates to the point of going around barefoot like his idol. Most important, however, is Plato himself, whose dialogues, in addition to memorializing Socrates, frequently criticize Athens and its people.

39d2 **ὅσῳ** "To the degree that."

39d4 **τοῦ ὀνειδίζειν** The case is dependent on the idea of separation implied by the verb of hindering (ἐπισχήσειν).

39d6–8 **ἀλλ' ἐκείνη (ἡ ἀπαλλαγὴ) καὶ καλλίστη καὶ ῥᾴστη, μὴ τοὺς ἄλλους κολούειν ἀλλ' ἑαυτὸν παρασκευάζειν ὅπως ἔσται ὡς βέλτιστος** "But that (relief) is very beautiful and easy, that of not repressing others, but instead preparing oneself to be as good as possible." παρασκευάζειν is parallel with κολούειν, thus describing another type of ἀπαλλαγή. The determination to take all steps to become as good as possible *could* be called a "relief" or an "escape" from the pain of living an evil life. Socrates argues much the same thing in the *Gorgias*, when he tries to convince Callicles that the tyrant who lives without restraint is the most miserable man alive (see also the *Republic*, books 1 and 9). Socrates does not argue that point here, however, and it is better to understand a slight anacolouthon that allows Socrates to contrast the two infinitives.

CHAPTER 31

(39e1–40c3)

"To those who voted for my acquital, do not be sad. Death is not a bad thing for me." For additional discussion of the chapter and questions for study, see essay 31.

Τοῖς δὲ ἀποψηφισαμένοις ἡδέως ἂν διαλεχθείην ὑπὲρ τοῦ e
γεγονότος τουτουῒ πράγματος, ἐν ᾧ οἱ ἄρχοντες ἀσχολίαν
ἄγουσι καὶ οὔπω ἔρχομαι οἷ ἐλθόντα με δεῖ τεθνάναι. ἀλλά
μοι, ὦ ἄνδρες, παραμείνατε τοσοῦτον χρόνον· οὐδὲν γὰρ

διαλεχθείην aor. pass. opt. < διαλέγομαι *converse, talk with*
παραμείνατε < παραμένω *remain with*

39e1 **διαλεχθείην** It is fitting that Socrates concludes with a reference to *dialogue*, that characteristic feature of his life and philosophical practice.
ὑπέρ "In regard to."

39e2 **ἄρχοντες** The Eleven (see on 37c2).
ἀσχολίαν ἄγουσι "Are busy." Presumably they needed to make arrangements for the transfer of Socrates to the prison. If they had expected him to go quietly into exile, they might have been caught unprepared.

39e3 **οἷ** Note the accent.
ἐλθόντα με δεῖ τεθνάναι "I must go and be executed." In fact, the execution of Socrates was delayed for a long time, as we learn from the *Phaedo* (58a–c) and *Crito* (43c9–d6). The Athenians annually sent a ship to the island of Delos in honor of Apollo and his role in the deliverance of Athens from King Minos and the Minotaur. During the time it took for the ship to go and to return, the execution of criminals was forbidden. As it turned out, the ship left Athens the day before Socrates' trial, and so he remained in prison for some time. It is easy to forget that when the *Apology* was written, Plato of course knew that the execution would be delayed.

39e4 **τοσοῦτον** That is, as long as the archons allow.

κωλύει διαμυθολογῆσαι πρὸς ἀλλήλους ἕως ἔξεστιν. ὑμῖν γὰρ ὡς φίλοις οὖσιν ἐπιδεῖξαι ἐθέλω τὸ νυνί μοι συμβεβηκὸς τί ποτε νοεῖ. ἐμοὶ γάρ, ὦ ἄνδρες δικασταί—ὑμᾶς γὰρ δικαστὰς καλῶν ὀρθῶς ἂν καλοίην—θαυμάσιόν τι γέγονεν. ἡ γὰρ εἰωθυῖά μοι μαντικὴ ἡ τοῦ δαιμονίου ἐν μὲν τῷ πρόσθεν χρόνῳ παντὶ πάνυ πυκνὴ ἀεὶ ἦν καὶ πάνυ ἐπὶ σμικροῖς ἐναντιουμένη, εἴ τι μέλλοιμι μὴ ὀρθῶς πράξειν. νυνὶ δὲ συμβέβηκέ μοι ἅπερ ὁρᾶτε καὶ αὐτοί, ταυτὶ ἅ γε δὴ οἰηθείη ἄν τις καὶ νομίζεται ἔσχατα κακῶν εἶναι· ἐμοὶ δὲ

κωλύει < κωλύω *hinder*
διαμυθολογῆσαι aor. act. infin. < διαμυθολογέω *converse, exchange stories*
ἐπιδεῖξαι < ἐπιδείκνυμι *show*
συμβεβηκός pf. act. part. < συμβαίνω *happen*
εἰωθυῖα pf. part. < ἔθω *be accustomed*
μαντική, -ῆς, ἡ *prophetic sign*
πυκνή < πυκνός, -ή, -όν *constant, insistent*
ἐναντιουμένη < ἐναντιόομαι *oppose*

39e5 **διαμυθολογῆσαι** This is a rare word in Plato, appearing only two other times, both in explicitly speculative contexts, once at the beginning of the *Laws* (632e4) and once in the *Phaedo* (70b6) in a discussion of proofs of the immortality of the soul. The shift from διαλέγειν (39e1) to διαμυθολογεῖν signals the shift to a more speculative register as Socrates prepares to discuss his views on the afterlife with those he considers sympathetic (Weber 1986).

40a1 **τό . . . συμβεβηκός** "The thing that has happened to me." Socrates' understanding of the verdict is based on his prior experience with the divine sign, which always had interceded to prevent him from acting in error. The absence of the δαιμόνιον from the day's proceedings offers Socrates indirect confirmation that he has acted in accordance with divine wishes. For a discussion of the δαιμόνιον, see on 24c1.

τί . . . νοεῖ "What it means." Note that the direct interrogative τί replaces ὅτι in this indirect question.

40a2 **δικασταί** Socrates now uses, for the first time, the word he has studiously avoided in addressing the entire jury. He addressed them instead as ἄνδρες Ἀθηναῖοι.

καλῶν ὀρθῶς "Calling you accurately" (i.e., by your right name).

40a6 **πάνυ ἐπὶ σμικροῖς** "In even quite small things." πάνυ may precede the preposition (Smyth 1956, 1663n.).

μή Take with ὀρθῶς.

40a7 **συμβέβηκε** The subject is ταυτί below, after the first relative clause. The sentence sets the stage for a reappraisal of the "dire" circumstances in which Socrates finds himself. If they really were as dire as they admittedly seem, the δαιμόνιον would have dissuaded Socrates from pursuing the course he followed. Since it did not, he argues, the sequence of events and their results must not be bad.

οὔτε ἐξιόντι ἕωθεν οἴκοθεν ἠναντιώθη τὸ τοῦ θεοῦ σημεῖον, b
οὔτε ἡνίκα ἀνέβαινον ἐνταυθοῖ ἐπὶ τὸ δικαστήριον, οὔτε ἐν
τῷ λόγῳ οὐδαμοῦ μέλλοντί τι ἐρεῖν. καίτοι ἐν ἄλλοις λόγοις
πολλαχοῦ δή με ἐπέσχε λέγοντα μεταξύ· νῦν δὲ οὐδαμοῦ
περὶ ταύτην τὴν πρᾶξιν οὔτ᾽ ἐν ἔργῳ οὐδενὶ οὔτ᾽ ἐν λόγῳ
ἠναντίωταί μοι. τί οὖν αἴτιον εἶναι ὑπολαμβάνω; ἐγὼ
ὑμῖν ἐρῶ· κινδυνεύει γάρ μοι τὸ συμβεβηκὸς τοῦτο ἀγαθὸν
γεγονέναι, καὶ οὐκ ἔσθ᾽ ὅπως ἡμεῖς ὀρθῶς ὑπολαμβάνομεν,
ὅσοι οἰόμεθα κακὸν εἶναι τὸ τεθνάναι. μέγα μοι τεκμήριον c
τούτου γέγονεν· οὐ γὰρ ἔσθ᾽ ὅπως οὐκ ἠναντιώθη ἄν μοι τὸ
εἰωθὸς σημεῖον, εἰ μή τι ἔμελλον ἐγὼ ἀγαθὸν πράξειν.

ἐξιόντι < ἔξειμι *go out*
ἕωθεν *early in the morning*
οἴκοθεν *from home*
ἠναντιώθη aor. pass. indic. < ἐναντιόομαι *oppose*
σημεῖον, -ου, τό *sign*
ἡνίκα *when*
πολλαχοῦ *in many places*
μεταξύ *in the middle*
γεγονέναι pf. act. infin. < γίγνομαι *be, become*

40b3 **μέλλοντί τι ἐρεῖν** The participle agrees with ἐμοι. The δαιμόνιον might have restrained Socrates as he was about to go out, an experience he might have interpreted as a sign that exile was preferable to death. Its intervention could also have been focused more narrowly, at some point in the speech, to prevent Socrates from saying something particularly inflammatory.

ἐν ἄλλοις λόγοις Or it might have induced him to speak further. In *Phaedrus* (242d–244a), Socrates reports that he experienced the intervention of the δαιμόνιον as he attempted to depart from the conversation. He interpreted the experience as a sign that he had to recant his previous speech and start again. Similarly, at *Euthydemus* 272e, the sign delays the departure of Socrates; consequently, he is still present for the arrival of the irrepressible brother duo of Euthydemus and Dionysodorus.

40b8 **γεγονέναι** Infinitive in indirect statement after κινδυνεύει: "It is likely that this thing that has happened to me is good." Since the δαιμόνιον did not prevent Socrates from getting convicted, it may well be that death is a good thing. Socrates has already spoken forcefully against the commonly held view that death is an evil (29a–b), but there he argued as an agnostic. Now the absence of the δαιμόνιον has given him further reason to think that death might not be so bad.

40c1 **ὅσοι οἰόμεθα** "All of us who think."

40c1 **μοι** Dative of possession, to be taken with γέγονεν (used impersonally).

40c2 **οὐ γὰρ ἔσθ᾽** "There is no way that . . ." (introducing a past counterfactual condition).

CHAPTER 32

(40c4–41c7)

"Death might be either unending, dreamless sleep or some form of afterlife as the traditional stories say." For additional discussion of the chapter and questions for study, see essay 32.

Ἐννοήσωμεν δὲ καὶ τῇδε ὡς πολλὴ ἐλπίς ἐστιν ἀγαθὸν αὐτὸ εἶναι. δυοῖν γὰρ θάτερόν ἐστιν τὸ τεθνάναι· ἢ γὰρ οἷον μηδὲν εἶναι μηδὲ αἴσθησιν μηδεμίαν μηδενὸς ἔχειν τὸν τεθνεῶτα, ἢ κατὰ τὰ λεγόμενα μεταβολή τις τυγχάνει οὖσα καὶ μετοίκησις τῇ ψυχῇ τοῦ τόπου τοῦ ἐνθένδε εἰς ἄλλον τόπον. καὶ εἴτε δὴ μηδεμία αἴσθησίς ἐστιν ἀλλ'
d οἷον ὕπνος ἐπειδάν τις καθεύδων μηδ' ὄναρ μηδὲν ὁρᾷ, θαυ-

τῇδε *in this way*
ἐλπίς, -ίδος, ἡ *hope*
αἴσθησιν < αἴσθησις, -εως, ἡ *sensation*
μεταβολή, -ῆς, ἡ *change*
μετοίκησις, -εως, ἡ *change of habitation*
ὕπνος, -ου, ὁ *sleep*
καθεύδων < καθεύδω *sleep*
ὄναρ, τό (no gen.) *dream*

40c5 **δυοῖν . . . θάτερον** δυοῖν is genitive dual; θάτερον = τὸ ἕτερον: "one of two things."

40c5–6 **ἢ γὰρ οἷον μηδὲν εἶναι . . . τὸν τεθνεῶτα** "For either the dead man does not exist" οἷον = οἷόν ἐστι. Literally: "For either it is such a thing as for the dead man not to exist."

40c6 **αἴσθησιν μηδεμίαν μηδενός** "No feeling at all." Note the accumulation of negations underlining the concept of absolute nonexistence.

40c8 **μετοίκησις** "A change of habitation." Socrates uses the same metaphor to describe the afterlife in the *Phaedo* (117c2).

τοῦ τόπου τοῦ ἐνθένδε "From here."

40d1 **μηδ'** "Not even."

ὁρᾷ Subjunctive in a general temporal clause.

μάσιον κέρδος ἂν εἴη ὁ θάνατος—ἐγὼ γὰρ ἂν οἶμαι, εἴ τινα
ἐκλεξάμενον δέοι ταύτην τὴν νύκτα ἐν ᾗ οὕτω κατέδαρθεν
ὥστε μηδὲ ὄναρ ἰδεῖν, καὶ τὰς ἄλλας νύκτας τε καὶ ἡμέρας
τὰς τοῦ βίου τοῦ ἑαυτοῦ ἀντιπαραθέντα ταύτῃ τῇ νυκτὶ δέοι
σκεψάμενον εἰπεῖν πόσας ἄμεινον καὶ ἥδιον ἡμέρας καὶ
νύκτας ταύτης τῆς νυκτὸς βεβίωκεν ἐν τῷ ἑαυτοῦ βίῳ, οἶμαι
ἂν μὴ ὅτι ἰδιώτην τινά, ἀλλὰ τὸν μέγαν βασιλέα εὐαριθμήτους ἂν εὑρεῖν αὐτὸν ταύτας πρὸς τὰς ἄλλας ἡμέρας καὶ e
νύκτας—εἰ οὖν τοιοῦτον ὁ θάνατός ἐστιν, κέρδος ἔγωγε
λέγω· καὶ γὰρ οὐδὲν πλείων ὁ πᾶς χρόνος φαίνεται οὕτω

κέρδος, -ους, τό *profit*
ἐκλεξάμενον aor. mid. part. < ἐκλέγω *pick out*
κατέδαρθεν aor. act. indic. < καταδαρθάνω *fall asleep*
ἀντιπαραθέντα aor. act. part. < ἀντιπαρατίθημι *compare*
βεβίωκεν pf. act. indic. < βιόω *live*
ἰδιώτην < ἰδιώτης, -ου, ὁ *private citizen*

40d2–e2 If someone counted up nights spent in pleasant, dreamless sleep, he would find them few in number when compared with all the other nights. The basic idea of this extremely complex sentence is that if death is like one of those restful nights, just longer, it would definitely be a good thing. Grammatically speaking, we have a future-less-vivid condition in indirect statement, introduced by ἐγὼ . . . ἂν οἶμαι (ἂν οἶμαι repeated at d8 for emphasis). The protasis remains unchanged, and the apodosis takes a subject accusative + infinitive construction.

40d2 **ἐγώ . . . ἂν οἶμαι** ἄν here and at d8 should be taken with εὑρεῖν (e1), as we expect in the apodosis of a future-less-vivid condition.

40d3 **δέοι** Impersonal use of the verb.

40d3–4 **οὕτω . . . ὥστε** "In such a way that . . ."

40d8 **τὸν μέγαν βασιλέα** The king of Persia is regularly referred to simply as "the great king" or even more simply as ὁ βασιλεύς. Both ἰδιώτην and βασιλέα function as the subject of εὑρεῖν in e1.

εὐαριθμήτους "Rare," agreeing with νύκτας

40e2 **κέρδος** Supply εἶναι.

40e3 **ὁ πᾶς χρόνος** "All of time."

δὴ εἶναι ἢ μία νύξ. εἰ δ' αὖ οἷον ἀποδημῆσαί ἐστιν ὁ
θάνατος ἐνθένδε εἰς ἄλλον τόπον, καὶ ἀληθῆ ἐστιν τὰ
λεγόμενα, ὡς ἄρα ἐκεῖ εἰσι πάντες οἱ τεθνεῶτες, τί μεῖζον
ἀγαθὸν τούτου εἴη ἄν, ὦ ἄνδρες δικασταί; εἰ γάρ τις
41 ἀφικόμενος εἰς Ἅιδου, ἀπαλλαγεὶς τουτωνὶ τῶν φασκόντων
δικαστῶν εἶναι, εὑρήσει τοὺς ὡς ἀληθῶς δικαστάς, οἵπερ
καὶ λέγονται ἐκεῖ δικάζειν, Μίνως τε καὶ Ῥαδάμανθυς καὶ
Αἰακὸς καὶ Τριπτόλεμος καὶ ἄλλοι ὅσοι τῶν ἡμιθέων δίκαιοι
ἐγένοντο ἐν τῷ ἑαυτῶν βίῳ, ἆρα φαύλη ἂν εἴη ἡ ἀποδημία;
ἢ αὖ Ὀρφεῖ συγγενέσθαι καὶ Μουσαίῳ καὶ Ἡσιόδῳ καὶ
Ὁμήρῳ ἐπὶ πόσῳ ἄν τις δέξαιτ' ἂν ὑμῶν; ἐγὼ μὲν γὰρ

ἀποδημῆσαι < ἀποδημέω *locate*
ἀποδημία, -ας, ἡ *relocation*

40e4 **ἤ** Used here in a comparison with πλείων.

εἰ δ'αὖ "If, on the other hand." αὖ, "again," refers back to the two possibilities suggested earlier. It is interesting to note that he does not mention here the doctrine of the transmigration of souls attributed to the Pythagoreans and (apparently) adapted by Plato in dialogues such as the *Meno*, which develops the idea of learning as the recollection of past lives, and the *Republic*, which ends with the myth of Er. The latter's near-death experience features souls in the process of choosing how they will spend their next incarnation.

οἷον ἀποδημῆσαι "A kind of relocation."

40e6 **ὡς** Introducing indirect statement after τὰ λεγόμενα.

ἄρα "I suppose (now that I think about it)."

40e7 **τούτου** Genitive of comparison.

41a1 **τουτωνὶ τῶν φασκόντων δικαστῶν** Genitives of separation after ἀπαλλαγείς. Socrates gets in another dig at his opponents. A consideration of the traditional Greek view of the afterlife, according to which the souls of the dead continued to exist in a bodiless form, whether in Hades or in a more or less precisely defined paradise such as the Isles of the Blessed, leads Socrates to mention three groups of inhabitants: judges, poets, and heroes, all of whom have important symbolic roles in the *Apology*.

41a3–4 **Μίνως . . . Ῥαδάμανθυς . . . Αἰακός . . . Τριπτόλεμος** Minos, Rhadamanthus, and Aiakos are commonly represented as judges or counselors in the afterlife, the best-known example being the reference to Minos in book 11 of the *Odyssey* (568–69). The presence of Triptolemus, more closely associated with the Eleusinian Mysteries, is less explicable, although he is referred to as an "administrator of laws" (θεμιστοπόλος) in the *Homeric Hymn to Demeter* (473).

41a4 **ἡμιθέων** For demigods in the *Apology*, see 27d–e.

41a6–7 **Ὀρφεῖ . . . Μουσαίῳ . . . Ἡσιόδῳ . . . Ὁμήρῳ** All four were regarded by the Greeks to have been historical figures, although most scholars now doubt the historicity of Orpheus and Musaeus. Within the *Apology*, poets such as Homer and Hesiod present a problem. Despite their enormous prestige,

πολλάκις ἐθέλω τεθνάναι εἰ ταῦτ' ἔστιν ἀληθῆ. ἐπεὶ
ἔμοιγε καὶ αὐτῷ θαυμαστὴ ἂν εἴη ἡ διατριβὴ αὐτόθι, ὁπότε b
ἐντύχοιμι Παλαμήδει καὶ Αἴαντι τῷ Τελαμῶνος καὶ εἴ τις
ἄλλος τῶν παλαιῶν διὰ κρίσιν ἄδικον τέθνηκεν, ἀντιπαραβάλλοντι τὰ ἐμαυτοῦ πάθη πρὸς τὰ ἐκείνων—ὡς ἐγὼ οἶμαι,
οὐκ ἂν ἀηδὲς εἴη—καὶ δὴ καὶ τὸ μέγιστον, τοὺς ἐκεῖ ἐξετάζοντα
καὶ ἐρευνῶντα ὥσπερ τοὺς ἐνταῦθα διάγειν, τίς αὐτῶν σοφός
ἐστιν καὶ τίς οἴεται μέν, ἔστιν δ' οὔ. ἐπὶ πόσῳ δ' ἄν τις,

αὐτόθι *right there*
παλαιῶν < παλαιός, -ά, -όν *ancient, old*
ἀντιπαραβάλλοντι < ἀντιπαραβάλλω *compare*
ἐρευνῶντα < ἐρευνάω *seek after, examine*
διάγειν < διάγω *live*

---

they represent a reliance on revealed wisdom that is fundamentally irrational and so inconsistent with philosophy as Socrates sees it. "They say many beautiful things," he says to the jury at 22c2–3, "but they do not know what they mean."

41a7 **ἐπὶ πόσῳ ἄν τις δέξαιτ' ἂν ὑμῶν;** "What would you give?" Lit. "at what price would one of you accept that?"

41b2 **Παλαμήδει καὶ Αἴαντι τῷ Τελεμῶνος** Palamedes and Ajax, the son of Telamon, were both heroes who were victims of the unscrupulous Odysseus. During the courtship of Helen, her suitors swore an oath to defend her against abduction. After she was carried off by Paris and the Trojan War expedition was forming, Odysseus feigned madness to avoid service. His trick was discovered by Palamedes, however, and he was forced to fulfill his oath. Odysseus later framed Palamedes on a charge of treason and had him executed. Later in the war, after the death of Achilles, a dispute over the great hero's armor arises between Ajax and Odysseus. Through some underhanded machinations, the armor is awarded to Odysseus. Ajax is stricken with madness by Athena and eventually commits suicide. One of Gorgias's great set pieces was a defense speech of Palamedes, and many scholars believe that the *Apology* is in part a reaction to it.

41b1–4 **ἀντιπαραβάλλοντι τὰ ἐμαυτοῦ . . . ἐκείνων** "Comparing my experiences with theirs."

41b5 **οὐκ ἂν ἀηδὲς εἴη** "It wouldn't be unpleasurable" (litotes).

41b5–c7 Socrates considers the possibility that if the traditional stories about death are true, he will be able to continue his investigations there with Homer, Hesiod, and the others (τοὺς ἐκεῖ), freed from the limitations of human life.

41b5 **καὶ δὴ καί** "Moreover." There is a slight anacolouthon after the dash, as the construction shifts to accusative + infin. after τὸ μέγιστον (ἐστι . . .). Supply ἐμέ as the subject of the impersonal construction and the antecedent of both ἐξετάζοντα and ἐρευνῶντα (b5–6).

41b6 **τίς** The direct interrogative takes the place of ὅστις in the indirect question introduced by ἐξετάζοντα and ἐρευνῶντα.

41b7 **αὐτῶν** Partitive with τίς.
τίς οἴεται μέν, ἔστιν δ' οὔ "Who thinks he is (wise), but isn't."

ὦ ἄνδρες δικασταί, δέξαιτο ἐξετάσαι τὸν ἐπὶ Τροίαν ἀγαγόντα
c τὴν πολλὴν στρατιὰν ἢ Ὀδυσσέα ἢ Σίσυφον ἢ ἄλλους μυρίους ἄν τις εἴποι καὶ ἄνδρας καὶ γυναῖκας, οἷς ἐκεῖ διαλέγεσθαι καὶ συνεῖναι καὶ ἐξετάζειν ἀμήχανον ἂν εἴη εὐδαιμονίας; πάντως οὐ δήπου τούτου γε ἕνεκα οἱ ἐκεῖ ἀποκτείνουσι· τά τε γὰρ ἄλλα εὐδαιμονέστεροί εἰσιν οἱ ἐκεῖ τῶν ἐνθάδε, καὶ ἤδη τὸν λοιπὸν χρόνον ἀθάνατοί εἰσιν, εἴπερ γε τὰ λεγόμενα ἀληθῆ.

λοιπόν < λοιπός, -ή, -όν *remaining, rest of*

41b8 **τὸν . . . ἀγάγοντα** "The one who led" (i.e., Agamemnon).

41c1 **Ὀδυσσέα ἢ Σίσυφον** The pairing of the two is not accidental. The prospect of Socrates commiserating with Ajax and Palamedes has already prepared us for an unsympathetic treatment of Odysseus. This was not unheard of. Although his character is celebrated in the *Odyssey,* other parts of the tradition emphasized his self-serving duplicity, among them Sophocles' *Philoctetes*. In the ethical context that Socrates develops in the *Apology,* Odysseus is the paradigm for speakers who are eager to *sound* good without really *being* good. He is appropriately linked with Sisyphus, who talked his way out of Hades for awhile before being assigned to his famous rock. A separate tradition, well represented in antiquity, has Odysseus as Sysyphus's illegitimate son. For the sources, see Gantz 1993, 175–76.

ἢ ἄλλους μυρίους Take the phrase as still the object of ἐξετάσαι (b8). οὓς needs to be supplied after μυρίους: "Or countless others whom one could mention. . . ."

41c3–4 **ἀμήχανον . . . εὐδαιμονίας** "An inexpressible [amount of] happiness."

41c4 **τούτου . . . ἕνεκα** That is, for conducting Socratic conversations.

41c5 **οἱ ἐκεῖ** "Those there." Since they are dead, the punishments available to the authorities are presumably limited. Lucian's send-up of Greek literature and philosophy, the *True History,* includes the author's miraculous voyage to the Isles of the Blessed. Lucian, who is heavily influenced by the *Apology* here, imagines just the sort of place that Socrates describes. There, where historical and mythological figures exist side by side, Socrates spends his days talking with young men from mythology such as Hylas, Narcissus, and Hyacinthus, much to the annoyance of Rhadamanthus (the judge), who threatens to throw him off the island (2.17).

41c6 **τῶν ἐνθάδε** Genitive of comparison.

41c7 **ἀληθῆ** Socrates' story is intended to console, but he is not willing to declare that it is true or even that *he* believes it. Here he makes the same qualification that he made at 40e5 and 41a8.

CHAPTER 33

(41c8–end)

"My last request, then, is that you treat my sons as I have treated you and rebuke them if they care for anything more than virtue." For additional discussion of the chapter and questions for study, see essay 33.

Ἀλλὰ καὶ ὑμᾶς χρή, ὦ ἄνδρες δικασταί, εὐέλπιδας εἶναι
πρὸς τὸν θάνατον, καὶ ἕν τι τοῦτο διανοεῖσθαι ἀληθές, ὅτι
οὐκ ἔστιν ἀνδρὶ ἀγαθῷ κακὸν οὐδὲν οὔτε ζῶντι οὔτε τελευ- d
τήσαντι, οὐδὲ ἀμελεῖται ὑπὸ θεῶν τὰ τούτου πράγματα·
οὐδὲ τὰ ἐμὰ νῦν ἀπὸ τοῦ αὐτομάτου γέγονεν, ἀλλά μοι
δῆλόν ἐστι τοῦτο, ὅτι ἤδη τεθνάναι καὶ ἀπηλλάχθαι πραγμάτων βέλτιον ἦν μοι. διὰ τοῦτο καὶ ἐμὲ οὐδαμοῦ ἀπέτρεψεν
τὸ σημεῖον, καὶ ἔγωγε τοῖς καταψηφισαμένοις μου καὶ τοῖς
κατηγόροις οὐ πάνυ χαλεπαίνω. καίτοι οὐ ταύτῃ τῇ διανοίᾳ
κατεψηφίζοντό μου καὶ κατηγόρουν, ἀλλ᾽ οἰόμενοι βλάπτειν·

εὐέλπιδας < εὔελπις, -ιδος, ὁ *hopeful*
διανοεῖσθαι < διανοέομαι *suppose*
ἀπέτρεψεν < ἀποτρέπω *turn away from, dissuade*
χαλεπαίνω *be angry at*

41c9 **ἕν τι τοῦτο . . . ἀληθές** "This one thing is true," in contrast to his colorful elaboration of τὰ λεγόμενα, which are only *possibly* true.

41d2 **ἀμελεῖται** The subject is τὰ τούτου πράγματα ("his affairs").

41d3 **τὰ ἐμά** "My experience" (i.e., "what has happened to me").

41d5 **βέλτιον ἦν** "It was better." Socrates treats his fate as having been preordained. He nevertheless distinguishes the divine decision from the human ill will that brought it about.

41d6–7 **καταψηφισαμένοις . . . κατηγόροις** Datives following χαλεπαίνω.

e τοῦτο αὐτοῖς ἄξιον μέμφεσθαι. τοσόνδε μέντοι αὐτῶν δέομαι· τοὺς ὑεῖς μου, ἐπειδὰν ἡβήσωσι, τιμωρήσασθε, ὦ ἄνδρες, ταὐτὰ ταῦτα λυποῦντες ἅπερ ἐγὼ ὑμᾶς ἐλύπουν, ἐὰν ὑμῖν δοκῶσιν ἢ χρημάτων ἢ ἄλλου του πρότερον ἐπιμελεῖσθαι ἢ ἀρετῆς, καὶ ἐὰν δοκῶσί τι εἶναι μηδὲν ὄντες, ὀνειδίζετε αὐτοῖς ὥσπερ ἐγὼ ὑμῖν, ὅτι οὐκ ἐπιμελοῦνται ὧν δεῖ, καὶ οἴονταί τι εἶναι ὄντες οὐδενὸς ἄξιοι. καὶ ἐὰν
42 ταῦτα ποιῆτε, δίκαια πεπονθὼς ἐγὼ ἔσομαι ὑφ' ὑμῶν αὐτός τε καὶ οἱ ὑεῖς. ἀλλὰ γὰρ ἤδη ὥρα ἀπιέναι, ἐμοὶ μὲν ἀποθανουμένῳ, ὑμῖν δὲ βιωσομένοις· ὁπότεροι δὲ ἡμῶν ἔρχονται ἐπὶ ἄμεινον πρᾶγμα, ἄδηλον παντὶ πλὴν ἢ τῷ θεῷ.

μέμφεσθαι < μέμφομαι *blame*
ἡβήσωσι < ἡβάω *grow up*
πεπονθὼς ἐγὼ ἔσομαι fut. pf. pass. < πάσχω *be treated*
ὥρα, -ας, ἡ *hour, time*

41e1 **τοῦτο αὐτοῖς ἄξιον μέμφεσθαι** Supply ἐστί for the impersonal construction with ἄξιον: "They deserve to be blamed for this" (lit. "It is worthwhile to blame them for this"). τοῦτο is explained by οἰόμενοι βλάπτειν.

41e1 **αὐτῶν** Socrates ironically calls on his accusers to take responsibility for the moral development of his sons, since he will not be there to do the job.

41e3 **ταὐτά** = τὰ αὐτά

41e4-5 **δοκῶσιν . . . ὄντες** For Socrates' description of his exhortations to his fellow Athenians, from which he borrows these words, see 29d7–30b4 and commentary.

41e5 **ἐὰν δοκῶσί τι εἶναι** "If they seem to be something." Even at the very end of the speech, Socrates continues to insist on the crucial distinction between seeming and being. So also at 41e6–42a1.

41e6 **ὥσπερ ἐγὼ ὑμῖν** "Just as I did to you."

ὧν The relative is attracted into the case of the unexpressed object of an assumed ἐπιμελεῖσθαι.

42a2 **ὥρα** Supply ἐστι.

42a3 **ἀποθανουμένῳ . . . βιωσομένοις** Future participles expressing purpose.

42a4 **ἄδηλον** Supply ἐστί: "It is unclear."

42a5 **τῷ θεῷ.** As at 19a6, no specific divinity is meant. Nevertheless, by choosing θεῷ as the final word of the speech, Plato reiterates Socrates' characterization of his life's work as divine service (cf. λατρεία 23c) and tacitly again rejects the charge of impiety.

Essays

ESSAY 1

In this opening chapter, Socrates confronts the accusation made by the prosecution that the jurors should not believe him because he is "clever at speaking." The concern with the deceptive qualities of speech and its ability to manipulate audiences was widespread at this time, owing to the growth of rhetorical education and to its being seen by adherents as a critical element in advancing one's status both politically and socially in the *polis*. In Plato, Socrates often criticizes this rhetorical education, however, and he here announces that he will speak merely in his accustomed way.

This concern with rhetoric is far from unique in the work of Plato. His dialogues, taken as a whole, offer a broad critique of public speaking, and of rhetoric generally, as a practice that is content with making things *appear to be* a certain way but less interested in how they really *are*. The successful rhetorician attempts to persuade members of his audience, not necessarily to educate them. In the *Gorgias*, Socrates likens rhetoric to cooking and says that the rhetorician's goal, like the cook's, is to produce pleasure for the listener/diner. Whether a cake is healthy for the one who eats it, or a rhetorical position is good for the character of the person who hears and believes it, is another matter altogether. Philosophy, by contrast, claims to be interested only in things as they *are* and sees rhetoric's preoccupation with pleasure as an indication that it is amoral and unscientific.

In the *Apology,* Socrates says that the job of a speaker is to tell the truth and that of a juror is to determine whether something has been said justly or not. To make that judgment might be harder than meets the eye, however. If rhetoric is like cooking, speakers will try to persuade by saying whatever they think will be most pleasurable for audiences to hear. It will take an extremely self-aware audience to distinguish the truth from something that has been manufactured to *seem like* truth, particularly if the speaker is unscrupulous about constructing a plausible falsehood based on his assessment of what he thinks the audience already believes.

What do you think Socrates expects from the jurors? How might they analyze the arguments so as not to be deceived by plausible lies and flattering rhetoric?

The problem is not simply an ancient one. Modern juries face the same problems, as do voters. How can juries best determine who is speaking τὰ δίκαια? And voters?

Further Reading

Habinek, Thomas. 2005. *Ancient Rhetoric and Oratory*. Oxford: Blackwell.
Kerford, G. B. 1981. *The Sophistic Movement*. Cambridge: Harvard University Press.

ESSAY 2

The fifth century is often referred to as the Greek Enlightenment. It is characterized by the founding, growth, and systematization of the disciplines of history, mathematics, rhetoric, medicine, and moral philosophy. Yet, as this chapter makes clear with its references to the "old accusers," there was resistance to these new ways of thinking. Fairly or not, some of it targeted Socrates. He was seen as a person who challenged the traditional understanding of what constitutes *arete* (excellence), and he caused irritation by asking pointed questions of people who had a reputation for virtue or wisdom, which he often revealed to be undeserved.

Athens was at the center of this cultural ferment, much of which was radically untraditional. The historians Herodotus and Thucydides, for all their differences, produced accounts of the past that, unlike Homer's epic, neither relied on the inspiration of the Muses nor portrayed the past as subject to divine decree. If they were right, what then was the value of traditional stories and the beliefs they implied? By the same token, if a sophist or teacher of rhetoric could teach you how to defeat your father in argument, as Aristophanes dramatizes in the *Clouds*, then why should you follow the traditional admonition to obey him unconditionally? If Socrates, finally, through his relentless questioning, could demonstrate that many of the men most honored by the community were blowhards and fakes, then why should anyone hold in high regard those men and the institutions they represent?

Such threats to the established order were deeply resented by some Athenians. They felt that their traditional way of life, the one that had forged men capable of defeating the vast forces of the Persian king at the battles of Marathon and Salamis, was under siege. The Platonic dialogues acknowledge the existence of these conservative forces, and some of their ideas make their way into Aristophanic comedy (see essay 3).

Are there contemporary parallels? Does the theory of evolution, and the position of science generally, play a similarly divisive role in contemporary life? Are there contemporary religious and intellectual movements that might be compared to the reaction of traditional Athenians to the intellectual advances of their day?

Further Reading

Aristophanes, *Clouds*.

Irwin, T. H. 1992. "Plato: The Intellectual Background." In *The Cambridge Companion to Plato*, edited by Richard Kraut, 51–89. Cambridge: Cambridge University Press.

Kennedy, George. 1963. *The Art of Persuasion in Greece*. Princeton: Princeton University Press.
Worthington, Ian, ed. 2007. *A Companion to Greek Rhetoric*. Oxford: Blackwell.

ESSAY 3

In this chapter, Socrates directly references Aristophanes' comedy the *Clouds*, which had portrayed him in an unflattering light. Comedy, it should be understood, was a civic institution in fifth-century Athens, not just a form of private entertainment. Comedies were perfomed by publicly financed choruses at the City Dionysia and the Lenaea, both annual festivals in honor of Dionysus. These comedies are characterized by abundant personal attacks on prominent individuals. Most scholars believe that five comedies competed in the years prior to and after the Peloponnesian War (431–404 B.C.E.), during which the number was reduced (for financial reasons) to three. The evidence, however, is both sketchy and contradictory.

Aristophanes, the foremost comic poet of fifth-century Athens and the only one for whom we possess complete plays, was born in the middle of the century and probably died in the late to mid-380s. He is believed to have been the author of forty plays, eleven of which survive. In the *Clouds* of 423, he portrays Socrates as an unprincipled sophist, although not one who seems to receive any money from his students. Incidently, the *Clouds* that we have is not the original play, but one that has been rewritten substantially. There is no reason to doubt, however, that the representation of Socrates remained essentially the same.

From the *Apology* we might reasonably conclude that Socrates regarded the *Clouds* as an important part of the public slander that had resulted in his being brought to trial. It is all the more striking, then, that Socrates' great admirer, Plato, does not appear to hold Aristophanes in low regard. The latter appears prominently in the the *Symposium*, where he is represented by Plato as being on friendly terms with Socrates. There he spins an outrageous fantasy about the origin of gender and concludes the evening by discussing the nature of comedy and tragedy with Agathon and Socrates (223d).

How might we understand the fact that Plato portrays Aristophanes as doing harm to Socrates' reputation while remaining his friend? What might his lack of obvious resentment tell us about the conventions and expectations of ancient comedy? What might it also say about the role of mockery in small, largely homogeneous societies such as that of Athens? To what extent should Aristophanes be seen as creating, and to what extent reflecting, an image of Socrates that was circulating among the larger Athenian public?

Further Reading

Dover, K. J. 1972. *Aristophanic Comedy*. Berkeley: University of California Press.

Halliwell, Stephen. 1991. "The Greek Uses of Laughter in Greek Culture." *The Classical Quarterly*, n.s., 41: 279–96.

MacDowell, Douglas. 1995. *Aristophanes and Athens: An Introduction to the Plays*. Oxford: Oxford University Press.

Nightingale, Andrea. 1995. "Philosophy and Comedy." In *Genres in Dialogue: Plato and the Construction of Philosophy*, 172–92. Cambridge: Cambridge University Press.

Platter, Charles. 2007. In *Aristophanes and the Carnival of Genres*, 1–41. Baltimore: Johns Hopkins University Press.

ESSAY 4

In this chapter, Socrates begins the effort to establish a systematic contrast between himself and those who taught rhetoric and other subjects for pay. The sophists and itinerant teachers of rhetoric were in many ways the rock stars of their day. They traveled from city to city, could command princely sums, and often carried with them an air of scandal. The historical Gorgias first came to Athens as a diplomat from Syracuse. His style is characterized by a heavy use of balanced antithetical phrases, rhyme, and assonance. Its self-conscious flashiness and ornamentation reflect precisely the type of speaking that Socrates contrasts with his own "plain" style at the beginning of the *Apology*, though Socratic conversation is in many ways no less self-conscious and, to judge by the capacity of Socrates to alienate his fellow citizens, equally unnatural.

Given the practices of such itinerant sophists and rootless cosmopolitans as Gorgias and Protagoras, is it ironic that Socrates is the one charged with corrupting Athenian youths, since he neither took money nor professed to teach? After all, while they were foreigners who owed no particular allegiance to Athenian society, Socrates was the equivalent of a decorated military veteran.

Both Socrates and the teachers of rhetoric could be seen as teaching skills and forms of thought that were corrosive to traditional values. The rhetoricians, however, at least taught a skill that could be useful in their students' political advancement, whereas Socrates' emphasis on the care of the self might have seemed simply perverse. Thus, wealthy citizens such as Callias were willing to spend vast sums to assure that their sons had every advantage in the competitive arena of Athenian public life. What was the skill Socrates had to offer? Would people normally be willing to pay for it? Would Socrates be more or less respectable if he were offering a concrete skill such as horse training or public speaking rather than the pursuit of wisdom (σοφία)?

Further Reading

Plato, *Gorgias*.

deRomilly, Jacqueline. 1992. Translated by Janet Lloyd. *The Great Sophists of Periclean Athens*. Oxford: Clarendon Press.

Schiappa, Edward. 2002. *Protagoras and Logos*. Columbia: University of South Carolina Press.

ESSAY 5

In the course of reading the *Apology*, it is sometimes useful to pull back from the text and try to put the issues in a larger context.

Plato was himself a rich man who traced his ancestry back to Solon the lawgiver on his mother's side of the family and to Codrus, the last of the legendary kings of Athens, on the other. It is therefore remarkable that from an early age he not only attached himself to Socrates, for whom pride in a noble lineage suggested spurious claims to ἀρετή rather than a social status to be admired. Moreover, he remained a loyal disciple long after the age when most of Socrates' other aristocratic followers, such as the brilliant Alcibiades, had given up philosophy to pursue their political and financial ambitions.

Plato, in fact, was uncommonly well connected. By his own testimony he appears to have had the opportunity to enter politics at an early age, during the oligarchic revolution of 404 B.C.E. and the subsequent reign of the Thirty Tyrants. In his *Seventh Letter*, regarded as authentic by most scholars, he says that some of the men involved in the revolution were relatives and that they invited him to join them. He says he decided to watch and see what they would do, but he was appalled by the abuses of the Thirty, including their attempt to involve Socrates in the crimes of the regime (see *Apology* 32c–e and notes). He withdrew from the political scene altogether at this point, never to enter Athenian politics again.

Throughout his life, however, he continued to ponder the meaning of the reign of the Thirty and the part played by his own family, a fact that he did not attempt to disguise. His uncles Critias and Charmides, leaders of the oligarchs, show up prominently in the dialogues as interlocutors of Socrates, as does Alcibiades, never a member of the Thirty but a wayward and dangerous force in the city.

Plato's interest in improving the function of government, however, never abated. He made several visits to Sicily in hopes of bringing about a government ruled according to philosophical principles. Most importantly, he composed lasting works of political theory, the *Republic*, and his final work, the *Laws*.

How should we interpret Plato's interest in good government in the light of his decision to abstain from politics? How should it be understood in light of Socrates' own claims? Is it morally incumbent upon all citizens to participate actively in government? Read *Apology* 32e–33b in translation. What might Socrates have said in answer to that question?

Further Reading

Plato. *Seventh Letter.*

Guthrie, W. K. C. 1975. "Life of Plato and Philosophical Influences." In *A History of Greek Philosophy. Vol. 4*, 8–38. Cambridge: Cambridge University Press.

Nails, Deborah. 2002. *The People of Plato: A Prosopography of Plato and Other Socratics,* 243–50. Hackett: Indianapolis: Hackett Publishing.

ESSAY 6

Socrates, in this chapter, represents himself paradoxically as one whose superiority to most people is based on the recognition of his ignorance. By this, he appears to mean that human beings are ignorant about the most crucial aspects of their existence, which are known only to the gods. Any understanding short of that impossible divine standard may be better than total ignorance, but does not really qualify as wisdom.

The highest human wisdom is the recognition of the limits of human understanding, yet human beings frequently represent themselves differently, as though they know something more. Socrates' service to humanity, in his view, is his willingness to show them that this is not the case.

In the Platonic dialogues, this service often takes the form of conversations regarding simple, everyday topics in which his interlocutors attempt to defend the conventional opinions they have never before questioned. Subjected to the critical questioning of Socrates, however, they are reduced to a state of perplexity, or *aporia*. This process is demonstrated in a number of shorter dialogues such as the *Ion*, the *Euthyphro*, and the *Laches*. There Socrates successfully demonstrates what he only asserts in the *Apology*, that those who pretend to knowledge are often unable to give a rational account of it. Many scholars view such dialogues as "protreptic" (< προ-τρέπω), a means of turning the interlocutor toward the pursuit of wisdom by making him aware of his ignorance.

Do you think such a strategy is typically effective? Are people whose ignorance is exposed grateful to those who compel them to acknowledge their lack of understanding, or are they resentful and sullen? Do they dedicate themselves to correcting their weaknesses, or do they attempt to disguise them more effectively? Further, what do you think the reaction of Socrates' contemporaries would have been to his claim of both ignorance and superior knowledge?

Nonetheless, how are people to change if they do not become aware of their ignorance? Encouraging feelings of self-worth in fellow citizens and students is no doubt a good thing, but can it encourage them to become individuals who are genuinely thoughtful and capable of analyzing seriously their own thoughts and actions? How would you attempt to address the problem that Socrates encountered?

Further Reading

Plato, *Laches.*

Penner, Terry. 1992. "Socrates and the Early Dialogues." In *The Cambridge Companion to Plato*, edited by Richard Kraut, 121–69. Cambridge and New York: Cambridge University Press.

ESSAY 7

To understand why Socrates went to the poets after the politicians—or perhaps why he went to them at all—it is necessary to have an understanding of the traditional place of poetry in Greek society. Poetry was not primarily an aesthetic phenomenon throughout much of archaic and classical Greece, nor was it considered effete or elitist, as it often is today. Instead, it was a means of education and communal acculturation for the Greeks. Children and adolescents memorized long passages of Homer, as well as the songs of the lyric poets. Further, they were expected to perform in choruses and to be able to sing at drinking parties (*symposia*) and on other occasions, both as children and as adults. In a society in which books were rare and expensive, this is perhaps not surprising. The Muses, Hesiod tells us, were considered the daughters of Memory, and as such functioned as the keepers of the culture's traditions, dominant narratives, and self-understanding.

Thus, when Socrates proposes to show that the poets only pretend to wisdom, he is calling into question one of the central assumptions of Greek society. He portrays poetry as a species of "automatic writing" in which the poet is a passive conduit for information that originates with the gods but is not himself wise. Their art is therefore the opposite of the philosophical drive for clarification and definition. Socrates wants to know what a virtue like courage *is* while the poet tells a story about courageous heroes.

Is such an absolute separation between abstract definition and concrete example necessary? After all, the work of Parmenides, Plato's great precursor, was written in verse. Is it possible to conceive of a poetry that approaches philosophical precision or a kind of philosophical approach that brings together the concrete and the abstract? Some of Plato's own dialogues make elaborate use of poetic myth, including *Republic*, *Phaedrus*, *Gorgias*, *Symposium*, and *Timaeus*. Can these myths be viewed as Plato's attempt to provide a satisfactory answer to this question?

Further Reading

Plato, *Ion*.

Hesiod. *Theogony*, lines 1–33.

Havelock, Eric A. 1963. *Preface to Plato*. Cambridge, Mass.: Harvard University Press.

Ledbetter, Grace M. 2003. *Poetics before Plato: Interpretation and Authority in Early Greek Theories of Poetry*. Princeton: Princeton University Press.

ESSAY 8

Socrates proceeds through the groups of citizens (politicians, poets, craftsmen) who might claim knowledge or wisdom in descending order according to their prominence in the Athenian *polis*. What he discovered, however, was that the order appeared to be reversed relative to the degree of ignorance he saw in them (cf. 22a3–6). The politicians merely presumed a general wisdom but in fact knew nothing. The poets claimed a general wisdom based upon divine inspiration but were unable to give a rational account of the "many fine things" (22c3) they said or of the other matters they deemed themselves worthy to pronounce upon. Finally, the craftsmen had a genuine skill and knowledge in certain limited practical areas that even Socrates did not possess, but they erred when they presumed to claim a more general wisdom.

What does this order tell us of the relation Plato assumes between knowledge and social prestige? How does this ordering fit with Socrates' earlier claim merely to speak whatever first comes into his mind? What effect does Plato achieve by ordering Socrates' speech in this manner?

Is this classification of professions and relative degrees of wisdom accurate in your view? How do we determine intelligently whether a speaker should be taken seriously? What knowledge must engineers or artists possess to do their jobs well? Does that knowledge give them any special authority to speak about matters outside their narrow field of expertise? What about service workers and tradespeople? Does their position outside the margins of traditional elite groups make their opinions especially worthy of our consideration? Why or why not?

Further Reading

Colaiaco, James A. 2001. *Socrates Against Athens: Philosophy on Trial*. New York and London: Routledge.

Crawford, Matthew B. 2009. *Shop Class as Soulcraft. An Inquiry into the Value of Work.* New York: Penguin.

Mara, Gerald M. 1997. *Socrates' Discursive Democracy: Logos and Ergon in Platonic Political Philosophy*. Albany: State University of New York Press.

ESSAY 9

Socrates says that the demands of his service to the god have left him no time to spend on politics or personal enrichment. This statement is perplexing if his original intention was simply to understand Apollo's oracle; his experience with the politicians, poets, and craftsmen should have been sufficient to allow him to conclude that they were not wise and so settle the matter once and for all. "I am the wisest, because at least I know that I know nothing." Instead of providing a firm answer to the initial question, however, Socrates' experience with the three groups seems to have convinced him that he had not reached the end, only the beginning of a lifelong "quest for wisdom," or φιλοσοφία.

The decision to continue his quest is all the more remarkable in light of the considerable material and social disadvantages that accompanied it. Indeed, not only does philosophy fail to provide an income, unlike the teaching of rhetoric, but Socrates' rejection of politics and most other forms of civic duty also provoked suspicion in democratic Athens. Yet this renunciation of all of the elements of what was commonly considered a successful life is exactly what the pursuit of wisdom demanded, according to Socrates.

Indeed, philosophy, as Socrates understands it, is not so much a theory or an intellectual investigation as it is a particularly demanding mode of life, one fraught with self-imposed dangers. Indeed, if Socrates had rested complacent with the results of his initial set of inquiries, he would have been guilty of the same self-conceit as his interlocutors, who thought that their limited knowledge qualified them to be competent judges of everything. In contrast, for Socrates the only honest response to the recognition of one's own ignorance is the pursuit of wisdom. It is far superior to the complacent confidence of one who, as Socrates says, "thinks he is something but is not." Thus, Socratic φιλοσοφία is not the end result of the process of question, answer, definition, and refutation but is the process itself.

Can such a pursuit have an end? What does this say about the possibility of human beings' possessing genuine wisdom? If

Socrates is right, is it possible for anyone to make ethical decisions and act on them? Or must one suspend judgment on every occasion so as not to *seem to know*?

Further Reading

Dover, K. J. 1974. *Greek Popular Morality in the Time of Plato and Aristotle.* Oxford: Blackwell.

Hadot, Pierre. 2001. *What is Ancient Philosophy?* Translated by Michael Chase. Cambridge, Mass.: Harvard University Press.

Plato, *Theaetetus.*

ESSAY 10

Why is Socrates on trial at all? In part, at least, it is because he appeared to have unusual religious beliefs. As this chapter indicates, the belief in Socrates' religious heterodoxy stemmed in part from the fact that many attributed to him the beliefs commonly associated with the materialist philosophers of the day who rejected traditional mythological explanations of the universe (23d4–7). Moreover, as Socrates makes clear, this charge cannot be separated from the political implications of corrupting the youth by teaching them how to question their elders and the traditional values they represent (23c2–d1; see essay 2).

In the early twenty-first century, when theocratic impulses are prominent both at home and abroad, such an example of religious persecution in ancient Athens might be unsurprising. Yet Athenians were not typically intolerant, and their religious life was hardly monolithic. In addition to the traditional pantheon, other exotic foreign cults had been brought to Athens with no more than moderate disapproval. Cybele, Isis, Sabezias, Asclepius, and Bendis were all worshiped in the time of Socrates.

At the same time, the ultimate authority of the *demos* in areas of religion was not seriously questioned. Nobody argued for a separation of church and state. This interpenetration of religion and politics can be observed in a number of ways. For example,

Socrates imagines his enemies referring to him as μιαρώτατος, "most foul" (23d2), a term of generic abuse often used without special religious implications. Nevertheless, the word derives from the same root as μίασμα, "pollution, ritual defilement," suggesting that, on a certain level, to be tainted religiously was to be tainted sociopolitically, and vice versa.

This conflation of ideas could have real-life political consequences. Around 432, according to Plutarch (*Life of Pericles* 32.1), Diopeithes proposed a decree, in language that clearly anticipates the indictment of Socrates, making it possible to prosecute individuals "who do not acknowledge divine things" (τοὺς τὰ θεῖα μὴ νομίζοντας). It seems that there was a political dimension to this legislation as well. Plutarch suggests that the bill was an attempt to attack Pericles via his friend, the philosopher Anaxagoras, a presumed atheist (see essay 14).

The trial of Socrates also appears to have had political overtones not strictly related to the ethical and religious issues mentioned in the indictment. The democratic faction may have seen an attack on Socrates as a way to get back at the oligarchs with whom he was linked by personal ties. Indeed, as Socrates mentions at the beginning of this chapter (23c3), many of his youthful followers were drawn from the upper reaches of Athenian society. However, the settlement between the democratic and oligarchic factions, which was imposed by the Spartan king Pausanias in 403, included an agreement that there could be no prosecution of individuals for offenses committed under the rule of the Thirty, with the exception of the Thirty themselves and a number of high officials (see introduction). Seen from this perspective, the trial of Socrates on a religious charge could have been one of the ways the democratic faction took revenge on their enemies without violating the amnesty.

What do you think are the most important issues in the trial? Is Socrates' service to Apollo, as exemplified by his dogged pursuit of the proper understanding of Chaerephon's oracle, qualitatively different from traditional civic religion? Does it have its roots in the status of philosophy's critical approach to civic life?

Consider the relationship of religion to political authority. What kinds of religion are easiest to harmonize with a political regime? Is Socrates' philosophical "religion" one of them?

Further Reading

Mikalson, Jon D. 1983. *Athenian Popular Religion*. Chapel Hill and London: University of North Carolina Press.

Morgan, Michael L. 1992. "Plato and Greek Religion." In *The Cambridge Companion to Plato*, edited by Richard Kraut, 227–47. Cambridge and New York: Cambridge University Press.

O'Sullivan, L. L. 1997. "Athenian Impiety Trials in the Late Fourth Century B.C." *Classical Quarterly*, n.s., 47: 136–52.

ESSAY 11

In this chapter Socrates begins his defense by reciting the charges against him as if he were reading from a sworn affidavit. Such trial scenes were familiar to his Athenian audience both from their experience of actual trials and from the dramatic stage. The law courts were a primary arena in which the drama of civic life was played out in democratic Athens.

The *Oresteia* trilogy of Aeschylus thus describes the story of a family trapped in an endless cycle of revenge. The commander-in-chief of the Trojan expedition, Agamemnon, finds his fleet unable to sail from Aulis because of contrary winds. He learns from a prophet that Artemis is angry and will not allow them to proceed unless the king sacrifices his daughter Iphigeneia. After much turmoil, he finally agrees to do so. When the deed is done, the fleet sails to Troy. The trilogy begins ten years later, when Agamemnon returns from Troy and is immediately murdered by his wife, Clytemnestra, who is seeking vengeance for Iphigeneia. Clytemnestra, in turn, is murdered by her son, Orestes, who returns from exile to avenge his father's death. He is then forced to flee his homeland by the arrival of the Furies, goddesses of vengeance who punish those who commit acts of violence against blood relations.

The *Oresteia* ends in Athens. Athena sets up a court, and there is a trial in which Orestes is acquitted. This action, in turn, serves as a foundation myth for the Athenian court system. Under the new dispensation, the old system of retributive justice ("an eye for an eye, a tooth for a tooth") is abandoned and replaced by the verdict of citizen juries who punish according to the law and their best judgment but are not personally involved in the case.

Yet the Athenian system was never truly impersonal. There were no public prosecutors, for example. The legal process was set in motion only by the direct action of private individuals who would undertake to prosecute someone they believed guilty. Naturally, such a system offered many opportunities for settling private scores. The defendant, too, acted directly in the trial. He was not allowed to engage a lawyer to speak on his behalf. It was in part under such conditions that public speaking became so important in Athens, and this was one reason the sophists were able to charge such high fees for their lessons. Defendants with means but without rhetorical ability might hire a ghostwriter such as the famous Lysias, although they would still have to memorize and deliver the speech on their own.

All of these features of Athenian legal practice conspired to make trials in general, and the trial of Socrates in particular, highly charged personal confrontations. As Aeschylus had seen when he dramatized the trial of Orestes, and as Aristophanes had parodied in his *Wasps* (a satire on the Athenian courts and juries), these confrontations were highly theatrical by nature. Modern legal systems retain vestiges of this originary drama, and the trial has long been a staple of movies and television. Such spectacles allow the viewer, who occupies a position similar to that of the juror, to see the participants as unique individuals and the contested issues as arising from a context, not simply as a set of abstract hypothetical concerns.

How, then, do the dramatic aspects of the *Apology* shape our perception of the personalities and motivations of those concerned?

Is this linking of the issues at stake to particular, often flawed, individuals important or healthy for the effective administration of justice? If the trial of Socrates were taking place today, would a jury chosen according to the rules of modern jurisprudence have decided differently? What about a small judicial panel or a tribunal?

Further Reading

Aeschylus, *Eumenides*.

Brickhouse, Thomas C., and Nicholas D. Smith. 1989. *Socrates on Trial*, 24-37. Princeton: Princeton University Press.

Sealey, R. 1983. "The Athenian Courts for Homicide." *Classical Philology* 78: 275–96.

ESSAY 12

Socrates appears to assume that most Athenians would agree with his implicit contention that one can only accuse someone else of corrupting the youth if one has taken special care in these matters oneself, and that one can only claim to have taken special care if one has also undertaken a rigorous inquiry into who "improves" the youth and how? In short, Socrates' questioning of Meletus would seem to imply that in his view, questions about what is best for our children should be left to the discretion of experts.

Such an idea cannot have sat well with the audience, however, for it calls directly into question an idea central to Athenian democracy—indeed, to all democratic societies—that average citizens, who by and large are not specialists, have the capacity to make good judgments for themselves and their families. Socrates' position could certainly have provoked resentment. Many members of the jury would have been fathers who would have felt few qualms about making their own judgments about what they perceived to be nefarious influences on their sons. Indeed, most of us would say that it is a duty to protect our children from corrupting influences, as we see them. It is not simply the job of "experts" but a moral imperative for all parents, from the best educated to the worst. For this reason, many in the audience would have found the standards to which Socrates holds Meletus as disturbing as any of the things with which he himself is charged.

The idea that common sense will always provide us with adequate solutions to the problems of daily life is one that few people question, for it affirms the basic egalitarian principles upon which modern democracies are founded. But there is another side to the issue that is less pleasant to consider. Common sense can also function as a screen, obscuring the hidden assumptions that many of us would be just as happy not to examine. This was certainly the case for many of Socrates' interlocutors, who grew angry at having their cherished beliefs questioned.

The issue is not simple, but let us return to this idea: what is required for a human being to live an ethical life as a responsible citizen in a democratic society? Is it enough simply to rely on common sense (or tradition, or public norms) in making the moral judgments that parents and citizens are required to make every single day? What are the costs of attempting to do so? Is there a middle ground between the rule of the experts and the appeal to unexamined traditional beliefs? Further, can questioning of the Socratic type play a positive role in making and disseminating these quotidian judgments, or by undermining traditional figures of authority does the Socratic approach threaten the ability of families to function as teachers of morality?

Further Reading

Plato, *Euthyphro.*

Strauss, Barry S. 1993. *Fathers and Sons in Athens: Ideology and Society in the Era of the Peloponnesian War.* London: Routledge.

ESSAY 13

Socrates implies strongly that his actions have been misunderstood and that he would never have intentionally corrupted the youth. Later he will assert openly that he has done nothing wrong (37a6–7).

In this chapter, however, Socrates makes a more dramatic claim that *no one* does wrong willingly. This argument can be found in a number of places throughout the Platonic corpus and seems to be one of the touchstones of both Socratic and Platonic ethics, although some scholars believe that in the later dialogues Plato is more pessimistic than Socrates was (Penner 1992). For various articulations of this argument, see, among other passages, *Meno* 77b–78b, *Protagoras* 345e, *Gorgias* 467c5–468e5, 509e5–7, *Republic* 438a3, 505d11, *Laws* 860d1–862a4.

The argument is based on two premises: (1) to do wrong to something, or someone, is to make it worse; and (2) when faced with a choice between things of varying qualities, one always attempts to choose the better and reject the worse. By doing wrong intentionally, however—and so making things worse (premise 1)—I am choosing to associate with that which is worse instead of that which is better. Therefore, either premise 2 is incorrect (an unlikely possibility), or I do not intend to do wrong. It may well be that I act *stupidly*, but it is out of ignorance and not from the desire to do wrong.

If we accept this argument, the appropriate response to "wrongdoing," as Socrates states, is not punishment but reeducation or persuasion. Is this a rational argument? Is it practical? What are its potential dangers? Does it sufficiently account for evil done through weakness of will (ἀκρασία)?

Further Reading

Slings, S. R. 1994. *Plato's* Apology of Socrates*: A Literary and Philosophical Study with a Running Commentary,* 113–18. Leiden, New York, and Cologne: E. J. Brill.

Weiss, Roslyn. 2006. *The Socratic Paradox and Its Enemies.* Chicago: University of Chicago Press.

ESSAY 14

The sources on the life and philosophy of Anaxagoras are rich and merit scrutiny if we are to understand the intellectual context informing the *Apology* and the specific difference Socrates introduces in turning from physical and cosmogonical speculation to the problems of moral philosophy and self-knowledge (see introduction). Anaxagoras is said to have been twenty years old when he came to Athens and began his philosophical career. He stayed for roughly thirty years, but he was was later tried on charges of impiety due to his presumed atheism (see essay 10). It is said that he was assisted in his defense by Pericles, who was his student and friend, with the result that he was fined and exiled rather than put to death like Socrates (Diogenes Laertius 2.7).

The fragments of Anaxagoras present a cosmogony that begins with primal chaos in which each element (hot, cold, wet, dry, bright, dark) was mixed with every other. This confusion was bounded by the infinitely small on one side and the infinitely large on the other (Kirk, Raven, and Schofield 1993, fr. 472–74). For Anaxagoras, the principle that ordered this chaos into the cosmos of defined entities we all perceive was νοῦς or "mind" (Kirk, Raven, and Schofield 1993, fr. 476).

As Socrates recounts in the *Phaedo* (97b–99b), he was initially very much attracted to Anaxagoras's theory of mind. Ultimately, however, Socrates found his explanations relied too much on physical causes and gave no real guidance on how this concept of mind might actually function in organizing the cosmos for the good or might lead a man to determine the best course of action. Socrates thus turned from seeking to know the external causes of natural phenomena to seeking a knowledge of the self, so that he might determine how best a man should live.

Socrates' decision suggests a gap between technical knowledge of the external world and the depths of the human soul. Does his understanding of this separation continue to be valid today, in a world where science is generally regarded as the most reliable approach to gathering knowledge and making decisions about the world? What are the implications of science for ethics, anyway? Is a scientist bound by ethical principles in the pursuit of his or her research? If yes, on what are these principles based? Are they themselves scientific, or must scientists borrow them from elsewhere (religion, potitical theory, etc.)?

Further Reading

Kirk, G. S., J. E. Raven, and M. Schofield. 1983. *The Presocratic Philosophers*. 2nd ed., 352–84. Cambridge: Cambridge University Press.

Woodbury, Leonard. 1981. "Anaxagoras and Athens." *Phoenix* 35: 295–315.

ESSAY 15

Socrates begins his line of questioning by trying to establish the validity of an argument by categories. He asks Meletus to agree that there is no one who believes in human affairs (ἀνθρώπεια πράγματα, 27b), without also believing humans and, likewise, no one who believes in matters pertaining to horses without also believing in horses. In each case, the existence of the larger class is used to deduce the existence of the individual entity. According to the same logic, Socrates' well-known belief in a divine sign, literally a "divine thing" (δαιμόνιον), must necessarily imply that he believes (like every other right-thinking Athenian) in the prior category of divinities (δαίμονες). Therefore, Meletus's accusation of atheism cannot be true.

Socrates' position on divinities may or may not be a ringing endorsement for traditional Athenian religious belief, but the argument by categories is an intrinsic part of his general approach to knowledge and is the basis for the Platonic Theory of Forms. The argument often goes as follows. A chair is an object fabricated expressly for sitting. Individual chairs may be of different colors and materials. They may or may not have legs and may have altogether different specific uses. Each chair, nevertheless, whether a camp stool or a La-Z-Boy, is part of a category that we could call "chairness" and that we appeal to, consciously or unconsciously, when we wish to distinguish a chair, say, from a hairbrush. Thus, the existence of a chair both implies abstract "chairness" and the fact of chairness implies the existence of individual chairs as a class. In a similar way, Socrates' belief in a δαιμόνιον implies the existence of δαίμονες. This way of thinking has important implications for ethics. For example, it is argued that good things of all sorts are good because they share in the category, or "form," of goodness. The existence of acts called "just" similarly implies that there is a larger category of justice of which each just act is a part and from which each derives its name. By the same token, the category of justice necessarily implies the possibility of just acts and those which fall outside that category.

The Theory of Forms does not make a direct appearance in the *Apology*, although its seeds are definitely present. Its historical development marks an important attempt to understand the way we know about and act in the world by compelling us to ground our judgments in precise and universally applicable definitions. Socratic questioning often begins from the assumption that such categories and definitions exist and are themselves foundational for ethical reflection.

Nonetheless, is such a precise understanding of terms necessary for us to be aware of the abstract qualities of the world that link our separate existences? Can we recognize ideas such as goodness and virtue without rigorously defining them, or will definition be necessary if we are to have confidence that what we mean by justice is consistent with what our neighbors, rivals, and enemies imagine (or should imagine) it to be?

Further Reading

Plato, *Republic*, Book 5.

Allen, R. E. 1970. *Plato's Euthyphro and the Early Theory of Forms*. London: Routledge and Kegan Paul.

Roochnik, David. 2004. *Retrieving the Ancients: An Introduction to Greek Philosophy*, 91–134. London: Blackwell.

ESSAY 16

"Someone will say" that Socrates should feel shame for acting in such a way as to bring a capital charge against himself. Socrates responds to this imaginary critic by invoking the Homeric tradition. Achilles was told by his mother that if he avenged the death of his companion, Patroclus, by slaying Hector, he would win eternal fame but an early death (*Iliad* 18.70–104). If the knowledge that your course of actions will lead to personal destruction ought to produce a sense of shame, Socrates suggests, then by this same logic would not Achilles' decision to avenge Patroclus also be shameful rather than heroic?

By associating his defense with a defense of the *Iliad's* greatest hero, Socrates cleverly suggests that he is the true defender of traditional Hellenic values. The heroes of old held their honor more dear than life itself. So does he. In this way, Socrates effectively turns the tables on his accusers and judges by invoking the values of an epic poetry sanctified by time and affirmed by Athenian cultural norms. He becomes the defender of traditional values and urges his fellow citizens to live up to the models they revere, suggesting that it is *they* who should feel shame if they do not.

But is the fear of shame and the obsession with honor (τιμή) that motivates so many of Homer's heroes a good image for describing Socrates' service to Apollo? Does not the epic system of values presuppose the existence of a community that shares a similar ideological orientation to the world? What would be the place for Socratic questioning in such a world? Would Socrates be welcome there?

To return to the *Iliad*, does Achilles belong to such a community of values, or does the quarrel with Agamemnon that brings about his "destructive wrath" shatter his confidence in that community once and for all? Does the epic tradition provide alternative models to heroism as Achilles understands it? What would Agamemnon have done? Odysseus?

Further Reading

Lucian, *True History*, Book 2.

Hunter, Richard. 2004. "Homer and Greek Literature." In *The Cambridge Companion to Homer,* edited by Robert Fowler, 235–53. Cambridge: Cambridge University Press.

Nagy, Gregory. 1979. *The Best of the Achaeans: Concepts of the Hero in Archaic Greek Poetry*, 13–210. Baltimore: Johns Hopkins University Press.
Nietzsche, Friedrich. 2003. *The Birth of Tragedy: Out of the Spirit of Music*, translated by Shaun Whiteside. London: Penguin.

ESSAY 17

The sentence οὐκ ἐκ χρημήτων ἀρετὴ γίγνεται, ἀλλ' ἐξ ἀρετῆς χρήματα καὶ τὰ ἄλλα ἀγαθὰ τοῖς ἀνθρώποις ἅπαντα καὶ ἰδίᾳ καὶ δημοσίᾳ is translated by Hugh Tredennick as follows: "Wealth does not bring goodness but goodness brings wealth and and every other blessing, both to the individual and to the state." What does Socrates mean by this? Does he really believe that ἀρετή invariably produces wealth? What about his own case? After all, Socrates has already cited his poverty as the result of his dedication to examining the oracle and neglecting both his public and private life (23b–c). Or are we to believe that a man who spends all his days exhorting his fellow citizens to excellence does not himself possess it?

An alternate reading of the Greek text proposed by John Burnet in his commentary understands ἀγαθά not as part of the subject phrase, but as the predicate along with τοῖς ἀνθρώποις (see also Burnyeat 2003, 2004). The result is a translation of the second half of the sentence that seems more in line with the standard Socratic idea that the pursuit of wealth and public honor are impediments to true ἀρετή, not its result: "It is goodness that makes money and everything else good for men" (Burnet 1924).

Both ways of construing the passage are grammatically defensible and have appeared in print. The first version seems most natural given the word order but produces a reading that is philosophically puzzling. The second must assume a less natural word order, but the result is a sentiment that is consistent with many other passages in Plato, where wealth for its own sake is not valued highly and the pursuit of it is regarded as a symptom of an unhappy soul.

As readers, we have the luxury of considering both ways of construing the passage, but ultimately we must make a decision. How should we go about doing it? What factors should be most important in attempting to resolve the crux? The naturalness of the grammar? Consistency of philosophical doctrine?

Further Reading

Burnet, John. 1924. *Plato's Euthyphro, Apology of Socrates and Crito.* Oxford: Oxford University.

Burnyeat, Myles F. 2003. "*Apology* 30b2–4: Socrates, Money, and the Grammar of ΓΙΓΝΕΣΘΑΙ." *Journal of Hellenic Studies* 123: 1–25.

ESSAY 18

This chapter contains the famous comparison of Socrates to a biting fly who has been sent to rouse the great and noble "horse" of Athens from its torpor (30e2–5). This is no idle figure of speech. The metaphor of "awakening" (ἐγείρειν) is central to Socrates' philosophical mission. He seeks to rouse his hearers and us from the slumbers of our complacency. In this view, the positive conclusions we reach from our inquiries are less important than the process of rigorous and unrelenting self-inquiry. This metaphoric complex, in turn, is directly related to the recurrence of forms of ἐπιμέλεια ("care"). But the process is not entirely directed at others. As he makes clear later (38a9–10), Socratic conversation and testing is directed as much at himself as it is at his interlocutors. The philosopher's mission is to awaken both himself and others to the need to care for themselves and to seek excellence (*arete*).

The central point, then, of the fly comparison is that the activity of caring for the self presumes self-consciousness. Socrates cannot awaken others if he himself is in a state of spiritual sleep or unconsciousness. At the same time, his efforts may be resisted by those who are unwilling to change and "wake up." Indeed, as we see, the Athenians grow angry with Socrates when he attempts to rouse them and, like a horse swatting a pesky fly with its tail, they strike at him in a variety of ways, literal and metaphorical.

Both Socrates' actions and those of the Athenians are aggressive: the one bites, the other swats. Yet where Socrates' badgering of his peers is part of a deliberate program of examining his fellow citizens and of seeking wisdom, their reaction is the product of resentment and annoyance. Despite the great gulf that separates them, the odd symmetry between Socrates' aggression and that of his fellow citizens is nevertheless striking. How should we account for it? Is a certain discomfort always part of any process of "waking up?" Is the possibility of provoking an angry response always the risk that "wakers" run, or could a gentler Socrates wake sleepers from their "dogmatic slumber" without provoking their wrath (see essay 6)?

Further Reading

Sayre, Kenneth M. "Plato's Dialogues in Light of the *Seventh Letter*." *Platonic Writings, Platonic Readings*, edited by Charles L. Griswold, Jr., 93–109. New York: Routledge.

Wilson, Emily. 2007. *The Death of Socrates*. Cambridge: Harvard University Press.

ESSAY 19

The precise nature of Socrates' divine sign (31d1), to which reference is made in a number of dialogues, is much debated (see essay 31). Plato gives us only a few details concerning Socrates' relationship to this peculiar being: it only works to discourage Socrates from pursuing a course of action he had otherwise determined to follow. Furthermore, its intervention is never accompanied by an explanation, leaving Socrates to speculate about what caused it. In some instances the reason for its appearance is clearer than for others. In the *Republic* (496c), Socrates talks about how the divine sign kept him from entering politics and concludes that the pursuit of the philosophic life requires one to keep clear of the inevitible "dust and sleet" of political life. In the *Phaedrus* and the *Euthydemus*, on the other hand, Socrates' decision to leave a particular place is checked by the intervention of the divine sign. In the first case, he interprets its appearance as a positive order to compose a speech opposite to the one he has just given. In the *Euthydemus*, he interprets (with presumed irony) the divine sign's delay of his departure as having given him the opportunity to meet and converse with the unscrupulous sophists Euthydemus and Dionysodorus. So there is no obvious pattern to the appearance of the δαιμόνιον, nor to its significance.

Yet the vocabulary Plato uses to describe the experience of Socrates has resonance in other dialogues outside references to Socrates' personal sign, most famously the *Symposium*. There Eros (Love or Desire) is described as a δαίμων, a being defined as a mediator between the divine and human realms. In that role, Eros comes to stand for the desire for the Good that is most clearly instantiated by philosophy itself. It has also been remarked by a variety of commentators that Socrates himself resembles the physical description of Eros given in the *Symposium*. Thus understood, one interpretation of the Socratic δαίμων might therefore be as the expression of "desire" or "force" that turns Socrates away from actions that would contravene a philosophic life and hence toward the Good. At the same time, however, the δαίμων does not dictate what the nature of that life should be, just as Eros in the *Symposium* has no specific positive attributes in and of himself but merely functions as an emblem for φιλοσοφία, the desire for wisdom.

How do you interpret Socrates' divine sign? Is it a supernatural being, the voice of conscience, or a convenient excuse to abstain from something that seemed contrary to reason? Can we use the *Symposium*'s theory of the δαίμων as a mediator between the human and the divine as a way to understand what is meant in the *Apology*? Why or why not?

Further Reading

Hans, James S. 2006. *Socrates and the Irrational*, 51–100. Charlottesville: University of Virginia Press.

Hunter, Richard. 2004. *Plato's Symposium.* Oxford: Oxford University Press.
Long, A. A. 2006. "How Does Socrates' Divine Sign Communicate with Him?" In *A Companion to Socrates*, edited by Sara Ahbel-Rappe and Rachana Kametkar, 63–74. London: Blackwell.
Smith, Nicholas D., and Paul B. Woodruff, eds. 2000. "Socrates and His Daimonion." *Reason and Religion in Socratic Philosophy*, 176–204. New York: Oxford Univesity Press.

ESSAY 20

In this chapter, Socrates recounts the risks he ran in standing up for justice against both the democratic regime and the rule of the Thirty in Athens. Socrates' democratic credentials have often been questioned, despite his well-attested military heroism in its defense.

Nonetheless, it is also clear from the beginning of the *Apology* and elsewhere that Socrates does not believe all people are equally qualified to do all things. Thus, in his opening conversation with Callias (20a7–b8), Socrates questions the wealthy Athenian about whether he has found someone properly qualified to educate his sons—in the same way that he might seek an expert in things equestrian to train his horses. Such a sentiment, which could be extended to argue that only some men are qualified to rule, while others are best suited to be ruled (see *Republic*, book 2), is clearly contrary to the principles of Athenian democracy, which was based on the concept of ἰσονομία, or the radical equality of all citizens and their competence to participate directly in the legislative, executive, and judicial processes. Indeed, many Athenian political offices were filled by lot, a practice that Xenophon records Socrates as criticizing on the grounds that these offices require a certain expertise. By the same token, Socrates argues, no one would trust a ship's captain chosen by lot (*Memorabilia* 1.2.9). Similarly, in the *Gorgias* he implies that it is foolish for the assembly to pick public health officials or elect generals based on popular sentiment, which can be easily manipulated by a trained rhetorician (455a–d; see also

Dodds 1966). Such positions require a sober analysis of the relevant qualifications of the individuals by those capable of making such an evaluation.

It seems clear from a variety of sources, then, that Socrates was in fact critical of Athenian democracy and, as the outcome of the trial reveals, not without some reason. He was thus lumped by many with the supporters of oligarchy and the Thirty. Yet Plato is careful in this section to distance him from both groups. This rhetorical move, however, raises several important questions. Is it possible to be a critic of democracy without being a supporter of oligarchy or tyranny? Insofar as Plato attempts to portray Socrates as apolitical, in the sense of being a supporter neither of democracy nor of oligarchy, does that mean his thought has no political importance?

Many modern readers of Plato have portrayed him as an apostle of the modern authoritarian state. Are they right? What place, if any, does Socratic and Platonic thought have in contemporary politics?

Further Reading

Larson, Thomas L., ed. 1963. *Plato: Totalitarian or Democrat?* Englewood Cliffs, N.J.: Prentice-Hall.

Platter, Charles. 2005. "Was Plato the Founder of Totalitarianism?" *Classical Studies and the Ancient World: History in Dispute*, vol. 21, edited by Paul Allen Miller and Charles Platter, 154–63. Detroit: Gale.

ESSAY 21

Socrates' statement in this chapter that he is the teacher of no man is in one sense true and in another obviously false. This passage has become a touchstone in scholarly discussions of Socratic irony. Most famously, Gregory Vlastos refers to it when he makes a distinction between "simple" and "complex" irony: "In 'simple' irony what is said just isn't what is meant: taken in its ordinary, commonly understood, sense the statement is simply false. In 'complex' irony what is said both is and isn't what is meant: its surface content is meant to be true in one sense, false in another" (31). Vlastos's distinction poses well one of the apparent paradoxes of the Platonic dialogues. On the one hand, the entire Platonic corpus would be senseless if Socrates had not been Plato's teacher. On the other, Socrates is clearly not a teacher as he defines the term: a professional who accepts money from students in return for transmitting positive knowledge to them. Socrates is not a sophist or a craftsman who claims to possess a defined τέχνη that he teaches others.

Further, the issue of whether or not Socrates teaches is tied to whether or not philosophy itself is teachable. Essay 18 discusses philosophy not so much as a set of skills that can be memorized, but as an approach to life that involves the careful examination of the self and its varying conditions in the company of others.

Is Socrates a teacher? If so, what does he teach? If you feel his disavowal of teaching is ironic, do you agree with Vlastos that there is a truth the irony disguises? If so, what is it? Or do you agree with Alexander Nehamas, who sees Socratic philosophy as an activity rather than a body of doctrine, and who regards Socrates' ironic approach as unlimited, even beyond the control of Plato himself?

Further Reading

Allen, R. E. 1980. *Socrates and Legal Obligation*, 3–16. Minneapolis: University of Minnesota Press.

Nehamas, Alexander. 1998. *The Art of Living: Socratic Reflections from Plato to Foucault*, 46–69. Berkeley: University of California Press.

Vlastos, Gregory. 1991. *Socrates: Ironist and Moral Philosopher*. Ithaca, N.Y.: Cornell University Press.

ESSAY 22

Socrates here argues that he does not recruit the young men with whom he associates, but that in fact they congregate around him because they love to hear the refutation of those who pretend to be wise.

This chapter acknowledges a range of attitudes. Socrates concedes that young men flock around him to enjoy the pleasure of watching their presumed elders and betters humbled. What young person does not enjoy the spectacle of authority being challenged and found wanting? For many an elder, however, this might seem a strong indication that Socrates encourages the youth of the city not to respect traditional figures of authority, in which case they might well believe that he is corrupting the young. Socrates, however, portrays the activity as part of his divine service, within which context the specific identities of the individuals with whom he converses are less important than their sincere dedication to the truth. Further, he justifies the contention that his behavior did not corrupt the youth by calling on the fathers and brothers of his associates present in the court to come forward and denounce him if he corrupted their relatives in any way.

Nevertheless, Socrates acknowledges that he also takes some pleasure in the activity (33e4). Thus, he is not motivated *simply* by truth or duty, but also by desire and enjoyment. Immediately after this surprising admission, Socrates reiterates his claim to be following a divine mandate (33c4–7), reinforcing it with claims of prophecies and dreams that go beyond the initial story of Chaerephon's consultation of the Delphic oracle.

What are we to make of this juxtaposition? What, then, does motivate Socrates? Are the claims of personal enjoyment and divine mandate contradictory or mutually reinforcing?

Further Reading

Miller, Paul Allen. 2007. "Lacan, the *Symposium*, and Transference." In *Postmodern Spiritual Practices: The Reception of Plato and the Construction of the Subject in Lacan, Derrida, and Foucault*, 100–32. Columbus: Ohio State University Press.

Reeve, C. D. C. 1989. *Socrates in the Apology: An Essay on Plato's Apology of Socrates*. Indianapolis: Hackett.

ESSAY 23

Plato's choice to have Socrates use forms of the word αὐθαδής (34c8, 34d10) is significant thematically. Composed from a compound of αὐτός and ἥδομαι, the adjective covers a range of meanings from stubbornness to self-satisfaction, both of which imply an intellectual inflexibility that might be taken as the opposite of the quest for self-knowledge. Socrates concedes that on the basis of his actions, jurors might perceive this quality in him. Ironically, however, the rhetorical structure of the passage shows that it is the jurors who might rightfully be charged with self-satisfaction and stubbornness, while Socrates tries to persuade them to abandon these ways.

In refusing to abase himself before the court, as Socrates implies most of the jurors have done in their own trials, he offers a dramatic contrast to their self-conception as virtuous, brave, and honorable men. Socrates is quite aware that such a demonstration may cause more resentment than self-awareness. The more his listeners insist on being satisfied with their own behavior, the angrier they may grow at Socrates and the more they may want to condemn him (see essay 18).

Socrates' refusal to practice the traditional rituals that characterized the Athenian courtroom serves as a kind of test of the jurors—one quite similar, in fact, to the kind of testing practiced by Socrates in his everyday life and exemplified in his interrogation of Meletus, the politicians, the poets, and the craftsmen. As in those conversations, the juror will show by his response whether he actually "is something" or only pretends to be. He will show whether he lives smugly self-satisfied or practices the unending examination of self and others that constitutes the pursuit of virtue, and hence a real care of the self.

Consider the parallel between the speech Socrates gives in the *Apology* and the Socratic conversations that have led to this trial. Is the similarity superficial or profound? Are Socrates' goals in each the same or different? And what about the stakes? Does it matter that Socrates is talking to save his life here, or are the issues he seeks to highlight for the jurors the same as those that have always driven his actions?

Further Reading

Brickhouse, Thomas C., and Nicholas D. Smith. 1989. *Socrates on Trial*, 24–37. Princeton, N.J.: Princeton University Press.

Brickhouse, Thomas C., and Nicholas D. Smith. 2004. *Routledge Guidebook to Plato and the Trial of Socrates*, 155–58. London: Routledge.

Sealey, Robert. 1983. "The Athenian Courts of Homicide." *Classical Philology* 78: 275–96.

ESSAY 24

In this chapter, the last one of his main speech, Socrates establishes a contrast between begging (δεῖσθαι) the jurors, on the one hand, and teaching (διδάσκειν) and persuading (πείθειν) them on the other. In so doing, he distances himself from what typically went on at an Athenian trial. This tactic is particularly apparent in the disdain he shows for the idea that he might beg for mercy: groveling would be an affirmation of the jurors' power. Socrates, by declining to participate in this ritual, refuses to ratify that power. The jurors cannot dictate what justice consists of nor how it should be pursued.

For Socrates, the concept of justice is subject neither to the procedures that define the judicial system nor to the opinions of his fellow citizens. This idea, however strongly held, is not the only one at work in the passage. By recommending persuasion and teaching, he clearly acknowledges that there is a social dimension to the trial that should not be rejected entirely. This recognition leads to a question, however. At the beginning of the trial, Socrates had denied that he was skilled in speaking (δεινὸς λέγειν), yet here he says that the proper job of the defendant is to teach and persuade. What are we to make of these seemingly contradictory statements? Are they merely a slip, or do they point to one of the basic paradoxes of Socratic philosophy? What must Socrates teach the jurors or any other interlocutor, and how does he seek to persuade them?

The idea of teaching is itself problematic. Earlier Socrates had denied that he taught anyone anything. Here he seems content with the idea that he could teach the jurors, provided that he had sufficient time. Does he contradict himself, or are two different meanings of "teaching" to be understood? If so, how can we determine which meaning is in play?

Further Reading

McCoy, Marina. 2008. *Plato on the Rhetoric of Philosophers and Sophists*, 1–55. Cambridge: Cambridge University Press.

Nightingale, Andrea Wilson. 1995. "Plato, Isocrates, and the Property of Philosophy." In *Genres in Dialogue: Plato and the Construction of Philosophy*, 13–59. Cambridge: Cambridge University Press.

ESSAY 25

This joke concerning the tabulation of the jurors' votes is complex. As almost all the commentators note, Socrates' calculations are part of a mathematical fantasy based on the assumption that each of the prosecutors was responsible for securing an equal number of votes. This would mean that Meletus's "share" would have been less than the one hundred votes necessary to avoid the fine of one thousand drachmas assessed for frivolous prosecutions. Yet we in fact have no true way of knowing whether the prosecution might not have obtained a similar number of votes for conviction if Meletus had been alone. Indeed, Athenian legal procedures were designed to avoid the kind of jury packing that would have been necessary for Socrates' fantasy to come true (see introduction).

In addition, Socrates' jest recognizes that while the indictment was filed under Meletus's name, he was in many ways the least substantial member of the prosecution. Anytus was more prominent, and Lycon's resentments were much more well-founded, owing to the death of his son at the hands of the Thirty.

Like many jokes, however, this one succeeds in part by distracting the attention of the listeners from something the teller wishes them to ignore. Socrates' opponents, who are congratulating themselves on his conviction, are treated to what is virtually a denial that he has been convicted at all. His supporters are comforted not so much by the logic of Socrates' argument, but by his refusal to despair.

At the same time, Socrates' remark is strange. Why does he choose this critical juncture of the trial for a display of irony? In not accepting the verdict of the jury with the requisite gravity, does Socrates demonstrate his fearlessness before death, and hence a certain heroic virtue? Does he also reveal a certain nonchalance toward, if not contempt for, the entire procedure? How do you understand the purpose of this joke? How would you, as a member of the jury, have reacted to it?

Further Reading

Nehamas, Alexander. 1998. *The Art of Living: Socratic Reflections from Plato to Foucault*, 19–45. Berkeley: University of California Press.

Reeve, C. D. C. 1989. *Socrates in the Apology: An Essay on Plato's Apology of Socrates*, 180–83. Indianapolis: Hackett.

ESSAY 26

Socrates' great service to the city, he explains, is to persuade his fellow Athenians to care more for themselves than for their political offices, their possessions, and the other outer accoutrements of ἀρετή. Thus, as at numerous places in the work, he makes a distinction between "being" and "seeming," between the outward signs of virtue and its substantial reality.

Such a distinction between inner and outer worth is fundamental to modern thinking, thanks in part to the *Apology* itself.

The voice of Socrates telling the Athenians that he will obey his private convictions rather than the public voice of the δῆμος has contributed significantly to this development. It would be difficult to exaggerate either the importance of his stand or the personal courage it took to make it.

Athens, for all of its success in innovation in both politics and the arts, was a traditional society by modern standards, and it is no accident that the word νόμος in Greek comes to mean both "custom" and "law." In the *Gorgias*, Callicles quotes Pindar's statement that custom/law is the ruler of all (νόμος ὁ πάντων βασιλεύς).

Within such a society, the assertion of individual rights is no small matter. Indeed, from the perspective of the Homeric poems, whose ideological assumptions almost all Athenians would have accepted, it is clearly the individual who must be understood in terms of the group rather than the other way around. Achilles chooses to withdraw from the fighting rather than endure the loss of public esteem (τιμή) implied by Agamemnon's decision to take away his war prize. He does not take solace in contemplating his superiority in isolation. Socrates' decision to value inner over outer worth is no mere commonplace of moral consolation, but a radical break with the cultural values of his fellow citizens.

Like everything else about Socrates, this action takes the form that it does because of his idiosyncratic approach to life. But it is worth asking ourselves whether or not Socrates' choice *also* leads us to a more general conclusion. Is it possible to adopt a philosophical approach to the world that is not ultimately hostile to tradition? Is there something about philosophy, as Socrates conceives it, that will always cause the philosopher to be a transgressive figure?

How does Socrates justify his decision to hold to his convictions in the face of the disapproval of many of his neighbors? What are his goals? What limitations, if any, should structure philosophy's search for truth?

Further Reading

Dodds, E. R. 1951. *The Greeks and the Irrational*, 207–35. Berkeley: University of California Press.

Hadot, Pierre. 1997. "Forms of Life and Forms of Discourse in Ancient Philosophy," translated by Arnold I. Davidson and Paula Wissing. In *Foucault and His Interlocutors*, edited by Arnold I. Davidson, 203–24. Chicago: University of Chicago Press.

ESSAY 27

At the end of chapter 27, Socrates acknowledges that if he went into exile, the fathers of the young men in his new home would undoubtedly drive him away. This statement seems to contradict his earlier claim that if he had truly corrupted the youth, then these young men's fathers and older brothers would have been lining up to denounce him and Meletus would now be calling them as witnesses (33e8–34b5). In the earlier passage, he took the fact that Meletus had not done so as proof positive that he had the support of the fathers and brothers of his young associates. Yet even there, not all the fathers and brothers of men who associated with Socrates were present, and not all would have necessarily had the same feelings as those who were present at the trial.

Here as in many places, Socrates appears to be playing with the audience, amusing his supporters while infuriating his detractors by pretending to enlist them as witnesses for the defense.

In the *Crito*, however, Socrates takes the question of exile more seriously. In response to his friend Crito's repeated urgings that he accept the help of friends and escape from Athens, Socrates imagines the Laws of Athens rising up to challenge him should he decide to leave. They scornfully point out that he has lived with them for seventy years without objection, but now, when they have decided against him, he suddenly needs to find a new city. This, they say, will be more difficult than he imagines, however:

> If you go to one of the neighboring states, such as Thebes or Megara which are both well governed, you will enter them as an enemy to their constitution, and all good patriots will eye you with suspicion as a destroyer of laws. You will confirm

> the opinion of the jurors, so that they'll seem to have given a correct verdict—for any destroyer of laws might very well be supposed to have a destructive influence upon young and foolish human beings. Do you intend, then, to avoid well-governed states and the most disciplined people? And if you do, will life be worth living? Or will you approach these people and have the impudence to converse with them? What subjects will you discuss, Socrates? The same as here, when you said that goodness and justice, institutions and laws, are the most precious possessions of mankind? (53b–c, translation by Tredennick and Tarrent)

What do you make of the Laws' argument? Are the citizens of a state bound to submit to its law even if applied unjustly? Would you want to live in a community where they were not? What would life in exile be like for Socrates? Would he be able to integrate himself into a new community, or would he have to live quietly, something he has already said is impossible for him to do in Athens and still remain true to Apollo? Could this issue explain his provocative refusal to propose an acceptable counterpenalty?

Further Reading

Plato, *Crito.*

Allen, R. E. 1980. *Socrates and Legal Obligation*, 120–28. Minneapolis: University of Minnesota Press.

Stokes, Michael C. 2005. *Dialectic in Action: An Examination of Plato's Crito*, 125–86. Swansea: Classical Press of Wales.

ESSAY 28

Socrates was clearly a divisive figure. He called into question the existing constitutional order and criticized the institutions of Athenian democracy. While superficially orthodox in his religious practice, his incessant questioning of all claims to knowledge, his tacit encouragement of the young to do the same, and his frequent mention of his personal δαίμων would certainly have been seen as undermining the received verities of Athenian civic religion. Moreover, his appeal to the young, who emulated his style of cross-examination with their elders, would naturally have been seen by many as encouraging disrespect and hence as corrupting the youth. Such a state of affairs is certainly implied by the representation of Socrates' student Pheidippides in Aristophanes' *Clouds*. In this light, Socrates' proposal that he be treated like an Olympic victor would have struck many as the height of impudence. It is little wonder, then, that an even wider margin voted for his execution than had voted for his conviction.

Given these circumstances, what do you think the jury should have done? How would we treat someone today whose intellegence we respected but who we sincerely believed was trying to overthrow the constitutional order, destroy our religion, and corrupt our young people? If that same person expressed a complete and utter lack of remorse, would we be more or less likely to vote for execution? Would we be willing to consider the possibility that he could be right and we might be wrong? Would we be willing to test ourselves and his line of reasoning by following it to its logical conclusion? Or would we rely upon the common sense of received opinion (see essay 12)?

Further Reading

King, Martin Luther, Jr. "Letter from the Birmingham Jail."
Thoreau, Henry David. "On Civil Disobedience."

ESSAY 29

Socrates here adopts the traditional position of the Greek hero: death before dishonor. Spartan mothers were said to tell their sons before they went off to battle, "come home with your shield or on it." Yet Socrates is no Homeric hero. The unquestioning adherence to the code of honor—which guides Achilles, Ajax, and Hector as members of an aristocracy based on the assumption that ἀρετή is transmitted genetically, not sought out—is not compatible with the Socratic dictum: ὁ δὲ ἀνεξέταστος βίος οὐ βιωτὸς ἀνθρώπῳ. Indeed, the Socratic emphasis on the care of the self takes what was an essentially other-directed ethos of honor and glory and transforms it into an internally directed commitment to moderation and self-examination.

Yet even the heroic tradition recognized a certain ambiguity in the range of ethical responses to a situation. As noted above, Odysseus, in one of the Cretan tales he tells Eumaeus the swineherd, portrays himself as one who threw away his shield. The story is a fiction, but it is told as truth and clearly was not unthinkable. Likewise Archilochus, a near contemporary of the Homeric poems, famously sang:

> Some barbarian is waving my blameless shield, which
> I left unwillingly under a bush. But I saved myself.
> What does that shield matter to me? Let it go. I
> will get another just as good. (fr. 5)

Archilochus is no Homeric hero either, but his iambic tradition is equally ancient and represents a comic and carnivalesque tradition that parallels and interacts with that of epic through such ambiguous figures as Odysseus and his Cretan persona. In this way, then, we can see that within the heroic world there is room for responses to a crisis that are virtually antithetical.

Socrates' own position recognizes no such range of attitudes. In some ways its insistence on "death before dishonor" is even stricter than the formulations we find in the poets. How are we to understand this reformulation of the heroic code? Is Socrates trying to outdo Ajax, Achilles, and Odysseus? How do Archilochus and Odysseus, by saving themselves, exhibit a different conception of the self from that which Socrates professes to care for?

Further Reading

Gentili, Bruno 1988. *Poetry and Its Public in Ancient Greece from Homer to the Fifth Century*, 179–96. Translated by A. Thomas Cole. Baltimore and London: Johns Hopkins University Press.

Miller, Paul Allen. 1994. "Epos and Iambos or Archilochus Meets the Wolfman." In *Lyric Texts and Lyric Consciousness: The Birth of a Genre from Archaic Greece to Augustan Rome*, 9–36. London: Routledge.

ESSAY 30

In this chapter, we have what is in many ways the essence of Socratic philosophy, at least as presented by Plato. If we want to escape from the blame and censure of others (39d4–5), then we must live rightly (39d4–5). The problem, of course, consists in how one determines the right way to live. If it is Socrates' position that no one does wrong willingly (37a6–7), then simply deciding to do the right thing is not enough to insure that one is actually doing what one should. We must first know what the right thing is. But how, if we do not already know it?

Socrates in the *Apology* presents no simple way around this dilemma (see essay 13). He offers no code, no law, no set of commandments one can follow to be sure of acting in a fashion that is beyond reproach. Instead, he presents us with something much more demanding: the proposition that each of us should be prepared at all times to present an examination of our lives, that we should be ready to undergo the crucible of Socratic interrogation (τοῦ διδόναι ἔλεγχον τοῦ βίου, 39c7). If our lives cannot stand up to this rigorous scrutiny, then we must change them or face reproach.

Would you be prepared to give such an account of your life? Should our leaders and those who claim to be wise be made to submit such an account? Would the heightened self-consciousness required to live up to such a standard improve our behavior or would it render us incapable of action as suggested by Callicles in the *Gorgias*? Could one be comfortable if one were actually to live this way? Might a certain level of discomfort be a positive thing and even, ultimately, a truer gauge of our happiness?

Further Reading

Foucault, Michel. 2005. *The Hermeneutics of the Subject: Lectures at the Collège de France 1981–1982*, edited by Frédéric Gros, 1–105. Translated by Graham Burchell. Series editors, François Ewald and Alessandro Fontana. English series editor, Arnold J. Davidson. New York: Picador.

Kraut, Richard. 2006. "The Examined Life." In *A Companion to Socrates*, edited by Sara Ahbel-Rappe and Rachana Kametkar, 228–42. London: Blackwell.

ESSAY 31

The nature of Socrates' δαίμων (40a5) has long been debated (see also essay 19). To many modern readers, it is easily assimilated to the voice of conscience. To those of us (unlike the ancients) who live in a world after the founding of the modern science of psychology and after Freud's analysis of the superego, ego, and id, the notion that there is an inner voice that warns us when we are about to do something wrong is anything but strange. Earlier writers have understood Socrates' δαίμων differently. The second-century-C.E. philosopher and biographer Plutarch, in *On the Personal Deity of Socrates*, actually posits a personal guardian deity who looks down on Socrates and other fortunate individuals from heaven and guides them (588b–593a). This is clearly a forerunner to the later concept of the guardian angel. Yet both the modern and the Plutarchan understandings may be seriously anachronistic. In Xenophon's version of the *Apology*, Socrates himself directly compares his δαίμων to other experiences of divination that were common at the time and attracted no special comment:

> Do I introduce new divinities by saying that the voice of the god appears to me signifying what I should do? For some

> men also conjecture the existence of voices using the sounds of birds, and others use the passing speech of men. Will anyone dispute that thunder, whether speaking or not, is a great omen? Does not the Pythian priestess at her tripod also announce things from the god with a voice? Furthermore, all say and believe, just as I say, that the god foresees what is to happen and foretells this to whom he wishes. Yet while they call these foretellings omens, voices, symbols, and prophecies, I call this thing the δαιμόνιον (12–14).

In short, Socrates here argues that his δαίμων is really nothing unusual.

How do you understand the δαίμων? Are the psychological, the angelic, and the divinatory explanations just different ways of describing what is essentially the same phenomenon? Or do these different ways of explaining assume fundamentally different conditions governing both the nature of the ψυχή or "soul" and its relation to what can be presumed to exist both within it and beyond it? Does Xenophon's account, in which Socrates' δαίμων becomes just another way of trying to tell the future, support or contradict that of Plato?

Further Reading

Plutarch, *On the Personal Deity of Socrates.*

Xenophon, *Apology*.

Brickhouse, Thomas C., and Nicholas D. Smith. 2004. *Routledge Philosophy Guidebook to Plato and the Trial of Socrates*, 178–81. London: Routledge.

Destree, Pierre, and Nicholas P. Smith, eds. 2005. *Socrates' Divine Sign: Religious Practice and Value in Socratic Philosophy*. Kelowna, B.C.: Academic Printing and Publishing.

ESSAY 32

This section constitutes a final mythological and poetic coda to the *Apology* as a whole. On the one hand, from the perspective of the dramatic situation its purpose is to comfort Socrates' supporters: this is no disaster that has just occurred. On the other, from the perspective of the dialogue as a composition, this chapter clearly plays a role in the architecture of the work as a whole.

Socrates devoted his life to advocating a rational approach to inquiry. It may seem odd, then, that Plato has him introduce this lengthy mythological digression. In fact, Xenophon's account of the speech includes no such material. But whether or not the historical Socrates ever talked about such subjects at his trial or anywhere else, it is clear that Plato thought this was an appropriate way to end the *Apology*. In many respects, it is similar to the mythological postscripts about the afterlife that he uses to conclude the *Republic*, the *Gorgias*, and the *Phaedo*.

His motivation for adopting this tactic is unknown, and certainly these three dialogues are far too complex to analyze in detail here. Nevertheless, we can say something about how this mythological digression functions in the context of the *Apology*. In it we move from the mundane issues of the trial, with its focus on petty human fears, anxieties, and jealousies, to a transcendental plane where such limitations are, if not completely surpassed, not the primary constraints on the state of our souls.

The myth itself represents a particular species of Socratic irony. It is not a logical proposition to which the supporters must assent as part of the process of Socratic question and answer. In fact, there is no philosophical examination of the problem at all, as Socrates develops his image of the afterlife by appealing to hearsay (τὰ λεγόμενα), the truth of which the supporters are invited to consider without being asked to affirm. With this kind of latitude available to him, Socrates is free to imagine a Hades that is a paradise for philosophers (through perhaps less pleasant for his immortal interlocators), unlike the Athens that will soon put him to death. Such a discourse, then, offers more an ironic perspective on the present than a demonstration of the nature of the unknowable future.

What do you think is the function of Socrates' speculations on the afterlife? Do you find them comforting? Do you think he believes them? How would the dialogue be different without them?

Further Reading

Brisson, Luc. 1998. *Plato the Mythmaker*. Translated and edited by Gerard Nadaff. Chicago: University of Chicago Press.

Veyne, Paul. 1988. *Did the Greeks Believe in Their Myths?: An Essay on the Constitutive Imagination*. Translated by Paula Wissing. Chicago: University of Chicago Press.

ESSAY 33

We know that there were various versions of Socrates' defense speech in circulation after his death, including retellings by Plato, Xenophon, and Andocides, among others. Each of these versions was clearly based on a real historical event, but no one of them was an authentic journalistic account of that event. Some of them, such as Xenophon's, appear to have been written years later and based on secondhand accounts. The case is very similar to that of the Gospels, where there are four canonical versions of the life of Jesus, each with its own specific characteristics and date of composition, together with other noncanonical versions of his life, such as the recently discovered *Gospel of Judas*, that were also widely read.

Why do you think different versions of the same event were in circulation? Should any one of them be considered more historically accurate than the others? How could you make that determination? What do you think was Plato's motivation in producing *this* version of the *Apology*? Was he successful?

What is there about the death of Socrates that has inspired people for the past 2,500 years to try to understand it and to attempt to claim that their understanding is the correct or the preferred one?

What is at stake in those claims? Now that you have read the complete text in Greek, do you care? Should you?

Further Reading

Danzig, Gabriel. 2003. "Apologizing for Socrates: Plato and Xenophon on Socrates' Behavior in Court." *Transactions of the American Philological Association* 133: 281–321.

Momigliano, Arnaldo. 1971. *The Development of Greek Biography: Four Lectures.* Cambridge: Harvard University Press.

APPENDIX

Changes to Burnet's Oxford Classical Text

21e3 Remove brackets from καὶ.

24e10 For οἱ δὲ ἀκροαταὶ print οἵδε οἱ ἀκροαταὶ.

26a2 Delete [καὶ ἀκουσίων].

26a8 For ἤδη δῆλον print δῆλον ἤδη.

28a7 For αἱρεῖ print αἱρήσει.

29b1 For καίτοι print καὶ τοῦτο.

29c4 Remove brackets from ἂν.

28d10 Paragraph break after αἰσχροῦ.

30c1 For ποιησάντος print ποιήσοντος.

31d1 Delete [φωνή].

31d4 For τοῦτο print τούτου.

32a7 For ἀλλὰ κἂν print ἅμα κἂν.

32c6 After ἀποθάνοι print a raised dot instead of a comma.

32e4 Punctuate as follows: καὶ, ὥσπερ χρὴ,.

33a7 For ἐπιθυμοῖ print ἐπιθυμεῖ.

35a1 Print the last part of this sentence as follows: γέ ἐστι τὸν Σωκράτη διαφέρειν τινι τῶν πολλῶν ἀνθρώπων.

38c7 Print comma after βίου.

38d3 Delete Ἀθηναῖοι, retaining the comma thereafter so that it now follows ἄνδρες.

41b5 For καὶ δὴ print καὶ δὴ καὶ.

Glossary

A

ἁβρύνω	adorn; *mid.* give oneself airs
ἀγαθός, -ή, -όν	good, brave, capable, virtuous
ἀγανακτέω	be angry
ἀγνοέω	not know; be ignorant
ἀγορά, -ᾶς, ἡ	marketplace, city center
ἀγροικῶς	coarsely
ἄγω	lead, bring, carry off
ἀγών, -όνος, ὁ	contest, struggle, trial, lawsuit
ἀγωνίζομαι	contend, fight
ἀδελφός, -οῦ, ὁ	brother
ἀδιάφθαρτος, -ον	uncorrupted
ἀδικέω	act unjustly, do wrong, do evil, harm
ἄδικος, -ον	wrong, unjust
ἀεί	always, on each occasion
ἀηδής, -ές	unpleasant
ἀθάνατος, -ον	undying, immortal
Ἀθηναῖος, -α, -ον	Athenian, person from Athens
ἀθρόος, -α, ον	all together
Αἴδης, -ου, ὁ	Hades
αἶνιγμα, -τος, τό	riddle
αἰνίττομαι	speak in riddles
αἱρέω	seize, take; convict
αἰσθάνομαι	perceive, learn
αἴσθησις, -εως, ἡ	perception, sensation, feeling
αἰσχρός, -ά, -όν	shameful, disgraceful
αἰσχύνη, -ης, ἡ	shame, dishonor
αἰσχύνω	shame, dishonor; *pass.* be ashamed

αἰτέω	ask, ask for
αἰτία, -ας, ἡ	cause, responsibility, blame
αἴτιον, -ου, τό	cause
ἀκολασία, -ας, ἡ	excess, extravagance; intemperance
ἀκόλαστος, -η, -ον	undisciplined
ἀκούω	listen to, hear
ἀκροάομαι	listen
ἀκροατής, -οῦ, ὁ	listener
ἄκων, -ουσα, -ον	unwilling, involuntary
ἀλήθεια, -ας, ἡ	truth; **τῇ ἀληθείᾳ**, in truth
ἀληθεύω	tell the truth
ἀληθής, -ές	true
ἀληθῶς	truly
ἁλίσκομαι	be taken, be caught, be convicted
ἀλλά	but
ἀλλήλους, ἀλλήλων	one another (*reflexive*)
ἄλλοθι	elsewhere
ἀλλοῖος, -α, -ον	of another sort, different
ἄλλος, -η, -ον	other; **ἄλλα καὶ ἄλλα**, again and again
ἄλλως	otherwise; vainly; **ἄλλως τε καί**, especially
ἀλόγιστος, -ον	unreasonable
ἄλογος, -ον	unreasonable, unexpected
ἅμα	together, at the same time
ἀμαθής, -ές	ignorant, foolish
ἀμαθία, -ας, ἡ	ignorance
ἁμάρτημα, -ματος, τό	error
ἀμείβω	change, exchange
ἀμείνων, -ονος	better
ἀμέλεια, -ας, ἡ	neglect
ἀμελέω	neglect, be careless about
ἀμήχανος, -ον	impossible, inconceivable, inexpressible
ἀμφί	around, about (+ *acc.*)
ἀμφισβητέω	dispute
ἀμφότερος, -α, -ον	both; **κατ' ἀμφότερα**, in both cases, in either case
ἄν	*indefinite particle*
ἄν	if (*contr. of* **ἐάν**)
ἀναβαίνω	appear in court
ἀναβιβάζω	bring into court
ἀναγιγνώσκω	read
ἀναγκάζω	compel
ἀναγκαῖος, -α, -ον	necessary
ἀνάγκη, -ης, ἡ	necessity; binding law
ἀναζητέω	seek out

ἀναιρέω	pick up, take up; (*of an oracle*) respond
ἀναισχυντία, -ας, ἡ	shamelessness
ἀναίσχυντος, -ον	shameless
ἀναίσχυντως	shamelessly
ἀναλαμβάνω	resume
ἀνάξιος, -α, -ον	unworthy
ἀναπείθω	try to persuade, seduce
ἀναφέρω	refer
ἀνδρεία, -ας, ἡ	courage
ἀνέλεγκτος, -ον	not refuted, irrefutable
ἀνελεύθερος, -ον	not fit for a free man, slavish
ἀνέλπιστος, -ον	unexpected
ἀνεξέταστος, -ον	unexamined
ἀνέρομαι	ask
ἀνερωτάω	question, ask again
ἀνέχω	bear up
ἀνήρ, ἀνδρός, ὁ	man
ἀνθρώπινος, -η, -ον	human, attainable by a person
ἀνθρώπειος, -α, -ον	human
ἄνθρωπος, -ου, ὁ	human being, person
ἀνόσιος, -ον	impious
ἀντί	instead of, in place of (+ *gen.*)
ἀντιβόλησις, -εως, ἡ	entreaty, prayer
ἀντιγραφή, -ῆς, ἡ	response to a charge, plea
ἀντιλέγω	reply
ἀντιπαραβάλλω	compare
ἀντιπαρατίθημι	compare
ἀντιτιμάομαι	propose a counterpenalty
ἀντωμοσία, -ας, ἡ	formal charge, affidavit
ἀξία, -ας, ἡ	worth, value
ἄξιος, -α, -ον	worthy of, deserving of, fitting, worthwhile
ἀξιόχρεως, -ων	responsible, worthy of credit, trustworthy
ἀξιόω	believe, consider, think
ἀπάγω	lead away; arrest
ἀπαλλαγή, -ῆς, ἡ	release
ἀπαλλάττω	free from, release from; *mid.* depart
ἀπαναισχυντέω	be shameless enough to say
ἅπας, ἅπασα, ἅπαν	all
ἀπειθέω	disobey
ἄπειμι	(will) go away
ἀπείρος, -α, -ον	inexperienced
ἀπελαύνω	drive off

ἀπεχθάνομαι	make oneself hated, become hated
ἀπέχθεια, -ας, ἡ	enmity, hatred
ἀπιστέω	disbelieve
ἄπιστος, -ον	unconvincing, not believing
ἀπό	from (+ *gen.*)
ἀποβαίνω	turn out
ἀποδείκνυμι	show, demonstrate
ἀποδημέω	relocate
ἀποδημία, -ας, ἡ	relocation
ἀποθνήσκω	die, be put to death
ἀποκρίνομαι	answer, reply
ἀποκρύπτω	conceal something (*acc.*) from someone (*acc.*)
ἀποκτείνυμι	kill
ἀποκτείνω	kill
ἀπολαύω	benefit from (+ *gen.*)
ἀπολείπω	desert
ἀπόλλυμι	destroy, lose; *mid.* be destroyed, die
ἀπολογέομαι	defend oneself
ἀπολογία, -ας, ἡ	defense
ἀπορέω	be at a loss
ἀπορία, -ας, ἡ	lack
ἄπορος, -ον	difficult, without resources
ἀποτίνω	pay
ἀποτρέπω	turn away from, dissuade
ἀποφαίνω	show, display
ἀποφεύγω	escape, be acquitted
ἀποψηφίζομαι	acquit
ἄρα	so, then, accordingly, as it seems
ἆρα	*untranslated adverb, introduces a question*
ἀργύριον, -ου, τό	silver, money
ἀρετή, -ῆς, ἡ	excellence, virtue
ἀριθμός, -οῦ	number
ἄριστος, -η, -ον	best, noblest, most excellent
ἄρουρα, -ης	ground, earth
ἄρτι	just now
ἀρχή, -ῆς, ἡ	beginning; government; office; **κατ' ἀρχάς** from the beginning; **τὴν ἀρχήν**, in the beginning, in the first place, at all
ἄρχω	begin; lead, command, rule (+ *gen.*); hold office
ἄρχων, -οντος, ὁ	commander; **οἱ ἄρχοντες**, the rulers, magistrates
ἀσέβεια, -ας, ἡ	impiety
ἀστός, -οῦ, ὁ	townsman, citizen

ἀσχολία, -ας, ἡ	lack of leisure, occupation
ἅτε	inasmuch as (+ *part.*)
ἀτεχνῶς	literally, completely
ἀτιμάζω	slight, dishonor
ἀτιμόω	deprive of citizen rights
ἄτοπος, -ον	out of place, eccentric, extraordinary
ἅττα	= **τινά** (<τις, τι)
αὖ	again, in turn, on the other hand
αὐθάδης, -ες	stubborn, headstrong
αὐθαδίζομαι	be stubborn, headstrong
αὖθις	again, later, hereafter
αὐλητής, -οῦ, ὁ	flute player
αὐτίκα	right away, at once
αὐτόθι	there
αὐτόματος, -η, -ον	on one's own
αὑτόν, -οῦ	himself, oneself; him, her (*reflexive*)
αὐτός, αὐτή, αὐτό	same
αὐτοσχεδιάζω	judge carelessly
αὐτόφωρος, -ον	caught in the act
ἀφθονία, -ας, ἡ	abundance
ἀφίημι	let go, release
ἀφικνέομαι	come, arrive
ἄχθομαι	be angry
ἄχθος, -ους, τό	burden

B

βαρύς, -εῖα, -ύ	heavy, onerous
βασιλεύς, -έως, ὁ	king
βέλτιστος, -η, -ον	best
βελτίων, -ονος	better
βιάζομαι	constrain, overpower by force
βιβλίον, -ου, τό	book
βίος, -ου, ὁ	life
βιόω	live
βιωτός, -όν	livable
βλαβερός, -ά, -όν	harmful
βλάπτω	harm
βοάω	shout
βοηθέω	help
βουλεύω	serve as a member of the βουλή; *mid.* plan
βούλομαι	wish
βραδύς, -εῖα, -ύ	slow

Γ

γάρ	for, since
γε	at least, indeed
γέμω	be full of
γενναῖος, -α, -ον	noble
γεωργικός, -ή, -όν	agricultural
γῆ, γῆς, ἡ	earth
γίγνομαι	become, happen; exist, be
γιγνώσκω	come to know, learn, recognize
γνησίως	genuinely
γοῦν	now, at least, at any rate (**γε + οὖν**)
γράμμα, -ματος, τό	thing written, letter; *pl.* letters, literature
γραφή, -ῆς, ἡ	writing; formal charge, indictment
γράφω	write; *mid.* present in writing, indict
γυνή, γυναικός, ἡ	woman

Δ

δαιμόνιον, -ου, τό	divine thing, divinity
δαιμόνιος, -α, -ον	divine, supernatural
δαίμων, -ονος, ὁ	divine being, divinity, god
δάκρυον, -ου, τό	tear
δέ	and; but; **μεν . . . δέ**, on the one hand . . . on the other
δεῖ	it is necessary, one ought (+ *infin.*)
δείδω	fear
δείκνυμι	point out, show, make clear
δεινός, -ή, -όν	terrible, to be feared; marvelous, strange; clever
δέκα	ten (*indecl.*)
δεσμός, οῦ, ὁ	bond; imprisonment
δεσμωτηρίον, -ου, τό	prison
δεῦρο	to this place, here
δέχομαι	accept, take
δέω	need, lack; *mid.* ask, beg
δέω	bind, put in prison
δή	clearly, apparently, manifestly, so, now, really
δῆλος, -η, -ον	clear
δημηγορία, -ας, ἡ	public speaking
δημιουργός, -οῦ, ὁ	craftsman
δημοκρατέομαι	have a democratic constitution
δημόσιος, -α, -ον	of the people; **δημοσίᾳ**, in public
δημότης, -ου, ὁ	resident of the same deme

δήπου	surely, no doubt
δῆτα	certainly, of course; **τί δῆτα**, what then?
διά	through; by means of (+ *gen.*); because of (+ *acc.*)
διαβάλλω	slander
διαβολή, -ῆς, ἡ	slander
διαγίγνομαι	pass through
διάγω	live
διακινδυνεύω	face all dangers
διακωλύω	hinder, prevent
διαλέγομαι	converse with, talk to
διαμυθολογέω	converse, exchange stories
διανοέομαι	think, consider
διάνοια, -ας, ἡ	thought, intention
διασκοπέω	examine, consider
διατελέω	continue
διατριβή, -ῆς, ἡ	pastime, pursuit, mode of living
διατρίβω	spend time
διαφέρω	be different from; be superior to (+ *gen.*)
διαφεύγω	flee, escape; be acquitted
διαφθείρω	destroy; lead astray, corrupt, ruin
διδάσκαλος, -ου, ὁ	teacher
διδάσκω	teach, instruct
δίδωμι	give, offer, present
διερωτάω	interrogate thoroughly
δικάζω	judge
δίκαιος, -α, -ον	just, right
δικαίως	justly, with good reason
δικανικός, -ή, -όν	characteristic of the law courts
δικαστήριον, -ου, τό	law court
δικαστής, -οῦ, ὁ	judge, juror
δίκη, -ης, ἡ	case, charge, trial, judgment, justice
διόμνυμι	swear
διττός, -ή, -όν	double, two-fold
διώκω	pursue, follow
δοκέω	think, think good; **δοκεῖ μοι,** it seems to me
δόξα, -ης, ἡ	reputation, glory, honor, opinion
δόσις, -εως, ἡ	gift
δουλεύω	be a slave to
δραχμή, -ῆς, ἡ	drachma
δρῦς, δρυός, ἡ	oak
δύναμαι	be able, can (+ *inf.*)

δυνατός, -ή, -όν	strong, powerful, effective
δύο, δυοῖν	two
δυστυχία, -ας, ἡ	bad luck

E

ἐάν	if (= **εἰ ἄν**)
ἐάνπερ	if in truth
ἑαυτόν, -ήν, -ό	himself, herself, itself (*no nom.*)
ἐάω	allow
ἑβδομήκοντα	seventy
ἐγγυάω	promise; *mid.* give a guarantee
ἐγγυητής, -οῦ, ὁ	guarantor
ἐγγύς	near (+ *gen.*)
ἐγείρω	rouse, wake
ἐγκαλέω	charge, accuse
ἔγκλημα, -ματος, τό	charge, accusation
ἐγώ, μου, μοι, με	I
ἐθέλω	be willing, wish
ἐθίζομαι	be accustomed to
ἔθω	become accustomed
εἰ	if, whether
εἶεν	very well then, okay
εἰμί	be, exist
εἶμι	come, go, will go; **ἴθι**, come!
εἰρωνεύομαι	dissemble, feign ignorance, speak ironically
εἰς	into, to, for, as regards, in regard to (+ *acc.*)
εἷς, μία, ἕν	one
εἰσάγω	bring in (to court), bring to trial
εἴσειμι	go into
εἰσέρχομαι	come in, enter
εἶτα	then, and then, next
εἴτε . . . εἴτε	whether . . . or
εἴωθα	be accustomed, be in the habit
ἐκ	out of, from (+ *gen.*)
ἕκαστος, -η, -ον	each, every one
ἑκάτερος, -α, -ον	each of two, each singly, on either side
ἐκεῖ	in that place, there
ἐκεῖνος, -η, -ο	that
ἐκείνως	in that way
ἐκκλησία, -ας, ἡ	assembly
ἐκκλησιαστής, -οῦ, ὁ	member of the assembly
ἐκλέγω	pick out

ἐκπλήττω	drive out of one's senses, strike with panic
ἐκτίνω	pay in full
ἐκφεύγω	flee, escape
ἑκών, -οῦσα, -όν	willingly, intentionally
ἐλέγχω	examine; refute
ἐλεεινός, -ή, -όν	pitiful, wretched
ἐλεέω	have pity on; show mercy
ἐλπίς, -ίδος, ἡ	hope
ἐμαυτόν, -ήν	myself
ἐμμελῶς	properly; at a reasonable price
ἐμμένω	stay with, abide
ἐμός, -ή, -όν	my, mine
ἐμπίπλημι	fill up
ἐμπνέω	breathe, live
ἔμπροσθεν	earlier, in front of
ἐν	in, among, in the midst of (+ *dat.*)
ἐναντιόομαι	oppose
ἐναντίος, -α, -ον	opposite, contrary
ἐνδείκνυμι	demonstrate, point out; indict
ἕνδεκα	eleven (*indecl.*)
ἕνεκα	for the sake of, because of (+ *gen.*)
ἐνθάδε	here, now
ἐνθένδε	from this place, from here
ἐνθουσιάζω	be inspired
ἐνθυμέομαι	consider
ἐνίοτε	from time to time
ἐννοέω	consider
ἐνταῦθα	here, there, at this point
ἐνταυθοῖ	here, to this place
ἐντεῦθεν	from there; from this, as a result of this
ἐντυγχάνω	happen upon, meet
ἐνύπνιον, -ου, τό	dream
ἐξ	out of, from (+ *gen.*)
ἐξαιρέω	take out, remove
ἐξαμαρτάνω	err
ἐξαπατάω	deceive
ἔξειμι	go out
ἐξελαύνω	send into exile, banish
ἐξελέγχω	examine closely, test
ἐξεργάζομαι	bring to perfection
ἐξέρχομαι	go into exile

ἔξεστι	it is possible to; **ἐξόν**, it being possible (+ *infin.*)
ἐξετάζω	examine, probe
ἐξέτασις, -εως, ἡ	close examination, scrutiny
ἔοικα	be likely, seem (+ *infin.*)
ἐπαΐω	understand
ἐπακολουθέω	follow after (+ *dat.*)
ἐπεί	since, because; when
ἐπειδή	since, when; **ἐπειδάν**, whenever (= ἐπειδή ἄν)
ἔπειτα	then, next
ἐπέχω	hold back, restrain
ἐπί	toward, at, near (+ *gen.*); to, toward (+ *acc.*); with a view to, on the condition that (+ *dat.*)
ἐπιδείκνυμι	show
ἐπιδημέω	reside
ἐπιεικής, -ές	good, suitable, reasonable
ἐπιθυμέω	desire
ἐπικωμῳδέω	mock, caricature
ἐπιλανθάνομαι	forget (+ *gen.*)
ἐπιμελέομαι	care for (+ *gen.*)
ἐπιορκέω	swear falsely
ἐπίσταμαι	know, understand
ἐπιστάτης, -ου, ὁ	trainer, master
ἐπιστήμη, -ης, ἡ,	knowledge
ἐπιτηδεύω	pursue, follow, practice
ἐπιτίθημι	place upon, put upon; *mid.* attack
ἐπιτρέπω	permit; trust in
ἐπιτυγχάνω	chance upon
ἐπίφθονος, -ον	hateful
ἐπιχειρέω	try (+ *infin.*)
ἐπονείδιστος, -ον	shameful, reproachful
ἔπος, -ου, τό	word
ἐργάζομαι	work, do, accomplish; do something (*acc.*) to someone (*acc.*)
ἔργον, -ου, τό	employment, work, deed
ἐρευνάω	seek after, examine
ἐρῆμος, -η, -ον	undefended
ἔρομαι	ask, inquire
ἔρχομαι	come, go
ἐρωτάω	ask, inquire of
ἔσχατος, -η, -ον	extreme, last
ἑταῖρος, -ου, ὁ	companion
ἕτερος, -α, -ον	one or the other of two, other

ἔτι	besides, still, further, in addition, again
ἑτοῖμος, -ον	ready, prepared
ἔτος, -ους, τό	year
εὖ	well
εὐαρίθμητος, -ον	easily numbered
εὐδαιμονία, -ας, ἡ	happiness, good fortune, joy
εὐδαίμων, -ον	happy, fortunate
εὐδοκιμέω	seem good
εὐδόκιμος, -ον	renowned
εὐέλεγκτος, -ον	easy to test
εὔελπις, -ιδος	hopeful
εὐεργετέω	do good service
εὐθύς	right away, at once
εὐλαβέομαι	beware, take care
εὑρίσκω	find
εὐσεβέω	be pious
ἔχω	have, possess, hold; be able (+ *inf.*)
ἕωθεν	early
ἕως	until, as long as
ἕωσπερ	so long as, ever

Z

ζάω	live
ζεῦγος, -ους, τό	pair of horses; chariot drawn by a team
Ζεῦς, Διός, Διί, Δία	Zeus
ζητέω	look for, seek into, investigate, search out
ζήτησις, -εως, ἡ	a seeking, search, inquiry, investigation

H

ἤ	either, or; than
ἦ	truly, really
ἡβάω	grow up
ἡγέομαι	consider, believe, think
ἡδέως	sweetly, gladly, pleasantly
ἤδη	already, by this time, now, at once, from now on
ἡδύς, -εῖα, -ύ	sweet, delightful, pleasant
ἥκω	have come
ἡλικία, -ας, ἡ	age, time of life
ἡλικιώτης, -ου, ὁ	contemporary, one of the same age
ἥλιος, -ου, ὁ	sun
ἡμεῖς, ἡμῶν, ἡμῖν, ἡμεῖς	we
ἡμέρα, -ας, ἡ	day

ἡμίθεος, -ου, ὁ	demigod, hero
ἡμίονος, -ου, ὁ or ἡ	mule
ἡσυχία, -ας, ἡ	peace, quiet; **ἡσυχίαν ἄγω**, live quietly
ἦτοι	surely
ἥττων, -ον	weaker, worse

Θ

θάνατος, -ου, ὁ	death
θαρραλέως	courageously
θάτερον, -ου, τό	one thing of two
θάττων, -ον	swifter, quicker
θαυμάζω	marvel at, be surprised
θαυμάσιος, -α, -ον	wonderous, marvelous, amazing, strange
θαυμαστός, -ή, -όν	wonderful, marvelous
θεῖος, -α, -ον	divine
θέλω	wish
θέμις, θέμιτος, ἡ	divine law, right
θεμιτός, -ή, -όν	lawful, righteous
θεόμαντις, -εως, ὁ	soothsayer
θεός, -ου, ὁ *or* **ἡ**	god, goddess, divinity
θέω	run
θνήσκω	die
θόλος, -ου, ἡ	Athenian public building also called the Prytaneium
θορυβέω	make a racket; interrupt; *pass.* be thrown into confusion
θρηνέω	lament

Ι

ἰδίᾳ	in private, privately
ἴδιος, -α, ον	private
ἰδιωτεύω	live as a private man
ἰδιώτης, -ου, ὁ	a private citizen
ἱκανός, -ή, -όν	sufficient, enough; competent
ἱκετεία, -ας, ἡ	supplication
ἱκετεύω	approach as a suppliant
ἵνα	where; in order that; **ἵνα τί**, for what reason?
ἱππικός, -ή, όν	equestrian
ἵππος, -ου, ὁ *or* **ἡ**	horse
ἰσχύς, -ύος, ἡ	strength
ἰσχυρός, -ά, -όν	strong, powerful
ἴσως	perhaps

K

καθεύδω	sleep, slumber
καθῆμαι	sit (as a judge)
καθίστημι	establish, set forth, bring
καί	and, even, also; **καί . . . καί,** both . . . and; **καὶ δὴ καί**, and moreover, what is more
καινός, -ή, -όν	new, strange
καίπερ	although
καίτοι	and yet
κακία, -ας, ἡ	evil
κακός, -ή, -όν	bad, cowardly
καλέω	call, summon
καλλύνω	beautify; *mid.* be proud
καλός, -ή, -όν	beautiful, excellent, noble
καλῶς	well, excellently
κατά	against (+ *gen.*); after, at, down, according to (+ *acc.*)
καταγέλαστος, -ον	ridiculous
καταγελάω	laugh at
καταγιγνώσκω	recognize
καταδαρθάνω	fall asleep
καταδέομαι	beg, entreat
κατάδηλος, -ον	manifest, plain
καταλαμβάνω	find, seize upon, understand
καταλύω	destroy, dissolve
κατανοέω	perceive, understand
κατασκεδάννυμι	spread
καταφρονέω	despise, hold in contempt
καταχαρίζομαι	gratify, do a favor
καταψηφίζομαι	vote against, condemn
κατέρχομαι	return, come back
κατέχω	restrain
κατηγορέω	accuse, charge
κατηγορία, -ας, ἡ	accusation
κατήγορος, -ου, ὁ	accuser
κελεύω	order, command
κέρδος, -ους, τό	profit, advantage
κήδομαι	have a care for (+ *gen.*)
κινδυνεύω	run the risk of; be likely (+ *inf.*)
κίνδυνος, -ου, ὁ	danger, chance
κόλασις, -εως, ἡ	punishment
κολούω	restrain, repress

κορωνίς, -ίδος curved
κρείττων, -ον stronger, better
κρίνω judge, try, decide
κρίσις, -εως, ἡ judgment, condemnation
κρούω knock, crush
κτάω acquire; *mid.* possess
κτῆσις, -εως, ἡ possession
κυών, κυνός, ὁ or ἡ dog
κωλύω hinder
κωμῳδία, -ας, ἡ comedy
κωμῳδοποιός, -οῦ, ὁ comic poet

Λ

λαμβάνω take, seize
λανθάνω escape notice
λατρεία, -ας, ἡ service
λέγω say, tell, mean
λείπω leave, abandon
λέξις, -εως, ἡ speaking, manner of speech
λίθος, -ου, ὁ stone
λογίζομαι reckon, calculate
λόγος, -ου, ὁ word, story, speech; discussion, argument; principle
λοιδορέω blame, abuse
λοιπός, -ή, -όν remaining, rest of
λυπέω cause pain
λυσιτελέω be beneficial

Μ

μά no, by . . . ! (+ *acc.*)
μάθημα, -τος, τό knowledge, instruction
μάθησις, -εως, ἡ instruction, learning
μαθητής, -οῦ, ὁ pupil
μακαρίζω bless, deem happy
μάλα much, greatly
μάλιστα most of all, especially; certainly, yes
μᾶλλον more, rather
μανθάνω learn, be taught, understand
μαντεία, -ας, ἡ power of divination; oracle, prophecy
μαντεῖον, -ου, τό oracular response, oracle
μαντεύομαι consult *or* inquire of an oracle
μαντική, -ῆς, ἡ art of divination

μαρτυρέω	testify
μάρτυς, -υρος, ὁ	witness
μάχη, -ης, ἡ	battle
μάχομαι	fight
μέγας, μεγάλη, μέγα	great, large, powerful, important
μέγεθος, -ους, τό	greatness, size
μέγιστος, -α, -ον	greatest, largest, most
μείζων, -ονος	greater, larger, more
μειράκιον, -ου, τό	youth, boy
μέλω	be an object of care
μέλλω	intend to, be about to
μέμφομαι	blame
μέν	indeed, on the one hand
μέντοι	but, however, in truth
μένω	remain, be unchanged
μέρος, -ους, τό	share, part
μετά	together with, with (+ *gen.*); after (+ *acc.*)
μεταβολή, -ῆς, ἡ	change
μεταλαμβάνω	obtain a share of
μεταμέλει	change one's mind
μεταξύ	between
μεταπέμπω	send for
μεταπίπτω	change
μέτειμι	have a share in
μετέωρος, -ον	in midair, above the earth
μετοίκησις, -εως, ἡ	change of habitation
μετρίως	fairly
μή	not, lest
μηδαμῶς	in no way
μηδέ	and not, nor, not even
μηδείς, μηδεμία, μηδέν	no one, nothing
μηκέτι	no longer
μήν	truly
μηνύω	disclose, indicate
μήτε . . . μήτε	neither . . . nor
μήτηρ, -τρός, ἡ	mother
μηχανάομαι	contrive
μηχανή, -ῆς, ἡ	means
μιαρός, -ά, -όν	impure, defiled
μικρός, -ά, -όν	small, little
μιμέομαι	imitate, mimic
μιμνήσκω	recall

μισθός, -οῦ, ὁ	pay, wage
μισθόω	hire
μνᾶ, -ᾶς, ἡ	mina, sum of money equivalent to a hundred drachmas
μόγις	with difficulty, reluctantly, barely
μοῖρα, -ας, ἡ	fate
μόνος, -η, -ον	only, alone
μόσχος, μόσχου ὁ	calf
μοχθηρία, -ας, ἡ	wickedness
μοχθηρός, -ά, -όν	bad, worthless
μυρίος, -α, -ον	without number, boundless
μύωψ, -ωπος, ὁ	horsefly

N

ναυμαχία, -ας, ἡ	sea-fight
ναύς, νέως, ἡ	ship
νέος, -α, -ον	new, young
νεότης, -ητος, ἡ	youthful recklessness
νή	indeed, yes
νικάω	win, be victorious
νόθος, -η, -ον	bastard, illegitimate
νομίζω	acknowledge, believe in
νόμος, -ου, ὁ	law, custom
νουθετέω	admonish
νοῦς, νοῦ, ὁ	mind
νυμφή, -ῆς, ἡ	nymph
νῦν	now
νύξ, νυκτός, ἡ	night
νυστάζω	doze
νωθής, -ές	sluggish

Ξ

ξένος, -ου, ὁ	stranger, foreigner, one from out-of-town
ξένως	strangely, as a stranger

O

ὁ, ἡ, τό	the; **οἱ μέν . . . οἱ δέ** some . . . others
ὅδε, ἥδε, τόδε	this, this here
ὀδύρομαι	moan
ὅθεν	from where
οἷ	to which place, where
οἶδα	know

οἴκαδε	homeward, to one's home
οἰκεῖος, -α, -ον	belonging to the household, family; **οἱ οἰκεῖοι** relatives, kinsfolk
οἰκέω	dwell
οἴκοθεν	from home
οἰκονομία, -ας, ἡ	household management
οἶκτος, -ου, ὁ	pity
οἴομαι (οἶμαι)	think, suppose
οἷος, -α, -ον	such as, what kind of
οἱόσπερ, οἵαπερ, οἷονπερ	just such as
οἴχομαι	go, depart
ὀλιγαρχία, -ας, ἡ	oligarchy
ὀλίγος, -η, -ον	small, little
ὀλιγωρέω	think little of
ὅλος, -η, -ον	whole, entire
ὄμνυμι	swear, take an oath
ὁμοίως	similarly, in the same manner
ὁμολογέω	agree to, promise, acknowledge, confess
ὅμως	all the same, nonetheless
ὄναρ, τό	dream (*only in nom. and acc.*)
ὀνειδίζω	rebuke, reproach
ὀνίνημι	help; *mid.* derive benefit
ὄνομα, -ματος, τό	name; word
ὄνος, -ου, ὁ or ἡ	donkey, ass
ὀξύς, -εῖα, -ύ	sharp, clever, swift
ὅπῃ	where; in what way, how
ὁπῃοῦν	in any way, whatever
ὅπλον, -ου, τό	weapons, shield
ὅποι	to where
ὁπόθεν	from where
ὁπότε	whenever
ὁπότερος, -α, -ον	which of the two
ὅπως	how, in what way; in order that; **ὁπωστιοῦν**, in any way at all
ὁράω	see
ὀργή, -ῆς, ἡ	anger
ὀργίζω	provoke, aggrevate; *mid.* be angry, grow angry
ὀρθός, -ή, -όν	straight, right
ὀρθῶς	rightly
ὁρμάω	rush into
ὅς, ἥ, ὅ	who, which, what

ὅσιος, -α, -ον	holy
ὅσος, -η, -ον	as much as; *pl.* as many as, all who
ὅσπερ, ἥπερ, ὅπερ	whoever, the very one who
ὅστε, ἥτε, ὅτε	who, which
ὅστις, ἥτις, ὅτι	whoever, whatever; who, what
ὁστισοῦν	anyone at all
ὅταν	whenever
ὅτε	when
ὅτι	that; because; whatever
οὐ (οὐκ, οὐχ)	no, not
οὗ	where
οὐδαμοῦ	nowhere
οὐδέ	and not, but not, nor, not even; **οὐδέ . . . οὐδέ**, neither . . . nor
οὐδείς, οὐδεμία, οὐδέν	no one, nothing
οὐδέποτε	not at any time, never
οὐδεπώποτε	never in the world
οὐδέτερος, -α, -ον	neither of two, neither
οὐκέτι	no longer
οὔκουν	and so . . . not, not therefore
οὐκοῦν	therefore, then, accordingly
οὖν	and so, then, therefore, accordingly
οὐράνιος, -α, -ον	heavenly
οὖς, ὠτός, τό	ear
οὔτε	and not, but not, neither, nor; **οὔτε . . . οὔτε**, neither . . . nor
οὗτος, αὕτη, τοῦτο	this, that
ὀφέλλω	help, be a benefit
ὄφελος, -ους, τό	use, good
ὀφλισκάνω	owe

Π

παγκάλως	absolutely, correctly
πάθος, -ους, τό	experience; bad experience, suffering
παιδεύω	teach, educate, train
παίδιον, -ου, τό	child
παίζω	play, jest
παῖς, παιδός, ὁ *or* **ἡ**	child; servant
πάλαι	formerly, long ago
παλαιός, -ά, -όν	ancient, old
παντάπασι	completely, absolutely
πάντως	wholly, altogether; at any rate, at least; by all means, certainly; yes

πάνυ	entirely, completely, very
παρά	from, by the side of, by (+ *gen.*); with, at the side of (+ *dat.*); along, during; by the side of, to the side of; by; contrary to (+ *acc.*)
παράδειγμα, -ματος, τό	example, lesson
παραιτέομαι	ask earnestly, beg, entreat
παρακελεύομαι	urge, exhort
παρακέλευσις, -εως, ἡ	exhortation
παραλαμβάνω	take in hand
παραμένω	remain with
παράνομος, -ον	lawless, unlawful
παρανόμως	illegally
παράπαν	absolutely, entirely
τὸ παράπαν	completely
παραπλήσιος, -α, -ον	similarly
παρασκευάζω	prepare, get ready
παρατίθημι	compare
παραχωρέω	yield, withdraw from
πάρειμι	be present
παρέχω	supply, offer
παρίεμαι	entreat
πᾶς, πᾶσα, πᾶν	all, every; the whole
πάσχω	experience
πατήρ, -τρός, ὁ	father
παύω	stop, cease
πείθω	persuade, convince; *mid.* obey
πειράομαι	try to (+ *inf.*)
πειστέον	one must obey
πέμπτος, -η, -ον	fifth
πένης, -ητος, ὁ	poor man
πενία, -ας, ἡ	poverty
πέντε	five
περί	about, around, concerning, with regard to (+ *gen.*); near, concerning (+ *dat.*); around, with regard to (+ *acc.*)
περὶ πολλοῦ (πλείστου) ποιεῖσθαι	to set a high (the highest) value on
περιάπτω	attach
περιγίγνομαι	be superior to (+ gen.)
περίειμι	go around
περιεργάζομαι	busy oneself
περιμένω	wait
περιττός, -ή, -όν	remarkable, strange

πέτρη, -ης, ἡ	rock
πιθανῶς	persuasively
πιστεύω	believe, trust, have confidence in, rely on
πλάνη, -ης, ἡ	a wandering
πλάττω	shape, fashion
πλεῖστος, -η, -ον	greatest, very great; *pl.* most, very many
πλείων, -ονος	more
πλῆθος, -ους, τό	multitude; democratic faction
πλημμέλεια, -ας, ἡ	error
πλήν	except, but (+ *gen.*)
πλησίον	near
πλούσιος, -α, -ον	rich, wealthy
ποδαπός, -ή, -όν	from where
ποιέω	make, act, do; compose
ποίημα, -τος, τό	poem
ποίησις, -εως, ἡ	activity of creating poetry
ποιητής, -οῦ, ὁ	creator, poet
πόλεμος, -ου, ὁ	war
πόλις, -εως, ἡ	city, city-state
πολίτης, -ου, ὁ	citizen
πολιτικός, -ή, -όν	of a citizen, political; *as a noun*, statesman
πολλάκις	often, frequently
πολλαχοῦ	in many places, often
πολυπραγμονέω	be meddlesome
πολυπραγμοσύνη, -ης, ἡ	interference, meddling
πολύς, πολλή, πολύ	much, great, large, long; *pl.* many; **οἱ πολλοί**, the many, the masses; **τὸ πολύ**, the greater part
πονηρία, -ας, ἡ	worthlessness
πονηρός, -ά, -όν	evil, worthless
πόνος, -ου, ὁ	labor, toil, task
πόρρω	far, further, in (+ *gen.*)
πόσος, -η, -ον	how much, how great? *pl.* how many?
πότε	when?
ποτέ	at one time, once
πότερος, -α, -ον	which of two; whether
πότμος, -ου, ὁ	fate
που	somewhere, anywhere; somehow
πρᾶγμα, -ματος, τό	thing, matter; *pl.* affairs, business, trouble
πραγματεύομαι	work over
πρᾶξις, -εως, ἡ	action, business, matter
πράττω	act, do, make, attend to, fare; *mid.* earn

πρέπω	fit, suit, be proper
πρεσβύτερος, -α, -ον	older
πρίαμαι	purchase
πρίν	before
πρό	before, in preference to; in place of, instead of (+ *gen.*)
προθυμέομαι	be eager, zealous
προῖκα	for free
προκρίνω	choose before others, prefer
πρός	from the side of (+ *gen.*); at, in addition to (+ *dat.*); toward, against, with reference to (+ *acc.*)
προσδοκάω	expect
πρόσειμι	go up to
προσέρχομαι	come to, approach, meet
προσέχω	apply
προσήκω	be near; be appropriate; **οἱ προσήκοντες**, relatives
προσκαθίζω	land on
πρόσκειμαι	settle upon
πρόσοιδα	know besides
προσποιέομαι	claim, pretend
προστάττω	command, assign
προστίθημι	place before; set as penalty
προσχράομαι	use in addition (+ *dat.*)
πρότερος, -α, ον	former; **πρότερον**, earlier, formerly
προτρέπω	urge on, persuade to do
πρυτανεῖον, -ου, τό	Athenian public building also called the Tholos
πρυτανεύω	hold office as a *prytanis* (member of the executive counsel of the *boule*)
πρῶτος, -η, -ον	first, earliest
πυκνός, -ή, -όν	constant, insistent
πῶλος, -ου, ὁ	foal
πώποτε	at any time
πῶς	how? **πῶς γὰρ οὐ,** certainly, how could it be otherwise?
πως	somehow

Ρ

ῥᾴδιος, -α, -ον	easy
ῥᾳδίως	lightly, easily

ῥῆμα, -τος, τό	word
ῥητέον	it must be said
ῥήτωρ, -ορος, ὁ	orator

Σ

σαυτόν	yourself
σαφής, -ές	clear, distinct, definite
σαφῶς	clearly, distinctly
σελήνη, -ης, ἡ	moon
σημεῖον, -ου, τό	sign, token
σιγάω	be silent, be still
σιτέομαι	feed
σίτησις, -εως, ἡ	feeding
σκέπτομαι	consider, examine
σκιαμαχέω	shadowbox
σκοπέω	examine, look at
σμικρός, -ά, -όν	small, little
σός, -ή, -όν	your, yours (*sg.*)
σοφία, -ας, ἡ	wisdom
σοφιστής, -ου, ὁ	sophist
σοφός, -ή, -όν	wise
σπουδάζω	take seriously
σπουδή, -ῆς, ἡ	haste, earnestness
στάσις, -εως, ἡ	faction
στρατηγία, -ας, ἡ	command; generalship
στρατηγός, -οῦ, ὁ	general
στρατία, -ας, ἡ	army, expedition
σύ, σοῦ, σοί, σέ	you (*sg.*)
συγγίγνομαι	be with, associate with, converse with
συγγιγνώσκω	forgive
συγχωρέω	go along with, collude with
συμβαίνω	happen, occur
συμβάλλω	put together; *mid.* contribute
συμβουλεύω	give advice
σύμπας, πασα, -παν	all
συμφεύγω	flee with
σύνειμι	be with, associate with, have to do with; **οἱ συνόντες**, companions, associates
συνεπισκοπέω	examine together with
συνοῖδα	be conscious, be aware
συνόμνυμι	swear along with, conspire
συντεταμένως	vigorously

συνωμοσία, -ας, ἡ	conspiracy; confederacy; one linked by an oath
συνωρίς, -ίδος, ἡ	two-horsed chariot
σφεῖς, σφῶν	themselves
σφόδρα	enthusiastically, exceedingly
σφοδρός, -ά, -όν	enthusiastic, passionate
σφοδρῶς	enthusiastically, exceedingly
σχεδόν	nearly, almost
σχολή, -ῆς, ἡ	leisure
σῴζω	save
σῶμα, -ατος, ὁ	body
σωφροσύνη, -ης, ἡ	moderation, self-control

Τ

τάξις, -εως, ἡ	battle station, post
τάττω	station
τάχα	perhaps, possibly
τάχος, -ους, τό	speed
ταχύς, -εῖα, -ύ	swift
τε	and, both; **τε . . . καί**, both . . . and
τεκμήριον, -ου, τό	evidence, proof, indication
τελευτάω	die, come to an end
τελέω	spend
τέτταρες, -α	four
τέχνη, -ης, ἡ	art, craft
τῇδε	here, in this way
τηλικόσδε	of so great an age
τηλικοῦτος, -αύτη, -οῦτο	of such an age
τίθημι	place, set, count; cast (*of a vote*)
τιμάω	honor, value; *mid.* propose a penalty
τιμή, -ῆς, ἡ	honor, respect
τίμημα, -τος, τό	penalty
τιμωρέω	take vengeance on
τιμωρία, -ας, ἡ	punishment
τίς, τί	who? what?
τις, τι,	someone, something, a certain one; *pl.* some
τοι	you know; doubtless
τοίνυν	well then, well
τοιόσδε, -άδε, -όνδε	such a thing as follows
τοιοῦτος, -αύτη, -οῦτο	such, of such a kind
τολμή, -ῆς, ἡ	daring
τολμάω	dare
τόπος, -ου, ὁ	place, region

τοσόσδε, -ήδε, -όνδε	so much, so great; *pl.* so many
τοσοῦτος, -αύτη, οῦτο	so great, so heavy, so much; *pl.* so many
τότε	then
τρέπω	turn
τρέφω	raise, bring up
τριάκοντα	thirty (*indecl.*)
τρόπος, -ου, ὁ	manner, mode
τροφή, -ῆς, ἡ	nurture, sustenance
τυγχάνω	chance, happen; happen to be (with part.)

Υ

ὕβρις, -εως, ἡ	insolence, violence
ὑβριστής, -οῦ, ὁ	an insolent or violent man
ὑμεῖς, ὑμῶν, ὑμῖν, ὑμεῖς	you (*pl.*)
ὑμέτερος, -α, -ον	your, of you (*pl.*)
υἱός, -οῦ, ὁ	son (also **ὑός, -οῦ, ὁ**)
ὑπείκω	yield
ὑπέρ	on behalf of (+ *gen.*)
ὑπέχω	offer
ὕπνος, -ου, ὁ	sleep
ὑπό	because of; by (+ *gen.*)
ὑπολαμβάνω	understand, suppose
ὑπολογίζομαι	take into account, calculate, consider
ὑπομένω	endure
ὑποστέλλω	withhold
ὕστερος, -α, -ον	later

Φ

φαίνω	show; *pass.* appear, be found, seem
φάσκω	say, assert, claim
φαῦλος, -η, -ον	worthless, insignificant
φείδομαι	spare
φέρω	bear
φεύγω	flee, be a defendant
φήμη, -ης, ἡ	report, saying, rumor
φημί	say, assert
φθονέω	begrudge
φθόνος, -ου, ὁ	envy, malice
φιλέω	love
φιλόπολις, -ιδος	patriotic
φίλος, -η, -ον	dear, pleasing, friendly
φιλοσοφέω	love wisdom, seek truth

φιλότιμος, -ον	ambitious
φλυαρέω	talk nonsense
φλυαρία, -ας, ἡ	nonsense
φοβέω	frighten, terrify; *mid.* fear, be afraid of, dread
φόνος, -ου, ὁ	murder
φορτικός, -ή, όν	vulgar
φράζω	point out
φρονήσις, -εως, ἡ	thought
φρόνιμος, -η, -ον	intelligent, wise, thoughtful
φρονίμως	wisely, sensibly
φροντίζω	think, reflect upon
φροντιστής, -οῦ, ὁ	thinker
φυγή, -ῆς, ἡ	flight, exile
φυλή, -ῆς, ἡ	tribe
φύσις, -εως, ἡ	nature
φύω	be born
φωνή, -ῆς, ἡ	voice, speech style

X

χαῖρω	rejoice, fare well
χαλεπαίνω	be angry at
χαλεπός, -ή, -όν	difficult, hard
χαριεντίζομαι	joke, jest, make fun
χαρίζομαι	gratify
χάρις, -ιτος, ἡ	grace, gratitude
χειροτέχνης, -ου, ὁ	artisan
χείρων, -όνος	worse
χίλιοι, -αι, -α	thousands
χράομαι	use (+ *dat.*)
χρή	it is necessary (+ *inf.*)
χρῆμα, -ματος, τό	thing; *pl.* property, money
χρηματισμός, -οῦ, ὁ	moneymaking
χρησμός, -οῦ, ὁ	response of an oracle, oracle
χρησμῳδέω	deliver an oracle, foretell the future
χρησμῳδός, -οῦ, ὁ	purveyer of oracles
χρηστός, -ή, -όν	excellent
χρόνος, -ου, ὁ	time
χωρίς	apart from (+ *gen.*)

Ψ

ψεῦδος, -εος, τό	falsehood, lie
ψεύδομαι	lie, deceive

ψηφίζομαι	vote
ψῆφος, -ου, ἡ	pebble; ballot, vote
ψυχή, -ῆς, ἡ	soul

Ω

ὧδε	thus, in this way
ὥρα, -ας, ἡ	hour, time
ὡς	as, how, that, since; as ___ as possible (*with superl.*)
ὥσπερ	as, like, just as, in the very way as, as if
ὥστε	so that, thus
ὠφελέω	aid, profit

Index

CPSIA information can be obtained at www.ICGtesting.com
Printed in the USA
LVOW090002070112

262833LV00002B/5/P